⌘ FINNISH
SHORT STORIES

Translated by
Inkeri Väänänen-Jensen
with **K. Börje Vähämäki**

Penfield Press

Inkeri Väänänen-Jensen

Inkeri Väänänen-Jensen (Ingrid Jensen), daughter of Finnish immigrants, grew up in northeastern Minnesota. In 1973, at the age of 58, she began an intensive study of the Finnish language, literature, and history. She has degrees in English and Finnish from the University of Minnesota.

One chapter of her life story, *Inkeri's Journey,* still in manuscript form, is included in the book, *Sampo: The Magic Mill,* published in 1989 by New Rivers Press. Three of her translations are also in *Sampo.*

In 1990, Penfield Press published two books of Inkeri's translations, *Finnish Proverbs* and *The Fish of Gold and Other Finnish Folk Tales.*

First published in 1982, this book, *Finnish Short Stories,* presents translations of 32 stories by 19 of Finland's short story writers.

Mother of three, wife of a retired University of Minnesota professor, Inkeri writes poetry about her experiences as a daughter of Finnish immigrants, under the title *Poems from Inkeri's Journey.*

K. Börje Vähämäki

K. Börje Vähämäki, Finnish born, received his Ph.D. at åbo Academy, Finland. Professor Vähämäki has taught Finnish Studies at the University of Minnesota, Stockholm University, and the University of Toronto. He has published books (e.g. *Existence and Identity,* 1984) and articles on the Finnish language, Finnish literature, Finnish folklore, and most recently on Finnish immigrant literature.

Cover trees by Inkeri Väänänen-Jensen
Cover design by Esther Feske
Copyright © 1991 Inkeri Väänänen-Jensen

The publication of this book has been supported by funds from the Commission for the Promotion of Finnish Literature and by the Finnish Literature Information Centre, both of Helsinki, Finland.

ISBN 0941016-82-X
Library of Congress Catalog Number 91-60699

FOREWORD

This collection of thirty-two short stories is the outcome of what began in January, 1976, as an assignment in a Finnish-to-English translation class in the Department of Scandinavian at the University of Minnesota. The project was challenging and engrossing, even though often difficult and at times arduous.

The earliest story in the collection was written in 1859, the latest in 1973. The arrangement of authors and stories is chronological, according to the birth of the author. Many short stories in Finland have been written in the Swedish language, and for them I refer the reader to Dr. George C. Schoolfield's SWEDO-FINNISH STORIES, 1974. Only those stories written originally in Finnish are included in this volume. The aim in the collection has been to acquaint English-speaking readers with the style of a number of short story writers writing in Finland in Finnish and with the subjects they wrote about.

Most of the biographical material on the authors was taken from A HISTORY OF FINNISH LITERATURE by Dr. Jaakko A. Ahokas published for the American-Scandinavian Foundation, 1973. It has proved an invaluable resource. Dr. Ahokas has generously given permission for the use of his material.

I wish to thank Otava Oy. and Werner Söderström Oy. for permission to use the stories from their publications. I am particularly grateful to Mr. Heikki Reenpää, Chairman of Otava Oy. and Dr. Esko Häkli, Director of the University of Helsinki Libraries, for arranging this authorization.

I wish especially to thank Professor K. Börje Vähämäki of the University of Minnesota Department of Scandinavian for his invaluable guidance and help during the translation process that resulted in this book.

I also with to thank Dr. Rudolf Jensen of the University of Maryland for reviewing the manuscript and Tuulikki Jaakola-Sinks, teacher of Finnish in the University of Minnesota Department of Scandinavian, for her advice and help.

Inkeri Väänänen-Jensen

GLOSSARY

A few Finnish words in these stories do not have English equivalents so the Finnish word is used:

AITTA: a building, and there often were several, on a Finnish farm separate from the main farmhouse. They were used for storage and also as sleeping quarters for the hired help.

LYSEO: Finnish eight-year school covering grammar school and the high school grades.

SAUNA: A Finnish steam bath, usually a separate building on a farm or at a cottage, often with a dressing room separate from the steam room.

Explanation of Finnish HEARTH: the older farmhouses in Finland had a large fireplace with an oven, on top of which was a large, warm shelf, where the elderly, the sick, or the indolent found a warm and comfortable refuge.

Contents

Aleksis Kivi (1834-1872)

Aleksis Kivi (Aleksis Stenvall), the son of a poor tailor from the village of Nurmijärvi, a short distance from Helsinki, became one of the greatest of Finnish authors. He was the first genuine writer, that is, a writer by profession who had no other career, to write in the Finnish language, publishing the first Finnish novel, THE SEVEN BROTHERS, in 1870. He had an inner compulsion to write, and it cost him whatever fortune he had, his physical and mental health, and his life--he died at the age of thirty-eight, insane. He wrote almost all of his works: three five-act tragedies, two long comedies, five short plays, five others not accounted for, about thirty poems, and a great novel--between 1860 and 1870. Aleksis Kivi is represented in this collection mainly in his capacity as a founding literary figure in Finland, not because he was primarily a short story writer, although he did write some short stories. *Eriika*, the short story in this collection, was submitted by Kivi in 1859, when he was twenty-five, with the hope of earning a stipend at the University of Helsinki; he did not get the stipend, but was given twenty-five rubles. The awarding committee stated that the story showed talent, and they felt the writer should receive some sort of recognition. The story was found in 1922 among University papers and gives the appearance of being hurriedly written in time for the competition. Even in this early short story, a number of Kivi's characteristics which were to appear again and again are already apparent. Although influenced by the dialect of his native region, he wrote in the old literary Finnish, archaic and solemn, rather than in the modern tongue other writers and linguists were developing. He describes nature and farm work in a broad, epic tone but does not omit familiar details; he combines realism and fantasy, building the supernatural with materials from ordinary life. His descriptions of nature, which he loved, are lyrical. In many of Kivi's writings, as in *Eriika*, the motif of the mountain and its view occurs many times, leaving clear images in the viewer's mind. Another frequent motif is the mother-child relationship, shown in *Eriika* first on the mountain top and then between Eriika and her mother. Kivi's sister Agnes died at the age of fourteen, when Kivi was nineteen, and clearly influenced not only *Eriika* but later writings as well, where he focuses on the yearning for death, especially among young women, and presents death as a beautiful, quiet place,' a dreamland of eternal bliss and immortality. His women are dreamy young girls, exalted and visionary, often expressing religious or moral feelings with great strength--Eriika being a forerunner of this type of woman. Eriika herself gives what may seem to modern readers an unreal impression of sadness and dejection, a yearning for death with the story itself ending in a grandiloquent style.

Eriika (1859)

Far from the village beyond the dark forest the house of Muistola [1] stands at the edge of a meadow. It is a wealthy farmhouse, praised by everyone, particularly the poor, since it has always served as their shelter and refuge. Rarely did a day pass there without some act of charity.

The house is attractive; the white window frames add to its charm. There are ten mountain ash trees in the yard, "a reminder of the ten commandments", as the patriarch of the family stated when he planted the trees to enhance forever the beauty of the house. A short distance towards the north lies a mountain; the ridge of this mountain is crowned by a dense forest of pine trees. Gazing at this forest, one sees the trees forming many strange pictures against the sky. There, a mother stands with a child at her knee; her breast is bared, and her scarf flutters in the northern breeze; with a smile on her face she looks at her little one, nourishing it with the divine wealth of her breast. There, two pines stand like two friends embracing. There, a rider spurs on his stallion, which plunges about in a fury. There, on the sky's battlefield, our great heroes who for hundreds of years have engaged in their brave deeds, swords in hand, are battling ghosts made of clouds. Yet highest of all, stands a pine, serene, like the king of all wisdom. There is still one picture at the top of the mountain; a downcast old man, staff in hand, sits at the edge of a grave, desolate and deserted, but beside him stands the angel of hope, whispering into his ear, pointing toward the East. Many other kinds of pictures appear there, whatever one wishes to see. But this is what the lovely Eriika, the only daughter of Muistola, saw. Thus the sleepless maiden dreamed during the

1 Manor of Memories

summer nights as she looked at nature from the window of the drawing room. Her pensive gaze revealed how her soul was filled with a vision of the beauty of the unknown, distant future. She was beautiful, this shy maiden of the valley. Her dark hair framed her forehead, which shone like a cloud before the sun, and the eyes beneath her forehead were like two windows in a chamber of peace. Her smile was as gentle as the touch of morning glow on the eastern shore, so full of joy, yet with a trace of melancholy. She was the love and joy of her parents, the spark of hope for many a young man, and a merciful angel to the poor. She went to church every Sunday. During the week she was always busy, aiding her mother in the care of the household. From the house to the storehouse, from the storehouse to the house, she stepped both morning and evening, diligent and quiet, full of life.

The maiden's life was beautiful, but yet more beautiful was her death, for untimely death called her from this world. Fullness of life lasts but a short while. Once, after raking in the hayfield during the heat of the day she felt her strength ebbing and her arms growing heavy as evening drew near. Her forehead burned, the blood churned in her veins, and she heard a soft ringing in her ears. She put down her hayfork, she left the fallen hay, and set out for home; with her hand on her forehead, she walked along the heath in the solitude of the evening. Wherever she looked, nature reflected only melancholy, for her mind dwelt on the evening of life. Reaching home, she quickly took off her kerchief, went immediately to rest and slept, awakened, and slept again; her bosom rose and fell, her cheeks burned, and beads of sweat dripped from her forehead. The maiden, usually silent and sparing with words, now chattered unceasingly, animated by her delirium. "My Mother, my Darling!" she said. "Sew me a new gown, bleach it and brighten it out on the beautiful fields, make it as bright as the sun itself. I must leave, for I hear the bell calling me. Its tolling echoes like a copse in the wind, like a distant copse echoing in the evening wind." So she spoke, but sorrow entered the house; her father grieved; with a melancholy mien, the mother sewed the gown for her daughter, and wept; all the servants wept. But Eriika did not weep; she worked hard as she approached death; her bosom rose and fell, her cheeks burned, and beads of swept dripped from her forehead. And so five bright summer days passed; five beautiful nights also slipped past, and when Saturday arrived and its sun began to descend in the West, the maiden's eyes began to flash. She rose from her bed, washed her face, put on the gown which her mother had made, and let the maidservants braid her dark hair. Her cheeks blazed like a flame of fire, and her speech was fiery. Now she said to the girl, her friend from childhood, "Make a crown of flowers for me. My Dear, run to Sharon and gather flowers into your lap. I want flowers from Sharon, for their soft coolness will soothe my burning forehead."

Wailing out loud, her friend went to the edge of the field to gather flowers for Eriika. She brought a beautiful crown from Sharon and placed it on the dying girl's head. Like a bride wearing a crown, Eriika sat up again in her bed and rested against her mother's breast. There, resting her head, tired and exhausted, she sighed softly, and her countenance no longer reflected strife, only peace. The Lord of Death, once he had besieged the fortress of life, refrained from shooting his arrows and allowed the few and powerless guardians of life still left in life's garrison to leave their fortress freely. The mother was silent, the father was silent, all who stood around her were silent. Quietly, they looked at Eriika, whose breathing weakened, and whose lips slowly turned blue.

Now there is vigorous activity at Muistola, work for the old as well as the young; everyone is busy and in a hurry, for it is the eve of Eriika's funeral celebration. From the house to the storehouse, from the storehouse to the house, the village maidens run briskly along the path in the beautiful yard, preparing for the celebration. The older women are busy working in the house: some are washing, some are brewing beer, and others are busy preparing food at the big hearth. The mistress herself, always careful about her work, is making wheat bread at the head of the table and casts glances through the window, awaiting guests from far-away villages. The sun shines through the back window, and on the hearth the fire is blazing. But in her blue casket Eriika rests in the silence of the drawing room, where no one disturbs her sacred peace. Yet from time to time, the mother goes in to see her bird of the meadow, to see this pale guest from the land of death. Adjusting Eriika's crown of flowers or smoothing her dress, she speaks to her child:

"Rest in peace, my beauteous One,
Soon you'll be at death's abode.
There the walls are lined with moss,
Fine sand lies over the floor.
How good it is for you to rest,
No need to turn you on your side,
No need to ease your shoulder pain."

Thus in the midst of her haste, she spoke to her daughter; once more she smooths her daughter's hair, and then hastens back to her cares.

Evening falls, the guests from distant villages are approaching. The carriages rumble and the smell of dust lingers over the winding road. In the house, the bustle increases; doors slam, dogs bark, and horses whinny. Some go to greet the guests, some go to gather leaves, others leave to get leafy saplings from the forest. The guests arrive, all in mourning clothes, the old as well as the young, from the highest in rank to the lowest. The little girls, wreaths of flowers around their necks, play in the yard. There is much activity, noise, and clamor in the house of the funeral celebration. But in the blue casket Eriika rests in the silence of the drawing room.

Night covers the earth with its wings, but sweet are the wings of the summer night; transparent, they glimmer gently in the valleys, hovering above little roses, moistening them with silver drops of dew. In the house of the celebration, all are resting quietly; a wonderful peace reigns everywhere; not a leaf stirs among the mountain ashes. The quiet of this night is disturbed only by the rapids, roaring in the distance, or by a nightjar flitting in the air. Stand quietly and look at nature in the festive mood of this night. From time to time it lightens suddenly and suddenly darkens; then in the southwest, lightning flashes, flashes without thunder. But look to the north, to the mountain, at the strangest of views. At the very top of the forest, with a cloud as a throne, the ghost of a maiden sits, as beautiful and grand as a princess. She sits silent and still, resting her elbow on the cloud and looking down at Muistola. When the lightning flashes in the southwest, it brightens her face and leaves her eyes in a shadow of beauty. The face is Eriika's, yet still more beautiful. She wears a crown of flowers on her head; it was perhaps plaited in Sharon, for such flowers are found nowhere but in the fields of Sharon. Her dress is white as snow, and the sash below her bosom is like the arch of heaven. Her countenance is most solemn, sealed with a gentle smile playing quietly on her lips.

Still she lingers, looking tenderly at her former home through the gentle night. And tenderly the windows of her home look back at her through the gentle night. Thus she tarries in her gazing, and how sweet it is for her to tarry, she, who will find eternal joy, who will know the land of hope. But, look! Now she is gone, quick as a flash she disappears. She has left Muistola forever.

Minna Canth (1844-1897)

"Freedom for the woman! Freedom to work, freedom to think! The weight of ancient, rigid ways and customs oppress and crush our spirit. The barriers set up against equal employment in many lines of work force us into a life of poverty. In this way, woman is reduced to a machine and deprived of her natural character, becoming someone else's slave. Life and the meaning of life is like a closed book in her hand." [1] Thus the firebrand, Minna Canth, wrote in the 1880's. This future champion of new ideas was born Minna Johansson in Tampere in 1844; in 1863 she entered the newly founded Finnish Teachers' College in Jyvaskyla, but instead of becoming a teacher, she married the professor of sciences there. When he died in 1879 she was left with seven children to support. She moved to Kuopio, where her father had established a drapery shop, took over the shop and managed it successfully. She became a well-known writer, primarily a playwright, and at times held what was almost a literary salon, where a number of Finland's liberal thinkers and writers discussed intellectual matters. At first she wrote descriptions, short stories, and articles on temperance and women's rights for newspapers, also writing two sentimental melodramatic comedies, MURTOVARKAUS (THE BURGLARY) in 1883 and ROINILAN TALOSSA (AT ROINILA FARM) in 1885. Her first important serious plays were TYÖMIEHEN VAIMO (THE WORKMAN'S WIFE), 1883-84 and KOVAN ONNEN LAPSIA (CHILDREN OF MISFORTUNE), 1888, both with touches of melodrama. Her short stories at this time, dealing with the position of the working class, the poor, and the position of women, included HANNA, 1886, KÖYHÄÄ KANSAA (POOR PEOPLE), 1886, KAUPPA-LOPO (LOPO, THE PEDDLER), 1889, and LAIN MUKAAN (ACCORDING TO THE LAW), 1889. In her early writings Canth railed against the existing society, blaming it for the ugly problems of the working class. Her work was often biased and propagandist, reflecting her intense interest in social and moral problems. Her themes, radical for the times, were: equal rights for women, sexual morals, evils of alcohol, exploitation of the working

1 Ripatti **et al** p. 81

class and the poor, and criticism of the traditional church and its conservative representatives. But her primary interest was always the position of women. She was a champion of new ideas, also a realist. In her later works she was no longer as radical as she had been earlier, having come to the realization that often people themselves, not society alone, also contribute to their problems. Although her plays were melodramatic, her characters either good or bad, her plots sometimes improbable, Canth had a talent for plot and dialogue, which helped to obscure her artistic and literary defects. Among the best of her later plays are PAPIN PERHE (THE CLERGYMAN'S FAMILY), 1891, SYLVI, 1893, and ANNA LIISA, 1895. Since Minna Canth was an important and influential writer, although primarily a playwright, her sentimental story, *Lapsenpiika* (*The Nursemaid*), 1892, is included in this collection as an example of one of her major themes, the exploitation of the poor by the upper middle class.

The Nursemaid (1892)

"Emmi, wake up! Can't you hear Madam ringing? Emmi! How that girl sleeps. Emmi, Emmi!"

Finally, Silja got a response from her. Emmi sat up, grumbled, and rubbed her eyes. She was still terribly sleepy.

"What time is it?"

"It's way after four."

Way after four? She had been in bed three hours; not until one-thirty had she finished wiping the dishes, for last night they had had guests, as they so frequently did. And before that, she had had to stay up for two whole nights because of Lilli; Madam had gone to a wedding and the child would not settle for the sugartit. Was it any wonder, then, that she was sleepy?

She was going on fourteen. Her legs always ached in the mornings, so that it was quite difficult to step on them at first. Silja, who slept with her in the same bed, said it was because she was growing. Her legs should be bled, Silja thought, but Emmi was afraid it would hurt. And they were thin even now. What would they be if blood was let from them? When she slept, her legs never ached, but as soon as she woke up, the aching would begin. Then, if she managed to fall asleep again, they stopped aching at once.

Even now, as she sat in the bed, her legs ached from the knees down to the heels. Her head dropped back into the bed, sank so heavily, that it was impossible to get up. Would she ever in this world be lucky enough to be allowed to sleep as long as she wanted to even for one single morning?

Sitting up again, Emmi rubbed her legs. Her head dropped so low that her chin touched her breast and her eyes closed. Her hands stopped moving, she breathed deeply and slowly. In no time, she sank back into the bed.

The bell jingled again. Silja poked Emmi in the side with her elbow.

"Isn't it strange that we can't get this little brat to obey. Get up!"

She poked Emmi once more with her sharp elbow, and it hit so sharply on Emmi's breast that she cried out in pain.

"What's the matter with you that you have to be called ten times before you'll get up?"

Emmi staggered to her feet, she felt dizzy and almost fell over.

"Rinse your eyes with cold water, it'll help you wake up," Silja advised.

But Emmi didn't have time to do that, for the bell sounded once again. She managed to put on her dress, smoothed down her hair with both hands, rubbed her eyes from time to time, and hurried in to Madam.

"I have rung three times," said Madam.

Emmi didn't speak, she just took Lilli, who lay beside Madam in the bed, into her arms.

"Put something dry on her and take her to the cradle, she won't fall asleep beside me any more anyhow."

Madam turned over on her other side and closed her eyes. The cradle was in the next room, where Emmi now took the child. After changing Lilli, she began to sing and rock the cradle. From time to time, an idea would pop into her mind, not a great or complicated one, but strong enough to break into the singing.

"Hs hss s. Aa aa aa a. --Sleep, my Child, sleep. --Hs hss s. Aa aa aa a. --Oh, god how sleepy I am. --I came along the Turku road, I rested on the Pori road.--Silja, lucky girl, is still sleeping--I came along the Turku road, I rested on the Pori road. --Hs hss hss s. Aa aa aa aa a--."

Lilli fell asleep. Emmi then stretched out on the floor beside the cradle. She put her arm beneath her head and before long she was sound asleep. Emmi was unaware that Lilli awakened almost at the same time as she fell asleep; Lilli rubbed her nose and looked around in wonder, for no one was with her. She tried to stand up, but couldn't; however, she managed to move to one side of the cradle and got her head over the edge. Now Lilli noticed Emmi, was delighted, and prattling, reached to touch her. The cradle tipped. She tumbled out and hit her forehead on the rocker of the cradle. The shriek of pain suddenly awakened everyone.

"God help me!"

Emmi turned deathly pale when she saw the child on the floor beside her. She grabbed the child into her arms, tried to quiet her, and still very pale, kept swinging her in her arms. Madam must have heard it, Emmi, terrified, kept thinking the whole time. In her panic she forgot to check whether the child was hurt, or whether she was just crying from fright. Madam opened the door.

Emmi thought she would faint, the whole world turned black before her eyes.

"What happened to her?"

"Nothing."

Emmi didn't know what she answered. Instinctively, she blurted out words which she hoped would, if possible, save her.

"Why is she crying like that then? Certainly there has to be a reason."

In vain Emmi tried everyting to calm the child.

"Give her to me," said Madam. "Oh, Child, my Dear, what is wrong? My god, she's got a black and blue mark on her forehead!"

She looked at Emmi, who stood helpless.

"How did it get there? Are you struck dumb?"

"I don't know..."

"You must have dropped her. From the cradle I suppose."

Emmi was silent and looked down.

"So, you can no longer deny it. What an incompetent and careless thing you are. First you drop the child and then, furthermore, you lie. Poor me, that I ever took you in. But now I want you to know that we will not keep you here next year. Get another place for yourself, wherever you can find one. I certainly don't want you, even if I never get a nursemaid again...Sssh, my Darling, sssh, mamma's own Child. Mamma will find you a better nursemaid next year. Don't cry, don't cry."

Lilli stopped crying when she found the breast, and after a little while, she smiled with contentment, even though teardrops still glistened in her eyes.

"Oh, my Darling, are you smiling at Mamma already? My own Child, what a good girl you are. And now you have that ugly black and blue mark on your forehead."

Lilli didn't cry any more that day; she was as happy as before, perhaps even a little happier. She laughed for Emmi, stuck her finger into Emmi's mouth, and tugged at Emmi's hair. Emmi brushed her own cheeks with Lilli's delicate hand, for teardrops the size of beads rolled down her cheeks all day. And when she remembered that in six weeks she would no longer hold this soft, sweet child in her arms, nor even see her except for perhaps just a glimpse at the window, when she, a miserable outcast, would walk past on the street; it was then, when she thought of this, or felt rather than thought it, that the teardrops followed each other so quickly that they joined together and formed a small pool on the table.

"Look at that, look at that," she said to Lilli, who began at once to splash in it with the palms of her hands.

Before noon, Madam received guests, Doctor Vinter's wife and Headmaster Siven's wife, elegant and refined, both of them, although they were not nearly as elegant as our Madam, Silja said, and Emmi thought so too.

When Silja brought in the coffee, Madam asked her to tell Emmi to bring Lilli in for the guests to see. Emmi put on Lilli's prettiest bonnet and also a brand new bib. These made the child look so lovely that Emmi had to call Silja to come and look before she brought Lilli to the guests.

How charmed the women were as soon as the two appeared in the doorway.

"Oh, how sweet!"

And then, vying with each other, they took Lilli into their arms, kissed her, and squeezed her, and laughed.

"How sweet, how sweet!"

Emmi stood in the back and smiled. She didn't really understand what "how sweet, how sweet" meant, since the women spoke in Swedish, but she concluded from it all that it must mean something really good.

But suddenly the women became very grave. Madam was telling them--whatever it was she was telling them. Emmi didn't understand it, since she spoke in Swedish. However, she suspected what it was when she saw the shocked expressions on the women's faces.

"My god, my god, no just think of it, poor Child."

Three pairs of eyes turned at the same time to look, first, with extreme compassion, at the black and blue mark on Lilli's forehead, and then, repulsed, at Emmi.

"What a wretched creature!"

Emmi looked down at the carpet on the floor and waited for

something to drop on her from the ceiling, something that in one swoop would dash her to pieces, or smite her deep into the ground. For certainly there was no one in the whole world as worthless as she, miserable wretch. She did not dare to look up, but she knew, and felt in the very tips of her fingers and toes, that they were still looking at her. These elegant, refined women, who themselves never made mistakes. How would that even be possible, since they were so very wise and so much better than ordinary people.

"You may take Lilli away," she heard Madam say.

Emmi's hands had suddenly become so limp that she was afraid of dropping the child if she took her into her arms now.

"Do you hear?"

"There you see now, what she is like."

Emmi staggered forward and somehow managed to take those few steps to Madam's chair. Her desire to get away from their sight back to the nursery provided the strength she needed. Or was it just her old routine that made her arms once again obey and carry out their tasks as always before. She lowered Lilli into the cradle, and sat on the footstool beside it and showed her playthings. But Lilli had lifted both feet straight up into the air and was grasping at them with her hands. She thought this was such fun that she laughed out loud. Emmi would have laughed too if her guilt and the choking sensation in her throat would have allowed it. As she sat there, she wondered why she hadn't remembered at all this morning the trick which she had often used to fight off sleep; namely, to prick and scratch her arms with a needle. This forgetfulness had caused the whole, horrible accident, which could not be undone, and which was now ruining her whole life.

Late that night, when everyone had gone to bed, Emmi went outside into the yard. It was gray and dark there and quiet, but above, the sky was filled with stars. She sat down on the lowest step to think about her present and her future. But just thinking about it didn't solve anything, for her situation was just as gray and dark as the night around her. So she left her cares behind and looked into the dark blue up high, where heaven's candles burned brightly. Who were the lucky ones near them? And who of those living now would get to go there? Probably no servant girls? But, of course, all the gentry. This was certain, since they were already so very much better down here. Furthermore, she wondered who lit those candles every night, the angels or the humans? Or did humans become angels there? What about small children who die very young? Who rocked them and cared for them? Or didn't they perhaps need care in heaven?

Silja opened the door and urged her to come inside.

"Why on earth are you sitting out there in the cold?"

"Listen, Silja," said Emmi later as she was undressing, "why is it that we servant girls are so bad?"

"Don't you know?"

"No."

"Because we have to stay awake so much. We have all the more time to sin. You see, since the gentry sleep late in the mornings, until nine or ten, they avoid many a bad deed."

That was probably it. If she, too, had been allowed to sleep longer in the morning, Lilli would not have fallen from the cradle because of her.

The following Sunday was the third Sunday for hiring servants. Emmi was given her reference paper, and told to go to the churchyard.

There was a big crowd there, those who were hiring and those who hoped to be hired. They were standing in their large sleighs; they all seemed to know one another and to be in league together. Emmi felt deserted and alone. Who would care to hire her, tiny and frail as she was? She stood next to the wall of the church with her reference paper, and waited. Masters and mistresses criss-crossed in front of her, but didn't even glance at her. Some young men were sitting nearby on the church steps.

"Ho, there, Girl, come over here," said one of them. The others laughed and whispered among themselves.

"Come, come, how about it? Come and sit beside me here."

Emmi blushed and moved farther away. At the same time, she happened to come face to face with a gentleman and his wife. Or were they real members of the gentry, since the woman was wearing a scarf over her head and the man's clothes were quite worn.

"What about that one?" said the gentleman, pointing at Emmi with his cane. "She certainly can't be asking very high wages. What do you ask?"

"Whatever the master and mistress wish to give me. I will be happy with that," answered Emmi softly. A faint hope rose in her breast.

"What use is she to us? Has she even got the strength to carry water tubs?"

"I do have the strength for that."

"And do you know how to wash clothes?"

"I've done that too."

"Let's take her; she seems decent and quiet," said the master.

But the mistress still was doubtful.

"She might be sickly, being so thin."

Emmi remembered her legs, but she didn't dare to say anything about them, for then they would have rejected her immediately.

"Are you sickly?" asked the master, looking at Emmi's reference paper, which he had snatched from her hand.

"No," whispered Emmi.

In her mind she decided never to complain again, no matter how much her legs ached.

The master tucked the reference paper into his pocket, gave her a couple of marks as wages paid in advance, and so the matter was settled.

"You are to come in the evening of All Saints' Day to the Karvonen estate and ask for the Hartonen family," said the mistress. "But be sure to be there by the evening of All Saints' Day!"

Emmi went home.

"You'll be going to a bad household," said Silja, who knew the Hartonen family. "Living there is miserable and poor, and the mistress is such a good-for-nothing that servants never stay for the full year. They say that she doesn't even give food except in portions, and very small ones at that."

Emmi blushed. But she recovered quickly and answered, "Not everyone can get the best places. Some have to settle for poorer places and be grateful that they don't have to go out into the world as beggars."

She took Lilli into her arms and pressed her face against the child's warm breast. Lilli grabbed Emmi's hair with both hands and babbled, "Ta, ta, ta."

Juhani Aho (1861-1921)

Juhani Aho (Johannes Brofeldt), perhaps the best known Finnish author of his time, was the son of a minister of cordial spirit and humor, who served parishes in the northern part of the Savo province. Aho studied at the University of Helsinki for four years without taking a degree. He began writing short stories and worked for many years as a newspaperman. His very short stories and sketches he called *lastuja*, or *shavings*, the byproducts of his writing, which dropped from his bench as he was shaping his longer works. In other words, they were incidental to his major works. Most of them first appeared in newspapers. He published eight collections of these *shavings*, one each in 1891, 1892, 1896 and five more between 1896 and 1921. Their subject matter varies from his contemplative philosophy of nature to realistic sketches and political pamphlets. His first stories were half-humorous descriptions of country people, later ones were ironic sketches of certain socially representative types and some were portraits of contemporary personalities. He often revealed his subjective point of view in the very first lines of a *lastu* by saying that they were told by an external observer. For instance, the story, *A Summer Dream*, included in this collection, begins with "My melancholy friend told me". He began as a realist with a short story, *Siihen aikaan kun isä lampun osti* (*When Father Bought the Lamp*), 1883, and two novels, RAUTATIE (THE RAILROAD), 1884, and PAPIN TYTÄR (THE CLERGYMAN'S DAUGHTER), 1885. Both *When Father Bought the Lamp* and THE RAILROAD deal with the reactions of simple people when confronted with new inventions. Aho made an effort to write simply and naturally and developed a very personal style, which reflected his dreamy, melancholy, sentimental nature. He and his literary friends represented the liberal current of thought in Finland and were critical of the conservative, oppressive, narrowminded and old-fashioned in art, literature, politics, religion and morals. He learned several foreign languages, read widely, particularly French and Norwegian literature, traveled in Europe. But he remained attached to his home country and its people. The novel, CLERGYMAN'S DAUGHTER, and its sequel, PAPIN ROUVA (THE CLERGYMAN'S WIFE), 1893, perhaps represent some of his best writing. His psychological analysis of the young woman in these novels is penetrating and sensitive. Although Aho was faithful to his liberal friends, he was basically a conservative who loved the good old days and watched their disappearance in the face of progress with regret, and a number of his stories reflect this attitude. Aho held an impartial view of man, had both a sad and yet humorous vision of life and a penetrating though humane realism. The irony in Aho's works is mild and understanding. He wrote other novels, among which are PANU, 1897, a result of his interest in the mythical past of the Finnish people; JUHA, 1911, the story of a middle-aged man with a young, beautiful wife; OMATUNTO (THE CONSCIENCE), 1914, a simple story about ordinary people, written in a straightforward style and one of his gayest stories, gently ironic and full of understanding of human weaknesses. His last work is MUISTATKO-? (DO YOU REMEMBER-?), 1920, a romanticized autobiography. One of the two stories in this collection, *Kello* (*The Watch*), 1884, an early short story, reveals Aho's satirical but understanding view of life; in it he displays his psychological intuition, working with different levels of consciousness. He remains, however, the dispassionate, resigned observer. Kesäinen *unelma* (*A Summer Dream*), 1892, shows his naive idealism, his love of Finnish nature and reflects a mood of compassion.

The Watch (1884)

Martti walked along the Esplanade. He thought about his watch, thought of nothing but his watch. He looked at Gronquist's many-storied stone building. His eyes scanned the shining windows, the shimmering red roof and its grand ornamentation. He looked at all this, but he thought about his watch.

Martti walked discreetly even on the Esplanade. He had always been an unassuming boy, quiet and thoughtful. He was an apprentice, respectful to his master and of good character.

Most of the time Martti looked down in front of him...at the tips of his shoes and at his vest, on which a copper watch chain was shining.

Martti had come from the country, had been an apprentice for half a year now, a shoemaker's apprentice.

He had been thrifty from the very beginning. He did not spend one penny more than necessary, and, yet, only now had he saved enough to buy the watch. Yesterday evening when he got his weekly pay, his savings had reached the required amount.

Yesterday evening upon leaving the shop he had gone to the watchmaker's to buy the watch. It had been picked out for many weeks...and the price agreed upon, twenty-five marks, without the chain. It was a cylinder watch with four jewels...which was just as good as if it had eight jewels. The watchmaker had said he had the same watch himself, and that the ordinary man didn't really need anything better.

It didn't actually cost twenty-five marks. At the time of purchase, the watchmaker offered it for twenty-four marks and fifty pennies. He even included the chain.

And now the chain gleamed so pleasingly across Martti's velvet vest.

For Martti had a velvet vest, bought from a Jew, and a jacket, open in the front so the vest would show and on it the copper watch chain.

Martti walked along the Esplanade; he looked in front of him, then at the tips of his shoes, and always, in passing, at the copper chain, which shone like gold.

Many people were walking on the Esplanade and there was quite a crowd in front of the Kappeli Restaurant, where music was being played. But Martti didn't want to walk in a crowd. He preferred walking where there weren't so many people. That was more appropriate for a man who had a watch...who had a watch and a shining watch chain. No one could see them in a crowd...not he, others even less.

Every so often it seemed to Martti that some people, in passing, glanced at his chain. And those who glanced this way did not have a watch themselves. They probably wished they had. It seemed that the majority did not have watches. Those whose coats were buttoned up certainly didn't have a watch, for most likely they would have had their coats open had they had one.

Martti didn't know where to put his hands. He tried to keep them crossed behind his back. It would have been more comfortable to keep them in his jacket pockets but the pockets in Martti's jacket were toward the back. That wasn't comfortable...nor was it comfortable to have them dangling straight down his sides, for then they swung back and forth awkwardly. The best thing was to keep them at his watch chain, one at a time.

Now it was easy to look at the watch. And then Martti had to look at the watch. Did it agree with the tower clock? Yes, it did, to the minute. What time was it, by the way? Twenty-five minutes past five.

Martti put the watch back into his pocket and all along his left side he could feel that he had a watch...in the left pocket of his vest. It felt a little strange. He could feel the watch right through the vest to his very flesh, yet it felt good.

Before, when walking on the street or the Esplanade without a watch, Martti had always stepped aside for everyone, particularly for the ones who had a watch. He had practically worshipped those who had a watch when he did not.

Martti, of course, had always been shy and meek, uncertain about how to behave. This he knew himself. But perhaps he had been that way just because he didn't have a watch. Now he had one. He didn't wish to appear too bold even now, nor haughty in any way, but he felt more confident than before. Nor was he now going to step aside for everyone. Others can yield just as well. Does he have to yield more than anyone else walking along the street? Of course not, he decided.

He decided this because the Esplanade didn't, of course, belong to one more than another. And he also paid the poll tax, didn't he?

Upon seeing him, everyone probably thinks that he is always the one who ought to step aside. But they are mistaken to think so.

Wherever a person happens to walk, he naturally walks in that space. Anyone else had better walk elsewhere.

And now Martti walked wherever he wanted to. And yet, he always yielded the way, but he assured himself that it was only the little bit that was absolutely necessary. If no one ever yielded, nothing would come of anyone's walking. And no longer did he step aside more often for people with a watch than for those without one. If he yields, he yields to just anybody...sometimes just because he likes to. Is it always necessary to walk in a straight line? It's much more fun sometimes to wind in and out, to walk now on one side, then on the other.

Martti would have liked, once in a while, to plunge into the midst of those guardsmen, to push his way between them and not yield an inch, as they walked in rows so arrogantly. But, of course, Martti didn't do it...for he could get pushed and his chain could somehow get caught on a button and snap, or the watch could drop to the ground and shatter.

Is the watch still in one piece?

It's still in one piece and still ticking. And those guardsmen didn't have a watch, at least not many of them. For no reason at all, they strut down the middle of the street and show off to the girls. Martti has never thought about girls...not even now that he has a watch in his pocket. Anyone who spends his money on girls is foolish. It's better to save and buy something, a watch, for instance.

There is nothing wrong, however, in spending a little on oneself. What if he had a glass of lemonade, ten pennies worth, or even twenty pennies worth...that wouldn't be too much.

And so Martti went to drink a glass of lemonade...as a toast to the watch.

Martti had his lemonade in a shop with doorposts of mirror glass, which reflected him in full, and his watch chain as well.

Martti sipped at his lemonade a little at a time and looked along the drinking glasses into the doorposts. Then Martti paid, gave a one-mark coin and got eighty pennies in change. The other drinkers seemed to pay with fifty-or twenty-five-penny coins. They probably didn't have a mark, nor did many of them seem to have a watch.

Martti did not wish to be haughty in any way. And anyone would have been mistaken to think that Martti would have become haughty just because he had happened to buy a watch. Only a fool gets haughty over trifles...No...But the other apprentices and the journeymen had probably thought him haughty yesterday. That's how it seemed to him now, as he thought about it, even though yesterday he hadn't...Only in jest had he asked them what time it was on their watches.

And they had begun to tease him for that and had kept asking all evening and even this morning, "What time is it on your watch, Martti? Please tell us what time it is on your watch."

They were probably jealous because they had no watches of their own. They could have had watches if they had wanted to. Anyone can buy a watch from the watchmaker's shop.

Here they're coming now!

Martti went to meet them and stopped beside them.

"What time is it on your watch, Martti?" they asked again and laughing, moved noisily past him.

That's it! They're jealous! Let them be jealous. What did Martti care...it was their own fault...they should have saved their money! And did they have to spend their money on beer? They'll just have to be without watches! When you live decently and save your money, you can buy a watch in no time, and then the money doesn't go to waste.

For a long time Martti had not remembered to look at his watch. How much time had passed by now?

"Out of the way, Boy!"

Who does that guardsman think he is? Does he think he's some lord who can push people around? Could he even have paid had the watch dropped to the ground?

And Martti looked angrily after the guardsman. But the guardsman just walked on, his skirts swaying.

"So there you are! I've been looking for you!"

It was Antti, another apprentice to the same shoemaker. They had come from the country at the same time.

They were good friends. Both of them had begun at the same time to save money for a watch, but Martti had reached his goal first. Antti was still far from his goal; he just seemed unable to save money and he admired Martti, who could. Martti, in turn, was fond of Antti, because he was different from the other boys. And when Martti had bought the watch, he liked Antti even more, for now Antti stared at him almost in admiration when he looked at Martti's watch.

They had gone together to buy the watch. Martti had wanted Antti to come with him, but they had not said anything to the others.

Antti had not wanted to hold Martti's watch in his hand even though Martti had urged him repeatedly, saying that he could even put it in his pocket. "Just try it!"

"What if I drop it?" Antti had said.

"You won't drop it; I'll hold on to the chain."

Only then had Antti dared to hold the watch; he turned it, looked at it in wonder and finally, with a sigh, gave it back, and Martti felt that there was no better boy in the whole world than Antti.

As for the other apprentices and the journeymen, they were dogs compared to Antti. As soon as they saw the watch, they just grabbed it from his hands, shoved themselves around it in a circle so Martti could not even see it himself. And they had opened the case although they should have known that the dust in the shop would damage the watch. But they didn't care even if it stopped running, since it was somebody else's watch.

"What time does your watch say?" asked Antti.

"Let's sit down here first and then we'll look."

Martti and Antti sat down on a vacant bench and Martti looked at his watch.

The watch was five minutes before six.

The chain hung across the velvet vest and Martti looked at it. Antti also gave it a sidelong glance. Then he raised his hand and touched Martti's chain. Martti even placed the watch in his hand.

"Try and see if you can open it."

"But what if it breaks?"

"It won't break."

"I can't get it open."

"You just don't know how. Here, let me show you. Like this...you just press your thumb over this button. Now try!"

"There, it sprang open! What does it say inside here?"

"Four jewels, 17,534...that's the watch's number in the world. That many men have the same watch as I have. You buy one like this too."

"I don't have the money."

"Would you like one very much? I guess you would."

"Not so very much."

But Martti saw that he craved one so badly that the corners of his mouth twitched.

Martti let Antti look at the watch for a long time, held it in front of him, and even let him look at it in his own hand. He wasn't at all afraid that Antti would break it or drop it. And Antti seemed much more insignificant to him than before. He didn't really understand it, but he also now felt bigger than Antti. He hadn't really noticed it before, only once in a while, when they had compared their savings and Martti had more marks than Antti.

"Shouldn't we put the watch back in the pocket?"

Martti put the watch into his pocket. But almost immediately he began to feel sorry for Antti. Perhaps he would have still liked to look at the watch, and he showed it once more to Antti. The poor fellow doesn't have a watch and sits there, almost falling off the edge of the bench, the tip of his nose as thin as the point of a knife, stroking the case and chain of somebody else's watch.

If Martti had been a rich man, he could have given this watch to Antti and bought a fulcrum watch for himself...that's how sorry he felt for Antti.

"Would a cylinder watch be good enough for you?"

"Sure...any kind, just so it's a watch."

"I intend to buy a fulcrum watch...one of these days."

"Then what will you do with this one?"

"I don't know; I might sell it to someone."

"Sell it to me."

"I'm not buying a new one just yet...when I get to be a journeyman. Don't I look a little like a journeyman now that I have a watch?" Martti said this attempting a joke.

"Yes, you do."

"But you still look like an apprentice."

"Because I don't have a watch."

"Is that why? Would you like some lemonade, Antti? I just had some myself."

All of a sudden a burst of generosity swept over Martti. He felt that somehow he owed Antti a glass of lemonade, for the poor fellow didn't even have a watch and goodness knows when he would get one. But almost immediately he regretted his offer; it would just cost money. It wouldn't be very much, though, only ten pennies. After all, one ought to do something for one's fellow man, one who doesn't even have a watch.

Martti drank some lemonade himself and clinked his glass with Antti's.

"Antti, now you should say: 'Good luck to my new watch,' " said Martti as a joke.

"Well, good luck, then."

Both of them gave a laugh and Martti's spirits rose. He had never experienced such a swell of emotion in his chest.

"There the guardsmen come again. Let's pretend we don't see them. No, let's not step to the side...they would think that we are yielding to them. Let's walk straight ahead and look squarely in front of us. We too can be proud."

Antti did not understand why he should do all this, but tried to comply.

"Are they turning to look at us? Why don't you look and see?" said Martti after they had passed by.

"They're not looking...they're just walking on."

Martti was a little annoyed by this.

The guardsman, who a short while ago had pushed Martti aside, was now approaching with a girl on his arm. They were walking in the middle of the street, and so was Martti. Antti stepped to the side but Martti didn't; he deliberately concentrated on his walking and struck the girl so that she was forced to stop.

"Look where you're going!" said the girl, and the guardsman cursed. But Martti just giggled to Antti and pretended not to know what had happened.

"Why did he do that?" Antti wondered, not understanding Martti at all.

But Martti's spirits rose even higher, "Let's go and have a bottle of beer."

Martti suggesting that they drink beer? Now Antti did not understand Martti in the least. Martti, who had never before...who had always disapproved when Antti would have liked to drop into a tavern once in a while with the others.

"What are you looking at? Let's go. Why don't we sit here." They were now outside the Kappeli Restaurant.

"We can't sit here."

"Why not?"

"Not on benches for gentlemen!"

"As long as we pay, we are just as good gentlemen as anyone."

"It's more expensive here."

"Where can we go then?"

"Let's go to the beer stand."

Martti would have liked to sit down on that comfortable wooden settee at the round table...lean backwards in the settee, his knees crossed, and his hand on his watch chain just like the gentleman on the other settee, who didn't even have a chain as shiny as Martti's. It was some kind of steel and the watch probably was no better.

"We can't hear the music there," complained Martti.

But he finally agreed to go to the beer stand, which was at the edge of the outdoor market. Antti knew the way.

"Here's how I toss up my watch and catch it in the air. You wouldn't ever dare do this! There! Ha-ha!"

"Don't, Martti, don't! It'll drop and break!"

"And now it goes into my mouth and I might even swallow it. Let's go and drink some more beer!"

"Martti! It's not good for your watch! Take it out of your mouth and put it in your pocket."

"It's my watch...haven't I paid for it with my own money?"

"Yes, yes you have."

"Didn't I pay for your beer even? Didn't I?"

"You did, you did...but I would have paid for my share myself if only..."

"Yes, but I'm the one who paid for it. You don't even have the money for it. What time is it on your watch, Boy?"

"But I don't have a watch...at least not until I buy one."

"Buy one? With what?"

"With my own money...when I've saved enough."

"You'll never save that much money."

"How do you know?"

"Look at you, how touchy you are. What are you so peeved about? I paid for your beer."

"You asked me yourself to drink to your watch."

"You could have paid for the second bottle."

"But you're the one who ordered it."

"You drank it, didn't you? You should have ordered it...since I ordered the first one. You're a greedy man...and you won't ever have money for a watch. I have a watch, but you'll never get one. You're greedy."

"You go on then. I'm not going with you. You're drunk, you're being mean. I'm going home."

"Go ahead. I don't care. You'll never get a watch, but I have one. Keep your mouth shut. You've got such a thin nose, such a pointed nose, your nose is like the point of a knife...so sharp."

The worst insult one could give Antti was to say he had a nose as sharp as the point of a knife. The only way the apprentices and journeymen could make him angry was to call him pointy-nose. Then he got angry, raving mad. He shouted, threw the shoe lasts around the shop, turned chairs and tables over and cursed. And when someone older than he tried to hold him to calm him down, he grabbed at the hand to bite at it, since there was nothing else he could do.

Martti was the only one who had been good to him when the others had treated him badly. Martti alone had never mocked him about his pointed nose and had always stood up for him against the others. And now even he was mocking him just like the others and for no reason at all. This made Antti feel so bad he started to cry. He felt they could never again be true friends and that there weren't any decent people in the world now that even Martti had turned out this way. This made him want to cry even more. He would not have wished Martti anything bad but he could not help thinking that Martti was bound to drop his watch and break it on the cobblestone street.

Martti walked along the stony market place at the shore toward the Esplanade, stumbling once in a while as he walked.

That Antti...what a pointy-nose. The beer must have gone to my head...no, no it couldn't have...not a small amount like that...a grown man. One, two, three...how many strikes? Seven. Yes, the watch said seven too. I'm just as good a gentleman as...There's music over there...

And Martti ran to the front of the Kappeli.

"Do you have a watch, young Man?"

"Me? No! Do you?"

"I have a watch although I'm nothing but an apprentice. What are you?"

"You don't have a watch. You're lying."

"Can't you see the chain shining on my vest?" Martti puffed out his stomach and his chest. "I have a velvet vest, and a watch, and a chain."

"A chain, maybe. But a watch, no."

"Don't I? Look at this. Ahah! Isn't this a watch?"

"You seem to have one. Good that you do."

"Don't leave. Look inside the case if you don't believe it's a cylinder..."

"You'll drop it."

Startled by this remark, Martti quickly put the watch into his pocket. Had he really been about to drop the watch? Something must be wrong with him. What is it? His head? Where did that Antti go? Did he drop the watch?...No, no it's safe in his pocket. Is it running? Oh, yes, still running. I'll put it away, I'll hang on to it so it won't drop.

Then the music began again and a crowd gathered about the music platform to listen. Martti found himself in the midst of the crowd. He also began to listen and started to beat out the rhythm with his head and his feet, and soon with his whole body, so he didn't even remember the watch, not even that he had ever had one.

But in a little while he forgot the music and its rhythm...just as if it had never existed. He noticed that someone was looking at him a short distance away at the foot of the platform. Why is that person looking at him? What is she looking at and smiling about and why is she winking at him as if she knew him? She doesn't stop looking even though he tries to look elsewhere. Then she whispers something into another girl's ear but doesn't turn her eyes away. They both gaze at him and smile. But then only the one stares, the one with gloves and a red dress and a cape and very red cheeks, and eyes which do nothing but look at him.

Martti felt as if he was somehow lifted off the ground and at the same time was being pulled and pushed. Some way or another he had to try to get to the girls. But the crowd was in front of him so he couldn't move.

Martti tried to force his way through the crowd, but he was only pushed still farther away. For a little while he lost sight of those eyes which looked at him and then he rose to his toes and tried to look over the crowd.

Then he saw her again and saw that she too had risen to her toes to look and was still looking. Something throbbed within him as never before. But he had no time to think about it. He pushed forward, using all his power, aching to get through.

The music suddenly stopped and the crowd broke up, carrying Martti with it.

Then he suddenly remembered his watch.

It flashed into his mind like lightning.

He groped for his chain.

His chain was dangling from its clasp.

Quickly he felt in his left vest pocket.

It was empty, and the other pocket was also empty.

No, he couldn't believe it. Yet he felt a cry of despair already rising within him, moving into his throat, straining to get out.

The watch was gone...it was gone. It was not in his breast pocket, not in his pants pocket, not in his vest pockets.

Then the cry, which had been forcing its way out, burst forth. "It's stolen! It's stolen! My watch! Thief!"

He grabbed the hem of the first coat he could reach, then the second, and the third, and finally he grabbed the coat of a policeman who had come to calm him down. He even called him a thief and in between his shouts, he wept.

But the policeman took him by the neck and led him out of the crowd.

"Catch him! The thief! Catch him!" screamed Martti.

The policeman told him to go home and to come to the police station the next day.

Martti went home, crying all the way and muttering to himself.

The whole of that week he muttered at his work so that the others thought he was going mad.

For many Sundays he did not go to walk on the Esplanade. When he finally went, he walked along the very edge and stepped aside for everyone. He didn't drink lemonade and never went as far as the music platform.

He walked along listlessly and didn't seem to be thinking about anything. But he was thinking about one thing and he thought about it with every step: how long it would be until he could save enough money for a new watch.

A Summer Dream (1892)

My melancholy friend told me: who among us has not at least once in his lifetime dreamed of becoming a farmer and marrying a farmer's daughter.

That desire seized me during my last year of school. Continuing until graduation felt unbearable and, in contrast, the life of a farmer was indescribably enticing. It's true I didn't know anything about that life except its joys: driving horses, making hay, reaping the harvest, fishing, hunting, and frolicking on the village green during luminous Sunday nights. But it seemed to me so absolutely noble to give one's self wholly to being one of the common people, to dress in homespun and high leather boots, and to scorn the upper class. And furthermore, I was in love...

We first met on a trip to church. I was living in my father's house on the shore of a large lake, and Mari was the hired girl in a small house across the lake. The churchboat from the other end of the lake passed by our house, and one Sunday I also joined the churchgoers.

I was seated in the choice spot at the feet of the man at the stern, and Mari sat rowing in the seat in front of him. She seemed a little shy, glanced at me covertly from the corners of her downcast eyes, but most of the time she followed the movement of her oar, every now and then tightening the knot in her kerchief, which tended to come untied.

"Why don't you take that thing off since it won't stay tied," I said as an introductory remark. She didn't say anything to that, but when at my request the rower sitting next to her gave me his oar, I sat down beside her to row.

"Are we well matched?" I asked and gripped my oar.

"I won't even try to match you," she answered, yet she quickened her rowing, which was a sign to me that she did not mind having me beside her and that she wanted to be my equal. This was like a gesture of esteem to me.

She was fair of face, her flaxen hair lying in a long braid, her strong hands energetically working the oar, and the heels of her lowcut shoes firmly planted against the ribs of the boat. The collar of her shirt was bright red. She had taken off her jacket, and a striped petticoat covered her knees.

At first we sat apart from each other, each one on his side. After a short while, we moved closer together and before either one of us even knew how it happened, we were joking away like old friends.

The people in the boat treated me as their equal and had accepted me as one of their own, which was a rise in rank to me. I returned the favor at the shore of the church by buying a mark's worth of biscuits, which all of us enjoyed beside the spring in the alder grove.

During the stay at the church, we each walked with our own group. The men relaxed on the shore in the sunshine, listening to the organ music, or stood beside the stone fence talking with farmers from other places about the summer work and the weather. They didn't know anything about me and when they asked, "Where are you men from?" I answered for all of us, "We're from the other side of the lake," and when they still inquired, "From just exactly where?" then I answered again, "From Selkäkylä, the village across the water."

Every now and then I saw Mari in a group of girls and when we had passed each other and I looked back, she did too. She was so pretty and attractive that I began to think about her more and more. I thought about her even in the church pew and when the sermon ended and I saw her go outside, I followed her in a little while. And when we gathered again at the boat and began to get ready for our departure, it happened naturally that we again sat side by side on the same seat to row.

On the quiet Sunday evening we made our way without haste toward the home village. There were boats ahead of us and behind us, the church cross dropped from sight, and the shores of the lake were reflected on the calm surface of the water. On one point there was a rather small house and I said to Mari, "That's really a nice place for a house."

"Yes, it looks nice."

"If only it were ours..."

"It doesn't hurt to think about things, even though they can never come true."

"Why couldn't they?"

"You couldn't live there like a gentleman even if it were your own."

"Who says one needs to live like a gentleman...one could live like a respectable farmer...stranger things have happened."

"I don't think there's an upper class girl who would come as the mistress to such a place," said the man at the stern, who sat in front of us and had heard our conversation.

"One would take one who would."

They didn't seem to really believe in my idea, but I decided definitely in my own mind that that *had* to happen.

Mari asked for the dipper from the prow in order to quench her thirst and when she had finished drinking, she offered it to me.

"Drink, it will do you good, too!"

It was a gesture of good will to which I responded by splashing a few drops of water on her skirt. And when I lifted the dipper to my lips, she retaliated in turn, jerked my elbow and splashed water on my neck and on my chest. And when on the shore of Lepo Island, halfway between church and home, where we made a stop both going and coming, I threw a spruce cone at her and she tossed the hat off my head into the forest, I no longer had any doubts about her affection for me.

The following evening I sat fishing among the reeds in front of her house. I sat there a long time without stirring, looking and listening for movement in the yard and every now and then pulling a perch into my boat. I saw Mari go to the gate, step from there to the meadow and from the top of a high boulder call the cows for milking. They answered from the forest and came, one by one, into sight along the edge of the forest. Then she walked in front of them to the cattle pen in the pasture, made a smudge fire, and began milking. While pouring the milk from the pail into the can, she seemed to notice me and stood with the empty pail in her hand, looking toward the lake. Then I heard her, back again in the shelter of the cows, singing and talking to them. But after milking, she carried the containers to the yard and disappeared for a long time. There was no sign of life from the house other than when the master plodded to his *aitta* to sleep and a little later when the mistress followed him. Even the cows lay down in the field and the smoke from the smudge fire rose straight into the air where it then spread out and descended in a broad fan in front of the threshing barn into the hollows of the meadow.

I began to feel sad and was going to leave when Mari appeared on the path to the shore where, halfway between the shore and the other buildings, her *aitta* was located. She passed her *aitta*, came to the end of the stone pier beside the seine drying shed and began to swish some clothes in the water. She acted as if she didn't even see me. And I acted as if I didn't notice her. However, I thumped the oar on the side of the boat and then cleared my throat. "Good evening," I said.

"Good evening," she answered, lifting her head a little. "Are the fish biting?"

"Not very well."

I steered the boat in front of the seine drying shed and asked, "Are they all sleeping at your place?"

"I guess they are," she answered as she swished the clothes, lifted them up, and wrung the water from them. "I see you do have a few perch in the bottom of the boat!"

"Why don't we go fishing, Mari?" I asked.

"Oh, no, not in the middle of the night."

"But if I come to get you during the daytime?"

"I have no time during the day!"

"May I come to Mari's *aitta* for a smoke?"

"If the master should see it, he'd be angry."

"He won't see anything, if we move quietly."

"There are some girl relatives in the other *aitta*, they'll hear."

"Will they be leaving soon?"

"They won't be leaving until next Saturday, when they will be going to the church with the master."

"Then I'll come on Saturday night."

"You mustn't come even then..."

But she said this so meekly that it was clearer than a direct consent.

"Why is Mari washing so late at night?"

"Because there's not time for another's slave during the day."

She began to climb to the yard and, elated, I turned my boat homeward and rowed slowly away.

That week was long and lonely. I wandered idly about the yard and along the lanes, sprawled on the slopes of the field, even tried to fish, but didn't catch anything. "Why don't you do something," my brothers said. But I didn't bother to answer nor did I engage in conversation with anyone. I just waited for Saturday. At last it came and it moved happily toward night. I had been on the shore watching and had seen the master row by. And so that no one would see me moving about during the night and guess my intentions, I took my boat from the home beach and to the shelter of a clump of alders below the field and hid my hat and jacket in the grass at the edge of the rye field.

I went to bed just as everybody else did. I pretended to be asleep and told my brothers to be quiet. When the whole house was asleep and when I heard the clock downstairs on the wall of the drawing room strike twelve, I rose cautiously from my bed, went downstairs into the hall, lifted the latch on the door, and bareheaded and in my shirtsleeves, I walked boldly across the yard and around the corner of the log cabin. My spine tingled, my ears buzzed, my legs barely held me up, but with a long jump, I leaped over the tobacco rows into the bottom of the ditch in the rye field.

No one had seen me, I didn't hear anyone moving about. Even the dog, who was lying in the yard, had just opened his eyes a slit and then closed them again without following me.

I found my boat among the alders and my clothes at the edge of the rye field. They seemed to know my intentions, were like fellow conspirators. As I rowed along the surface of the water and as the small ripple of wave glided under the prow, it sounded to my ears like a message from the mouth of one who understands and approves and wishes me luck. A night thrush twittered from the trees on the shore, "Go, go...there is no need to worry...all are sleeping, all are sleeping...no one hears, no one, no one!" And from the opposite shore the night mist rose protectingly before me, hid the grass and the trees on the shore, rose to the ridge of the cabin but still did not reach the crest of the hill, where a tall fir tree pointed its crown against the clear sky, so I would not stray from my course.

I heard some rowing but I couldn't tell exactly where it came from but to my joy, it seemed to be moving toward the other end of the lake. And I was out of danger, when a little later I slipped into a ball of mist and at the same time the reeds began to slap against the sides of the boat.

I beached my boat between two willows, hid my oars under a nearby hay shed, and began to steal along the meadow fence up to the yard. Again there was a rye field in front of me and a ditch which led straight to the back of the *aitta*.

Will she let me in, will she open the door, will she let me sit on the edge of her bed, will she let me kiss her, will she believe that I love her...?

There was not a sound, not from the *aitta*, not from the yard. A cowbell clanged. The cows were in a field a short distance away, although through the mist I could see them only vaguely.

I took a lump of earth from the field, threw it against the wall and pressed my ear against a chink in the wall. There was some movement in there now. I threw another lump of earth, a larger one. Now she got up and went to the door. I hurried around the corner to the door and heard her whisper through the crack in the door, "Who is it?"

"It's me...let me in, Mari!"

"You still came, even though I told you not to."

"I told you I would come..."

"Please go away, someone might see you."

"Let me into your *aitta,* then no one will see."

I gently pushed the door open with the tip of my shoe. She did not resist, and I got in.

It was pitch dark in there, just a tiny streak of light peeped in at the edge of the roof. She had slipped somewhere into the back of the *aitta*; it sounded as if she had jumped into her bed and pulled the covers over her. I groped my way toward the sound, my hand happened to touch her hair and she seemed to be giggling when I finally managed to sit down on the edge of her bed.

"Now, why did you come here?"

I was so short of breath that I couldn't say a word. And all of a sudden I was overcome with shyness, I didn't know how to act or how to say that which I had come to say.

Finally I managed to ask whether the master was home.

No, he wasn't, he had gone to the church already this morning, no one else was home except the old mistress.

"So what about it?" she asked a little sarcastically from inside the cover when I still couldn't make myself clear.

I had never before kissed any woman. But I had dreamed about it and fantasized about it for a long time. I groped for her head and leaned toward her. She drew the cover over her eyes, I tried to take it away. She turned toward the wall, I tried to turn her back.

"Mari, now listen to me, Mari!"

I got my hands around her neck, drew her toward me and kissed her fiercely and clumsily on the lips, on the cheeks, on the forehead, and on the nose.

"Don't, let go now, let me be!"

But I did not let go of her.

"I love you, Mari, listen, I love you, do you hear?"

"You're just fooling me..."

But on the verge of tears, I assured her that I loved her and demanded that she *must* believe it.

"You'll love me a while and then leave me."

"You mustn't say that. I'll marry you right now, if you'll have me."

She didn't say whether or not she would, but she now allowed me to kiss her freely, let me put both my arms around her neck, and did not even pull away her head from below mine, where I had placed it. I was even allowed to lie down beside her after she had first wrapped her covers tightly around her.

I wonder if I have ever been as happy as I was that night. I wonder if I have ever since loved as completely, as wholeheartedly, and as purely as on that cool summer night in the half-darkened *aitta*, through whose flimsy roof a tiny streak of light peeped in, from whose beams her meager wardrobe hung, where her strong arms hugged me with almost childlike tenderness, where only her cheeks became a little warm from kissing, where our innocent words were accompanied by the call of a faraway cuckoo and the whistle of a sandpiper along the shore.

When the first morning sparrow fluttered in the mountain ash behind the *aitta*, she asked me to leave and I obeyed upon getting permission to come back another time.

"Is all this in good faith?" she asked.

"Yes, it is."

She opened the door for me, reached out her hand through the crack, and with happy thoughts I rowed slowly home, where everybody was still asleep, and without being noticed, I reached my bed. At that moment, the sun rose and the first breath of morning air rustled the aspen leaves beneath my window.

This was repeated for many nights. She believed me now. We built cottages, we bought houses and cows and horses and drove with our own carriage to be married in the church. Ever longer I lingered with her, coming earlier and leaving later. She no longer feared her master nor I my home folks. I went there even during the day, sat with the master in a room to which she brought the coffee, and she visited us on Sunday nights.

I had decided to leave school and to tell my father everything when the time came for me to go off again to school in the fall.

But he learned about it from someone else.

One morning as I again returned home at daybreak, he was sitting on the porch steps waiting for me. Somebody had evidently seen me moving about at night and had informed my father.

"Where are you coming from?" he shouted in a stern voice.

"From nowhere...I've been fishing..."

"You're lying...you've been on the prowl."

"Who told you that?"

"Do you dare to deny it? You're on the wrong track, Boy...and you'd better watch yourself if you care to save your skin. What were you doing the other night in the *aitta* of Rantala's hired girl..."

"In the *aitta* of Rantala's hired girl?"

"You have been seen leaving there in the middle of the night...Isn't that true?"

"Yes, it's true. But there's been nothing wrong in it."

I stood before my father thinking that I would have liked to say, "Hit me, if you want."

My father was a kind man, we had never spoken a harsh word to each other. My straightforward confession must have impressed him. He controlled himself, evaded my look, and motioned me to sit beside him on the step.

"I believe you, since you yourself say so...if you have not spoken the truth, you'll have your own conscience to answer to."

"I have spoken the truth. And I intend to get married and quit school."

My father gave me a long, searching look. "You plan to leave school?"

"To start being a farmer!"

I don't know whether my father had perhaps in his time experienced the same thing, or whether he just could understand my position. I expected him to laugh at me and to make fun of everything, but he took the matter calmly and seriously and began to talk to me as one does about something which is worthy of discussion.

"The matter is not so urgent that you can't finish school first, is it? You can still do it after that, can't you?"

Of course I couldn't say that it couldn't be done later. And so that is what we kind of agreed upon, that when I had graduated from school, we could take the matter under discussion again.

But now that the matter had been brought out into the open, it lost its lure of secrecy, and when I began to think more carefully about it, I was a little ashamed. I had prepared myself for opposition and there had been no opposition. Then, again, I was still afraid that perhaps my father was laughing to himself over my plans, thinking they were childish. Why would he, otherwise, have treated me so protectively.

I did not see Mari after this, she did not come to visit us and I did not dare to go to see her either. And then after a few weeks I left for school.

And when in the following spring, I returned home from Helsinki, my graduation cap on my head, no further talk about my plans of last summer ever came up. And I was not very deeply affected when I heard that Mari was married.

Nevertheless, that summer dream has never faded from my memory. Mari and her husband lived as tenant farmers in a small cottage beside the country road. Almost every time I drove past it I saw her face through the low window. It seemed to get paler from year to year. And every time, a number of flaxen-haired little girls ran out of the door of the cottage, whose porch served as the summer kitchen, to the gate at the country road to watch me, the passerby. I was told that they lived in poverty and I always felt pity for them as I passed in my bouncing cart. At the same time I felt sorry for myself and my own life. I still often thought that if my "summer dream" could have come true and if I had been a keeper of those great promises Mari and I had exchanged in her cool *aitta,* perhaps I would have become a farmer and an upright citizen, contrary to what I am now...I am nothing of what I wanted to be nor what I should have been.

Teuvo Pakkala (1862 - 1925)

The early years of Teuvo Pakkala (Theodor Oskar Frosterus) were spent in poverty and misery in the slums outside the city of Oulu in northern Finland. His father, a goldsmith, was a restless man and from time to time deserted his family to wander about, leaving his family in dire straits, even during Finland's famine years of the 1860's. Sometimes he took his son Theodor with him on these wanderings, acquainting the boy with the rough, outdoor life and the lumberjacks, tarmakers, and the boatmen along the Oulu River. Later, the son was to use these people and places in his writings. Like his father, Pakkala was restless, emotionally unstable, living in many cities and trying many professions--working as a journalist, translator, traveling salesman, teacher. Pakkala's sensitivity and his acute powers of observation are among the few constant elements of his character. They run through his literary production, which reflects radical shifts just as does his personal life. As a young man, Pakkala read and was influenced by the Norwegian authors Henrik Ibsen, Björnsterne Björnson, Alexander Kielland, Jonas Lie, trans- lating Kjelland into Finnish. Pakkala's first work, LAPSUUTENI MUISTOJA (MEMORIES FROM MY CHILDHOOD), 1885, is a se- ries of pictures of his early memories of difficult times. In it he uses the local dialect and popular speech, even though he knew literary Finnish. The book is rich in popular sayings and proverbs. In an- other early work, OULUA SOUTAMASSA (ROWING ON THE OULU RIVER), 1885, he uses the dialect of the boatmen working a- long the Oulu River. It represents another contribution to the rural, humorous type of realism Juhani Aho had initiated two years earlier with his RAUTATIE (THE RAILROAD). After stating in a letter in 1888 that his ambition was to be a "kansan kirjailija", a writer of folk life, and nothing more, Pakkala's next two works, VAARALLA (ON THE HILL), 1891, and ELSA, 1894, were social protests. ON THE HILL was a series of loosely connected realistic sketches, subtitled PICTURES FROM THE OUTSKIRTS OF A TOWN. After ON THE HILL was published Minna Canth warned him against permitting his sympathies for the oppressed to foster wrongs against others; in other words, not to make the same mistakes she had made in her early writings. In ELSA his artistic grasp is more secure and he molds a well-defined psychological portrait of the main character. In 1895 he published his masterpiece, LAPSIA (CHILDREN), delightful short stories about children. Pakkala is at his best in describing people moved by their imaginations and feelings rather than by reason. He does not moralize and his stories are half-humorous, simple descriptions about the daily lives of children from his own childhood background. Later, in 1913, he wrote another book about children, PIKKU IHMISIÄ (LITTLE PEOPLE) but did not reach the same heights as he had with CHILDREN. Pakkala also wrote plays. The best known one--a popular classic of the Finnish stage and even of the Finnish-American stage--is TUKKIJOELLA (LOGGING ON THE RIVER), 1899, with songs by several poets and music by Oskari Merikanto, a well-known composer. Rural humor and lumberjack romance are the trademarks of this four-act play. His other two plays, KAUPPANEUVOKSEN HÄRKÄ (THE MERCHANT'S BULL), 1901, a satirical farce about small town life, and MERIPOIKIA (SAILORS), 1915, with music by the composer Toivo Kuula, never became popular. In 1902, he published a novel, PIENI ELÄMÄNTARINA (THE MODEST STORY OF A LIFE), which differs from his other works. It has no humor or dialect and his earlier abundant and unrestrained language is more conscious and controlled. It is sharp and lively, almost impressionistic, with brief flashes and quick sketches, due partly to the influence of the Norwegian writer, Knut Hamsun, whom Pakkala had translated, and due partly to the French influence after his trip to Paris in 1896. The novel was not favorably received, perhaps because it deviated radically from what was expected of a psychological novel at the time. Pakkala's greatest contributions to Finnish literature were his psychological analyses and also his ability to present intuitive insights which would later become the "facts" in psychological theory. His short stories and THE MODEST STORY OF A LIFE have these qualities. *Liars?* from his 1895 CHILDREN collection and *The Bishop's Pointer* from the 1913 LITTLE PEOPLE collection both demonstrate his psychological insights into behavior and also his social criticism. *Liars?* shows Pakkala's skill in describing girls at play as contrasted with the adults in the story. *The Bishop's Pointer* is an understanding portrayal of boys from Pakkala's childhood days in the outskirts of Oulu.

Liars? (1895)

Hanna and Lyyli were excited.

Yesterday their cousin Olga had come to show them her new overcoat and had explained that when she had gone downtown on an errand for her mother, all the people had looked at her. Especially people of the upper class. For she had on a spring coat, which is something only upper class children and some rich people's children have. In her own mind, Olga was a little like an upper class child, and her cousins thought so too.

Excited, they marveled at Olga. They had gone to the gate to watch her leave. The hem of Olga's dress swayed so beautifully.

Oh, oh if only they, too, had spring coats! But since they had only long jackets, the hems of their dresses did not even show and thus could not sway.

"If God would only let us find seventy-five pennies on the street, then we, too, would buy spring coats!" said Lyyli.

But Hanna explained that you can't get a coat for so little money; you have to have much more than one mark.

"If God would only let us find a hundred and fifty marks!" Lyyli immediately wished. Walking to the house, she leaned over and carefully looked on the ground as if searching for a needle. When she went to sleep that night, she prayed that God would drop the money in front of their gate, where she would find it in the morning. Immediately after waking up, she had gone out to look, had grubbed in the dirt, even dug holes, and became angry when she didn't find anything. This had happened before, that no matter how much she prayed for something, she did not get it, but, then, she had never wanted anything so devoutly as the spring coat. She almost cried.

Later in the day, when Mother had gone somewhere on an errand, and the two were at home alone, Hanna took Mother's red coat-sweater, which Mother wore working around the house, and tried it on to see if it wouldn't serve as a spring coat. She walked around the room and swung her body so the hem of her dress swayed. Lyyli was utterly fascinated, and began to feel sad that she didn't also have a sweater.

Hanna got Mother's good, black, Sunday sweater from the attic and gave the red one to Lyyli. And then they tried walking and moving together. Even Lyyli could sway her skirt nicely when Hanna showed her how. They both thought it was fun, especially Lyyli.

"Everybody will think these are real spring coats, won't they?" asked Hanna.

Lyyli strongly agreed. And to her, they were very real. Even the sleeves, which were so long they dangled to the knees when they held their arms straight down, and which hung like empty sacks when they bent their arms, were, in Lyyli's mind, just beautiful. That was how it was supposed to be with spring coats. They had better and more beautiful spring coats than Olga! This is what they now were so excited about. They started to walk downtown.

They looked at all the people, to see if they were noticed. And when somebody did look at them, they were happy and swayed their skirts even more. Whenever some upper class women met them, they looked at the two girls with a smile. And after the women had passed, the girls decided that the ladies must certainly have believed them to be rich. In meeting some farmers, they walked with great dignity, in the firm belief that they were members of the upper class!

On one street they saw their aunt walking ahead of them. They walked over to the other side of the street in order to meet her. Lyyli thought, "Now we'll see if Auntie recognizes us!" And as they approached their aunt, Hanna smiled, but Lyyli looked solemn and dignified.

"Where are you coming from?" Auntie asked, looking surprised.

"From an errand for Mother!" snapped Lyyli, confident that this was an appropriate answer, since Olga, too, had been on an errand for her mother.

"What are those rags you're wearing?"

"These are our new spring coats!" Lyyli asserted confidently but a little annoyed that Auntie had called them rags. She started to explain, "We have just gotten them today. Mother bought the material from Sunila's store and Josefiina Juustinen has made them. And Josefiina has been terribly busy, since she has made new spring coats for all the upper class children. Josefiina made our coats before those for the colonel's children, since Josefiina is our godmother."

The aunt listened so amazed that she didn't know what to think. She could have believed everything to be true, if she had been stone blind and hadn't seen they had on their mother's sweaters! And so solemnly and without the slightest hesitation, Lyyli was lying right to her face. And on top of that, Josefiina had supposedly made their coats before making coats for others because she was their godmother!

"But Josefiina isn't your godmother!"

"But she's Olga's godmother."

"Yes, but not yours!"

"Well, but Josefiina likes us as much as if she were our godmother," explained Lyyli, without a shred of embarrassment.

"Those aren't spring coats, you've got on your mother's sweaters!"

"No-o-o," assured Lyyli. "These have long sleeves, because that's the new style. All the ladies and gentlemen have been looking at our coats, and one lady even asked how much they have cost. They have cost 'fifty marks hundred' ".

The aunt would have laughed if it had not been so terrible that such a little twit of a girl was lying so readily, even when it didn't make sense. Sternly, she ordered the girls to go home and said she herself intended to come there to explain their awful behavior to their mother.

Hanna wondered out loud to Lyyli why Auntie was so peculiar that she didn't believe them! However, they didn't care about Auntie and her orders, but went to Olga's to show her their spring coats.

On the way, Hanna suggested that Olga, being taller than they, could be the mother and they could be her children, and they could go somewhere.

Olga immediately agreed to their suggestion. She took her brother's straw hat, on which they sewed beautiful patches of cloth and ribbons, paper flowers, and whatever else seemed to be fitting decoration. They wound up scarves as hats for Hanna and Lyyli. And thus they went downtown once more.

All the people looked at them and smiled, which delighted them. They decided what the people must be thinking and imagining: I wonder who they are? Who might that woman be? My, aren't they pretty! I wonder who has made those stylish new spring coats?...

They returned very satisfied and excited. Olga didn't want to go home yet but went along to her cousins', since she still wanted to talk about herself. In her mind she was the most outstanding of them, as she had an honest-to-goodness spring coat, so that she was just like a real upper class lady.

Hanna's and Lyyli's aunt had already arrived at their house and had explained to Mother and even to Father, who was home for his lunch, how she had met them on the street and how Lyyli had lied. This had seemed quite unbelievable to the mother. But the aunt had assured them that if she had not heard with her own ears Lyyli herself explaining about their spring coats, she would not have believed it either. The aunt had concluded that Hanna must have made up the lies and told them to Lyyli. In any case, it was terrible, and the mother had decided to punish them severely.

Yet, when the girls came in, the mother found it difficult to remain stern. Everything tended to dissolve into laughter. She had never seen anything so funny.

Olga began at once, very seriously, and as if it were something special, to explain the situation; they had walked over the whole town, and everybody thought she was an upper class lady and Hanna and Lyyli her daughters.

"That's what they thought, naturally!" remarked Auntie. "Everybody must have just laughed at the scarecrows you are!"

But nobody had laughed. Everybody had just smiled in a very friendly way. And Lyyli explained, "There was a lady and a gentleman who met us and even they asked each other about us, 'Who might that beautiful lady be, who has such lovely daughters!'"

By now some doubts about her companions had entered Olga's mind, and she started to defend herself. She did indeed have a real spring coat, made by Josefiina Juustinen, who makes all gentlemen's children's clothes...

"Well, and what are these?" asked Mother pointing at Hanna's and Lyyli's sweaters.

And as if it were the purest truth, Lyyli answered with confidence, "New spring coats. They are of the same material as Mother's sweaters, and for that reason even Auntie thought they were Mother's sweaters, but they are not. Mother can certainly borrow these, whenever she needs to..."

Mother was at a loss as to what to say or do. But Father told her and Auntie that the children were not liars, they were just firm in their make-believe.

The Bishop's Pointer (1913)

Santeri Tiura, son of the blind widow, was the best reader among the poor boys who lived in the outskirts of the city, and some boasted that there was not a better reader even among the sons of the well-to-do. He had memorized the whole catechism from cover to cover, and he could read from any book while other boys his age were still struggling with the ABC book. He was called the bishop. This was a title of respect.

Aukusti Stark was as well known for his lack of reading ability as Santeri Tiura was for his reading ability. Aukusti was the oldest boy in the class and did not yet know all the letters in the alphabet. He was called the godfather of a castrated horse. This was a harsh, ugly nickname. And what was worse, anybody could use it. And as strong as Aukusti was, he had a vulnerable spot, an Achilles heel. It was in his neck. The hairs on his neck were so devilishly sensitive, as he himself said, that even if a comb were pulled through his hair with the greatest of care, cold shivers ran up and down his spine and tears welled up into his eyes. If somebody began to pull, or even just pretended to pull, the hairs on his neck, Aukusti grimaced with pain and turned away, his shoulders hunched.

Aukusti had two ways in which he left his boy friends when his mother called him. Sometimes he left running happily, but at other times he left with his head sunk down between his shoulders, staggering as if he were blind. Then his friends knew that now Aukusti was going to read.

Learning to read was an extremely trying task for Aukusti. Sometimes his mother punished him by having him fast for a whole day. This did not bother Aukusti in the least. In fact, he would gladly have made a contract to eat only once a week, if only he didn't have to read. And he certainly would have even consented to sitting down beside the book at any time, even in the middle of his sleep at midnight and as long as necessary; his mother could even pound him on the head with a large spoon or with the end of a weighing scale; she could pull the hairs on his forehead and those on the top of his head...if she just wouldn't pull the hairs on his neck! And that was the problem; his mother pressed her fingers into his neck, grabbed hold of some of the hairs and pulled up...ouch, ouch, ouch!

During the winter and even some time into the spring, the hairs on Aukusti's neck had had quite a long and peaceful rest, but when summer came, his daily ordeal had begun. During the summer the other boys were able to relax from their reading lessons, but for Aukusti, on the contrary, they became even more stressful.

The truth was that Aukusti's mother had received a letter from her husband saying that he would be coming home this summer. He was a seaman and because of the good pay had been on his last voyage for a number of years. When Stark had left, Aukusti had been a little boy. And this little boy was the apple of his father's eye, about whom he had written in every letter, asking the mother to take good care of him and to raise him well. For that matter, Aukusti would have been a good boy, above reproach, except for that learning to read. How disgraced the mother would feel over her husband's distress upon hearing his son's friends call him the godfather of a castrated horse. For that reason, the mother had persevered with the reading. But with little success.

It had been another hot week. And the hottest day was Saturday, a beautiful summer day, but for Aukusti there was no breakfast, no lunch, no supper, and every little while his mother's fingertips were in the hairs on his neck. Nevertheless, the day ended happily when at its close, his mother snatched the ABC book from in front of Aukusti, tapped him on the head with it and said, "As far as I'm concerned you can grow up without ever learning to read." Aukusti understood this to mean that the hairs on his neck would never again be pulled.

On Sunday morning his mother placed on the breakfast table a thick, beautifully browned pancake which, having just been taken off the stove, still sizzled in its fat and filled the room with its delicious aroma.

"I have made this just for you," said his mother good-naturedly. "You may have the whole pancake."

What a wonderful treat after a difficult week, and especially after Saturday's fast. Aukusti's mouth began to water. With a smile on his lips he had already folded his hands to give his table grace...as he had been taught. But his mother, in a gentle and persuasive voice, said, "Let's read a little first."

In the twinkling of an eye, Aukusti's head sank down between his shoulders and his cheeks turned pale. He got his book and staggered to the table.

"Now let's begin," said his mother, still in a sweet, gentle voice as she sat down beside Aukusti.

Aukusti began to read the alphabet. It went smoothly, as easily as water pours. But when his mother began to point at random here and there at the letters, Aukusti began to make mistakes and then became so confused by his mistakes that he didn't even recognize the first letter. His head sank down into his shoulders and he squeezed his eyes shut, opening them a little every now and then as stealthily as a thief.

"This letter you must know," said his mother, sure that Aukusti would know it.

" 'A' ", answered Aukusti. When he didn't hear the sound of his mother's approval, he hunched his shoulders and shut his eyes even more tightly and hurrying to correct his mistake, said, " 'P' ".

" 'P' ", said his mother in a strange voice, but not at all angry, so Aukusti opened his eyes. How dreadful! His mother's finger was near the 'A' and the 'Ö'! Aukusti hunched himself down so far that he was as round as a ball. He waited for his mother's strong hand to press down on his neck to grab hold of the fuzz. But nothing happened. After a long time, Aukusti, surprised and frightened, opened his eyes. His mother was sitting across the room beside the window near the street and seemed to be crying.

The silence in the sunfilled, freshly-cleaned room was grim. Through the open window facing the yard came the distant chanting of a child's voice. At home Santeri Tiura was reading the day's gospel and epistle to his mother. He read so distinctly and with such a clear voice that in the Sunday morning quiet it was as audible over the whole neighborhood as the minister's sermon was in church.

After Santeri's reading ended, the silence in the room continued for a long time. Then Mrs. Stark spoke as if to herself, "I don't understand. I have tried everything. Let his father try when he comes."

She dressed and left for church saying pleasantly to Aukusti as she went, "Eat now, my poor Child."

Aukusti was left sitting with his thoughts.

"Father?"

He didn't remember much about his father. His father seemed just like some huge giant who could lift him up with his fingers by the hairs on his neck and dangle him in the air as the boys dangled flies by their wings.

Aukusti began to think about running away. As he sat thinking about this, the sound of Santeri's reading came once again. After listening to it for a while, Aukusti thought out loud, "What in the deuce is the trick to this reading?"

He had often wondered about this before...there must be some easy method, which some are not aware of, as there was in other activities in which his boy friends engaged and in which Santeri, in particular, was a real master, teaching the others in exchange for pieces of bread.

Aukusti wrapped his pancake in a piece of paper, thrust it into his shirt, put his ABC book into his pocket, and went outside. He went to Santeri Tiura's, not into his house, but peeking through the opening of the door, he signaled for Santeri to come. When Santeri came into the hallway his eyes were like saucers and he breathed heavily through his nostrils for he recognized the fragrant aroma of the wheat flour and the delicious fat...an aroma that is not more fragrant even in the kitchen of the finest manor house. And then, as if he were being led on a short tether he followed Aukusti, who, without saying a word, went through the yard, stepped into the street, and then walked in a very roundabout way into a small alley, which was so narrow that arms spread out reached from wall to wall, and into which only a thin streak of sky showed itself. It really was a secret place!

Santeri thought that in this very quiet place Aukusti wanted to share the sweet tidbit with him in order to get him as an ally against the other boys who teased Aukusti, frightened him about putting him into the stocks, and jeered that he would never get a wife.

Aukusti took the pancake from his shirt and extended it to Santeri, "You can have this whole pancake."

"The whole pancake?"

Santeri did not put out his hand to take the pancake for he began to fear that this was a dream. He was so frightened that he was on the verge of tears.

"Just show me the trick."

Now Santeri roused himself, took the pancake, and began to explain that he had just learned a brand new trick, one which no one knew yet. He had read about it in a library book. He knew the trick in which one could get a needle, a sewing needle, to float on the water just like a splinter of wood.

"I don't care about that," said Aukusti scornfully, pulling his ABC book from his pocket, and continuing, "Show me by what trick you learned to read."

Santeri was baffled. "By what trick I learned to read?"

Now he would never get the pancake! For he did not know of any trick in learning to read. He himself had learned in this way: with a pointer in his hand, he had followed the letters of the alphabet in the order in which his blind mother had pronounced them. Trying as hard as he could, he just did not understand that there was any special trick to it. Choking with tears, he began to explain, "You just have to have a kind of pointer..."

"Get me that kind of a pointer," interrupted Aukusti.

Santeri looked around to see if there was any kind of wood splinter. But when he saw nothing that could serve his purpose, he handed the pancake to Aukusti for safekeeping, ran out of the alley, and soon returned with a pointer which, with a few slashes of his knife, he had made from the first piece of wood he had picked up.

"Now you just start to point at the letters with this," he told Aukusti, who was sitting in the passageway, his book wide open in his lap.

Aukusti examined the pointer on all sides and after carefully inspecting both ends, began to point out the letters, pressing so hard with the pointer that a small hole was left at each letter; firmly and confidently, he pronounced the names of the letters.

"You know how to read now!" shouted Santeri joyfully.

Aukusti burst out in a laugh.

Together they studied the Lord's Prayer and Aukusti learned it.

Santeri and his mother were enjoying the delicious pancake for their dessert after their meager meal when Mrs. Stark brought them all kinds of good food, thanking them profusely and calling God's blessings on them. She explained lengthily and in great detail to Santeri and his mother all the trouble, worry, and heartache she had suffered in trying to teach Aukusti to read, believing that Aukusti was incapable, somehow defective. Then imagine her joy, when after returning from church today she met Aukusti, who without any help, read at full speed, just as a good horse moves at full speed over an obstacle.

Soon the story spread around about the miracle that Aukusti Stark had very suddenly learned to read. It wasn't long before Aukusti took aside many of his former tormentors, turned his ABC book to the last page, to the page with the rooster's tail, and pecking away with his reading pointer, read completely on his own the Latin poem printed below the tail.

One after another the boys came to Santeri Tiura to order a reading pointer. For the pointers he got a piece of bread, or half a piece, a tea rusk, and sometimes even some money. When he heard them praised, heard that the students learned with them, and since new ones were continually being ordered, he raised his price and set a fixed price of ten pennies. They continued to be bought even then. Every child had to have one, and since they either broke or disappeared, the demand was constant. Santeri sold some pointers every day.

But a rival appeared for Santeri. A workman's son, who had moved from another city, also began to make reading pointers. He had them for sale at five pennies apiece. They were well made and attractive. By comparison, Santeri Tiura's best reading pointers were just ugly splinters. And the maker himself was a good reader. Within Santeri's earshot, the other boys began loudly to praise the new master's products. Santeri could not help but admit defeat and had already made up his mind to give up the making of pointers and to leave the field entirely to his rival, when Aukusti Stark blurted out, "It doesn't matter whether the reading pointer is ugly or pretty." What he meant was that with any kind of a pointer used to point with, the reader can point out the exact spot, since the pointer is not as wide as a thick finger, which is like a shovel and points to many letters at the same time so the reader doesn't know which letter is the one in question. But because he was so slow, Aukusti wasn't able to even begin to explain, when Santeri Tiura shouted,

"The beauty of the pointer doesn't matter, the only thing that matters is whether a person learns with it. That's the trick!"

The boys stared. First they looked at each other, then they looked at Santeri, who now stood looking like a winner. Santeri continued, "Aukusti Stark is already reading the catechism and ROBIN'S SON, which his father has bought for him."

"Robin's son? What's Robin's son?"

The questioners were scornful and some even laughed out loud, thinking that Santeri was making up some kind of a story. But Aukusti began to show them with his hands how thick, wide, and long the book was and gave the name, ROBIN'S SON CRUSOE.

The boys became silent and serious so Aukusti had a chance to explain that the book tells the story of a sailor who was the only survivor of a shipwreck to reach a deserted island, and the book even had pictures.

The boys wondered to themselves. ROBIN'S SON CRUSOE! And they were still in the ABC book! Aukusti had been so far behind all of them and now he was so far ahead.

Every boy was ashamed that he had cast aside the reading pointer he had bought from Santeri and bought one from that other boy. Each felt he had done a foolish thing, perhaps even committed a sin, and for this reason had not progressed in his reading as Aukusti had. It was of some comfort that each one had not intentionally committed the sin, but had done so unknowingly. No one had realized that there was some "trick" in the reading pointer but had just believed that the pointer was a good one if it had been made by a good reader.

Santeri would have received many reading pointer orders if only he had remained silent. But stimulated by the effect which he noticed he had made on the boys, he continued, "Whoever makes and sells reading pointers must himself be able to read well, otherwise the reading pointer will have no effect."

With one voice, about five of the boys yelled in delight, just as if they had been freed from a heavy load of sin, that the new reading pointer master was an excellent reader, reading both Finnish and Swedish.

Santeri felt as if he were sinking into the ground. Swedish also! Without a doubt, his reputation was ruined. But suddenly he stood up straight and with his body proudly erect, exactly as if he were challenging that master who was not here, he shouted, "But can he read English?"

The boys hooted with unrestrained laughter and jeeringly

shouted, "You yourself, dear Brother, don't even know how to read English!"

When Santeri reached home, he swore to himself and tossed his whole supply of reading pointers into the stove. He really wouldn't have minded too much if only the boys hadn't laughed at him. Why had he asked about that English when he himself didn't know English. How stupid of him! Now they would laugh at him and mock him whenever they saw him, just as they had laughed and called after him when he left, "Santeri is going home to read English!"

Santeri wept. But suddenly he struck his knee with the palm of his hand. He had thought of something!

Aukusti's father knew English. He had said that for the last five years he had spoken only English so that even now at home English words kept slipping into his speech. He was a friendly, jolly man. Surely Mr. Stark would teach him. And then he would show the boys just whom they had taunted!

The next day Santeri went to the Starks. A bearded and powerful man was showing Aukusti a very large book, a beautiful picture book.

"Is it an English book?" Santeri asked excitedly, but keeping his distance.

"Yes, my Boy," answered the bearded man.

Santeri craned his neck to look. He saw enough of the picture to recognize it as a picture from the Bible.

"Is it an English Bible?"

"Yes, an English Bible," answered the seaman.

Santeri moved closer to get a better look. Then he was overcome with joy and blurted out, "Well I'll be dog-goned! The letters are the same as in regular language!"

"Oh yes."

"It can be read just like a Finnish book," reflected Santeri, happily confident.

"No, no," warned the seaman, and he explained that in the English language one does not read at all as the language is written but quite differently.

Santeri was crushed. In a disappointed tone he asked, "I suppose it's very hard?"

"Yes. And you have to hold your mouth just as if you had a hot potato in it."

"Now, don't you go telling stories," said Stark's wife.

Stark began to read from the Bible. Santeri listened with his eyes like saucers, his mouth open. Aukusti grinned and Stark's wife stood with her hands on her hips and laughed.

When Stark had finished, his wife said, "Never in this world is that God's word! It's just as if you were jabbering nonsense and indeed with a hot potato in your mouth."

"Yes, it does sound strange. That's what I said," remarked Stark. "A language which you do not understand does sound like jabbering, and you think that the speaker is just mischievously contorting his mouth. And that's how Finnish sounds to an Englishman. Once on the ship they asked me to read out of a Finnish book. How they laughed when I read! And it would have been the same even if I had not actually read Finnish but had just jabbered some nonsense."

Santeri asked Mr. Stark to read some more from the English Bible.

"Read a whole page," he urged.

Stark was willing and Santeri was all ears.

After Stark had finished reading, Santeri went home, took the Finnish hymnbook and imitating what he could remember of the contortions of Mr. Stark's mouth and his garbling of the words, he let them come at full speed.

"Goodness gracious! Is that you, Santeri?" asked his blind mother.

"Yes."

"But what are you reading, English?"

"Yes, the English Bible."

"Where did you learn that?" questioned his mother.

But Santeri had no time to answer for he had seen boys coming along the street. He opened the window and in a loud voice began to rattle off as fast as he possibly could, happy to see that the new reading pointer master was among the boys.

Santeri's reading had a remarkable effect on the boys. One of them was able to assure the rest that it was English that Santeri was reading since Englishmen often say "yes", just as Santeri was doing in his reading. Santeri was reading pure English!

Yes! That boy can read whatever language he wants to. Since he can now read English, then certainly he can read whatever is put in front of him, Russian, African, anything!

That same evening one of the boys came to buy a reading pointer from Santeri. Meekly, he confessed that he had bought a pointer from the other boy. But he had learned nothing with that pointer. But he knew he could learn with Santeri's pointer, he was certain of it! Santeri promised to make him a reading pointer for the next day and a very good one at that. Santeri explained that a good reading pointer, one with which to learn to read, must not be made of just any piece of wood but from a special tree and at a special time, just as he had made Aukusti's reading pointer. There were ever so many steps in its making, new steps, which he had learned.

The new reading pointer which he now made for this buyer had one flat end; he carved a cross on both sides of that end.

Santeri's rival laughed at this reading pointer and at Santeri's methods. He said it did not make any difference in the learning of reading what kind of pointer it was nor who made the pointer; you would get the same results if you took a broken twig or an old pipe stem, or anything else. But usually the pointer is whittled beautifully, as beautifully as one can make it.

"What about the sign of the cross?"

"The sign of the cross! It wouldn't matter even if you carved a goat's horn."

To this someone pointed out, "But the devil would get the reader with that kind of a pointer."

The reading pointer master laughed.

"He doesn't believe in the devil," someone in the group remarked.

"He's not even afraid of God," added someone else.

The reading pointer master was left alone and he was never able to sell another pointer.

All bought Santeri's new reading pointers which, it was said, he whittled on Saturday nights and then carved the sign of the cross on them on Sundays during the church service. They were called bishop's pointers. Santeri then began to make the kind with three crosses. They cost twenty-five pennies and the well-to-do boys came to buy these.

Joel Lehtonen (1881 - 1934)

Joel Lehtonen was born in Sääminki, close to Savonlinna on Lake Saimaa, the illegitimate son of a country servant girl. Kind people helped him through secondary school, he attended the University of Helsinki but dropped out to work as a journalist, later as a free lance writer. In 1904-06 he produced his first literary works, three novels and a narrative poem: PAHOLAISEN VIULU (THE DEVIL'S FIDDLE), 1904, VILLI (THE SAVAGE), 1905, MATALEENA, 1906, and PERM, 1904. In all of them the characters know they fight overwhelming odds and will be overcome. Lehtonen began his literary career as a romanticist, as was the fashion, but his romanticism was robust, sarcastic, fantastic, and terrifying. The old folk tales of his home region appealed to him and he published two collections of them: TARULINNA (CASTLE FABLES), 1906, and ILVOLAN JUTTUJA (TALES OF ILVOLA), 1910. Restless and filled with inner disharmony, he traveled extensively from 1907-14 in France, Switzerland, Spain, Italy, and North Africa, writing newspaper articles about his experiences, books about the places he visited, and translating from French into Finnish. In 1911 he published MYRTTI JA ALPPIRUUSU (MYRTLE AND RHO-DODENDRON), a series of short stories from his travels. After a stay in Paris, which for some unknown reason was a disillusioning experience, he wrote PUNAINEN MYLLY (LE MOULIN ROUGE) in 1913, a book about his visit there and two collections of poetry, RAKKAITA MUISTOJA (DEAR MEMORIES), 1911, and MARK-KINOILTA (FROM THE MARKET), 1912, which were broadly humorous, descriptive, realistic. Two other poetry collections, NUORUUS (YOUTH), 1911, and MUNKKIKAMMIO (THE CELL OF A MONK), 1914, were more conventional. In 1919 he wrote his last collection of poems, PUOLIKUUN ALLA (UNDER THE CRES-CENT), alluding to his travels in North Africa. Lehtonen's works always contained something disharmonious and strident; he attacked sham idealism and "niceness" as not a part of real life, yet he yearned for peace and happiness, which he knew he would never find. In 1905 Lehtonen had bought a small estate he was to name Putkinotko (roughly translated, Weed Valley), and his visits there between 1914 and 1920 resulted in a series of four books about the region and its people: a novel, KERRAN KESÄLLÄ (ONCE IN SUMMER), 1917; A short story collection, KUOLLEET OMENAPUUT (THE DEAD APPLE TREES), 1918; and two novels, PUTKINOTKON METSÄLÄISET (THE BACKWOODS PEOPLE OF PUTKINOTKO), 1919, and PUTKINOTKON HERRASTELIJAT (THE FINE PEOPLE OF PUTKINOTKO), 1920, later published in one volume as PUTKINOTKO and looked upon by many as his major work and which has proved lastingly popular. In an unglossed representation of country life, it tells the story of the antagonism between an idealistic landowner and his lazy tenant farmer. Lehtonen eventually sold Putkinotko, buying another place, Lintukoto, haven of peace. In 1923 he again described the characters of PUTKINOTKO in a collection of short stories, KORPI JA PUUTARHA (THE WILDERNESS AND THE GARDEN), which served as an epilogue to his PUTKINOTKO series. The stories are mainly a search for peace and harmony as they also are in ONNEN POIKA (THE HAPPY MORTAL), 1925, in which Lehtonen returns to happy childhood memories. He wrote a number of other novels and in 1929 he wrote LINTUKOTO, a novel about the haven of peace he had hoped to find. His last novel, HENKIEN TAISTELU (THE STRUGGLE OF THE SPIRIT), 1933, was a criticism of the Finland of his time. His last work was a collection of prose and poetry, JÄÄHYVÄISET LINTUKODELLE (A FAREWELL TO LINTUKOTO), 1934. He committed suicide the same year. Lehtonen's writings were the subject of the literary critic Pekka Tarkka's doctoral dissertation published as a book, PUTKINOTKON TAUSTA (THE BACKGROUND FOR PUTKINOTKO) in 1977. The story, *The Gentleman and the Boor,* was selected from THE DEAD APPLE TREES, 1918, which, with the 1917 collection, ONCE IN SUMMER, served as a prologue for his PUTKINOTKO novel and uses the same characters in whom human weaknesses are caricatured. Lehtonen also makes use in this story of the technique of inner monologue, in which a character's thoughts intrude into the narrative without the use of a formal device to introduce them. The story also reveals his conscious opposition to the idealization of common people and the excesses of neoromanticism. The name *Aapeli* translates to *Abel, Juutas* to *Judas. First love* from THE HAPPY MORTAL, 1925, is a return to Lehtonen's childhood memories, that happy, sunny time when he was protected by kind foster parents. However, even in this story the feelings of loneliness and isolation persist.

The Gentleman And The Boor

(Or What You Sow You Shall Reap) 1918

The name of Aapeli Muttinen's summer estate is Putkinotko. [1]
He has a caretaker who is to look after the estate and its garden and
guard the summer house during the winter while the caretaker
himself lives in a small cottage a short distance away. The man's
name is Juutas Käkriäinen.

It is a summer morning, still quite early. Käkriäinen is standing
in his master's garden, at the bottom of its long slope. In front of
him are several large rocks he has dug out of the ground, and with
which he will have to build a garden fence. He looks down at the
rocks and then, in turn, looks around him with dull eyes. The sun's
morning rays, as they beam deeper and deeper into the cool hollow,
shine into his eyes.

The cold mist is slowly lifting off the shore of the bay.
Immensely long shadows spread out over the drained swamp. The
thrushes are scolding and smaller birds, whatever they all might be,
are twittering shrilly.

Käkriäinen stands there, a slightly stoop-shouldered man. His
arms are unusually long, like those of a gorilla; his hands are broad,
his legs quite short. He is wearing a fur cap, even now in the
summer. His head is already hot for the early sun has begun to give
off heat; this is why, in scratching his head, he has pushed his cap
over one ear so his hair sticks up on one side, hair, which is as
messy as a bed of straw. Between his spittings, brown juice drools
from his mouth into the coarse stubble of his heavy jaw. The seat of
his pants hangs in tatters, some of which, as long as rags cut for
rugs, touch the dew-wet grass.

At this moment, Käkriäinen's eyes -- two small eyes below a
stubborn forehead and set between his high cheekbones -- are
gleaming, angry and sullen. When the rays of the sun strike them,
they occasionally glitter as red as the eyes of a dog, or some forest
beast.

He is frustrated and angry. For now he is supposed, as has

1 Weed Hollow

already been said, to build a stone fence, put up a high wall of rocks around Muttinen's garden, at first just on one side. He has to roll more and more rocks from that rock pile. As a protection for his master's, that fancy Mr. Muttinen's, currant bushes, and for his apple trees, which have all died anyway, for reasons that Käkriäinen knows all about, heh, heh. There they stand now, black against the sky. But at their roots the master planted new shrubs, which Juutas now has to take care of. And then there are his lilac bushes, which grow above, close to the walls of the summer house, in fact, attached right to the walls, rotting away good walls. What rubbish! The growing lilac jungle fills Juutas Käkriäinen with disgust. And the same is true for all the other pretty things...useless flowers, whatever they all are, for which this fence must now be built so the animals cannot trample them down.

And he had better start! There's no way out of it. For Muttinen has finally forced him to build this fence: brought witnesses out here into the country...gentlemen friends of his...and with the support of a contract, orders him to build it. Even says he'll drive him off the place if he does not obey the orders.

Drive him, Käkriäinen, off! He, who has kept this place, Putkinotko, as if it already were his own. Yes, almost like his own, for ten years. And that's a fact. But Muttinen is a regular devil. A gentleman and a fraud. He has deceived him, Käkriäinen.

This is how Muttinen had deceived Käkriäinen: some ten years ago, this Aapeli bought this place. At that time there had been no building here other than that cottage back of the forest, the one where Käkriäinen now lives. There was no summer house -- nor was one needed. There wasn't even an outhouse -- and one could have managed even without that -- but Muttinen forced Käkriäinen to build one. He had built that outhouse...and hadn't he otherwise fulfilled his obligations as well, built the outhouse, and cleared more land? Ten years ago there had been nothing here. That is why Muttinen was able to buy this place cheap; he knew to buy when things were cheap.

Then he built this summer house of his. And in the worst rocky ground...He simply wouldn't have it anywhere else. So he would have a pretty view! But then he lets lilacs cover his windows! And then right on this spot he began to clear land for a vegetable garden for himself. Among the rocks. What a place for a garden!

After Muttinen had finished his summer house, with verandahs on the ground floor and even on the second floor, so he could sit on them alone, a single man, he had gone into the village and had inquired at the cottages where he could get a man to guard the vacant summer house during the winters so thieves could not tamper with his things. And whatever other things he wanted the man to do there. He promised that the caretaker could live in the cottage, from which he had already asked the tenants to leave.

At about that time, Juutas Käkriäinen had just been married. He was living in a cottage owned by an innkeeper, and what a shrewd man he was, this innkeeper. He demanded eighty days of work a year from Käkriäinen and Käkriäinen would have to use his horse for as many of those days as the innkeeper might want. And Käkriäinen's wife had already had a baby, and life had been very hard there...It had been different from this place--if only that Muttinen had not deceived him.

Käkriäinen had heard that this bookkeeper, or whatever Käkriäinen at the time had thought him to be, wanted an overseer or caretaker for his summer place. And at his wife's urging, he had gone to ask what the working days and other conditions would be for the caretaker.

Muttinen replied that there wouldn't be many in a place like this. In a place like this! Only a hundred and fifty acres, he said. He was rich even then, the devil, or he just didn't understand about conditions on a farm. That's why he suggested that the caretaker wouldn't have to do anything but watch over the summer house and care for the garden. The what? The garden. A garden, a kitchen garden. This garden, which at that time was just being planted here, was ridiculously large. It was large then, yet he did not ask for more than the hauling of some one-hundred loads of dirt every year; it would take about one week out of a year, part in the winter, part in the summer. Muttinen, for his share, promised to furnish and pay for additional helpers, the planters and harvesters, mind you. In addition, Käkriäinen was only to guard the vegetable garden against lambs and rabbits. And within five years he was to have built a stone fence around the garden to keep out the animals. And in all of this Muttinen has kept his word. Only in Käkriäinen's hauling of the dirt and building of the fence has Muttinen been insistent. And this garden has become much smaller than first planned, very much smaller. This Aapeli had no other conditions. He said he would pay the taxes on Käkriäinen's cottage himself, also pay for keeping the road in good shape, and everything. And he has done so. In return, he expected Käkriäinen to take care of Putkinotko's land just as if it were his own, for his own benefit and according to his own wishes.

Käkriäinen was so astounded at such conditions that at first he had stood with his mouth open. Then he pricked up his large ears and asked, "What were those working days again?" Muttinen gave

a short laugh, laughed out loud, and repeated the conditions. That's the kind he was, --a good man, then. One week's work for this place, for which Muttinen could have gotten seven-eight-hundred marks in rent each year! Now, did Muttinen have some mischief in mind? Or was he just foolish, to give so much away for practically nothing?

Furthermore, Muttinen even promised to settle with the innkeeper so Käkriäinen could move out of his cottage before the end of the rent period. Muttinen said he himself would bring news of this settlement to Käkriäinen's cottage, where they would then make the final arrangements for the caretaker's move to Putkinotko.

In great joy, Käkriäinen ran home to bring his wife this news. It was so wonderful to the wife also that she didn't know yet whether to rejoice over the good news or whether to suspect that there was something wrong somewhere. Anyhow, she finally thought the same as Juutas, that the bookkeeper was too inexperienced in these matters, an ignorant, good man. Just so he wouldn't back out now from his offer!

But Muttinen did not back out. He came to the innkeeper's cottage, he had cancelled the rent agreement, paid the innkeeper for the loss in rent. And he now repeated his earlier promises. Then Käkriäinen's wife said the conditions were good and she hastily moved the coffee pot off the fire to the fireplace shelf, becoming more talkative, particularly since Muttinen treated her and Juutas as his equals; he had pulled a big bottle from the breast pocket of his large overcoat and poured a little something into their coffee; he looked at the children with tears in his eyes and said that he loved the common people, understood the poor. He wanted to help and that was why he was giving over the care of Putkinotko with such generous terms...And in the end he said -- by god, if only there had been witnesses -- he said that at some time he would give Käkriäinen the whole place, since he himself was a bachelor...Or at least he promised part of the land as Käkriäinen's own...if the caretaker fulfilled Muttinen's expectations satisfactorily.

Juutas Käkriäinen almost fell off the narrow bench he was sitting on, so astounded was he at such a promise. But even then he wondered: what did Muttinen really have in mind for him, since he gave such good terms. But he was that kind of man, he didn't understand. And it was easy for him to give, he was rich, the rascal.

That is why he, Juutas Käkriäinen, agreed. But he hasn't gotten this place for his own, not even a piece of it.

And that Muttinen keeps nagging about the fulfillment of expectations. Hasn't he fulfilled them then? Hm, but what expectations! To shovel manure for the trees and the flowers. It really takes all kinds...Muttinen had deceived him.

After Muttinen had had the Putkinotko cottage repaired, Käkriäinen moved in. It had been a struggle during the first snowstorm of the fall to pull behind him his old rattle-bones of a horse with his wife, children, and a sack of potatoes as the load in the wagon, the cow walking behind.

And during that first winter, Käkriäinen did not get around to hauling dirt to Muttinen's garden -- a job that would have taken three days. He had to provide food for the animals and the children and the wife. And his own fields needed dirt, while Muttinen's apple trees...And it also took time to get used to the new place and to reflect on their new position: for once they were renters of a house, even better. It was so pleasant to sit at the neighbors, telling them that Aapeli, the good man, had said he would give Putkinotko to him...if...But he had chased rabbits away from the garden, that he had done!

Nor did the delay in the hauling of the dirt seem to perturb Muttinen in any way when in the spring he came from the city to his land to laze around for the whole summer. Käkriäinen watched him carefully, to see what he would think when the dirt intended for the trees and the shrubs was still in the ground down below in the marshy meadow. But no, Muttinen just pursed his thick lips a little and looked with a long face at his shrubs, which he probably thought should have been in full bloom, heh, heh. And when Juutas explained he had not yet had the time, now in the beginning, since his little ones needed food, then Muttinen said no harm was done, and there was still time to haul the dirt even now in the summer. And thus Muttinen had confessed to the truth of the whole matter: why haul dirt to these trees and bushes at all? Käkriäinen's wife had actually laughed at how good a man Muttinen had been, then.

So not even in the summer had Käkriäinen been in too much of a hurry about getting the dirt for the trees and the berry bushes. For there were other things for a man to do in this new cottage. If Muttinen would have demanded the dirt, he would have answered, exactly as he thought, that it was not good to shove dirt under the bushes during the summer as it would wither them. But Muttinen did not make that demand. What did he do but get men and horses from elsewhere and had them do it. Well, he had the money.

The following spring Muttinen worked in the vegetable garden himself. He pried up rocks, dug around the roots of the shrubs with his fingers, like a pig with its snout in the dirt. Just as if that was necessary. For the sake of the flowers, and things like that. The gentleman was enjoying himself...

And in the meantime, Käkriäinen did real work, worked for himself. The time passed so quickly now as he arranged his life to suit himself, opened new fields and slashed and burned so the trees went crashing. Muttinen, of course, complained at first about the slashing and burning, but when Käkriäinen explained to him that this is what is needed when new fields are opened, he was satisfied; he admitted that he didn't understand such matters. And if some slashed and burned-over slope didn't happen to get planted, well, the cattle could always use pasture.

There was nothing to worry about, living here. The land produced potatoes almost wastefully and even if it didn't grow enough rye to last for the whole year, well, then he could buy more of it, even other stuff, with the potatoes. And with fish. He had his own fishing waters. From the forest here he could even give a few trees away to those in need; there's still plenty of wood here, even if some of it is rotting. This is a good place to live. That could not be said of the innkeeper's cottage, where you had to put in eighty days of work each year.

And yet, the gentleman deceived Käkriäinen. Yes he did.

For he had said ten years ago when he had come to lure Käkriäinen here that he might perhaps give some land to Käkriäinen as his own, if...And that had planted into Käkriäinen's mind the idea that Muttinen would give him the whole place, since he was so good, and so ignorant. And then Käkriäinen had begun to think the place was really his. At least Muttinen had told him he could take care of the place as if it were his own. At first, Muttinen did not pry into another's business. When in the summer he came here to the country from the city he stayed properly on his verandahs, in his hammock, or wherever else he may have lazed around, burning his stomach red in the sun. During the winters, Käkriäinen's life was even more peaceful, even though during the rest of the year he also could take care of Putkinotko pretty much as he wanted. And hadn't he taken care of it? Even expanded the fields at first. He grew a fourth more potatoes now than before. During the winter they had potatoes, their stomachs were stuffed with them, and without worry he could lounge on top of the hearth or even on the bench, for Käkriäinen can grab forty winks on a bench only ten inches wide. And as he had just been thinking, he did have other things with which he bought flour and sugar...fish, for instance. And he had trees; they're no good here in the forest anyway...

Thus the years went by.

But then after a long time, Muttinen began one spring to

complain that Putkinotko's boundary fences were neglected. Käkriäinen had let them fall down to rot as piles of brushwood. At first Käkriäinen was so surprised that he could not manage a single word in answer. And then Muttinen complained that the windows in Käkriäinen's cottage had been broken and last winter had been patched with shingles and rags, with one of the windows plugged shut with a straw mat. With what? With a mat? Should the window then have been left open to the freezing cold and the sting of the north wind? Käkriäinen understood his own situation...Those windows were good enough for him, if not..And as for the boundary fences: Käkriäinen had let them fall down so his cows could get to the neighbors' lands...How could they get through all those twenty-foot wide gates? This way the animals got a larger pasture on the neighbors' lands. But the neighbors' cows have no business coming here, though; Käkriäinen's children are sure to give them a good chase...

But when Muttinen still went on nagging that in the last few years Käkriäinen hadn't even cared to gather firewood for himself during the summer but chopped down clumps of birches during the winter, then Käkriäinen's temper finally flared and he shouted straight out what right has Muttinen to come here and nag him in his own cottage. He, Juutas Käkriäinen, will not put up with such nagging. This had dumbfounded Muttinen at first, his eyes had almost popped out of his head. But then he had snapped his lips shut tight and shaken his head nastily and remarked, "Is that so..." And he had waddled away with such an expression on his face that Käkriäinen was frightened. He was so afraid of what Aapeli might do now. But he did nothing, particularly since Käkriäinen, in order to please Muttinen, hurriedly mended those fences just a little.

Nevertheless, he then set about cautiously to find out if it really was true that Muttinen had not given Putkinotko to him, in spite of their agreement. And then Käkriäinen realized that Muttinen did not intend to give it to him after all.

And why not? Because Käkriäinen supposedly had not fulfilled the expectations: he had not taken care of the shrubs or the flowers, had not done a number of things like hauling dirt and whatever else Muttinen might have requested at some time in the past. Dirt for such things as shrubs and flowers -- and he was supposed to guard them from rabbits, huge Russian rabbits. If only they had been rutabagas, cabbage, but no, they were just rubbish, red and blue flowers. And after the apple trees had died, Muttinen planted currant bushes of a kind the little ones can't even eat from because the berries are black and bitter.

No, Muttinen deceived him, even though Käkriäinen had already thought how comfortably he could live here if he sold the whole forest. And now Muttinen was dispossessing him.

This deceit infuriated Käkriäinen. There was, however, nothing he could do to Muttinen since in his stupidity, he had not demanded a written agreement that this place...But then he knew other ways...he'd show Muttinen's flowers and other silly stuff. What nerve. The master made such senseless demands...a rich man...who had gotten his money easily from selling books. He sucks like a bloodsucker...even though his belly is big. And he doesn't have kids. Käkriäinen has accumulated quite a few...Twice in the last few years the Creator has blessed them with twins...added burdens. But Muttinen sleeps late. What else do gentlemen do? He sits there on his verandahs book in hand, with a hired girl waiting on him. And to Käkriäinen's annoyance, he drags all kinds of visitors here, who make merry and laugh. No wonder they laugh; they drink liquor from early morning; that makes men laugh, if anything. And, moreover, he invites them to play on the piano and other instruments. Käkriäinen has no sympathy at all for such instruments.

And Muttinen shows no mercy even toward Käkriäinen's poor little children; there are eight of them now. Muttinen would have them sent to school. He once had shoes made for a couple of them for school, but they wore out at home. And now he won't give shoes any more, rich and stingy as he is. He wanted them away at school so they wouldn't howl around here like wolves for the gentlemen visitors to listen to. Even though one of the visitors, the singer Valkki, is always howling away himself. And what did Muttinen once say about Käkriäinen and his wife? That they smell like a rotting carcass, that they have bedbugs. What difference did it make if they had dung beetles! And Muttinen had also said that with such lenient conditions they could easily have become rich here had they only wanted to.

Get rich! He, Juutas Käkriäinen, get rich while making somebody else rich, taking care of his forests, his fences!

No. Beginning with the year in which Käkriäinen realized that Muttinen would not give him the place, he had not expanded the fields further. Nor did he take care of Muttinen's flowers and bushes. Nor did he chase rabbits any more during the winter cold...well, the rabbits no longer had the apple trees to nibble at. To annoy Muttinen, Käkriäinen had let his sheep gnaw at the apple trees more than ever before. Then he discovered another means of destroying the trees before the cold finally killed them. When

Muttinen had once undertaken to fertilize his apple trees, Käkriäinen got him to do it with fresh cow manure, and for this reason, Käkriäinen believed, the trees had been eaten away by worms.

So, for some years now, Käkriäinen has been in a persistent troublemaking mood. He has not taken care of Putkinotko. He has not protected the forest but has just permitted thieves to freely haul away trees. He has done nothing about mending the fences but has claimed that the neighbors' cows keep wrecking them. It is true that he has not been able to neglect the fields for if he did, they would not provide him with crops. But he has improved his cottage just enough for the bedbugs to survive the winter cold. Since Muttinen has been grumbling, and since Käkriäinen did not have any written contract to protect him from being evicted, and since there were so many advantages to living here, he had given the impression of complying with Muttinen's conditions. He had promised to begin to care for Putkinotko in earnest...as soon as his swarm of kids would allow. Secretly, however, he has been looking after his own interests, against those of the rich and powerful Muttinen. To earn bread, he had gone to work for others, making sauna stoves. Finally he had hit upon making whisky. If he had just thought of that sooner! Then he would not even have needed to bother with these fields! And there was nothing to making whisky. He has been left alone and has made money off the whisky. He has added to his other earnings so he has been able to live quite well, much to the annoyance of others. He has even put money into the bank against a rainy day.

And this is how Muttinen deceived Käkriäinen. He would have him fertilize his flowers, trees, and bushes, all of which Käkriäinen hates. They make it so dark around the house! Now Muttinen even had roses planted in place of the apple trees. For such things the man wastes his money. It was good that Käkriäinen had not cared for them even from the very beginning.

For he hates embellishments, just as he hates the very air Muttinen breathes. When Muttinen stays in his summer house, Käkriäinen tells his little children, "Remember now, children are happy in the summer, so just holler, 'Whee!' " When Muttinen has had very important guests, he has gone over to the summer house to talk to him wearing his worst rags, even though nowadays he has very good rags, and giving off a stench among the flowers. And in a matchbox he once even brought some little creatures, plucked from his armpits.

But now...who would have thought their disagreement would

reach this point. Just how did it happen?

Not long ago, Muttinen demanded that he sign a contract. When Käkriäinen heard this, he disappeared. For a week he hid in the forests and villages. He finally had to return home. The witnesses, of course, were still there...those fancy gentlemen. Muttinen called him in and read the conditions out loud.

To hell with such conditions, Käkriäinen had thought at first. It's true, they were not hard. They were just as easy as the earlier ones, those agreed on orally; but these conditions, in very plain and exact words, had definite rules about caring for the garden and the building of this stone fence, besides the care of the forest and his cottage, as well as other jobs. Even about the making of whisky. It was never to reach Muttinen's ears that Käkriäinen was making whisky. What did he mean by that? And finally, at the very tail end of the paper there was a statement that Käkriäinen was to leave Putkinotko on May 1 of the year following the one in which he does not fulfill the conditons to the letter.

That's how hard the conditions were. But what choice did Käkriäinen have? The conditions were good...especially in view of what they would be anywhere else. And Käkriäinen would have been chased off like a rabbit had he not agreed, not approved the contract by putting down his cross. He does not know how to write at all nor does he even care to know. And finally, Muttinen, in the presence of the witnesses, had once again warned that he would have to leave if he didn't remember particularly the section about making whisky. And to top it off, he had laughed, the devil.

That's the kind of devil that Muttinen is. And that is why Käkriäinen now has to build this stone fence around these trees and bushes, which he has tried with every possible trick to destroy. Useless, ugly things! The apple trees have grown nothing but worms, fortunately.

Is Muttinen really serious about doing such an evil thing?

Käkriäinen is brooding about this at the foot of the garden, looking at the rocks, which he should begin to tackle. And all of a sudden he becomes frightened. A window in the summer house creaks and flies open, but perhaps it is just one of those gentlemen visitors, one of those wicked witnesses? But no, it is Muttinen himself. Between the birches he now appears on the balcony in his red gown, in his long woman's gown. What in the hell is he doing up so early? flashes through Käkriäinen's mind. He should stay in bed, Muttinen. That's what he, Käkriäinen would do if he were Muttinen, a rich man. And usually Muttinen does stay in bed, or sits in his rocking chair...exactly as Käkriäinen would.. Käkriäinen is quite frightened, for he has even been drowsing in his brooding, standing there getting ready to build the fence. He is even more frightened when Aapeli comes right up to the railing and looks out, right at him. He's so serious, his eyes are so grim under his swollen eyelids. Käkriäinen remembers the contract, he gets very busy, turns this way, turns that way, looks at the huge rocks, getting ready to take them into his arms. But at the same time the thought enters his mind: is Muttinen really serious? Isn't there any way he could be appeased, even pleased? So he would not be so unreasonable in his demands in the contract. Perhaps one could try to make him laugh a little...since he is such a good-natured man. That is why Käkriäinen now, half in anger and half in fright, grabs a rock so enormous that it barely fits between his arms, and lifts it -- he is as strong as a bull -- up above his head, holds it there a long time, and from under the rock he peers at Muttinen, and grunting, he attempts to laugh, "Hahaha!"

But Muttinen does not even smile, he turns his back and walks inside. He is serious; Käkriäinen will have to build the stone fence, and that is just the beginning. And he will build it. He will build it high and straight. For...Muttinen is a shrewd one...that contract of his...yet it's not a bad one after all.

First Love (1925)

It was fair time, fall fair time. Antti, who now attended the *lyseo*, was wandering in the big market square with his classmate Uuno. It was night, it was dark, but yet lighter than usual; here and there old-fashioned street lamps burning lamp oil, glimmered faintly, but the tents and booths gave off brighter light. People were swarming everywhere. Horses were running. Some gypsies were maneuvering their chargers through the crowd. Here were some Tartars, there were some German Jews, selling furs. Uuno started to provoke them; under their very noses he squeezed the hem of his coat into the shape of a pig's ear, shook it, and said, "Madam, buy the skin of an old Siberian woman!"

Then a Jew or a Tartar would rush out snarling, measuring stick in hand, and chase Uuno away...a few moments, and Uuno would appear again to tease them...

Whistles blew, piercing the air. The wild animals roared in their cages...Some man sang something called a fair ballad. This was almost the first fair Antti had really seen; only a couple of times before had he been to town for the fair, when he was smaller. He wasn't very big even now -- in his second year at the *lyseo*. Then the fairs had seemed quite strange. But this fair was -- wonderful. When he had first wandered about the market square with his foster father, a sleigh bell close to the wall of a tall building had clanged and beside the bell, the head of a *living* person was hanging down, talking -- a severed head. It talked, it invited people inside. What was it? It looked terrible -- a red, bloody head. And a man at the entrance to the same building called out, inviting people inside to see the talking head...Strange, horrible, Antti thought. How did the head get there? Was the sleigh bell rung from the inside, since it rang by itself? Did a string run through the wall to that bell? Everything was strange...like a dream.

There was still something dreamlike about this fair. Antti walked beside Uuno, or behind him, small, helpless...There were fancy coffee breads. There were cardboard play horses, gray and dapple-gray horses, -- toys, which Antti still liked even at this age. There were so many wonderful things.

Uuno was not yet such a rogue as he was later to become, the prematurely uncanny Uuno, whose insolent comments and slightly affected, brazen maleness Antti instinctively feared; Uuno didn't even smoke yet.

Fair time, or actually the evening before the fair...

But Antti could not stay there very long; he would have to go to his room to do his homework. Only the day after tomorrow, the second day of the fair, would the *lyseo* have its fair holiday.

His room seemed gloomy to Antti, it was so solemn and almost grimly silent. Antti lived in the home of an honorable, friendly family. But to Antti, the place was somewhat lonely. The food was good--but there were so few people, just the man and his wife, who had no children his age, and two servant girls. It was very quiet there. Only once in a while did Antti hear someone playing the reed organ in the drawing room on the other side of his wall. Antti sat at his table and studied, studied his lessons, night after night. School was frightening, the teachers seemed to demand the impossible. Antti was very ambitious and, furthermore, he did not want to cause his foster parents any grief; he had to fulfill his duty. He studied -- studied until his mind was all muddled. At times the solitary boy was invited to go for a walk. He did not go, such and such still had to be memorized, and he was not forced to go. Antti sat quietly in his room under the lamp, his back hunched over. Antti was considered an industrious boy.

But now it was fair time and Antti was excited over the freedom.

But the joy was short-lived, soon he had to go back home, into the silent house, where the ticking of the wall clock could be heard from one room to another; into a strange life, whose purpose he had begun to doubt in some vague way: perhaps it was not so purposeful after all, but accidental, somehow tragic...his constant companion the sadly humming lamp. Lessons, which one had to wrestle with unceasingly just for the honor of it. Outside, darkness -- the city went to sleep early at night, it was as if half-dead; each person got up and went back to sleep, busying himself with something in between...like a machine. And the children, for their part, studied their lessons; if they could just get through tomorrow, take just one day at a time, then the battle would be won for the moment.

Now he had a short, wonderful holiday. Ah, that it had to end so soon!

But Uuno said they still had one more place to visit, the best was yet to come. Uuno had money, given him by his mother, and generous Uuno now took Antti into a large tent, in front of which, on a stage of boards, men and women dressed in many-colored clothes called out in the mysterious lantern light. Actually, only one woman! The costumes sparkled with silver stars.

Uuno and Antti went inside.

And there, in that tent, Antti fell in love with that woman. In the dim tent, snakes were being exhibited---Uuno said they were made of wooden pieces joined together with hinges---snakes, which that woman charmed from a chest, touching them with a golden magic wand. Of course, Antti already knew the Circe myth. And there in the reddish light of the torches, many other things were also exhibited, though nothing as awesome as those snakes. The torches flickered in their shining bowls on decorated stands. It was hazy and dark in the tent. There was only a small crowd. Soon Antti saw nothing but the woman who performed tricks of magic. She was dressed in a long, white robe -- Uuno called it a shirt. A golden diadem glittered on her head. She stood on a red platform near an altar with a black curtain as background and a fluttering torch flanking each side. Antti's eyes devoured the priestess; his chest ached---it pained him when the male actors' hands touched the sorceress in helping her into that white robe. Antti would have been prepared to do anything. He did not hear Uuno's mocking words. In Antti's eyes, the woman had beautiful, curly hair---black hair, which, in reality, was probably dyed and damaged from burning with a curling iron; beautiful hair---and a high, noble forehead which shone more nobly than the golden diadem on it. A beautiful, white forehead---radiant cheeks. And even more radiant, her bosom.

Antti was consumed by fire, overcome by agony---excited, blinded,---madly in love.

After the show he hurried to his room. But he did not begin to study. He told one of the servant girls, the housemaid, that he now had a mistress.

The girl was stunned and she laughed, "Antti! What do you know about those things, you!"

And she laughed even more heartily.

Antti was not at all hurt by her laughter. In that laughter there was some kind of understanding---as if the housemaid were in agreement with him, as if they had something in common; it almost felt as if he could have spoken quite boldly about such things with her. And then Antti went to work---but not to wrestle with his lessons. No, under the oil lamp, which cast a faint circle of light over his books, he settled down to compose a love letter to the divine circus lady.

It was agonizing work. But he managed. The letter had to be written in Swedish, for the charming and wonderful lady spoke Finnish only poorly; she probably understood very few words of Finnish. But Antti had already studied some Swedish, and he now had to search his memory for the vocabulary to use. The letter was fire, adoration, it was worship, praying on bended knees, tenderness, fidelity, holy sacrifice. What did Antti wish to sacrifice? That he did not know but he wrote about sacrifice. He begged the fascinating goddess for a meeting. With what words? At this time he had not yet learned the word *rendez-vous*---he had not studied the refined and cultured French. But he revealed his thoughts in other ways. The letter was written in very small handwriting, for he intended to slip it secretly to the goddess tomorrow night, perhaps even directly into her hand. And the goddess would press the letter to her warm bosom. If Antti did not dare to do this, then he had another plan ready. In the tent, the goddess made coffee using magic---made coffee in a way that no coffee beans or anything was needed. She served the audience the coffee made in a few seconds from nothing. To show that it was real coffee, she walked among the rows of benches set in a curve in front of the stage, carrying a tray with small cups. Antti had decided to put his letter into one of those cups, after first drinking the coffee. The beloved woman would find it in the cup.

Antti knew his lessons the next day, even though for once he had hardly studied them at all; love, and the presence of the goddess in his mind, made him particularly alive, alert, confident. His ambition was to distinguish himself so the noble woman would in no way come to shame because of him, so she would not come to suffer from Antti's fantasies. Antti gave his vigor and his wit as a sacrifice for his loved one, and he was proud of it.

Finally even this school day came to an end. This evening Antti was completely free; tomorrow was a holiday. Antti's foster parents came to town for the fair, perhaps to hire servants, perhaps to buy livestock, but certainly to get gifts for the hired help, woolen kerchiefs for the girls and scarves as colorful as the rainbow for the hired men. When the mistress came to town, Antti tugged at her skirt and asked for some fair money. He got a whole mark.

With the mark Antti intended to buy a ticket to the circus tent; it was almost impossible to sneak in there without money. By no means would he have asked Uuno for the money. Even if it hadn't been otherwise unthinkable, Antti wouldn't have asked Uuno for the simple reason that he might have come with him and perhaps have guessed everything.

Antti slipped into the tent. He trembled when he saw his beloved. So beautiful was the adored woman that Antti closed his eyes when, for a moment, Circe looked back toward the black curtain ---closed his eyes, thinking only of her splendor. Then once more with his eyes, his soul, he devoured the woman's dark hair, radiant skin, divine bosom, which appeared to him so tender. Antti had arranged for a seat in the front row, sacrificing most of the mark.

Finally, the sorceress once again made coffee; hocus-pocus, a wave of the magic wand, and the coffee rose steaming to the empty altar, which Circe had lit with a torch to prove to the audience there was no coffee there and that she had no means of help, no coffee beans, no serving tray or cups, nothing. And now the goddess ceremoniously descended in her long, star-studded robe, which swayed about her hips and revealed her bare feet, clad in Greek sandals---descended into the crowd, close to Antti, a mere mortal.

"Who want hot coffee?" the goddess asked in broken Finnish.

Nobody wanted any; what pigs these people are, thought Antti. Beautiful Circe should turn them into pigs. But Antti wanted some; he bought a cup of coffee, twenty-five pennies. Trembling, he grabbed the small cup---his hand shaking so the coffee splashed over the brim. The goddess stood in front of him. Antti drank. He didn't care if the people stared at him or not. The goddess before him gave off a fragrance---an intoxicating fragrance. Oh, if only he dared touch her, her robe. But he didn't. He didn't dare. Dejected, he quietly swallowed that little bit of coffee, which was lukewarm and bitter, but tasted delicious to him. He felt as if he were in this way sacrificing something, drinking the vile coffee---just as ancient heroes were sometimes required to undergo lowly tests.

He drank very slowly. In his left hand he held the love letter, folded into a very small packet; it was as small as a packet of aspirin powder. After drinking the coffee, he mustered up his courage---the courage of Achilles, and quickly pressed the letter into the empty cup.

"Thank you," he said, actually he sighed. He was thanking her for the coffee.

The circus lady saw the small boy put something into the coffee cup. She glanced to see what it was, snarled in anger, dug the paper out of the cup, tossed Antti's letter to the sawdust-covered floor of the tent, into the wet dirt. And then she left.

Pain tore through his chest---a deep grief began to gnaw at him. The goddess had not grasped his intention, even though the writing on the outside read in Swedish: "Oh, my Beloved!" Or, perhaps the woman was too proud...

And now the letter, the precious letter, lay there in the dirt, in the sawdust, in the filth---trampled upon!

What if it should be found, if someone from the audience should find it! It's true, the writer's name was not on it, for that he would give the sweet woman later, somewhere and somehow---Antti had not yet thought that part out. But Antti could be recognized from his handwriting! This added to his anxiety. But the anxiety, however, was nothing compared to his deep grief...

Sad, Antti left the tent. He went to his home, to his old room, his heart filled with pain and sorrow. That night, unseen by anybody, he wept out of love. The next day he suffered much agony; he did not go to the circus tent again. He had no money left.

He mourned for a long time; he mourned for many days, a whole week. Then he forgot; that normally happens with love.

Frans Eemil Sillanpää (1888 - 1964)

Frans Eemil Sillanpää is the only Finnish writer to have won the
Nobel Prize in literature, receiving it in 1939. Reflecting the spirit of
the 1920's and 30's, his writings combine a feeling for the deeply
philosophical and majestic with descriptions of very simple,
primitive people in simple surroundings. Sillanpää was the son of a
small farmer at Hämeenkyrö, west of the city of Tampere. With
financial help from friends he finished secondary school and spent
almost five years at the University of Helsinki, studying science and
medicine with the intent of becoming a doctor. However, finding
that his interests were literary, he dropped out of school, returned to
his home region, worked as a farmer, married, and continued his
literary activities, which he had begun as a student. His first novel,
ELÄMÄ JA AURINKO (LIFE AND THE SUN), 1916, was favorably
received and, encouraged, he collected his short stories entitling
them IHMISLAPSIA ELÄMÄN SAATOSSA (THE PROCESSION OF
LIFE), 1917. Sillanpää's subject matter consists of the farmers and
tenants of his rural home district, its maids and farmhands, its
children and animals, and the surrounding nature as it changes with
day and night and the seasons. He describes people realistically and
is not blind to their weaknesses, yet his stories carry a
lyrical-romantic feeling for nature and an appreciation of life that is
almost mystic. On occasion he animates nature, making it observe
and take part in human actions. As a result of his training in the
natural sciences, Sillanpää looked upon man first of all as a
biological being, a part of a large whole, existing within the
framework of the biological laws that govern all species, and in
which man instinctively fulfills his destiny without weighing the
causes and effects of his actions.

He felt the ruling force of all human life is love, or sex, and the
reproductive instinct has moral values unconnected with social
rules. His characters submit to the forces of nature rather than act
voluntarily. His other works include the novel, HURSKAS
KURJUUS (MEEK HERITAGE), 1919, a story from Finland's 1918
Civil War. It is a book without Sillanpää's usual lyrical descriptions
of nature nor his philosophical considerations. Then followed a
collection of short stories, RAKAS ISÄNMAANI (MY BELOVED

COUNTRY), 1919. In the 1920's Sillanpää wrote several collections of short stories which some consider among the best in Finnish literature. Most important are HILTU JA RAGNAR, 1923, ENKELTEN SUOJATIT (UNDER THE PROTECTION OF ANGELS), 1923, MAAN TASALTA (ON GROUND LEVEL), 1924, TÖLLINMÄKI (THE HILL WITH THE CABIN), 1925, RIPPI (THE CONFESSION), 1928, and KIITOS, HETKISTÄ, HERRA...(I THANK YOU, LORD, FOR THESE MOMENTS...), 1930. By this time Sillanpää was facing a crisis; his creative powers seemed to be failing. He was invited to edit a periodical, which proved exhausting. But in 1931 he produced his best known book, NUORENA NUKKUNUT (FALLEN ASLEEP WHILE YOUNG, also called THE MAID SILJA), a story of young love and premature death. Only two books written after this one are considered on the level of his best compositions: MIEHEN TIE (THE WAY OF A MAN), 1932, and IHMISET SUVIYÖSSÄ (PEOPLE IN THE SUMMER NIGHT), 1934, his most complexly structured work about a group of people, each of whom fulfills a fundamental natural role. In the 1930's he published two more collections of short stories, VIRRAN POHJALTA (THE BOTTOM OF THE RIVER), 1933, and VIIDESTOISTA (THE FIFTEENTH), 1936, both unremarkable. By 1939, when he received his Nobel Prize, Sillanpää was disillusioned and failing, and his devoted wife had died. In 1941 a novel, ELOKUU (AUGUST) was published and in 1945 he wrote IHMISELON IHANUUS JA KURJUUS (THE BEAUTY and MISERY OF HUMAN LIFE) about a poet whose creativity is failing--much of it appearing autobiographical. In 1953 and 1955 he wrote three volumes of memoirs, grew a bushy beard, was called "Taata" (Grandpa) by the people, gave talks and read Christmas messages on the radio. He died in 1964 at the age of seventy-six. In *The Hired Girl* from THE PROCESSION OF LIFE, 1917, Sillanpää tells the story of a simple girl in simple surroundings who submits to the forces of nature rather than act voluntarily. Nature, as it changes from winter to spring, receives a lyrical-romantic treatment, and from time to time Sillanpää animates nature to observe and take part in the actions of the story.

The Hired Girl (1917)

On Easter Monday Sanni, the dairymaid and the only hired girl at the Liutu farm, was free after the noon dinner until evening milking. After helping the farm's sixteen-year-old daughter Elli in the kitchen with the dinner dishes, she entered the large, clean living room, where the only sound was the ticking of the wall clock and where the dozing furnishings seemed to start when the door opened, almost as if apprehended in brooding about forbidden things. With complacent steps Sanni walked past the stove to her bed in the corner of the room. There she paused beside the window.

The wide window sill was her very own. On one side of the sill lay her catechism and hymnbook, one on top of the other; there was a square mirror which, although cracked in two, was still held together by its frame. There also were two reddish hair pins, a comb, and a double-folded Christmas message. All this, plus the four-poster bed with her clothes hanging on the wall beside it and a pair of shoes tucked casually under the bed, created a homey space. Whenever she came here during her free time, Sanni felt as if she were at home; she could look out of the window, even hum a little.

But now, after watching the melting world for a while, Sanni began to comb her hair. She did it so quietly that if someone had come through the door, he would have thought he was entering an empty living room. A strong feeling of holiday spirit pervaded the room which, in a strange way, mixed with her idle thoughts and feelings. The benevolent sunlight was like the soundless singing of hymns still lingering as a tolling in the peaceful mind of one just returned from church. The sound came perhaps from the tiny, little rivulets which streamed along the dark roads like veins winding about and then branching out. Their gentle rippling and gurgling filled the air outside and streamed with the daylight into the living room, where once in a while came the soft sound of the comb being drawn through Sanni's brown hair.

Having wound her hair into a knot, Sanni yawned, placed her hands on her hips, and glanced at her body. The languid quiet of the two-day holiday began again to press pleasantly upon her. She lay down on the bed, turned on her side to face the wall, and felt the heat of the afternoon sun in her blood. Her Sunday blouse felt a little tight as she lay there so she unbuttoned it at the breast and her heavy white undershirt fell into generous folds. And so her thoughts slipped again into a pleasant, half-mystical mood; in its solitude, her mind surrendered itself to attend to its own matters, taking pleasure in the images which seemed to flow from her rounded limbs to her closing eyelids. The images continued without invitation, without permission, adding to her languid pleasure. Half asleep, she stroked the nearby crack in the wall and now as so often before, lying on her bed on Sunday evenings, she surrendered completely to this mood.

This mood had first appeared during the past spring. It usually appeared as she lay on her bed on a Sunday afternoon as if challenging the solemnity of Sunday with its sinfulness. Sanni felt that only now was she becoming an adult, becoming a true hired girl, one who has her own bed, her own affairs. This was all the more strange since she already had a child over a year old whom, in fact, she had just now begun to remember. And at the same time she began to feel good about this son, almost to her own embarrassment, since she didn't have to take care of him but could, as an unencumbered girl, lie on her bed in this spacious living room. Concealing her secret joy, with her eyes closed she held her breast tightly and finally for once she said it, "Let the boy grow up in his grandmother's cottage. I'll go out and enjoy myself, I'll go to the village..."

The ticking of the clock no longer reached her ears; it had changed into a vague lapping of waves. The room around her grew more silent, finally leaving her conscious mind altogether. Her mind wandered to the dusky corners of the village, to the fragrant boughs of evergreens, to the straw in the haylofts. Finally, her mind completely left her body, left it with mouth ajar, stretched out on its back on the corner bed, breathing the fragrance of the woolen Sunday clothes and the healthy flesh...

It was already dusk when Sanni suddenly awoke, turned in her bed, and smacking her lips, groped beside her. Even though half asleep, she almost had to laugh when she realized where she was and in the dusk saw the familiar window panes and behind them the familiar bit of evening sky. It had been so pleasant as he had turned in the bed and wrestled with her so that her blood was still on fire. But suddenly something had crashed, she had wrenched herself free and cried out, "No, no!" She awoke.

Sanni yawned slightly, rubbed her face with her hands, and tried to doze off again to recapture her dream. But it did not come back. Only the musings of the afternoon kept swimming in her head as if strengthened by her dream, spreading a pulsating feeling of satisfaction throughout her body. Oh, oh how nice. Being a young hired girl...

Just as Sanni was planning to get up she heard the footsteps of two people coming quickly toward the living room as if searching for something. They stopped right at the door and a boy's voice said,

"Come on, let's try it now." It was the *lyseo* student, a guest at the farm, and the other person was Elli. They began to dance and the student breathlessly hummed a melody. They stopped in the middle of the floor, stayed there a while, and the student said with emotion, "You don't know how to do anything." A little later, with Elli laughing excitedly, he said, almost in a whisper, "You don't know how to do anything--or do you?" Now with quick strides they approached Sanni's bed and carried along by their fast pace, with their arms around each other, they landed on Sanni. This delighted the student immensely, he fell into the bed dragging Elli with him and in the confusion he began pressing against Sanni's body, hugging her ardently. Elli pushed her head between them and hugged them both. When for a moment they stopped, intertwined, Elli said, "Shouldn't you be going to the barn, Sanni? Mother has already gone there."

Then Sanni, disentangling herself, rose from the bed, twisted and stretched her lissome body, buttoned up her blouse and left for the barn. As she moved toward the barn humming a dancing song, parts of her dream still lingered in her mind and her body still felt the boy's recent ardor. An oddly shaped full moon had appeared in the sky while she slept. It rose from the village as if trying to hide and seemed to entice Sanni like some familiar boy behind a post...

A blissful recklessness, which she had never felt before, seized her soul and body. After her chores were finished, she would go to Kivelä to visit with Alina.

She went through the barn door. In the pale light of the early moon the farmyard and the sky seemed to be in complete harmony, as if nurturing secret plans.

Sanni's transgression had happened about two years ago, just at Easter time, which that year had fallen a little earlier in the spring. Her suitor had been one of those college students who occasionally would come to the country for visits of varying lengths. It wasn't yet quite clear to Sanni who he was, where he had come from, or where he had gone afterwards. The event itself had also become much like a dream in her mind. The boy, who was born afterwards, was a totally separate matter; he was some kind of unfortunate mishap in the course of her life, an accident, which had to be accepted as the price for past moments of pleasure. When she sometimes reminisced about those moments she had spent with the student, the child never entered her mind. Or if toward the end of her reverie he came into her thoughts, she roused herself from her daydreaming and began to work with increased zeal.

Everything had happened in one night.

She had gone to the neighboring farm at dusk as the pale Easter moon peeped over the top of the barn from behind the birch grove and the thawing earth was crusting over in the chill of the evening. With a wool kerchief over her head and rubbers on her feet, she waited in the kitchen until the hired girls had finished their work; then they went to the village green to the swings. The student had also come there; he stood, handsome in his white woolen sweater, beside the swaying swing and in the sheltering dusk looked at her, at Sanni. Then he stopped the swing and in the most gentle voice asked if he could sit beside her. Sanni had never heard a young man speak in such a way. But after getting on the swing the student did not say a single word to Sanni but began to kick and laugh with the girls who sat on the opposite side of the double swing. But the more zealously he did this, the more definitely Sanni could feel how his arm kept pressing against her shoulder and how the side of his strong chest warmed her breast.

Just then the moon rose, large and silent, but anticipating and promising, like some approaching moment of joy. Those on the swings disappeared into the dusk among the dark evergreen branches, and in the clear air the creaking of the swing could be heard far away; the ring of their voices fell on the ears of a solitary wanderer who had been charmed into listening. A drop of water fell every now and then from eaves, turning to ice as it touched the earth.

A feeling of fellowship had developed among those on the swings and they decided to go to the village to dance. The student jumped off the swing, pulled Sanni with him and neglecting to withdraw his arm from around her waist he asked, "We're going, aren't we?" They went.

It was already quite late; the large houses in the village and the small cottages ringing it were settling down for the night. But they didn't miss their young people on such a beautiful holiday night.

It was the time when the moon was at its fullest and it was shining even in the early morning when the student walked Sanni home. The air had remained mild the whole night through, everything was soft and still, watching and listening as the drops of water fell from eaves and turned into ice as they struck the earth.

Sanni felt as if she had already known the student for a long time, somewhere on the other side of childhood, in some muted past. They simply had never come together until this night when, during the dance, the student had taken her on a kick sled far along the country road, where he had kissed her. Even now they did not speak, for what should they have said to one another. It would have been like speaking with only one voice in the moonlight; it would have been absurd.

The walk home went slowly, for Sanni could not bear the thought of withdrawing her arm from around the student's waist. Furthermore, time after time the student stopped and wanted to kiss, and this always took a long time. The clock must surely have been at least two when they came into the yard at Sanni's home.

Until now Sanni had never had a real suitor. She had grown to adulthood as the naturally shy daughter of good parents; she had developed a strong, beautiful body and had moved to sleep in a small *aitta* on the opposite side of the yard. Nor did her parents watch over her at all but were happy to see her go to the village on Sunday evenings. But in spite of these advantages, the neighbors waited in vain for her to get a suitor. No young man had yet come to her door.

Although this now happened to Sanni for the first time, there was nothing strange or frightening about it. She would scarcely have been alarmed had her father stepped outside. Jokingly, she asked the student, "Guess where I sleep." He happened to guess correctly and so Sanni took her key, opened the door, and they went inside.

Sanni felt that everything that happened was just what she had been waiting for as long as she could remember. It was just as when a spring grass shoot waits for something, for the rain, which it has never felt before. It is true that she resisted a little but never enough to prevent it from happening. It was all so thrilling.

This is the way Sanni's transgression had come about. She never saw the student again, although later in a very casual way she learned what his name was. And she had no keepsake from the student except the ten-mark gold piece he had given her upon leaving. And, of course, later on, the child.

After this dance Sanni did not go to any evening gatherings or dances. During the first weeks after the student had left, she lived in a strange, wonderful daze, her whole being reminiscent of one of those gentle women who for some reason have suddenly become pious. Noticing then (Actually, her mother noticed it.) what was happening to her, she could no longer go anywhere nor did she want to. She stayed at home through Christmas and then, leaving her newly born son in her mother's care, she went as the hired girl to the Liutu farm. It was a small, isolated farm, a good place to serve in, especially suitable for someone like her. After this she had gone home only a few times to bring money for the boy's upkeep and occasionally she went to visit Alina.

That winter and the following summer she remained placid in the solitude of the farm. The uneventful life at the small farm did not disconcert her mind, which, after that momentous event, had fallen into a state of peaceful slumber. And as if not wishing to disturb the dreamer, the world around her moved quietly farther from her, turning its eyes away from her. On her part, Sanni longed for no one, waited and hoped for nothing as she walked along the grassy forest path to fetch the cattle. Perhaps she was slightly puzzled at how the birch grove changed during the summer. She did not understand what it was, only that it was not as it had been. Her languid glance did not perceive the world's turning away from her.

But then fall arrived, the nights grew darker, they seemed ghostlike in the moonlight. As might be expected, this began to disturb Sanni, for after going to bed she now sometimes felt as if she had been sleeping the whole day through only to be awakened by the desolate night. She could not remember that there had ever before been such nights. A faint feeling of loneliness seized her. She could lie for several hours with her eyes open and even though she did not think about anything in particular, she found her pillow moist; she had been crying. This was odd since she did not feel that she lacked anything in this good place. She had not thought about the big event and, anyway, that never brought about a tearful mood. But now this happened to her more and more often. At times she thought of talking to Alina about it, but she immediately felt that would not be appropriate...

Then the snow came and unknowingly Sanni fell again into the old slumber.

Just when people had become used to winter, spring swept over the land. The snowdrifts began to shrink away and in their midst blades of brown grass peeped out, and the dry fibers of the bark on the trunks and branches of the birches quivered with the breath of the invisible wind. Again Sanni felt as if she had awakened from sleep, but that feeling no longer came at night when she lay in bed but in the middle of the morning as she carried evergreen boughs into the barn. Their fragrance was so heart-warming; the sound of the cows' contented chewing and the clanking of their chains floated through the open door into the blue world, where everything was melting and dripping. She found herself humming and talking to Elli, who was in the back of the barn feeding the small animals, the lambs and the calves. The lengthened days passed quickly, and at night she again was unable to sleep. But now being awake was a joy and if her eyes sometimes grew moist, she felt that the tears came from deep inside her, where quite clearly something was melting.

Her uneventful childhood and the past two years faded from her memory; she felt herself timidly rising to where new worlds and experiences awaited. The beginning of her dream brought them closer and unveiled many images; the memory of them made her glance shy even during the day. In the evenings she hurried through her work to have time to go to Kivelä to ask Alina to come out and then arm in arm they would walk along the country roads for a long time chatting together.

As the spring wore on this new mood possessed her more and more. She could feel it in her body. It ached and pained her so that she often had to turn and twist, beginning for the first time to notice her body's shape. As she looked at her body she had to smile as she remembered what it had been like when she was a little girl. When Sunday afternoon arrived, she was drawn to her bed as if by some irresistible impulse and as she stretched out on the bed she felt as if she would have gone willingly to a man. Sanni's peaceful, slightly proud mind had, despite the recent happenings, remained just the way it had been shaped by the life in the loving and gentle shelter of her simple cottage home. Now a stream of adult thoughts rushed into her mind, shattering its composure, tantalizing her...She was a hired girl, healthy and strong, at her very best. Whom was she lying here for, behind walls on Sunday nights, weeping and wrapping her empty arms around her bosom? Wasn't it her own affair? Come what will...

Sanni brooded about such things although no one who saw her face and eyes as she moved about on those warm spring days would have believed it; her outward appearance seemed a gentle reflection of the day's brightness.

But now at the end of April, on Easter Monday, she decided to go out in the evening. She hadn't been out to enjoy herself for two years.

That is why Sanni was pleasantly excited as she and Alina were approaching the dance hall. Her eyes were shining and she giggled frequently as they chattered about many things.

But when the gable of the dance hall came into sight, the same dance hall where they had danced then, a feeling of desolation suddenly seized her. She felt as if she had been forced to leave a dear friend in the midst of happy plans to go to a dreary place, where the walls and even the gateposts appeared grim. Even Alina there beside her seemed like a stranger with whom she had been forced to walk. A most peculiar thought flashed through her mind: at this moment she wished she were sitting in her small room in her parents' home.

They had, however, already reached the road running through the village and could hear the music through the windows, from which uneven lights were flickering. Bursting with laughter, a man dashed out of the door to the yard bringing with him a gleam of light and the buzz of voices. At the same time another man, bareheaded, and two laughing women also came outside and down the steps. There was music and noise. And there she was, Sanni, once again at the dance...

"Alina from Kivelä," one of the women whispered.

"Yes, and Sanni from Liutu. My goodness...Oh, for heaven's sake..." Both women came towards Sanni and Alina, and both young men followed them, trying to pull them back. "Come on, Girls, let's hurry inside, the good waltz is going to waste." They went in. One of the women took Sanni by the hand, asked some questions, whispered, and laughed.

Even inside, Sanni did not feel comfortable at first. Something there seemed different from last time just as something had seemed different on the path through the birch grove last summer, even though nobody noticed Sanni particularly and everything else was just as usual. It was intermission and the musician was tuning his instrument in a back corner, and around the door the young people were competing for seats. Sanni stood with Alina in front of the stove in a crowd of girls which began to thin out slowly as the dancing resumed and serious looking couples appeared on the floor to dance. The more awkward boys bounced up and down as they danced but the boys from the big farms and those who had been out in the world danced even the polka so smoothly that their heads did not jerk from side to side. They knew how to dance and their faces showed that they knew people were watching them.

But then two rugged-looking fur-capped men cleared a path from the door, placed their hands on each other's shoulders and began to dance more gracefully than any other couple. They plainly were showing off their dancing, their faces reflecting deep concentration, for now everyone was watching them. And many had to admit that the pair knew how to dance. Two hired girls who were of the same height also danced all the dances together. Even during the intermissions they stood hand in hand without speaking.

Perhaps the light was dimmer now but to Sanni it seemed that on that other Easter it had been much brighter in here. When they had come in then, the light had sparkled everywhere, in the air of the room, in the eyes of the people sitting on the benches. Then it had seemed as if everyone had, on the spur of the moment, decided to go dancing. Then it had not been so serious. Now there was no talking, there was only the music and even it played old themes...about drops of water which now and then dripped into the moist earth, in the moonlight...

Sanni of Liutu just stood there. Her gay recklessness vanished into the music's flow, her gentle glance seemed to be seeking some small token of sympathy. A young man passing by noticed this. It was Yrjö, Eeva Pirtti's son, slender, good-looking, blue-eyed, who didn't spend his time hanging around the door but danced energetically. He was no more than twenty but had already traveled about in the world and had long since forgotten his mother. He gave a sidelong glance at Sanni's hairline, her shoulders and...She was prettier than the others...The road to Liutu's and all the places along it flashed through his mind. He didn't even feel like dancing now but sat down on a bench, a pleasant feeling running through his body...

"Let's have a circle dance!" shouted the girls.

"The mother thought the thieves had come.
For her daughters dear swains had come."

The man who had been in the yard when they came took hold of Sanni. The song ended and another began. Sanni noticed Yrjö's blue eyes and chose him. Alina came inside with some man, her eyes still shining from something that had just happened. They joined in the dance without looking at each other, and Sanni was glad that she happened to be in the middle of the circle.

Many songs were sung--

"The road is smooth with sand
The wandering boy is roving--
Hey, hooray, hooray--Yrjö...Yr...
My sweetheart is young and pure,
I cannot bear to leave him.
Hey, hooray, hooray..."

The music joins the singing, which then ends in applause. They dance, even Yrjo dances and at this very moment one of them feels as if the university student of two years ago is there in one of the adjacent rooms and that is why she dances so well. Yrjö is easy to follow.

By midnight it seems as if the lamps are shining more brightly and the people dancing better. And it seems as if the student is still sitting in the side room talking and laughing with others. Alina has again disappeared somewhere; she has completely forsaken Sanni; who knows where she has gone off to this time. The moon is still shining...And now Sanni feels a poignant helplessness but yet a confidence in her desire to surrender. With downcast eyes, quite unaware, she presses closer to her dancing partner and with the fingers of her left hand squeezes the strong arm as if she wants to feel what it is like.

Time has stopped moving; it is standing still. It is early morning.

Sanni goes toward the room where the refreshments are served.

"Where are you going?"

"I'm going to get Alina."

"What for?"

"To go home."

"Don't go yet...Let's go together..."

Silence. A waltz begins and at the door someone slaps his palm against his boot: ladies' choice!

Sanni nods at Yrjö for the dance and says, "Then we'll go."

On a quiet April night one sees far in the moonlight, sees two people come out of a hay barn. First a woman comes out and starts to walk slowly toward the road without looking back, back to the man who a little later strides out of the barn and pauses before it. The woman keeps on walking but the man stands for a moment, hands in his jacket pockets, the glow of a cigaret lighting up his face. He doesn't seem to know whether to follow the woman or remain standing there. He doesn't seem to feel like doing either, he moves uneasily about, peers around him and the tip of his cigaret glows even redder. It seems as if their relationship is not quite clear, even though they are two young people who have stayed together for at least an hour in a hay barn. And on such a moonlit night, in the morning hours!

The woman has already gone so far that whatever the man will do, he must do soon. His situation is awkward. It does not seem proper to separate from the girl as if she had been cast aside. But there she goes all by herself as if she were just returning from some errand; she doesn't look back, doesn't slow down her pace. He was foolish to rush out to stand there; why didn't he remain lying in the hay long enough for her to disappear from sight. But he had not intended to let her go yet, what the devil got into her. He had by no means seduced her, he had gone with her since she was willing, and she had been passionate herself. But then she breaks away and leaves, and he did not even get a chance to grab her arm to make her stay. They could still have stayed on since everything had gone so well. Damn it...

He begins to walk behind her; at first he just walks casually but upon reaching the shade of a threshing barn he starts to run; he finally catches up with her and in a playful voice, trying to catch her eye, he sputters, "Just where do you think you're going?" In the moonlight the woman's flushed face appears indifferent, almost complacent. She does not alter her pace in the least even though the man has reached her side. She looks down in front of her as if she had heard nothing of the question except its sound, hardly even that.

And so they walked silently side by side, the woman with short, even steps, the man with slightly longer strides; the rough black road crunches beneath their feet. The man keeps looking at the woman's face constantly, but when she does not·look at him, he begins to hum a polka, one that had been played many times last night. All this does not perturb her in the least; she is completely alone and the man realizes that talking is fruitless. This is most mortifying to the man, but he cannot bring himself to turn back, or to pretend to become angry, for there is absolutely no reason for *that*. And so he just keeps on humming his polka, pretending to be very content, just as if this sort of thing were natural between them.

The curves in the road follow one after another through the quiet countryside until the cluster of buildings on the Liutu farm become visible at the edge of the rocky hill. The small roof over the dinner bell is outlined against the lightening sky, and a dog barks. They go up the side road past the woodshed to the passageway through the barn. The man knows that the woman will go into the house without stopping, but he still remains standing at the entrance of the passageway as if waiting for the woman to look back so he could once more charm her into coming to him.

And she does look back. In closing the door behind her, she turns and her glance glides over the man standing at the passageway entrance but it does not stop there. And the door closes.

The man gives a short laugh and with light steps walks back the same way, glancing occasionally at the moonlit sky.

Parting from her companion of the night, Sanni entered the living room. She was completely calm; her eyes were immediately drawn to the pale light at the window, and the stillness of the night fell sharply upon her ears. The unhurried ticking of the clock was like an old man's serious voice, not loud, but direct and calm. It spoke to her for a few moments with the whole silent living room listening but then it disappeared somewhere and left Sanni looking out of the window at the barren fields and the threshing barns. She could not see the moon but the moonlight fell beneath the window like a living spirit. She began to hear the heavy breathing of Taave, the hired man, from his bed near the door. Sanni listened to it closely for a moment and upon hearing that it was deep and steady, she felt that she was alone at last.

Everything that had happened seemed to her to be in some distant past, as if someone else had lived it, someone almost a stranger to her. She still felt the nervous excitement of this night; yet it felt as if this night from some distant past had, in passing, just casually touched her. For a moment everything stood still, just as did the moonlight over the darkened earth.

Looking at the familiar horizon, she suddenly had the impression that the house, the village, the whole world was empty, that she was the only inhabitant. She had experienced this before and had always wondered if anyone else had ever felt the same way. A night like this has no end; she does not stir, she sees only the contour of the forest. As she keeps on looking into the forest, Sanni is captivated by her mood. She is standing beside the window of her room, into which the distant world of people is only dimly reflected. Although a deceiving emptiness lurks behind every corner, it is comforting to look at since it is so far away.

But suddenly she awoke and, repulsed, saw all that had recently happened, the dance, the men...She almost smiled to herself remembering the man who had moved like a shadow beside her as far as the barn and had then vanished from sight like a rat into a corner hole...They're all like that she felt herself saying silently, but at the same time she was startled as if it had been someone else whispering those words into her ear. Was it the university student? He suddenly appeared from somewhere to stand near her in the dark. He stood there and looked at her. Even though Sanni did not glance in his direction, for the first time she saw his face clearly. She saw his eyes and mouth smiling and inviting her into the dark. Sanni was repelled; she fixed her gaze near the corner of the threshing barn, and then the image of the student began to plunge about in the air and finally disappeared. Sanni remained there staring.

A feeling of infinite loneliness, finally released from deep within her, now overwhelmed Sanni. She is ten years old, no longer in her own room but in a distant, and forbidden, wilderness on a cloudy summer night. A repressed cry raged within her--like that of someone sinking into a bog. She felt her arms reach out and then, embracing only emptiness, she crossed her arms against her breasts as if craving something unknown, yet long desired. But nothing in the universe responded. Then slowly, as if fearing to disturb the discreet peace of the living room, a tear appeared in the corner of her eye. Unhindered by her widely open eye, the tear rolled down her cheek; other tears soon followed. The beautiful stillness quivered and broke, the glow in her eyes blurred, and the moonlight shattered into tiny beams. Sanni undressed and went to bed to weep beneath the covers.

What was she weeping about? Certainly not over her new transgression, for at this moment she felt it to be so insignificant that she was almost amused thinking about it. Nor was she crying over her first love; that also seemed to glimmer far away, dim and fading. It was nothing like that at all, but she could not grasp just what it was she yearned for. In her feverish mind everything was muddled -- the loneliness of the fall, the recklessness during the spring which had ultimately led her to the dance. -- Who am I? I am Sanni, here is my hand, I am a hired girl. -- She raised her head. -- This is Liutu's living room, the clock is ticking over there, it has been ticking the whole time. -- She held her head up for a while and gazed at her tears reflected in the window. The air vibrated with signs of the approaching morning. Sanni laid her head back on the pillow and her eyes closed in sleep.

--She is sitting on the steps outside her room in the evening. She does not know whether it is spring or summer, but the sky is full of soft clouds, foretelling a lovely rain for the night. She feels someone drawing near. She goes quickly into her room, slips into her bed and waits. He comes through the door, approaches in the half dusk and she allows him to lie beside her. Tenderly she embraces his slender body, which is so young that no one else has yet embraced it. A pleasant thrill flows through her body; it is as if a great ache has been released. Then someone is rattling at the door. It is the university student with money in his hand, drunk. An acute anguish seizes Sanni and she presses herself tightly against her companion. The cover on the bed is snatched off, she shivers, for she is naked; she rushes off somewhere; Yrjö dances alone in the air, dances a polka in the air above the floor of the room.

The *lyseo* student sleeping in the room next to the living room, who had awakened when Sanni came in, fumbled vainly, trying to open the door leading into the living room, but that door was never used; the key was missing. Sanni no longer heard him repeatedly clearing his throat behind the door. After awaking from her first restless dreams, she had finally fallen into a deep sleep. Deep sleep at last brought an end to Sanni's state of confusion.

Outside, the moonlit April night was fading away. The air was filled with the scent of melting ice, a sign of spring, as, unperturbed, the world moved from holiday night to workaday morning.

Maria Jotuni (1880 - 1943)

Maria Jotuni (Maria Gustava Haggren) was born in Kuopio, the capital city in the province of Savo. In 1900 she entered the University of Helsinki, where she studied aesthetics and general history for some years but then devoted herself, without taking a degree, to writing. After her marriage in 1911 to V. Tarkiainen, one of Finland's foremost literary scholars of his time, she divided her time between homemaking and writing short stories, novels, and plays. Maria Jotuni began her writing career with two collections of short stories: SUHTEITA (RELATIONS), 1905, and RAKKAUTTA (LOVE), 1907. These stories are short, concise, terse and her handling of her subject matter is firmly realistic. In 1908 she published an essay on the Norwegian writer, Knut Hamsun, whom she admired and who had some influence on her acceptance of the subconscious and instinctive forces in man. In her later short story collections, KUN ON TUNTEET (WHEN YOU HAVE FEELINGS), 1913, and TYTTÖ RUUSUTARHASSA (THE GIRL IN THE ROSE ARBOR), 1927, her natural style of writing changed as her intellectual grasp of language grew stronger. She became a master of the concise short story, often used dialogue or monologue, even letters, to unveil the speaker's personality. Her characters speak of love, but pursue selfish ends, which they discuss openly. They describe their lives matter-of-factly but reveal the frustrations and feelings that lie behind their disillusioned words. Through her characters, Jotuni often expresses her belief that women were denied the right to an independent life. Her short novel, ÄRKIELÄMÄÄ (EVERYDAY LIFE), 1909, is one of the major achievements in Finnish literature as a realistic, seemingly humorous description of rural people. The public considered her a humorous author who wrote about funny people from the country. She may have described her characters humorously but the undertone of her writing was earnest, if not bitter. Some of Jotuni's plays are: MIEHEN KYLKILUU (THE RIB OF MAN), 1914, her most successful play, TOHVELISANKARIN ROUVA (THE WIFE OF THE HENPECKED HUSBAND), 1924, a bitter and satirical comedy, and the posthumous work, KLAUS, LOUHIKON HERRA (CLAUS, MASTER OF LOUHIKKO), 1946. She also wrote three collections of aphorisms, in which she reveals very personally, her world of ideas. As late as 1963 a posthumous work was published, a novel dealing with married life, HUOJUVA TALO (THE TOTTERING HOUSE), which has aroused much attention. In all her work Jotuni is a psychological realist. Her style is stringent; she outlines quickly and sharply what she wants to describe. Often both comic and tragic elements merge together into intellectual humor. Her most important object of description is always man. She is especially adept in illustrating with deep insight the relationship of women to two major factors in life, love and death. The motif of most of her stories is love or the absence of it. The action is often set in the past and narrated by the main character in a long monologue interrupted only by brief remarks by the listener. The stories in this collection are excellent examples of her concentrated brevity. *Love*, the title story from her 1907 collection and a good example of Jotuni's use of dialogue, reveals the personality of the speaker through her open discussion with her friend of her matter-of-fact pursual of material ends of marriage. *When You Have Feelings*, the title story from her 1913 collection, is also in dialogue form and reveals some of the speaker's frustrations and feelings when she speaks of love, yet pursues material, selfish ends. *Death*, also from WHEN YOU HAVE FEELINGS, graphically portrays the conflict between emotional reality and the practical, material necessities revealed at a time of death. *The Girl in the Rose Arbor*, the title story from her 1927 collection, which some consider one of her best achievements, is a long short story. It also uses dialogue, some of it imagined. Both love and death graphically enter the story as it presents some social realities of the time.

Love (1907)

-Well, in the end everything turned out all right. But he sort of made a mess of things right at the beginning when he started out, as it were, at the wrong end. Men...they just don't understand about things like that.

-They just don't seem to notice how...

-That's just it. But let me tell you about it from the beginning, how everything came about.

-Please do.

-First he said, "May I ask if the young lady has ever been in love?"

-And what did you say?

-What did I say? I said, "Mr. Shopkeeper, what difference does that make? If, when I was younger I did some foolish things, that is of no importance now."

-How true.

-He had placed his hand here on my knee like this and said that he would like to learn how to love.

-And what did you say to that?

-What did I say? Not a thing. At first I was going to shove his hand away but then I thought that perhaps it might be better to take my time and wait, so I began to put up with him a little. Then he said I had gained weight. "Mr. Shopkeeper, you're just kidding," I said. "You really have," he said and then he placed his other hand on my back. "May I make love to you?" he said. "What?" I asked. "Would you let me get close to you?" he said. "And then?" "Make love like people usually make love." "And for what purpose, may I ask? No, Mr. Shopkeeper, you ought to stop and consider that no longer at our age...if when one is young, curious, and so on, one gets infatuated and so forth...but if what you want, Mr. Shopkeeper, is to propose to me, just ask me straight out and not in any roundabout ways, so I can understand and answer accordingly. Is that your intention?" I asked. It was, that was his intention, but he hadn't yet thought about making any definite contracts; if only he could first be allowed to, as it were, make love a little.

"No, not until after the wedding," I said. "Only then, in the lawful way."

"Of course, only then," he said. Nor had he had anything unlawful in mind. His thoughts moved only along proper lines. He said that he had always thought that when he had enough means so he could afford to support a wife, then he would support one. Comfort and joy are well worth that price.

"Of course," I said. And then I told him I could get along very well without getting married. Of course I could. I already earned seventy-five marks a month at the office, and I had close to five hundred marks in the bank as savings for my old age. But, of course, better is always better. As far as my legs are concerned, I mean. Soon they will not tolerate standing in a draft. I have rheumatism in my legs. And now that he knows this, he can't say afterwards that he didn't know about my legs when he married me. There's nothing else wrong with me, and if next summer he would be willing to spend a couple of hundred marks on those legs, I could go for treatment at a health spa, so that in the future there would be no further expenses for them.

"Oh yes, of course," he said. He would give the money, if we got married. And things would probably work out all right since he had to marry some time, and especially when he would be getting such a solid person as me, who won't mess up his life, then he would prefer to go to some expense. For he had seen that much in life, that the cheaper you get something, the poorer it is.

"Well, that's your business, do what you want," I said.

"The house is there, ready."

"And I will provide all the linens," I said.

"And there's money, if it's needed."

"No thank you, not until after the wedding. That's the usual custom."

"Everything's settled then."

"No matter what happens," I thought to myself, "it can't be too bad." And, of course, in time I'll get used to the man. It's best to do at the proper time what must be done. And since this one is well-to-do and even-tempered, I have nothing to complain about there, and the other things I can easily handle. It isn't that I wouldn't have been a good wife to a poor man. I was made for a poor man. And I would have made a good wife for a poor man. I would have understood a poor man's condition better and worked without complaining in order to improve our condition. But it didn't happen that way. The man I had in mind didn't notice me. He did not know, I am sure, the ideas that filled my mind and haunted me for years. "Don't think about him," I said to myself. "Don't waste your time thinking about him, he doesn't care about you." But what if he did care, I always said to myself. And I did think about him. When you are at an age when you should get married, you think about it. But what is not to be, is not to be. It's as simple as that. And there are, after all, many other men. And among them one is no more special than another. Nor was he any special kind of person. For I saw what he was. But, anyhow, I keep thinking about him and it gives me a feeling of loss. So then I told this one that a man must be clearheaded and understand the order of the world to which he is subject, so that for example, when the woman whom he has taken as if for his own pleasure does not demand yearly pay for her position, then the work which she puts in for the home is like a voluntary contribution, and there will be no talk about pay...*that* can be called *love*, if you wish. "Do you understand?" I asked.

"I do, I understand perfectly," he said. And he would also give generously of his money. No narrow limits would be placed on it, and *that* can be called *love* as well.

"Yes, it can," I said. And with this, it was settled. The next day we went and bought the rings.

When You Have Feelings (1913)

-Me, happy? No, indeed---why should I be happy? No, I'm not happy.

-But you've just been married, and everything.

-Just married, you say? That's true, I have just been married. But I got married against my will.

-Against your will?

-When you're poor you sometimes have to do things against your will.

-Did your parents make you do it, Viia?

-What do I care about parents? Besides, I don't even have parents. I did have a mother, but a father I never had. There just aren't enough fathers for all the hired girls.

-What made you do it then?

-Necessity. You see, when you're poor, you get married without even thinking. Of course a poor person knows that a stupid act is a stupid act, yet she goes and does it anyhow.

-That's true.

-That's true. You see, the story of my life goes like this: out there in the country there was this Antti from my home village, and he was as handsome and ruddy as a balsam flower, and he kept calling his feelings love, and I also called my feelings love, but for no reason. You see, calling it love makes it nice--but nothing more. Still, when you're young you say anything, even if it is just in fun. Well, this Antti brought me fancy coffee bread from the fair and everything, and I was considerate and sweet to Antti. And why not? At least I care about people, and even now, when somebody is talking to me and says, "That's right," I also say, "That's right." Why should I disagree? But this Antti particularly appealed to me. This one is mine, I thought and he would have been too, if this rascal of a Matti hadn't come in between us. Matti happened to show up at a very bad time and, wouldn't you know, he began to like me. You see, when I got a job in town, then wasn't this Matti the hired man in the same place. At first I didn't even notice him, even though I do notice men, especially if they're handsome. But this Matti--he was just a little man, a pip-squeak. But that didn't prevent him from suddenly popping up in front of me and saying, "Viia."

"Oh, it's Matti," I said.

"Matti, Matti, yes."

"And how are you, Matti?"

"Can't complain."

"Can't complain."

"Here, take this," he says and presses his hand into mine and then scurries off to the barn.

-Oh my, a ten-mark piece. Did he give me this for keeps, I wonder. I guess he did. And since I was a poor girl and my pay was only six marks a month, all of which went for shoes, I thought it really was a lucky thing he gave it to me. Now I'll buy Antti some mittens and I'll make myself a blouse in the city style. I had only plain blouses, which had been perfectly all right up to now. Well, I made a new blouse and I even made it out of red silk. And it was a pretty one.

-But what if he gave me that money just as a joke, I suddenly asked myself and might want his money back. Well, I started to worry about that, so whenever I saw him I would sneak away. But he kept following me around. If he says anything, I think to myself. I'll rip the blouse off, throw the darned thing in front of him, and say, "Keep your rubbish." But he didn't say anything; he didn't even have the chance because I always ran away. But doesn't he call to me once on the street, "Viia, don't run away." I didn't. I just didn't dare to.

"Where are you going?"

"To Tiihonen's store to get meal for the hog. That stupid hog really gobbles up the meal. I would never feed a hog like that; he's a real devil..." and I talked about that hog for a long time so Matti, the rascal, wouldn't get a chance to ask for his ten marks back. But what does he do when we get near the watchmaker Viik's shop but suggest, "Let's go in, Viia, and buy rings."

"All right, let's go," I said. How would I, poor girl, have dared to say anything else? Besides, I'll look just for the heck of it, I thought, and see if he'll really buy them. And the rascal did buy them, I have to admit.

"Now we're engaged." said Matti as we came out on the street.

"I guess so," I said. But I thought to myself, just wait, when I get my pay, I'll show you if I'm engaged or not. You'll get back your money, your rings, and even your blouse. "Keep your rubbish," I would say. "I won't sell myself for such trifles." But I kept this to myself, for why should I say anything now, he might just have asked for the ten marks back, the devil.

-Well, at home the mistress congratulated me, since I was now supposedly engaged, and I curtsied. And the others congratulated me, and I curtsied to everyone. What else could I do? And the mistress kept saying that she hadn't known anything about it, and I said I hadn't either, but this Matti wanted to get engaged so what else was there to do?

"What else, that's right," said the mistress. "And Matti's a good man."

-That could be, but what did I care about his goodness. I wasn't going to benefit from it anyhow.

-And everything could have still gone all right, if this Matti, the rascal, hadn't pushed his way that evening into the *aitta* where I was sleeping.

"Now, Matti, you mustn't get mad," I began cautiously. "I'll pay you back your money as soon as I can. We're not really engaged, I guess."

"And why not?" said Matti.

"Perhaps I'm still waiting for someone else," I said.

-That's when Matti got mad. His eyes rolled in his head like spinning tops, and he shouted that he would not be made a fool of.

"Stop it!" he yelled. "And don't make any more trouble now that you have promised yourself to an honest man. Remember that. I will not put up with any trickery."

-What could I, a woman alone, do but let things be. Who knows but what he might have stabbed me in the stomach if I made trouble.

-Well, Matti stayed overnight in the *aitta*, and the banns were read the following Sunday. For the wedding Matti bought me some fine, black dress material and gave me a corsage with an angel sewed to a gauze star. The gauze was like mist, and there was even a verse on the back. Well, that was a nice thing to do, and I still have it on top of the dresser. And Matti was good too; it wasn't that. He did his best. He bought soft drinks for the wedding, and everything. And when I said he was throwing his money away, he just said that when the bride is a pleasing one, one should toast her with something better than water.

-Everything would have gone all right, but as luck would have it, Antti happened to write from the country, and I got the letter on the very morning of the wedding. Well, didn't he write that he would be coming in the fall to claim me. As I stepped forward to my wedding

I felt like crying when I thought that now there would no longer be anything left for Antti to claim.

-I cried so much at the wedding I could have wrung out my handkerchief if I had wanted to. The minister even told Matti he had better be kind to this wife of his, since she seems so sensitive.

"That I will," said Matti.

And he has been.

"What in the world made you pop up in front of me that first time, and what on earth made you give me those ten marks at that time?" I asked Matti later.

"Why, don't you know? Because you were so pretty and your cheeks were red," he just said.

-It should have been Antti looking at those cheeks, I thought, but said nothing.

-Well, I might have forgotten about Antti, who knows, but doesn't he come to town that fall, just as he had promised in the letter. He even came to our house, where I stood beside the stove mashing potatoes for our hog; we already had a hog of our own by then. So he showed up there and said, "As a man of my word, I have now come to claim you, Viia, but I gather others have already done the claiming?"

"Yes, others," I said. "Others have claimed me." And my heart ached, for Antti, I always knew, was kind of made for me.

-Well, I wiped the potato from my hands, and we shook hands.

"Sit down, Antti. Let's have some coffee," I say. "Let's not carry any grudges over this."

"No, there's no reason to," says Antti and he sits down.

-So we drank the coffee, but it didn't taste good, even though I thought I had made good coffee. I had put in a generous amount of ground coffee beans and even a big chunk of chicory--just for Antti. But it didn't taste right; I don't know what was wrong. Was I upset since there was supposed to be this love--or call it what you will, it doesn't matter. In your dreams you think you yearn for something, when you're young, when you have feelings..."

Death (1913)

Old woman Pärsky stood with her hands on her hips near the stove, where the blackened coffee pot boiled and bubbled. Kaisa, the village drudge, sat on the bench at the door, moaning and sighing. Pärsky himself lay in his straw bed in the corner, wrestling with death. His weak limbs trembled. For over a month he had not taken any food to speak of. Occasionally he fell into a long stupor, and the rattle of his breathing sometimes seemed to subside altogether. One would think his end had come. But not yet. Life does hang on...sometimes.

Hands on her hips, old woman Pärsky strode toward the dying man and listened. "No, he's not finished yet. Let him live for all I care. He might as well. He doesn't even eat any more."

Secretly, she wished the end would come soon. He might as well die, she thought, since he is already so feeble, a heavy burden, in the way of those who are well. He might as well die, if only God in his mercy would take him; he can't work any more anyhow.

This is how she thought now, but she had once thought otherwise. At first she had pitied him. Sorrowfully, she told everyone, "Pärsky is just sick all the time."

"What's wrong with him?"

"I don't know, some trouble with his insides."

"Haven't you taken him to the doctor?"

"No, what would be the use of that? If God finds it best to take him away, it is useless to fight against His will. If His intention is to give Pärsky a longer life, the doctor's permission is not needed."

But one tires of everything. Old woman Pärsky tired of sympathizing with him and pitying him when the illness continued on and on. She began now to wait for the time when the Grim Reaper would cut the wilted stem of Pärsky's life. If it had happened in good time, the parting would have been a beautiful one. A lovely memory would have remained with her both of her husband and of her own goodness. But when this did not happen, the whole idea of a beautiful ending was ruined. Well, that's how it goes.

Secretly elated over her own good health and survival, the woman stood with her hands on her hips near the stove and watched while the pot boiled and bubbled. With deep breaths, she drew in the fragrant aroma of the coffee.

"For some," she remarked, pursing her lips together, "for some a husband has been a source of riches. For me...well, if I had not looked out for myself, no one would."

"That's so," sighed Kaisa.

"I would have led a dog's life if it were not for my own efforts."

"That's right."

"A dog's life my whole life...even if my life hasn't been much better anyhow."

But this was only what she said. In her mind she was thinking that she was not in such bad straits; she was still alive, and she had even been able to save money secretly for herself. Let's see, wasn't there nearly four hundred marks? For she had always known that the old man would die before she did. If one did not save, from where, then, after a husband's death, would one get money? For this reason in their cottage it was through the woman's hands that the pennies moved; it was she who held the purse strings. The woman took care of the everyday expenses and for his labors, the man got his food and his clothing, what little a shoemaker needed.

The old man turned and tossed on the straw.

"What's wrong now? The flies are probably bothering him. Or could it be the end?"

The old man stretched out his arms and moaned quietly.

"Things must be pretty bad now," said Kaisa.

"They've been as bad before." But anyhow, she walked across the floor and bent over the invalid.

"What? Perhaps the end is near? You certainly do seem to have the look of death. Just bless yourself now and remember your sins."

The old man moved his lips, tried to say something, but nothing came out.

"You don't have money in some kind of secret hiding place, do you? Speak, speak more clearly. Do you?"

She saw that the end was not far off and she began to fear that her husband might have secretly saved money from his earnings and that it would remain in an unknown place. If only he would speak. There was certainly no longer any need for concealment.

She shook the dying man's shoulder and tried to get him to regain consciousness to answer, but he did not have the strength to make a sound. The woman continued to shake him.

Suddenly, the man's body stiffened, becoming a heavy weight in her arms. His mouth fell ajar, his eyes were open. He was dead. The woman lowered him from her arms.

"Now Pärsky is through."

"Oh, oh, that's too bad."

"Come, Kaisa, and let us look through his clothes, in case he had some hidden money. He must have had some somewhere."

She pulled the stockings from her husband's feet, turned them inside out. She examined his underclothes; she and Kaisa poked through the straw, opened the rag pillow and searched through it. They found nothing. She began to sweat and the sweat streamed down her plump cheeks. Yet she went on searching.

"There are his boots," said Kaisa, pointing under the bench. There in a dark corner under the bench was a pair of old boots. The old woman pulled them out. She examined one, found nothing; she examined the other, and there, in the dirty toe of the boot, she felt a small lump. She wiped the sweat off her brow and holding her breath, examined the lump.

"Look at this. Didn't I say so? He did have hidden money. And he would have been foolish, too, not to have any to take care of himself. Isn't this clearly a five-mark note and isn't that more than a mark in silver? Look at the rascal; he wasn't as stupid as I thought he was. He looked after himself, just as a man should."

"But he probably didn't get his sins forgiven."

"I'm sure he did even that."

"I suppose he did."

"It surely must have been God's merciful wish, since he sent me a signal about that money. But what if I had burned the clothes or given them to a stranger? So there is reason to be thankful. Kaisa, take the coffee pot off the stove. Because of all things to do, I forgot about it, and it has boiled too long. It's time now for coffee, for the laying out."

Smoothing out the wrinkled five-mark bill, she sat at the end of the bench, wiped the sweat from her face with her sleeve, and rested.

Finding that money still made her feel good. It made her feel thankful that even if the late Pärsky had not been exactly a man's man, he at least was not the poorest of men. The time they had lived together was over, but she was still alive. Now she had only to take care of his burial and to observe the period of mourning with honor.

Kaisa placed the cups on the table and they drank the coffee. The hot coffee added to their contentment and enjoyment. Together they lifted the body to the bench, and Kaisa prepared the water and began to wash the body, a job for which she had long ago been promised one mark.

Hands on her hips, old woman Pärsky stood and watched Kaisa as she worked. It struck her that Pärsky's body was so yellow and small, as shriveled and rough as a worthless, dried pike. Well, the main thing was that the Creator had taken him to heaven.

"You rest now in peace and be thankful that you are free of all hardship," she thought. "Just sleep away, Pärsky. How does it feel when you don't have pain any more? You can see now that death is still the best thing at the proper time."

The Girl In The Rose Arbor
or The Dying Sister (1927)

"Please go and ask my sister and her husband to come here," said Hedvig, fifty-years old and single, to her maidservant, who had been taking care of her during her illness.

"Should I tell them anything else?" asked the maid.

"Nothing but that I am ill and would like to see them once more."

"I'll go at once," said the maid and left.

For almost ten years Hedvig had not seen her sister, even though they lived in the same city. It was almost ten years since Hedvig had last visited her childhood home, which now belonged to her sister and her sister's husband. And she had so longed to see at least the trees in the garden. But now she wouldn't see them. She would soon die. She would have to leave everything. It was so decreed. And what was decreed must surely be good. Hedvig did in no way complain about this. She had only hoped to be able to go in peace on her last journey and to be allowed the time to sort things out before then. She hoped that she would no longer misjudge life nor carry any grudge against those who would survive her.

During her lifetime Hedvig saw only the wrong she had suffered, and she felt the blows which had struck her. Solitude and poverty had not blessed her, nor had they cleansed her. Grief and melancholy held her their victim. She understood that this was due to her weak spirit. She had clung too strongly to her own little experiences and her own little disappointments. And they were nothing, really. But they had nevertheless been her destiny.

As a young girl, she had been engaged to her sister's husband, Konrad, but her sister had taken Konrad from her. Those things happen. They had then purchased Hedvig's share in the family home. But when the value of money had decreased, she had been reduced to poverty. She had had the impractical upbringing of girls in the old days, and thus had difficulties in making a living, particularly since she was often ill. That is how it was.

In her mind Hedvig repeatedly churned over her fate, as if she were memorizing a lesson. But this did not gratify her. There were other things, all those things which had hurt her, that secret searching and wandering spirit which had made her timid and shy and had separated her from other people, and which had also made her inner life nothing but a series of disappointments.

Thus her life had become a heavy burden. Her life had been a misfortune from start to finish, she thought. She wondered whether many people could boast about being happy. She did know that for many their visible and outward life was neither of meaning nor of consequence because all their trials in life existed only as a proving ground and a preparation.

It often gave her pleasure to think about those who had been more successful than she. She heard their voices in the silence, and she seized upon their comforting thoughts in her extreme despair.

And in her bed, as she fell to disparaging her past life, it felt as if someone said to her, "It is not important to achieve happiness."

"What is important?" she asked.

"To think the right thoughts."

"And love?:"

"It is not important to seek love, which does not exist. It is more important to seek the truth and to endure all the humiliation."

He, this invisible comforter, knew all this, and they also knew it, the invisible ones. She believed them. They had been seekers. They had flogged themselves with secret tortures in their days on earth, testing their humanness. They had crucified their own flesh in order to find the way to truth and purity. Out of their disappointments they had built a temple under which they had buried their forbidden, futile lives. They returned from earth as victors. On earth they had not been recognized as victors. Because of their striving they were damaging to others, hence they were attacked. They did not defend themselves, hence they were envied. They had taken a stand for which there was no room in the struggle for survival inherent in nature, so life struck them in the face and rejected them.

Hedvig thought of these invisible comforters in order to ease her physical pains. And even if she said she wanted to suffer patiently all that had been set as her share, her body won out. When her physical anguish was severe, she forgot everything else. She felt as if she were being burned at the stake. Pain, like a searing whip, pierced her body. She was being whipped into shreds. She tossed about on her bed and wished only that all would be over and that she could die.

Exhausted and unconscious, she then sank for a while into a coma and found relief in the world of dreams. Her thoughts and her dreams, as in a fever, changed so quickly and became so jumbled together, that at times she didn't know what was real and what was dream. And then sometimes, exhausted, consoling herself, she repeated, "I will never see the evening. I will soon get away from all this, get away!"

Then it was clear to her. It was as if she had never existed! Soon all traces of her would be covered up. No one would remember her. As if she were explaining to someone she thought, "I was poor and disappointed. I did not have any friends."

"You have friends, as long as everything goes well with you. But when things go badly with you, your friends turn their backs on you."

"That's how it is."

This invisible someone suggested to her, "In turning their backs on you, they do you the biggest of favors. You learn, then, something you otherwise would not learn, you learn to see what a person really is. You have seen this. And do you still love him?"

"But only a human being is worthy of love. I love human beings desperately. But I hate deceivers and liars -- therefore I have been as if ill from the time of my youth."

She pondered on these things in the midst of her pain as she waited for her sister.

Upon realizing that she would die from her illness she had, at first, when she was still quite strong, planned to die alone. Nobody would be concerned about her passing away, nor did she have anything to say to anyone. But then she began to doubt herself. If she had been mistaken, she wanted to correct her mistake. If there had been misunderstanding, it no longer had the same significance as it had before. She was leaving, the others would remain here.

Although she said this her heart did not accept it yet. She became upset as she thought of how she had been treated. And she blamed her sister now, as before.

Her sister had wanted to get her away from home and had driven her away, just as one drives a troublemaker away. Her sister wanted to get the family home for herself, and she blamed Hedvig with regard to Konrad. Her sister claimed that Hedvig wanted to get Konrad back. At first Hedvig did not understand, thinking this to be fear or jealousy. But then she realized that it was actually a plot.

Home became a place of torment for her. When the two were alone, her sister began to harass Hedvig.

"You should have taken him. You were enchanted by him," said her sister.

"That was then. We were all enchanted by him."

"You still love him," said her sister.

"You don't have to be afraid of that!"

"Can you live under the same roof with him and not love him?"

"But this is my home. Where else could I live?"

"This is also my home," said her sister.

And so Hedvig began to feel that she was superfluous. This she understood well. And then her sister asked her outright if she wanted to sell her share in the house to them, so they could settle the estate. Hedvig agreed and set a very modest price; she wanted a few pieces of their late mother's furniture and some of the family's heirlooms, for she loved them because they were old. They would be a comfort to her. They had an air about them which others did not sense. When she touched them it was as if she touched a living, ever living past to which she too now belonged, a past which this bickering had now rendered commonplace.

So she left her home and settled in the outskirts of the city, where the poor lived; she began to work, to sew and embroider, which she knew how to do. Her sister did not seek her out. And thus Hedvig became completely abandoned. The world now opened to her, new and frightening. She felt that the world would come to destroy her. She recognized her powerlessness and shied away from life. She felt that a poor person, simply because he is poor, suffers many agonies. No one honors him as being with full human value. Everything bad which is said of him *is* true. If it is proved not to be true, he is still treated as if it were true. Hedvig came to experience this many times in her searching for work and in trying to sell her handwork.

So the best years of her life had been a struggle to make a living, illness, inner conflict and searching, depressing thoughts, but nothing had become clear. Life in her had become disgraced. And the burden of sin which she carried weighed her down, even in her youth. But wherever she looked, she saw the same sin, shame, and lies.

She tried to seek the truth from those small happenings which enveloped her gray days, and which kept recurring through the monotonous years. But she became more and more bitter. She found herself in a maze, going helplessly around and around in the same circle.

War came. The value of money changed. Her small savings lost their value. Her handwork did not sell. She became hard-pressed and suffered hunger. She could not bring herself to sell the family heirlooms. Then she decided to humiliate herself for once and go to her sister to ask for help.

"So, hunger now drives you to me, does it?" the sister asked.

"When one is needed, one is remembered, but when one is not needed, one is forgotten."

"How would it be possible to forget you?" said Hedvig.

"Have you tried?"

"Always," said Hedvig.

"You have some heart," responded her sister.

"I am not here to offer my heart. I am here to ask for help."

"You don't offer your heart to me, but perhaps once again to my husband."

"You know very well that is not true, not before, not now."

"But people talked," said her sister.

"Since you told them things. Let us for once ask Konrad himself what he thinks."

"The matter is no longer of such importance," said her sister.

"It's important to me."

"I will forgive you anyhow," said her sister.

"I don't want your forgiveness. There's nothing for which I need to be forgiven," said Hedvig.

"You're ungrateful."

"Why should I be grateful to you? In certain respects you were my guardian, since you were older, and yet, how did you use that guardianship?"

"Do you mean that I took your fiancé away from you?" said her sister.

"We were engaged."

"Can anyone really take anybody away from anyone--the taker himself does not determine anything," said her sister.

"That may be true. What existed between us was youthful folly. I don't mean that. What I mean is the way you drove me away from home."

"But that's how it is in life--people part," said her sister. "Some leave of their own accord. It is unnatural to make estates that are too large. And didn't you sell your share legally?"

"Yes, I did."

"There wasn't any wrong done, was there?"

"No."

"What, then?"

"The value of money went down."

"Is that my fault?" asked her sister. "I was fortunate, you weren't. They say that everyone gets the happiness he deserves."

"I didn't know you could buy happiness with a lie."

"Now you know it," said her sister. "I am happy. If I have lied, I have bought my happiness with a lie."

"Once you told Konrad, when we were still engaged, that it was too bad I was ill and doomed to death; you said there supposedly was something wrong with my lungs. I knew nothing at all about that. You didn't think I heard you."

"Ha-ha-haa, you must be dreaming!" said her sister.

"We could ask Konrad, if you don't remember."

"I beg of you, stop dredging up the past."

"And after you were married, you told people I was still in love with Konrad, and that's why you had to drive me away. I heard it. And everyone believed it, as it seemed so likely, since I had been engaged to him."

"Wasn't it the truth?"

"You do not yourself think about me the things you said about me then!"

"Is that so?" laughed her sister.

"It was contemptible!"

"Should I say what was contemptible to you? That he left you and took me. If he had left me and taken you, that wouldn't have been contemptible, would it? You are jealous, and also evil."

"I prefer to be evil, if you are good."

"Who knows, you might want to look at my husband again in the same way as before." said her sister.

"Then I would be exactly like all you good women."

"Ahaa, now I understand; you love him still and came to see him again. I'm sure you often recall with pleasure how you used to sit on his lap," said her sister.

"Stop it! You are dreadful! I was a child then and we were engaged."

Her sister now retreated and realized that she could not go any further without bringing about a confrontation with her husband. And she said, "That's true, that was in those days. It was nothing. And that is how I have understood it."

But Hedvig knew that even if her sister saw it that way, she did not want to admit it as the truth. It gave her sister satisfaction to torment her and to distort matters. And flinging her malice into the begging Hedvig's face, the sister said, "If you had asked nicely, perhaps you would have got a loaf of bread."

"I don't think the bread would have tasted like bread any longer. You have a heart of stone."

"That heart was good enough for your fiancé then, and still is."

"I am glad about that."

"I don't believe it! If you were, you wouldn't have told people I broke up your engagement," said her sister.

"You know very well I have not said that to anybody. You're just afraid I did, and you want to hear me say I didn't. I am not as contemptible as you think I am."

"I don't think I believe you."

"You believe me completely."

"He loves me!"

"I believe that. But that is your affair."

She left her sister's house, never to return.

Never again, never again would she see her home. She remembered it with pleasure from the times when mother and father were still alive. It was light and beautiful. It was still beautiful when she and her sister lived there as orphans, sustaining each other. Now there was shame, sin and shame, between them.

"I yearn for my home!"

She said this, putting her loneliness into words, and she said it thinking of this home, but at the same time her thought broadened; she actually meant another home. She longed to get away from here. To go home!

But she was evil and she felt so bad; she was still filled with sin. What could redeem a person from her sins? What could cleanse her tainted soul? What could heal her anguished heart? When would she be good enough to see the truth and earn forgiveness? Only then, when she has stripped off these alien trappings, lowered the heavy burden from her shoulders, been summoned from her misguided life, only then can she get rest and peace?

From deep within her breast, Hedvig heaved a sign, "Give me a humble heart!"

If only she could feel as pure as a child. She had once been as pure as a child. She still remembered the past. It was just like a faraway dream. It filled her soul with sorrow and a sense of loss, as it had so many times before. Once she had lived that past. And blessing her memories, she opened her heart to them once again.

It was a sunny summer day; the garden was full of flowers. The roses had just begun to bloom. Konrad came to their house for the first time; then he had come for her sake. They had seen each other many times before that. He was a lieutenant from some distance away and had been wounded in the war. This made him even more attractive. He told them so beautifully of other countries and peoples. He had seen many lovely and strange things in faraway places. When one listened to him it seemed as if one heard strange music, which overcame and captivated one and sent one's mind soaring. No one could tell stories the way he could. There was no one like him.

Then the two stayed alone in the rose arbor. She had on a white dress, she remembered it so well, and in her arms a bouquet of roses, which she had picked for the dinner table. Konrad took one of the roses and pressed it to his lips. She could understand this, for they loved one another. And Konrad said that even though he had seen many people in the world, he had never seen anyone with eyes as blue as hers; they were like the sky and the stars. He was filled with joy as he looked at them and knew he had reached the end of his search. And when he touched her hair, so very blond, it felt as if he were caressing the radiance of the sun, and pure bliss flowed from it.

"Beloved, I will take you into my arms, my Love, and whisper something softly to you, little One." And he said, "Do you know that I love you?"

"I know."

"And do you love me?"

"I do."

"Tell me, how much."

"The earth and sky cannot contain it."

"And I, I until death, and even beyond death and time, forever."

And the fragrance of roses filled the whole world, for they sat in the rose arbor, and the roses were blooming.

But scarcely had autumn come and the leaves fallen from the rosebushes, when she knew more about love than she had that summer.

It was another day later in the summer. Sister came from the wedding of one of her friends. She was beautiful, young, and still in high spirits from the wedding. She met Konrad in the garden and she laughed so strangely and enticingly; she spoke and was so radiant, it was as if she were not herself. And her joy affected Konrad. At that time, Konrad forgot Hedvig. Therefore, he forgot her often.

Sister was just acting, but the acting became the truth. Soon Konrad was engaged to sister. And so sister walked hand in hand with Konrad in the rose arbor, and Hedvig sat in her room alone.

And then she began to fade away. She heard them talking once, and Konrad wondered at how she had changed.

"I told you at the very beginning that there is something wrong with her lungs," said sister. "She will not live long."

"It would have been wrong to bind her," said Konrad. "The

poor little thing. She is like a melody that keeps running through my mind.''

But when the two were alone, sister said to Hedvig, "I don't understand what's come over you." Her eyes flashed strangely, and she didn't even care to conceal it.

"I don't know.''

"Don't be sad. We will soon have a wedding. For once you can dance as much as you want to.''

But after that, Hedvig never danced again. She had had more than she wanted.

The heart--her heart continued to be restless and agitated, unaccustomed as it was to life's harsh discipline. Even though her mind matured as grain matures for the reaper, she forgot the passage of time. She often forgot, had forgotten, that before her lay old age. Only when she looked in her small mirror did she see how her skin had turned yellow and wrinkled as mother's had been. Her hair had grayed. And her smile, the helpless smile of an old woman, submissive and humble--it was mother's customary expression! It was mother who looked at her from the mirror. Her mother's face, how well she now remembered it. Those eyes, the wrinkled, drooping chin, which used to make her shudder--there they were again! This old and sick woman, who was she?

All of a sudden she felt as if only her mother was there. Mother had come into her to live again. Was it she, then, who troubled her spirit? Was that why she shrank from herself and could not find peace? Was that why her life had become a nightmare? Two beings, which could not be reconciled, in the same body.

"Go out of me, if you are in me,'' she said to her mother. "Why do you keep my body as your dwelling place? I don't want this, I don't want this! Go wherever you want to in your worlds, but don't destroy me! Am I your last place of refuge? And whom can I turn to, since I have no child to destroy?''

She became agitated thinking about her own freedom, and expelled the dead in order to struggle alone with her own strength. She would not cling to the possibility that she would return to earth.

And now, when she sighed alone, she kept remembering mother's sighs, which had formerly disgusted her. And now she sighed in the same way. Was there no progress, no movement forward, no healthy spiritual life in succeeding generations? They took their torment so seriously that they sank beneath its small weight.

"No more of this sighing,'' she said. "I won't permit it! Away from me, you dead Ones,'' her soul cried out. "I will not be the refuge for cowards.''

Then she seemed to see a row of those who had passed on; they offered their hands to her in friendly gestures and assured her that she was mistaken. She did not yet understand life. She bowed her head and asked forgiveness from these invisible ones. So, whatever was right, she was willing to accept. She was merely a lowly stepping stone. But when she raised her head she said, terrified, ''That is not enough!'' What am I thinking? I must be mad. Thus loneliness breeds a world of fantasy. It was all a dream, full of mysticism, toward which the human mind always tends.'' But she had succumbed to it anyhow, for it helped her like a stimulant in her difficulties and got her to belittle the transient happenings in life, those happenings which keep the human spirit captive and fill it with futile matters.

But wasn't this retreat of the mind to the safe refuges of the dead a sign of the weakness of the human spirit? Since it did not have the strength to create anything itself, the human spirit repudiated real life and catered only to death, which it thought of as its master. Thus a person strangled the chances for her own growth and became a lifeless body without purpose here. This lifeless body, waiting for death, and with death as its purpose--it was a heavy burden to carry. This was she. She had just let go of life. She was like a withered leaf, which waited for the wind of its benefactor to separate it from the large mass of leaves and which felt that its falling to the ground was more important than its living. But even though she was as if she were dead, deep within her she still was not quite ready. At times, an unfulfilled frenzy for life burned within her. She loved life, which she had spurned; a vague hope struck its claws like a wild beast into her aching heart, twisted it, and did not wish to release its grip.

If only one could turn back the wasted past years! How differently she would love life. Out of each day she would create a song of thanks. How differently, how wisely, she would look at the world, accepting people as they were. She would love them as children are loved. As a mother takes into her lap the child who has erred, as she mourns over the boy who has slipped into crime, her heart full of pain and hope, bearing her grief in silence and alone, just so should a person be accepted here. To love all people despite their differences, to forgive those who do you wrong. This was the old, eternal truth; yet it was always new. Her heart had not yet mellowed to that point. When would it? Only then, when she removed life's gray, everyday garments, these unfamiliar clothes, this prisoner's garb, which concealed her soul, which longed for freedom, was dark and confused, full of despair, and yearning for love? Hedvig fell into these reveries when her pain abated. Her mind gradually calmed. Her thoughts swung to a world where man's life seemed like a child's wandering, like a dream.

Then she had dozed off and awakened. The air was filled with the fragrance of roses, of roses and life. Her mind was stirred by a feeling of warmth. She remembered that she was waiting for sister and her sister's husband. Her maid returned.

"Are they coming?" asked the invalid.

"They'll be here soon."

"Good, good."

"Do you want anything?"

"I would like my gown for dying; you know which one it is."

The maid helped Hedvig put it on. Hedvig had sewed it herself, long ago. But then her bodily pains began. They became unbearable.

"Can I be of any help?" asked the maid.

"No, no." Hedvig panted and tossed in her pain. She forgot where she was and who she was. The minutes were as long as hours, and then time no longer had any boundary or any limit. It was as if crowds of people walked past her and trampled on her. She heard the faint murmur of a voice. And then someone helped her and said, "You must be in terrible pain."

"Oh, no, it is nothing. It is just the body," she said. "Let them trample me, if it makes them feel good."

"She's delirious," the faraway voice said.

"First one must get to know man, then one must learn to love him. This is difficult. He is the enemy; he tramples you into the ground; oh, it doesn't matter, just let them trample." She groaned in her delirium.

"That must be painful."

"It doesn't matter anymore--it's easier now."

Her anguish left her and she became herself again, and her mind began to wander about in its former mazes, as if seeking clues to something she had forgotten a short time ago. But she did not find herself completely. Something odd and numbing had remained with her from her pains. She felt her head, but her hand was a little stiff. And wondering, she asked, "What has been put on my forehead? It presses so."

"There's nothing there, nothing at all."

Hedvig did not believe it. She felt pressure on her forehead.

"Perhaps I should sponge it with water," said the maid, and she sponged Hedvig's forehead. It felt good. Her breast rose and fell more easily. She fell asleep for a moment.

"Haven't they come yet?" the invalid soon asked.

"No."

"Yet so many hours have passed already."

"Not more than half an hour has passed since I returned."

"Don't deceive me, my Friend, as if I didn't know."

"Why should I deceive you?"

"You deceive me out of compassion, because I will die soon."

"I wouldn't do that."

"Oh," Hedvig laughed oddly and chided, "I know everything, I see everything."

"I must be mistaken," the maid said. "One loses track of time here."

"Don't lie to me. Stick to the truth," and suddenly the invalid understood the situation and continued, "I was the one who was mistaken. The minutes seem long as hours. I probably slept a little in between?"

"Yes, you did, and some time has passed."

"You have a watch. I forgot where I was and who I was. Did I speak strangely?"

"Not at all."

"If I do, don't be afraid. Sick people do get delirious, they say. Don't be afraid!"

"Of course I won't. But you seem fine now."

"Because I'm expecting visitors."

"I hear steps now; they must be coming."

"They're coming?"

"You're getting very pale, don't--Are you strong enough to receive them?"

"I have no choice. I can't afford to choose."

But then it was as if a large, invisible hand began to press upon her; it pushed her down and she was unable to rise. She tried to resist it, but she was overcome by weakness. She lapsed into a coma. Then, as if from far away, she heard a voice which called, "Hedvig, Hedvig dear!"

And someone said, "She falls into a coma now and then. It lasts just a few seconds. She'll wake up in a moment."

She awoke. She saw her sister bending over her. She looked at her sister, and it seemed to her that no time at all had passed since she had last seen her.

"Are you so very sick?" asked her sister. "Why didn't you let us know before this?"

"Konrad didn't come?"

"He'll come soon; word has been sent to him. Are you already so very ill?"

"I am not quite that ill," said Hedvig, for something in her sister's voice restrained her from telling her sister more about her illness. "You're the same as ever," thought the invalid. "You are full of deceit."

"You have had to suffer."

"Does that make you feel good now? thought Hedvig, but said nothing.

"Perhaps you will still get well; surely you will get well," said the sister.

"No, I won't," said the invalid lightly, but she thought to herself, "And it's all the same to you, that's what your voice is saying."

"What else should my voice be saying?" she seemed to hear her sister say. "You certainly are in great distress now."

She remembered that voice from the old days, flippant and cold, always lacking feeling. And the invalid answered, "I'm not in as great distress as you think."

"No. But what would you have to lose anyhow?"

"If I should lose everything that you in truth possess, I would not be losing anything."

"Little sister does have a heart!"

"And you a sister's love. You are colder than death!"

"Ha-ha-haa!"

Hedvig was horrified by that laugh. She awoke from her coma and asked, "Who laughed here?"

"No one, my Friend, no one at all," said the sister.

"I must have been dreaming."

"You must have. You are being tested now, poor little Sister. Try to be courageous, won't you?"

And humbly the invalid replied, "I'll try."

She felt so good now that someone was talking to her. And her sister's voice was now without deceit. This gave her great relief and comforted her. Somebody had words even for her.

Her condition changed for the worse. Her pains began to increase and her strength to diminish. She repeated to herself, "I will soon leave; I will never see the evening." And then it was as if these pains had never existed. She longed to be allowed to dissolve, to be allowed to leave this unbearable burden behind. She longed for rest; her soul yearned for rest. "Take this cup from me. However, not according to my will, but Yours."

Who said these words? It was precisely her life's sigh, the

contents of her whole life, its very essence.

She still lived in her delirium. She was walking up a mountain, dragging a huge cross, under which she was about to collapse. She was flogged and reviled. Tears of blood flowed from her eyes. A crown of thorns pressed on her head, beads of blood rolled off her forehead. She stretched out her hands as if to say that she was only a human being, but they whipped her, mocked her, and nailed her to the cross. At this point, she wailed and awoke. She held out her paralyzing hand to her sister and spoke complainingly in a child's thin and clear voice, "They have now driven the nails through my hands."

"They have? They are wicked."

"That hurt me," she said and tried to explain with a smile what she could no longer say with words.

"She's delirious," said the maid.

"She had a dream," said the sister. "She had a terrible attack."

"The end seems to be near now," whispered the maid.

"Yes, it does."

And the invalid, who understood their conversation, was so happy about it and wanted to show them that she was conscious, that she said, "It must be summer?"

"Oh, yes, it is summer."

"The fragrance of roses," and she looked at her sister with such joy, and smiled with one corner of her mouth.

"Little One," said her sister now, using the name she had always used when Hedvig was a child.

"I'm so cold."

The maid covered her gently. But soon the pains came again. She begged, "Let me down from the cross; oh, lower me to the earth, bury me in the grave, bury me there!" Her breast heaved. Then she quieted down. A radiant smile spread over her face.

"Did she die?"

"No, she's asleep."

"She'll wake up soon."

And Hedvig awoke. She had seen something bright in her dream. She knew now that she would see it again. It waited for her there, when she was free of these bonds. There was life. The life she longed for. She would be born into it soon. She waited for it. She greeted her body's pains now as blessings and purgers of her torment. In her quiet moaning there was no longer fear nor impatience; her moaning, as her breathing, was now only an involuntary action of her body, which could not be stopped or withheld. But a small matter still kept her here. Now she remembered, "Hasn't Konrad come yet?"

"No, he hasn't. But he'll be here soon."

She still waited for Konrad. Konrad was her sister's husband. And she had loved him. That was how it was. In that she had sinned throughout her life. And that is why her whole life had been a trial, and she had deserved nothing else. But now it would be longer offend anyone. She would be leaving. Everything would be set right. Everything was fine. Her sins had been forgiven. "It was such a small offense," they had said. That is why she was given peace and rest, which she longed for. She felt this a short while ago, when, for a moment, her soul left her body and she saw the brightness which awaited her. Its sweet peace lured her with its strains, which flowed over her and supported her. They healed her sick soul from its anguish--her soul, which was like a melody gone astray, a lamentation, and joyfully her spirit rose as if on wings and drowned in the purity of the universe.

A moment ago, it seemed to her that she had already left her shackles and her beaten body on the earth, and that she had reached home. Did someone cry? There was nothing to cry about. This was her moment of birth, her triumph, and her reward. It was truly a great reward.

But she did not leave yet. She returned from her journey and came back into the world. She settled again into her body and remembered her own insignificance, which she had a moment ago been allowed to forget and leave behind for a while. Life puzzled her. For it was so strangely unreal. She wondered about that little creature who lay ill, waiting for death. Was that she? That creature was strange and unfamiliar to her, as strange as someone else who carried life's burdens. She lay there, exhausted from her journey. But wasn't she just starting on her journey?

"Little One," she heard a voice coming from afar. "Are you already asleep?"

She did not have the strength to open her eyes now; she just tried to say, "I'm asleep." Who was asking? It was mother's voice. Mother asked if she were asleep. She was a child and lay in her little bed, pretending to be asleep; mother bent over, doubting that she really was asleep. Her little deception amused Hedvig and she whispered, "Mother!"

"She does not recognize me any more," said the sister.

Now the invalid remembered aright. It wasn't mother after all. Mother had died long ago. She herself was old and ill and lay on her deathbed. And her sister was there and waited for her end.

And she had already been far away from here, to the place toward which she was now journeying, but her sister did not know this, no one did, and she could no longer tell anybody. But she made a great effort and said. "I know you."

"She recognizes me. She said, "I know you."

But again it seemed to her that she was a child, had been ill for a long time, and was in an isolated, dark room, and had now recovered from her illness. Father carried her into the sunny living room, where mother and sister sat waiting for her. Sister asked whether she recognized her and Hedvig said, "I do." Father placed her in mother's lap. And they all rejoiced that she had survived. For they all loved her. No? She was not loved? She had just imagined it? She had lived this long, long ago. And those who had loved her had died long since. Now there was no one--now she was old and dying. Wasn't that how it was? And to confirm this to herself, she said, as convincingly as if she were giving a memorized lesson. "I will die--soon."

"She said, 'I will die soon'. She is conscious again. Hedvig dear, Konrad is here. May he say goodbye to you?"

"Yes, he may," she said softly.

"Konrad, give her your hand; you can see that she cannot lift hers."

Hedvig tried in vain to lift her hand, but she couldn't, it was paralyzed. Sister took Hedvig's hand in hers. It was cold and small, it slid from her hand to the cover. Then Konrad took her other hand, the hand that was not paralyzed, and pressed his lips to it, and tears fell from his eyes. The invalid opened her eyes and looked at him as if in reproach, and then a sob rose from her breast and a shudder ran through her whole body. Sister saw two beautiful, deep blue eyes of a child, which opened as if awakened from sleep; she saw a reproachful, yet gentle look, which spoke of love and purity, and then she saw two tears roll from the deep blue eyes and fall down the pallid cheeks.

"Little One, little One," said Konrad.

"Let us not disturb her."

The invalid had closed her eyes. She became restless.

"Are you afraid?" asked sister.

"No, I can--die."

"Yes, each of us dies in our time. Try to be courageous a little longer, won't you?"

"I'll try."

"I'll tell you what the world is like, if you still care to hear it. It's a warm day, the sun is shining. Your roses are blooming beneath your window. Your towels are drying on the stepladder, and your sheets are on the line, I recognized them at once. For you made them at home long ago.''

And when Konrad turned his head away, she continued, ''So this is the way it has turned out. You have now reached the end of your journey.''

The dying Hedvig tried to say something, but she could no longer bring forth any words, only some faint sounds and some movement of her weakened lips.

''Konrad, she still wants to say something.''

''What is it you want to say, little One?'' asked Konrad, and he took her hands between his.

The invalid kept trying to say something, but it was unintelligible. Konrad followed this hopeless struggle. Then, suddenly, as if from her eyes' deep, bottomless blue, flowed a strong, clear thought, which reached Konrad, ''We are all parts of the same--we are like children of the same Father--we belong together--it is life's great unity--isn't that so?''

She quieted down. Then she looked at her sister as if she wanted to tell her of all the sufferings and humiliations to which there had never been any witnesses. Now the older sister could get to know them all. But her strength ran out. Waves of light rolled toward her, she sank into them. Someone called her; she knew the voice and hastened towards it joyfully, ''Mother!'' She understood the fullness of her joy. Even if life had been hard and painful, she had now reached its end safely--that she knew. Her eyes opened a little. A pair of vital, beautiful eyes looked at them wisely and gently, as if expressing all her love. She gasped and her eyes closed. She now left her body.

''Did she die?''

Konrad restrained his wife's hand and said softly, ''She can still hear.''

But then the dead one's lips twitched and she sank into everlasting rest.

''She is dead.''

''Yes, she is dead.''

Motionless, they looked at her. And Konrad said, ''How beautiful she is.''

''She should be straightened out before she stiffens in that position.''

Konrad adjusted her position, lifted her hands, and crossed them on her breast. Sister stroked her sister's hand. She was dead. Cold matter. She remembered stroking her mother's hand in the same way long ago. It had felt the same. And now that hand no longer existed. And this hand was also vanishing. And the hand which touched this one--when would its turn come? "Everyone has his turn. Nothing is more clear. Death is clearer to the living than birth ever was," she thought. "It is just the final stage, which we know is certain to come. So why be sad?"

To her, the event of death became a simple and natural one. She had known about this before and had thought about it before. But that it was such an inevitable result of the body's loss of power--this she had never seen before. An inevitable stage, which should not be difficult to submit to. This was the truth. To her, it was almost consoling, almost honorable and exalting in its simplicity. "How life as a journey was short and simple. How natural and simple was death," she repeated to herself, and it gave her satisfaction. For this to her was the truth. "This was a more useful lesson than any other."

But the day with its cares called them.

"We must take care of the last duties here," she said to Konrad. "She will have to be lifted to the board and then placed in a casket after the doctor has given the death certificate.

She sent the maid to order the casket and to get the doctor to come.

"It's so sad," said Konrad.

"Yes it is," said the sister.

"Her share in life was so little."

"Life must be faced with more spirit."

"She looks so contented now, almost happy. She left here so beautifully."

"Perhaps death itself is easier than we think it is."

"When I look at her, I feel as if she is alive and is listening."

"You are just imagining things."

"Of course. But anyhow--I don't know, everything seems so unnatural."

"You're afraid of the dead."

"Not really. I'm just filled with dread," said Konrad.

"Feel her hand, then your dread will disappear."

Konrad felt the dead one's hand and bent down his head. "We will all lie like this some day," he said.

After the doctor had been there the sister said, "She should be lifted to the board so the bedclothes will not be ruined. They will be ours now."

"Is it really necessary? The casket will be here soon."

"But in this hot summer weather."

The sister rolled away the carpets and made room for the board.

"We can lift her, just the two of us, she's so light."

"Would she herself have wanted it this way?"

"Of course."

They lifted her to the board. There little Sister lay on the floor, on a sheet-covered board. Her face had changed, and because her head had tipped backward, a discontented expression like that of an unhappy child had appeared at the corners of her mouth.

"She's not comfortable there," said Konrad uneasily.

"But she can't feel anything."

"She looks uneasy."

"Her face is just puffing up."

But Konrad was seized by fear. He looked at the dead one. She had changed. Something extremely strange and unnatural had happened. This human being, which a short while ago spoke and lived, now lay here. They acted and handled her as if she were not a human nor had ever been one. That was why her expression had changed, wasn't it? She was not happy. She suffered from the way they treated her.

"Konrad, go out to the rose arbor," said his wife. "You're very pale, and it's hot in here."

"I feel bad," said Konrad, and he pressed his heart. "I have pain--in my heart."

"Spare your heart. You can't bear this."

"There was a time, remember--when I loved her," said Konrad, as simply as a child. "If she could only hear!"

"And what then? Is there something else you need to say?"

"Don't be cruel. We were engaged, so is it any wonder I say that now?"

"Well, tell her, there she is. If I'm in the way, I'll leave."

"Now you are cruel."

"Go outside, otherwise you'll get ill. I'll call you when the casket comes."

Konrad went out and sat on the bench in the rose arbor beneath the window. The day was at its brightest. The summer sun shone on the hot garden path and made it shimmer. The air was stifling hot. The fragrance from the roses felt oppressive and filled the air. He was reminded so much of a morgue, funerals, and death. The same fragrance had filled another rose arbor once, long, long ago. Then, the fragrance meant love. A young girl had stood in the rose arbor in a white dress, her arms full of roses. A young boy had taken her into his arms and promised to love her "until death". Now he had lifted the girl in the white dress to the board--in between were thirty long years. A whole life. They had lost one another. And they had yearned for each other. How cruel life was. He had remembered that girl always, when his life was joyless and gloomy. And he knew now, more certainly than before, that it was that little one to whom he had first been devoted, whom he had loved the most. He would never have admitted this before. Soon he heard the rattle of the hearse. The casket was brought in a black carriage. His wife called him in to help.

"But what if the deceased would not have wanted me?"

"She isn't a human being any more. Someone has to help even the dead."

They went inside. Those who brought the casket had opened it, fluffed up shavings and spread the bottom sheet over them. The headrest was small and hard. The deceased had turned darker. The head had slid helplessly to one side, the face had swollen, and the corners of the mouth still had the expression of an unhappy child.

"She looks so much like a little child now."

"The face has become rounder."

"It seems as if she is blaming us."

"And what wrong would we have done her?"

They moved toward the men, who had finished preparing the casket.

"The body is falling apart now," said one of the men. "It won't keep in this kind of weather."

"It has a strong smell already," said the other.

"We've got to hurry to the cemetery storeroom with it."

"I suppose so," said the sister.

One of the men had placed the deceased's stiff, white leg on his knee and the other handed him a rolled white stocking, which he pulled up the deceased's leg. When he let go of the leg a little carelessly, it fell and thudded strangely on the board. They handled her quickly and skillfully, as if she were just matter.

"May she stay in her death dress?" asked one of the men.

"It is indeed beautiful," said the sister.

"It's like a bride's dress," said the other.

"She loved beautiful linens," said the sister to her husband. "She sewed this death gown herself."

The deceased was then lifted into the casket. Konrad helped with this. The sister noticed how the odor from the body upset him. It would perhaps bother him for a long time, she thought. Would he still love her, even after he has endured the odor from that decaying body? Was there anything still left? Had there ever been anything? And had something remained, even after they had separated? No one really knew Konrad's heart; he hardly knew it himself.

The cover was put in place and the hands were crossed.

"Should we close the casket now?" asked one of the men.

"Not quite yet," said Konrad.

"Perhaps you should get some roses for her hands," said the sister. "They are her own bushes."

Konrad went to get a fresh rose. It had just opened. He stood a moment in the entry, pressed the rose against his cheek, caressed it, and a bright teardrop fell on a petal. Then he went into the room and placed the rose between the crossed hands of the dead one. And the hands, white and unnaturally peaceful, rested like lilies on the sheet of the casket, holding the rose; on the fingers a womanly grace and sensitive movement stiffened for all time--a movement which no longer had anything to do with life or the flowing of life's blood.

Dead. Little Sister was dead. The body was like an empty shell which she had cast aside. They bade farewell to the deceased with their glances. The men lifted the lid up and nailed it shut. Then they carried the casket to the hearse. And without any escort the hearse left for the cemetery.

Konrad went out into the rose arbor to wait for his wife, who with the maid, stayed to put the room in order.

"Madame is certainly having a lot of trouble now because of her" said the maid.

"She caused so little trouble while she was alive. Everyone needs a little help in death."

"Yes, I suppose so."

"Did she leave any papers, any will, or--?"

"No, she didn't. Only an old, faded letter. The money is in the dresser drawer; there isn't much. But she did have silver."

"It's the old family silver. She got it as part of the family estate. She wanted it."

"Madame can take the silver with her now."

How happy she now was to move them back into her own house. For she had missed them, the beautiful, old pieces. She tried to hide her pleasure and said, "Death does snatch us away from here suddenly. It's a wonder, though, that we get used to it so soon--I mean, the empty place is soon filled. I have seen that often."

The sister sat in her sister's rocking chair to rest. Through the window she saw Konrad sitting on the rose arbor bench, helpless and sad, deep in his thoughts. He looked old and as if he himself were about to die.

The maid kept working in the room. So the furniture will now be mine, thought the sister. In the room were some good, old pieces which had been passed on in the family from its better days, and the younger sister had not sold one single piece. There was the dresser which had been given to sister, the only piece whose true value had not been assessed during the sharing of the estate. Now it was hers. It had been on loan here for nearly thirty years. Her eyes caressed its curved lines and its beautiful ivory inlays. Once before she had wanted it for herself. And now it was hers. "You're not someone's sister for nothing," she smiled to herself.

She opened the top drawer of the dresser, and her hands touched a faded paper. It was a letter to sister from Konrad, written when he was a young man, thirty years ago. She read,

"The Girl in the Rose Arbor
Whom does the boy dream of?
The girl in the rose arbor.
Whom does he love?
The girl in the rose arbor."

"Nothing is as powerful as death. But even stronger than death is love. People without love are the unfortunate in life. People without feelings are living corpses. People without heart neither love nor hate. To hate or to love--isn't it the same thing? For love breeds hatred, and without hatred there is no true love. I hate evil and love the good. You are good, so I love you. I pity those whose rose gardens here have no roses. Their days are gray, and they know nothing of the beauty of life. Come, my Beloved, and open the door of your rose arbor to me, for I will give you a box of jewels, which is my heart, and I will open it for you and show you the best of what the human heart conceals. Come, my Beloved, my Little Friend, and reach out your hand to me, your hand which is as white as a lily, so graceful and pure."

Sister gave a short laugh, Why do they write like that? What do they know of death or of life--of love! She laughed oddly. Then her own laughter made her shudder a little.

The girl in the rose arbor, she was the one who had just been taken from here--to her own rose arbor--with Konrad's small flower in her hand.

Toivo Pekkanen (1902-1957)

Toivo Pekkanen was the first member of the working class in Finland to make his living as a writer. He was born in Kotka, a city founded in 1879 on the Gulf of Finland, east of Helsinki. Because of its good harbor, railroad, communications system, and its nearness to the Kymi River, Kotka developed quickly as an industrial city. Pekkanen's father was a factory worker and Pekkanen himself was a metal worker until he was thirty. His family was poor and uneducated, wholly proletarian, but one in which fundamental human values were held in deep respect. Pekkanen finished elementary and vocational school, read and studied foreign languages, writing his first stories at night after work and during whatever free time he could muster. He began his literary career by writing short stories for magazines and published a first collection, RAUTAISET KÄDET (IRON HANDS) in 1927; then followed the collections SATAMA JA MERI (THE HARBOR AND THE SEA), 1929, and KUOLEMATTOMAT (THE IMMORTALS), 1931. All the stories describe work and attitudes toward work, most of the attitudes indicating that work is usually burdensome even though at times it can be pleasant, providing opportunities to show strength, skill, and energy. In 1930 he published a novel of Lapland, TIENTEKIJÄT (THE ROAD BUILDERS), in which a city springs up and then disappears with equal speed. In 1932 his novel, TEHTAAN VARJOSSA (IN THE SHADOW OF THE FACTORY), the story of a young steel-mill worker fighting for the growth of his mind, his sensibility, his knowledge, and imagination, received nationwide attention and enabled Pekkanen to give up working in the factory. He moved to Helsinki and worked part-time as a publisher's reader but devoted himself primarily to his writing. His next novel, KAUPPIAIDEN LAPSET (SHOPKEEPERS' CHILDREN), 1934, is about middle class life. In his writing Pekkanen was free of dogmatic working-class prejudices even though he wrote about the people from the social class of his origin--industrial workers. He remained the dispassionate observer, writing most often sympathetically about the workers, most often critically about the middle class. His writing was serious and demanded a formal, correct form. Writing was an effort for him so his texts are often stiff and awkward. He did not follow free patterns of emotion and thought. Wishing to indulge in lighter writing, he introduced nonrealistic elements into a number of plays in the 1930's, some of which are: SISARUKSET (THE BROTHERS AND SISTERS), 1933, TAKAISIN AUSTRAALIAAN (BACK TO AUSTRALIA), 1936, UKKOSEN TUOMIO (THE JUDGMENT OF THUNDER), 1937, RAKKAUS JA RAHA (MONEY AND LOVE), 1937, and DEMONI (THE DEMON), 1939. However, Pekkanen's basic earnestness made even the plays he wrote for relaxation deal with serious and tragic subjects. During the 30's he also wrote several novels: IHMISTEN KEVÄT (HUMAN SPRING), 1935; ISÄNMAAN RANTA (MY COUNTRY'S SHORES), 1937, which he and critics and scholars considered one of his best works, the main character being Pekkanen's favorite among all his characters; MUSTA HURMIO (BLACK ECSTASY), 1939; NE MENNEET VUODET (THOSE PAST YEARS), 1940, rewritten and published in 1946 as JUMALAN MYLLYT (THE MILLS OF GOD). Pekkanen's writing during World War II was not outstanding but after the War his short story collection. ELÄMÄN JA KUOLEMAN PIDOT (THE FEAST OF LIFE AND DEATH), 1945, and the novel NUORIN VELI (THE YOUNGEST BROTHER), 1946, are on the level of his works of the 1930's. He also started writing a series of novels about the development of his home town, Kotka, and published the first two parts in 1948, when he suffered a serious cerebral stroke. Amazingly, he recovered and in 1952 published the third part. Other volumes were to follow but he never finished the task. He wrote some more short stories and in 1953 published his memoirs, LAPSUUTENI (MY CHILDHOOD). In 1955 he published his last book, a volume of poems, his first and only poetry. Both *Food for the Winter* and *Building a Bridge* are from his 1929 collection, THE HARBOR AND THE SEA. Both stories are serious, about work, and about the working class characters' attitudes toward work and present the working environment, particularly in *Building a Bridge*, as a joyless place. In their solid and serious style, they reveal Pekkanen's humanism, his social concerns, his rational seeking for truth.

Food For The Winter (1929)

In the growing dusk of the November evening the rain, which had been threatening all day, finally began. It started as a gentle, thick, foggy drizzle but quickly developed into a cold, pounding, autumn rain which forced its way into every corner and crevice, soaking those who were without shelter.

Since the ship's cargo had almost all been loaded on the deck, the captain did not permit a break in the work and demanded that the ship loading be completed. The captain wanted to get out of this dark and rainy hole as soon as possible since there wasn't even a decent saloon nearby. Besides, the sooner he got the cargo to its destination, the more money he would earn.

The ship rocked heavily in the ground swell. Some of the loading crew showed obvious signs of seasickness as they staggered up the ever-increasing pile of cargo. Two of the women loaders had already been taken below into the lounge to rest. The ship's sailors, as they went past the women, sneered at them, their faces green and pale, their eyes rolling from the anguish of their nausea. With the loaders spurred on by a small addition in pay and by the rain, the work moved rapidly. Carried by tireless hands, an unending stream of long boards of lumber rose from the rocking barge alongside the ship. (Loading was accomplished entirely by hand since at this time, the last decade of the nineteenth century, cranes were not yet in general use). The men below in the barge set each stack of boards in motion, and it passed from hand to hand until it found its place on the deck. If the stack occasionally stopped even for a moment on its way, the foreman or the ship's mate shouted an order, spicing it with a curse, which sent the stack moving even faster.

Two hours after dark, the work was done. In the light of the smoking and creaking lanterns of the ship the loading crew descended into large boats and started rowing toward the blinking lights of the harbor pier. Soaked to the skin, the loaders wrapped themselves tightly in their coarse homespun jackets and huddled as closely together as possible for warmth. But in spite of this, only the rowers, who pulled and struggled with the heavily loaded boats amid the rolling waves, kept warm. The teeth of the others soon started chattering. Even though the pier was not far away, many were so numb when the boats finally reached the shore that they barely managed to climb from the boats to the pier. But in spite of this, their spirits were lively and cheerful and a continuous buzz of voices rose from them. They had loaded yet another ship, and their wages were waiting for them. The small lights of the city twinkled in the distance; there were homes, wives, children, warm fires, food.

Wages were paid at the loading company's office at the shore immediately after the loading was finished. While the treasurer and the foreman together figured out the wages from the foreman's wage lists, the loading crew gathered into a tight knot in front of the office door, pressing as close as possible to the wall to get shelter from the pounding rain. Finally, the shutter in the door opened, and the cashier's head appeared. The buzz of voices ceased among the waiting loaders, and all turned to stare at the cashier's pale face. The cashier cleared his throat and began to call out names one by one. Dressed in soaked homespun, one wet shape after another appeared before the light from the open shutter, got a bundle of money into a fist, and disappeared.

The Kämäräinens had both been working on the same ship. They were a sturdy couple in their forties, who in no way seemed different from the rest of the loaders. But after getting their wages into their hands, they did not hurry toward the city but turned back to the pier. There their boat was waiting for them, tied to the pier. They were among the first city people to move across the bay to the islands and had built a small cottage on a rocky and barren shore. In other respects, they were also more enterprising people than others and always had many irons in the fire at the same time. They knew each other's thoughts so well already that they hardly ever had to speak to one another. With half a word, or a scarcely audible grunt, they often got along for many hours. They didn't talk, they acted. In the boat were two large tubs and a staff with a crossbar. The man descended into the boat and lifted the tubs and the staff to the pier. They set the crossbar through the handles of the tubs, hoisted the staff to their shoulders, and started stepping one behind the other toward a dimly visible lantern some distance away. They had an agreement with the saloon keeper who, for a small fee, permitted them to get leftover food scraps for their pigs.

Half an hour later both tubs were back in the boat and full of sour, foul-smelling food scraps. They untied the boat and each settled into a rower's seat to row. The rain still continued and as the waves hit the bow, every now and then a cold water spray splashed on the rowers' necks. As the ships rocked in the bay, their twinkling lights bobbed up and down as if someone was using them to give secret signals in the dark. The ships themselves could not be distinguished until they were close by, but from time to time the creaking of their anchor chains and their masts could be clearly heard above the roar of the wind and the rain. And from the

direction of the pier sounded the endless splashing and crashing of
the breaking waves. The city's small and moist, fog-shrouded lights
slowly receded and finally seemed to blink as if from some
boundless pitchdark outer space.

For many hours there had not been a single dry thread in the
Kämäräinens' clothing. They had eaten their simple sandwiches
during their lunch break nearly twelve hours ago. They had two
kilometers to go over the surging and rainswept sea. The heavily
loaded, clumsy boat moved ahead very slowly. Even though the
rowers struggled with all their strength, the boat crawled like a snail
from one wave to another and from time to time a cold spray
splashed over them. But not for a moment did they think of their
hardships. They thought about the approaching winter. Soon an icy
cold would descend on these shores, the sea would freeze over, the
harbor would close, the loading company's office would be locked.
Then those who did not have anything put aside for the winter could
go to fairer fields, or starve. The Kämäräinens did not complain, for
they felt they were in control of life's powers: the changing weather,
the absence of ships, the loading company's closed office. They had
food for the winter.

Food for the winter. That was life's purpose. If, then, at the
same time, they labored for new and better times, of this they were
not aware. They did not know that they were building a new city in
the world.

But they felt a kind of superiority over the people in the city.
There, many would soon face disaster. When they ran out of money,
they would also run out of food. The people would walk meekly,
their heads drooping, hunger pains gnawing in their stomachs. But
for the Kämäräinens the quiet winter days would now begin. From
their wooden tub they would slice pork for their frying pan, and they
would sit beside their warm stove. On beautiful winter days the
husband would go fishing, seeking variety in their food. The city
and its sawmills and harbors had existed for such a short time that
their existence did not yet provide stability nor dependable
continuity of work. They followed the rhythms of the seasons as
does the bear, who sleeps in his lair during the coldest time when
food is difficult to get. But for people, who couldn't do this, life
would be difficult indeed.

They rowed in silence, the veins in their necks swelling and
shrinking, sweat pouring from every pore and blending with the
rainwater on their soaked bodies. The lights of the city faded away,
and little by little the ships' smoking and swinging lanterns also
disappeared from sight. For a while only the jet-black darkness and

the roar of the wind and the sea surrounded them. But even in the dark, with the rain and the wind, they instinctively knew how to stay on course. After struggling yet a while, they caught sight of the blinking light in the window of their cottage. This gave them more strength. The oars started to move as if by themselves, in longer and stronger strokes. The surging sea had begun to subside little by little since they had now entered the shelter of the calm bay. Finally, the boat slid into a quiet cove, where the water glistened as black as melted pitch. The bow of the boat crunched on the home shore.

They stumbled on to the land as wordlessly as they had rowed, pulled the prow of the boat further up on land, and grabbed the heavy tubs. The wind whistled and howled through the woods, and the rain continued unabated. The staff sagged squeaking between them as they, staggering and stumbling along the rocky path, carried the tubs to their pigs. Smelling the food and the people, the pigs began to squeal and jump against the palings of their pen. The man lit the tallow candle in the blackened lantern and while he stayed to measure out the food, his wife hurried to the house.

The smallest children were already asleep, but with swollen eyes, ten-year old Liisa and eight-year old Kalle sat beside the stove. They had already boiled the potatoes and fried the meat. They had been so frightened that they had been compelled to alternate between singing out loud and sitting quietly, not uttering a sound. But now all at once, everything changed. A feeling of joy entered the house. The mother quickly took off her wet clothing, wrapped something dry around herself, and added wood to the fire. For, of course, they had to have a little coffee to finish off their meal. Besides the potatoes and meat, bread and salted fish also appeared on the table. There was no milk even for the smallest ones, since there were no cows nearby. They had milk only when the parents found time to get some from the city.

When the father came in, they seated themselves at the table. They ate eagerly. The hard bread and the fishbones crunched in their teeth. In the pale light of the lamp, many gray hairs already showed in the wife's hair, the husband was almost bald. They both had the faces of old people, but their hands, as they reached for more food from the table, were strong and firm. And their minds were filled with contentment and peace. The roar of the sea and the wind outside only added to the intimacy and security of the home. The forest on the island, even though it did not belong to them, provided plenty of dead branches, stumps, and fallen tree trunks, so they did not need to conserve wood. From the fields which they had cleared among the rocks on Sundays and during other occasional spare moments, they got a good crop of potatoes. They had a good supply of salted fish and they had three pigs squealing in their pen. And with their wages, they got flour, sugar, coffee, tobacco, and a few other delicacies.

They had food for the winter.

Their aching and tired limbs were relieved by the thought that after they had loaded one or two more ships, their winter rest would begin.

After the meal was over, the older children went to bed, but for the parents there still remained many things to attend to. The mother cleared the table and prepared food for the children for the next day and lunch for herself and her husband. With the light of a lantern, the husband went to chop wood and to carry water from a spring some distance away. Only then, when all was finished, did they crawl into bed, one beside the other. They sank into immediate heavy sleep.

Little by little the cottage was filled with the smell of wet clothes drying in the heat from the stove and with the breathing of seven sleeping people. The rain stopped, but the wind continued to blow briskly through the night, rattling the roof of the cottage and whistling down the chimney. The forest murmured, crashed, and sighed and the sea pounded incessantly on the rocky shores. For the Kämäräinens, this was a cradle song, a lullaby, which helped them sleep even more soundly. In the midst of the fall night's storm and the depth of their sleep, the comforting and cheerful thought filled their minds: we have food for the winter.

Building A Bridge (1929)

A strange ache and longing always seizes me when I think about people whom I have at some time grown attached to but whom I will never see again. It feels so strange and distressing. To think, that something, such an important thing as a person, can disappear from our lives forever. But that is human destiny.

For instance, I remember two men, whose friendship I enjoyed for almost a year. I remember that during that whole time I was bored, and yet I am now almost panic stricken when I realize that I will never see them again. They live somewhere and I live somewhere, but we once worked together and lived together for the time it took to build a bridge. We have not heard from one another since.

The bridge was to be built for the railroad over a river. It was winter when the project started and the work on the footings was to be completed by spring so the concrete could be poured as soon as the weather warmed. It was out in the country, and the men were lodged in a village about two kilometers from the bridge site. It was just an ordinary country village, which had dozed in the same place for who knows how long, and which now upon suddenly waking up to the racket and the horde of workers, appeared confused and awed. But the people of the village, having unusually healthy and strong business instincts, soon accepted the situation and realized what could be gained. Money could be made. So they rented their rooms and sold their food to the bridge builders while their daughters, to the great indignation of their sons, found other benefits in the situation.

The two men roomed together. When I got a job as the helper in their blacksmith shop and, coming from far away, had no place to stay, they took me in as the third roomer. It was a small room in a large house and allowed little room for individual pursuits. However, it was a better place than what many of the other bridge builders had, since the room was in a large house. And, of course, I now lived in the company of blacksmiths, no less.

On weekdays we worked from dawn to dark. It was the most pleasant part of these days although we always wished the work would end. We wished the strain of the work would cease so we could have the evening to ourselves. And what did we do in the evenings? We just were bored. We ate, drank, read newspapers and books, went dancing, but yet, what else could we have done except feel bored during those evenings? The village streets were filled with snow, the stars twinkled distantly in the sky, the forest stood dark and motionless. We looked at all this through the window, reduced to silence, sinking deeply into our thoughts. It is not good for a bridge builder to look out into the winter night and sink into his thoughts. Thinking suits him poorly. It only arouses yearnings and fears. But what else could we have done? We didn't care to go to the village dances too many times in a row just for the sake of dancing, if there was no prospect of other things. And these village dances failed to offer memories of any girl which would occupy our thoughts as we fell asleep. These girls danced so well and dressed so beautifully that they were capable of arousing yearnings in us, but they lacked the power to appease these yearnings. Consequently it was best to stay away from them.

It took half an hour to read the newspaper. A book--of the kind available there--poor novels, books about farming and home economics, the collected works of celebrities--could sometimes fill up a whole evening, but never two evenings in a row. And there were so many evenings, there was so much time; sometimes it felt as if there was an endless amount of time, of darkness and time. When we were more bored than usual, we played cards but even though card playing is an excellent way of killing time, we were never able to rid ourselves of the feeling that it was dull. One of the smiths had another remedy; he went into the village for most of the night and came back drunk. The other smith never did that since he was an unusually tidy man and did not want to destroy his body with poison. The following day he clearly outdid his friend in performance, for in this life we are paid according to our merits.

We were bored. The winter seemed as if it would never come to an end and spring was the only thing that we had to look forward to. To be sure, we didn't know what spring would bring with it in these surroundings. But if one has nothing to look forward to, nothing to hope for, life is a calamity. And so, having nothing else, we waited for spring. We always had some fun on pay day, for everyone who did not worship Lady Luck too ardently began to pile up money. Money is something that is easy to enjoy. You don't recognize its value until it stays in your pocket with some constancy. But then it begins to demand more, ever more, and so we became quite frugal. But underlying even this pleasure there was always the boredom. Something was lacking and we often thought: if only spring would come soon.

And it came. But we had not considered the possibility that it would be just another ordinary spring. One day a crack appeared in the river, the fiery disc of the sun glowed in the sky, water dripped from the eaves of the houses. Ah! The nights were still cold but not nearly as cold as the week before, and yet how bright they were even in their darkness. There were thousands, millions of stars. Above the little village floated exciting patches of light and the breath of the wind carried with it the smell of a faraway sea. Now even the days, the hours at work, lost their appeal. They just made us sweat. Something in the forest, in the muddy roads, and in the bright crusts of snow summoned us. A short while ago we had been filled with yearning, now we were filled with tormenting restlessness. It felt almost inevitable that something unusual had to happen and we waited for it with unceasing restlessness.

But what could have happened? We, who had lived long enough, were doubtful from the very beginning. Spring had already deceived us too often. It just makes people act impulsively and then it goes its merry way. And summer, despite our expectations, never fulfills the promises of spring. But with spring seething in our blood, our doubts were of little consequence. The habits of a lifetime and rigorous discipline had brought us to the point where we were able to continue our work in an orderly way. But it was hard. Some could not do it, they just left, but they were few and from year to year their number decreased because the spirit of modern times disdains them and denies them livelihood and a good life. The vagabonds, the knights of the open road, are dying out. We who stayed on, sweated, and somehow the days passed. But what could we do in the evenings? The books had lost their appeal and the newspapers were dull for it was the slack season in politics and sports; even the smugglers were just waiting for the ice to melt. The evenings were now still longer than in the winter, there was even more time. We walked around in the village, dropped in at our neighbors, danced, played cards, but still there was too much time. The one blacksmith went more frequently on his nighttime forays and more and more often he fell behind in his work.

When the ice and snow had gone, the bridge structure began to rise in huge arches out of the river. The concrete mixers began to churn. But we in the blacksmith shop knew almost nothing about this. We just shoved iron and steel into the fire, forged drills, steel beams, bolts. Every now and then some angry looking engineer would come to see us bringing drawings, arguing a while at the costs of the piece work, and then leave. The grass began to turn green and buds appeared on the trees.

We got used to sweating. The smiths stopped swearing. It was summer. And so our time passed, so our lives passed. Day by day the bridge neared completion. We walked in the forest and swam in the river. Again we read, played cards, and went dancing. The drinking smith did not drink as often. And we were bored, for we didn't know what to do in the evenings. Playing cards, dancing, drinking and reading newspapers are not really doing something, are not events. They are just incidents which are simply absorbed into a void. There is nothing else. There has to be something to give content to life. The bridge meant nothing; we had merely lent it our hands, but we did see the river flowing, the forest surrounding the village, and the unmoving face of the universe over our heads, and we could not solve their puzzles...Some pursued politics. They were happier, for they had something to look forward to, to hope for, even in the summer. The others of us did not.

The bridge was almost completed. Toward the end of September it was so close to being finished that it was decided the blacksmiths were no longer needed. We got our money, gathered our things together, and started out to look for new jobs. At the nearby railroad station, our ways separated, and we cast a last glance at the bridge.

The drinking smith said, "And so we got another bridge built."

"So we did," his friend agreed.

"We put six months into this one. That's another six months of our lives."

"Yes."

"Well, so long then, Boys."

"So long to you."

Since then we have not seen one another. They live somewhere, I live somewhere. It feels strange to think of these words: never again. They are like two parallel lines. But perhaps something of us, of the three of us, was left in the bolts and the steel beams, even though it is buried so deep in the concrete that no one will ever see it. Somehow it's comforting to think that way.

Pentti Haanpää (1905-1955)

Pentti Haanpää was born in northern Finland in what is known as North Ostrobothnia and lived as a free-lance writer in his home district, writing about the small farmers, lumberjacks, and hoboes of this region. He never had more formal education than elementary school but he took correspondence courses in English and philosophy, and he read widely. Haanpää describes these northern Finns and their environment, which he considered crucial, with a primitive strength as they struggle with the conditions of their lives. Without much success, they struggle against overwhelming odds, yet they do not surrender. Haanpää's stories reveal his feelings about the futility of life's struggle for the people he writes about. His writing is simple and straightforward, intense, without affectation, colored by original humor. It is also poetic. He developed to unique mastery a type of miniature short story, "a yarn", which has a sketchy easiness and freshness both in language and in treatment of subject matter. He published ten collections of "yarns", some of which are: MAATIETÄ PITKIN (ALONG THE ROAD), 1925, TUULI KÄY HEIDÄN YLITSEEN (THE WIND BLOWS OVER THEM), 1927, KENTTÄ JA KASARMI (THE FIELD AND THE BARRACKS), 1928, LAUMA (THE CROWD), 1937, NYKYAIKAA (MODERN TIMES), 1942, HETA RAHKO KORKEASSA IÄSSÄ (HETA RAHKO AT AN ADVANCED AGE), 1947, and ATOMINTUTKIJA (THE ATOMIC SCIENTIST), 1950. He has also written a number of miniature novels: KOLMEN TÖRÖPÄÄN TARINA (THE TALE OF THE THREE TÖROPÄÄS), 1927, NOITAYMPYRÄ (THE MAGIC CIRCLE), 1939, KORPISOTAA (WILDERNESS WAR), 1940, YHDEKSÄN MIEHEN SAAPPAAT (THE BOOTS OF NINE MEN), 1945, and JAUHOT (FLOUR), 1949. THE MAGIC CIRCLE and FLOUR are considered his best novels. At one time Haanpää was looked upon as an anarchist because of his treatment of the military in his short story collection, THE FIELD AND THE BARRACKS, written in 1928 and for almost ten years no respectable publisher would publish his works. However, he continued to write. The controversy around Haanpää's alleged anarchism has been resolved by time and perspective. He is currently being re-evaluated in Finnish literature and his life and works await a major biographical treatment. Each story included in this collection presents the main character in a given situation and in given surroundings. The stories represent the major characteristics of Haanpää's personality, style, and humor: his "anarchism" in *Military Splendor*; his tendency toward meditation in *The Last Tree*; his view of life's futility in *The Unneeded Paradise* and also in *The Last Tree*. All three stories end in terse, ironic statements revealing an accepting and sympathetic pessimism.

Military Splendor (1928)

Captain Lelu sat drinking his morning coffee in the officers' mess, silent as usual, as if lost in deep and serious thought. Yet his mind was not occupied by conscious thought--it was filled only with the gray dreariness of life, the irritating, debilitating, consuming bitterness of it.

He got up and walked in the direction of his company, to his work. The gravel crunched under his shoes, the light, dry gravel of spring. A gentle breeze was blowing and wisps of clouds floated in the wide blue sky. The shrill cry of a bird rang among the pines, the exuberant cawing of the garrison's crows split the air, almost as if rejoicing. The whole springlike world was designed to raise people's spirits, to sweep away the dust, to drive away the gloom, melancholy, and bitterness. But Captain Lelu's soul was like that of a downtrodden beast which no longer cares about anything, the corners of his mouth drooping downward in bitterness, his dull, yellowed teeth bared in a sneer.

And it was no wonder. The wind and the clouds--they seem so free, yet they can go nowhere. Theirs is an endless, everlasting journey across the arch of the blue sky just as is Captain Lelu's journey in the yellow gravel of the garrison.

About ten years had passed since Captain Lelu as a young second lieutenant first walked on this brown, barren gravel. At that time he was young and supple, clean and well groomed, as gay and resilient as a kitten. A cheerful enthusiasm for world affairs and for the good things in life filled his innocent mind. There had then followed countless steps in the garrison's gravel, several minor events, and two new stars had, at different times, been added to his collar. So now he was "Captain, Sir". No longer was he the same clean, happily innocent, kittenlike second lieutenant. The heavy burdens of the world had changed his face, his whole appearance, which now bore the marks of trials and sufferings, and too much heavy drinking. Even though his uniform was still militarily correct, its earlier neatness and trim fit was gone. Some rather undefinable shabbiness was apparent. It was particularly noticeable when he wore his topcoat, which hung on his body as if hung on a pole, its rain-washed and sun-faded hem flapping. The soldiers had given this worn-out coat a name: Fishcape. In time, the name transferred from the coat to its wearer.

In these ten years, Captain Lelu's nature had gone through a radical change both inside and out. The once youthful second lieutenant had been quite a different person from the man now known as Fishcape. Then, his face had been bright and smooth, shining with good humor. Nowadays his face was never brightened by a smile, nor did the angry cursing through his teeth make it any gloomier. His face always had the dull, listless bitterness of a down-trodden beast. The time was long past when he would chat happily and playfully with the soldiers, when he would open his cigarette case and wade through the snowdrifts to offer cigarettes to the men of his ski patrol. Nowadays he might just grab a clumsy young recruit by the nose, turn him about, kick his buttocks, just as a worn-out horse, an embittered animal, sometimes gets an inexplicable urge to kick something with his run-down hoofs.

This change had occurred gradually and almost imperceptibly. In the beginning his former good humor and cheerfulness had sometimes shone through like the sun between dark clouds, but soon the dark clouds shrouded his soul completely. There were no breaks in the clouds, no sweeping winds. How did this happen? Who knows. It took him by surprise, like a fog: the weight of life, the gray and the monotony of the small military town. Then came the alcohol, night after night of sitting beside a bitter glass. His blood and his heart became poisoned. His nature changed completely; he became gloomy, suspicious, irritable. Joy no longer touched him, nothing interested him. But he carried out his professional duties in an orderly way; he taught and shouted, dissipated and half asleep after a night of drinking. The only satisfaction he now felt was the knowledge that he was feared and hated by his men. There no longer appeared any prospect of other sources of satisfaction, of fulfillment of other hopes. He had become the army's proletariat, shabby, poor, having somehow fallen into disfavor. For the rest of his life he would never rise one step higher, no new and bigger star would be attached to his collar, no new stripes would be sewed on the sleeve of the fishcape. But it felt good that even he was feared and respected by someone. Let them hate him, just so they are filled with fear and just so the fear remains greater than the hatred.

And yet there had been a time when he felt good that the soldiers did not hate him, when they said, "He's okay." And the maneuvers had gone well. His company was the best in the whole garrison and he had rapidly been awarded those two new stars. It wasn't that the maneuvers didn't go well now. They had to. At least his men knew what they had to do and how, except when, angered beyond limits, they sometimes did everything all wrong.

There was once, for instance, a review of marksmanship. Captain Lelu's company didn't hit a single bullet into the target. But the red marking flags on the edge of the bank were as full of holes as sieves. The officer in charge of the review had inquired of the men why the bullets were going into the flags and not into the targets. He was able to surmise that too rigorous practices and harsh discipline had made the men defiant enough not to aim at the targets. The men had assumed that this would somehow be annoying to the officers. And indeed it seemed to be; the reviewing officer first cursed at the men and then shouted at the captain. Lelu had raised his hand to his hat and tried to explain, "Sir, Colonel, Sir..." But the colonel snapped. "Stand at attention!" And so Captain Lelu had to press his palms against his thighs and stand as straight as a ramrod, regardless of what he might be thinking. Bread is precious to everyone. One has to have a means of livelihood. One must subject oneself to one's superiors. The soldiers had secretly sneered, "The master found his master." Just let them sneer. They will soon see who is their master.

And they did. However, nowadays the captain had to be more careful, had to curb his temper. Some years ago he happened to kill a man, had gotten into trouble, into the courts, and out of his meager income he had to pay a pension to the deceased man's mother. They had been out on field practice and the whole company had been ordered into a prone position. Then Captain Lelu had noticed that one soldier's back was hunched, just as if he were maliciously aiming his buttocks at his superiors standing behind him. What? Is such a thing tolerated? Won't that back straighten out along the ground? Captain Lelu leaped on the man's back and then the man did straighten out, but at the same time the stump beneath him rent his body. After this, Captain Lelu had to be a little more careful, a little more observant. But there was no doubt that this incident considerably increased the men's fear and respect for him.

But did they really fear and respect him so very much? At least one of them had played a devilish trick on him a few days ago. Well, he was someone, the only one, who would dare to do such a thing. The Captain had come walking into the barracks area late one night with a sack of potatoes over his shoulder. He was a strange man, he did not always make use of his subordinates. He himself would do what other officers had their men do. So, when his family needed potatoes, he had gone outside the barracks fence, bought a sack of potatoes and started to carry it to his living quarters. But the sentry at the gate stopped him, "Captain, Sir, halt! What is in your sack?"

Captain Lelu knew the man. It was one of his own men. He had been held in the service for years of overtime, by turns serving time in prison, in the guardhouse, in the company. Captain Lelu remembered quite clearly how this lengthy service had originated. It was in the days when he had started drinking. This soldier had gone once to get some liquor for him. In those days Captain Lelu was still occasionally light-hearted, even cheerful. And so he had given the soldier a small bottle, saying, "Enjoy it." The man had done this, had become drunk, had been taken to the guardhouse but had escaped. He had screamed, "I'm not going in there! The Captain got me drunk. Get him too…"

Captain Lelu came close to being brought to trial again at that time. However, everything was silenced and buried. Neither the Captain nor the soldier were punished for trafficking in liquor. But Captain Lelu, whose nature was turning mean and petulant, damaged by alcohol, had punishments inflicted upon the soldier for many small infractions and then for recurring infractions, imprisonment. Through perceptive and clever cunning this was easy for a superior officer to arrange against hated subordinates. And so the man was still in the service. And now he stood as the sentry at the gate and said, "Captain, Sir, halt! What is in your sack?"

The Captain cursed and told him to step aside and not make trouble, and continued walking forward.

But the guard released the safety catch on his gun and repeat^d, "Halt! I am the guard and it is my duty to check that nothing not properly authorized is brought into the barracks area."

The captain released a stream of curses and threats which would have petrified a weaker man. But this man did not flinch.

"Captain, Sir, it cannot be helped! Open the sack!"

Captain Lelu realized the man was serious. That man won't stop at anything. He'll shoot, the devil. And in the dusk of the evening he was overcome by fear. He opened the sack.

"Dump everything on the ground so I can see what's in the bottom."

Fear conquered the Captain's ire and he dumped his potatoes on the ground and started to leave.

"Halt, Captain, Sir. Pick up the potatoes and put them back into the sack and take them away. A sentry cannot permit any foreign matter to be left at the sentry gate."

The Captain knew that the bullet in that guard's rifle was set for firing. Life is precious even to a soldier. It is not to be wasted on petty matters, even though one is prepared to give one's last drop of blood for one's country and for the established order. The Captain picked up his potatoes, lifted the sack to his shoulder and walked away, telling the sentry before he left that he would remember this.

"I believe you, Sir."

And he had reason to believe it. He knew he could not be punished for being overly conscientious in following the rules and regulations but of one thing he could be sure, there would be arrests and imprisonments enough for seemingly other reasons.

These days gave Captain Lelu some diversion in his life as he pondered and reflected on how to retaliate for the humiliation he had suffered. It was not always easy to think of something on the spur of the moment and so in recent days he had become extremely ill-tempered, fanatic. The whole company had borne the brunt of his anger; sweat had poured off them and steam had risen through their wet clothes.

This was the kind of man Captain Lelu was and, on the whole, such had been his story until this moment when he walked toward his company on this spring day, the gravel crunching under his shoes.

The company, a construction troop, was standing all lined up in front of their barracks with their hoes, shovels, axes, their trucks loaded with other necessary tools. When the Captain appeared around the corner, the men all turned their eyes toward him, and every face reflected, "Here comes the son of a bitch!"

The routine drills and announcements were carried out and the company started to march to their field practice.

They were digging trenches. There was a huge boulder blocking their way. Holes had been drilled into it. They planned to blast it into bits. The explosive had been set in place, the fuse lit.

Lelu, the company commander, stood there looking sullen. Everyone was supposed to run for cover. Captain Lelu was just turning to leave when behind him he felt arms encircling his groin. He was lifted into the air and rushed to the top of the boulder, where the fuse was sputtering at the base. He knew they were the arms of the old veteran who had been the guard at the gate and that he lay in his arms, his back pressed tight against the veteran, helpless as a child. At the base of his ear, the Captain heard him call, "Boys, write home that I have gone to give the Captain a ride to heaven!"

All of this happened suddenly, with no warning. No one suspected anything. The non-commissioned officers and their men, petrified, peered from behind the shelter of their barricades. The sun was shining, a soft breeze was blowing beneath the blue sky, and from the pines the shrill cry of a bird pierced the air. But they were all, with white, rigid faces watching these two men, the soldier and the officer, on the top of the gray boulder. Then someone suddenly recalled last night, when the field practice had ended and the company, steaming with sweat, had reached their barracks. Someone had remarked, "That Fishcape is a real devil, a madman, on the loose only for lack of rope." Someone else had said, "I wonder how many men would find relief if we hanged him from a branch of a tree?" But the old veteran had said, "Be patient, Boys! It won't last long!" Nobody had noticed anything unusual in this. Each one had thought, "That's right, just over a hundred more days, but there is a lot to be put up with even in that time."

Now the old veteran lay on his back on the huge rock, holding Captain Lelu on top of him. And he had shouted out that he was the driver. They were on the way to heaven.

None of the soldiers had the time to wish them a good journey. Time was short. At first, Captain Lelu had lain as if paralyzed. But now he seemed to be tearing at the old veteran's unyielding wrists, and he shouted, "Help!"

But no one ran to the gray rock. Everyone knew the length of the fuse which sputtered at the base of the rock. They knew the sudden violence of the substance waiting there in its crevice. The Captain's shout served as a last command to his company; all the heads ducked into hiding. At that moment the explosion came. Gray chunks of rock burst through the air. In the pines the shrill cry of a bird ceased. But the sun shone and under the blue sky the gentle summer breeze blew through the branches, just as before. But the two men who had lain on the rock had left on their journey.

The Last Tree (1947)

Juho Pernu, a hulk of an old man, dropped heavily down to sit on the frost-covered ground, gasped for air; he fumbled for his chest with a hand that had slipped out of his patched mitten and was almost as white as the frosty ground. There, somewhere inside, was the pain. For a while it was absolutely unbearable. But little by little the pain gave way and the old man could breathe a bit more easily, fill his pipe bowl with dried moss, and puff a little.

He was in low spirits. The sad thought had flashed through his mind that it was now time to go, to let go once and for all. He was no good any more, hadn't been for a long time. He had become slow and weak. "This is disease at work", one could say about his sawing, and the blows of his ax were no longer real blows, only futile chopping. Ever smaller stacks of wood and ever greater weariness. He had to face up to the fact that his time was past. The forest was no longer for him, nor was any other place. He was nearing the end...

Often before, thoughts like these had passed through his mind, but then again, he had felt he was still a vigorous and tough old fellow. The chips flew, the tree fell, and the stack rose. It was no use for a person to let go. For then the devil would take him...

But now, Juho Pernu, the old woodsman, suddenly was convinced he had to let go. And that right now, at this very moment. He would fell one more tree, the one over there which is marked for felling, just as it should be.

And so old man Pernu tapped the ashes out of the bowl of his pipe, and his saw began to hiss and buzz at the base of his last tree.

He had come this far. And in his lifetime Juho Pernu had felled many trees, a great many trees. This was the last one. But he did not remember his first tree, which he had sent crashing to the ground some time more than fifty years ago. What kind of tree had it been, and where had it been? It had happened somewhere farther to the South, while he was still but a boy...

Then he had not done much of anything except to fell trees, even virgin timber, logs for sawing, mine posts, railroad ties, pulpwood, beams, whatever was needed. Sometimes in the springs and summers he had guided the logs along the rivers and over windy lakes. He had gone just like a mourner in a funeral procession with those wooden bodies which would go travelling all over the world along the flowing waters.

And then he had returned to his endless felling of trees. He had also cut up tremendous amounts of cordwood. Later they crackled in the stoves in homes, heated steam boilers, drove trains so that dark smoke belched out. He had even chopped wood for charcoal, black charcoal for the blacksmith's forge. And in recent times, the power from charcoal moved cars on the highways...

So being a woodcutter, a feller of trees, was Juho Pernu's occupation, and he had done more than his share of the work. He had felled, even stripped, nature's mightiest creations of the North as if they were his enemies. But that was not really how it was. He felt a kinship with the trees, and the forest's eternal murmur soothed his cares and his bitterness in life's struggle. For that is what Juho Pernu's life had been, a struggle, a constant wrestling with want and poverty. For chopping down trees never brought in much money, and a lumberjack's way of life was often questionable... especially the life of a wild lumberjack such as he had been in his youth and early manhood. Then he had built a house, real log house, foursquare, to which he could return from his tree-felling trips, and where the wife and children lived off his toil.

No less than four sons had Juho Pernu's ax and saw raised into stalwart young men who, then, from the youngest through the oldest, fell on the battlefield. This was a fate which cast a heavy gloom over old man Pernu's later years, a gloom that even the forest's endless murmur could never completely dispel...to grow to manhood in poverty so extreme that only Juho Pernu understood it, and then to be dragged to some battleground like an animal to be slaughtered. The blood was just drained from the body, like dew on some faraway brush heap, and then the body sent back home to a grand burial ground for heroes.

More than once a childlike idea had passed through old Pernu's mind that he had felled many trees with which he had felt kinship...perhaps too many. And that was why his sons were not allowed to die as people, but were felled just like trees. Antti Pernu, fallen in Syvari, it read on a white cross in a row of white crosses...It had taken the swinging of Father Pernu's ax to accomplish this. This was some world! Trees fell and men fell. If heaven did not send deadly frosts, then people themselves managed their lives so hunger was never far away...

Now, not very much more could happen to old man Pernu. His last tree had already crashed to the ground so that the white frost swirled. He would go to that four-sided cottage and live whatever was left of his life. He would still have the pension, given in behalf of his dead heroes. But it was very lonely and desolate in the cottage. His wife, Mari Pernu, was also dead and buried. A small rock, a grave stone, had been put over her stomach so there was no way she could get out of there...Would she even care to come back? One could easily believe that she...

Up until this time, old man Pernu had by no means been a ready believer. The forest held some secret power, which had no name, but which helped a man's mind stay free of cares, taught him to understand that needless worry does not lengthen the woodpile. Old man Pernu had always been a cheerful man, and his shoulders had shaken with laughter more often than with chills. For in the forest and in the lumber camps it was often cold and trying and hard and monotonous. But there was always the fresh smell of pitch. The worry of providing a livelihood did not defeat his spirit...

In the forest his ancient forebears had hunted for game, relying on the goddess of the forest. There his grandfather's and also his father's tar pits had smoldered. Even though they were, as the old saying went, "in debt as all tar distillers are", they had still managed to live so their shoulders now and then shook with laughter. And the modern lumber companies, whose saws screeched and whose factories smoked and sent out a stench, had made a feller of trees out of Juho Pernu. He had felled them and felled them and raised sons, who all fell at Syvari, and who knows where else...

And now it was very lonely in that four-sided cottage. Now he had felled his last tree, the northern forest's mighty creation. He lopped off its branches, cut it up, and stacked it...weak, clumsy, old.

The last tree! This thought filled him with sorrow. For more than fifty years he had felled trees, lived his life among them. Now he would walk away from them with his saw and his ax, and he would never return.

Sitting on the stump of the last tree he had felled, giving a farewell glance to his last clearing, Juho Pernu felt as if he died.

Even if he should live on for some time yet in that four-sided cottage, or somewhere else, it would no longer be living, but something else, whatever it would be, lingering...

Juho Pernu, former feller of trees, began his walk toward the village with steps more deliberate than ever before, his working tools under his arm, the dried moss smoldering in the bowl of his pipe, which he was still able to carry clenched between his gums.

The Unneeded Paradise

(Published posthumously, 1958)

On the day that Samppa Mäki saw Antti Takalo, who had just returned from America, he became restless and dissatisfied. For Antti Takalo walked like a gentleman, was well dressed, had an elegant tie around his neck and fancy shoes on his feet. There was a rumor that he had bought land, the neglected Leiviska farm. That upset Samppa the most. The clothes, and even the grand yellow watch fob and chain across Antti's vest, he could accept. But this land buying, this farm ownership, was more than he could bear.

Only too well Samppa Mäki remembered what Antti Takalo's origin had been: just plain Antti Takalo, a boy from a wretched hovel, a shepherd, with the manners of a boor. And now he walked like a gentleman and was the master of Leiviska. How was this possible? That sort of thing originated and was encouraged in America. Antti Takalo had gone there to make his mighty and incredible leap upward.

Dissatisfaction and restlessness smoldered in Samppa Mäki's heart. For him, things were as they had always been. He was the son of the Mäkis, as he had always been, now a grown man, and, without any doubt, a confirmed bachelor. And there was no prospect in sight of his becoming the master of the farm, nor of his getting any kind of inheritance. His parents kept on living, tenacious as juniper bushes on a hill. They managed the farm and kept on living. And they should live! You are supposed to honor your parents so you may prosper and live long upon this earth...But did he prosper? Samppa Mäki had always worked, worked very hard, the results of which, however, seemed to dissolve into thin air. You chop wood and it is burned, you turn over the earth and you just get your feet all dirty. He hadn't managed to get ahead one bit. His life and his time seemed to have passed for nothing when you compared them with Antti Takalo's accomplishments. There must be a flaw somewhere, and a bad one. For Samppa Mäki believed that he was the equal of Antti Takalo, the present master of Leiviska, in working capacity. But he had been putting in his work in the wrong place. That was it.

In the former complacent heart of Samppa Mäki, discontent

smoldered and smoldered. He caught the incredible America fever. He could, just while waiting to become master of the farm and getting his inheritance, go across the ocean and accumulate money, which seemed so easily accessible that it was within the reach of even the Antti Takalos of the world.

Tough, wrinkled, and ill-tempered old man Mäki still treated his son as if he were a child.

"So, you want to go to America! It's only the poor who go over the sea and into the cold world..."

"The poorest and dumbest can stay here," said Mäki's son. "You can't get ahead here."

"Go then! Go and search for the world's riches. The dog will know he's been swimming when his tail gets wet."

And Samppa Mäki left the only home he had ever known, left his father's house, left for America.

But already on the ship, when for days there was nothing to see but sea and sky, when life was agonizingly empty and of a very strange flavor, from the very beginning of the trip, he bitterly regretted his decision. He did not get seasick, yet he was desperately ill. He was used to working regularly, and the imposed idleness oppressed him. He couldn't help constantly thinking about how many days of good ploughing weather were being wasted. For it was fall. Restless, he walked the deck. The ever present mass of water repulsed and frightened him. Even the food did not taste good...and the kind of food it was too, not worth eating by human beings. The time just dragged for him, and he thought that he had actually stepped of his own free will into hell's entrance hall. Drinking and carousing, which some of his travel companions fell into, were totally foreign to him. Samppa Mäki had not gone out into the world to seek only pleasure, adventure, to live and act just any old way, but to earn big money, to get rich...

But now, for some reason, the dreams and illusions of riches and prosperity had lost their glitter and their power to excite. They had lost their glamour. A verse from the Bible forced its way into his mind: "What does it profit a man..."

Samppa Mäki's mind filled with extremely clear pictures of the faces of people he knew, of the life at home, of Mäki's gray house and its spacious living room where perhaps right now the boiling potatoes were steaming away; where, after eating, it felt so good for a person to lie down on the floor and with confidence in his own strength, raise his legs and relax.

Samppa Mäki felt as if he were somewhat like the prodigal son; in fact, quite a bit like him. He was just about ready to see himself for what he was, to turn and go back to his father. But that was not possible. The ship steamed ahead along the open sea, which seemed as endless as eternity itself.

But there is a limit to everything. The sea ended and land began to appear. Before them was the harbor and the disembarking place, America, the rich land. Samppa Mäki sighed with relief. The idle, mind-confusing, boring existence would end and one would again feel solid land beneath one's feet and would get in touch with real life: go to work, work, then go home, eat, sleep, and see, perhaps, how the money piles up from the work of one's hands.

But on the American shore there was a terrible, mind-boggling city. It was packed with people and the streets were overrun with all kinds of vehicles. In addition, people were carried underground like moles and they glided in the air like birds. The buildings stretched so high into the sky that the humming of the righteous probably could be heard on the rooftops. The pace and noise were horrifying. Even the people's speech was like the meaningless twittering of birds. It seemed as if their tongues were wrung out of their throats and turned wrong side out.

The confusing sounds constantly pushed their way violently into his ears, and there didn't seem to be anything solid on which to rest his eyes. Only with the greatest difficulty did Samppa Mäki realize that there now stood in front of him a man he knew, knew from home, the appointed greeter and guide for the first steps in the new world. It finally became clear to him and he again felt some sort of relief and shouted into this familiar man's ear, "Listen, do these people live like this of their own free will, or have they been sentenced to it as a punishment for something?"

"Each to his own liking," smiled the familiar man. "You find it strange? One gets used to it..."

"Those who have to perhaps," added Samppa Mäki skeptically.

It now became clear to him that everything would be arranged for him here through the effort of this man he knew, even a job was waiting for him.

But when Samppa Mäki saw the place of work he was terrified. The mine shaft seemed to him the blackest of the black, the gate to hell itself. And the people who stepped out of the mine shaft to the surface of the earth were as if condemned to damnation, completely worn out, panting through open mouths, their skin wet with sweat.

Was this a place to work? Now Samppa Mäki remembered more clearly than ever before the family home, where he had taken his ax or his spade and had gone to the big forest or to the open fields or had harnessed the horse in the farmyard with its old familiar smell.

He looked at a man who rose from below the earth, his mouth open, panting like a dog, his tongue hanging out of his mouth, and Samppa Mäki made a hard decision.

"This is no place for me to work," he said.

"Isn't it?" said the familiar man. "And what then?"

"I guess the ships move in the other direction too. It seems that my coming here was nothing but a trip to the land of death. I can manage to survive at Mäki's farm. It even supports seven horses."

The man went right away with Samppa to help buy his ticket. For the son of Mäki had not had to go traveling so poor that he had only money for a one way trip out into the world. He felt all his craving for riches and profits to be dead. He got on the first departing ship and spent his time sleeping or staring dully in front of him as the ship steamed toward the faraway Finnish shore.

Here on the shore of Finland, Samppa Mäki, for the first time in his life, and perhaps for the last, felt what it meant to be poor. He no longer had enough money to buy a ticket to the station closest to his home. He bought a ticket as far as his money would take him and then got off the train. He did not dare to ride any further. Who knew how the railroad bosses might swear at him and even kick his backside.

He now had ahead of him a walk of over a hundred kilometers. He no longer had money to buy food. Samppa Mäki did not spend his time looking at the sides of the road, but tightened his belt and said quietly, "You live like a king for a day, a slave for a week." And so he trudged along the muddy autumn roads.

It was night when he reached the Mäki farm, the home place. The doors were open, as usual. Robbers were not feared here, for there weren't any. The returning son went quietly inside, climbed to the warm spot above the large hearth and with a sigh, stretched out his limbs and fell asleep on the delightfully warm, familiar spot.

The next morning Samppa's mother started the fire at the hearth and the master, sitting on the bench, pulled on his boots intending to step outside, when someone, or was it just a phantom, descended from the top of the hearth.

But it was human after all, Samppa himself. It even spoke, "Greetings from the unneeded paradise," he said.

Mika Waltari (1908-1979)

"When Mika Waltari died at the end of August, 1979, Finland lost one of her best known writers--a man for all times, unusually varied and prolific in his output. His list of works is impressive, both in quality and variety of style. He wrote massive novels, plays and poetry, was a master thriller writer, an essayist, a critic and film-script writer. He worked as a translator and journalist. His novels have been published in twenty-nine countries, translated into twenty-five different languages. Mika Waltari's working life spanned fifty years; he was a living link between several generations, from the 1920's to the present day." [1]

Mika Waltari was born in Helsinki and considered a child prodigy, publishing a volume of poetry, JUMALAA PAOSSA (THE FLIGHT FROM GOD), at the age of seventeen. He entered the University at eighteen and received his master's degree at twenty-one. Until 1949 he produced one or more books each year. Some critics consider his early works his best ones: the novels, SUURI ILLUSIONI (THE GREAT ILLUSION), 1928, APPELSIINI SIEMEN (THE ORANGE SEED), 1931; the short stories, JÄTTILÄISET OVAT KUOLLEET (THE GIANTS ARE DEAD), 1930, and the description of his journey to southeast Europe, YKSINÄISEN MIEHEN JUNA (THE LONELY MAN'S TRAIN), 1929. In some of his early work he wrote about the young people in the gay 1920's in Helsinki. In the 1930's he wrote serious, moral books, among which are: a trilogy about a Helsinki family which witnesses the growth of the city and was eventually published as one volume in 1942 as ISÄSTÄ POIKAAN (FROM FATHER TO SON); a novel about Helsinki in the 1930's, SURUN JA ILON KAUPUNKI (THE CITY OF SORROW AND JOY), 1936; one on violent passions in a rural setting, VIERAS MIES TULI TALOON (A STRANGER CAME TO THE FARM), 1937. After World War II, he discovered the colorful, romantic, thrilling historical novel and has written the following, all of which have been translated into English: SINUHE, EGYPTILÄINEN (THE EGYPTIAN), 1945, which has been filmed in Hollywood; MIKAEL KARVAJALKA (THE

ADVENTURER), 1948; MIKAEL HAKIM (THE SULTAN'S
RENEGADE), 1949; JOHANNES ANGELOS (THE DARK ANGEL),
1953; TURMS, KUOLEMATON (THE ETRUSCAN), 1955. He has
also published short novels: FINE VAN BROOKLYN, 1941; EI
KOSKAAN HUOMISPÄIVÄÄN (NEVER A TOMORROW), 1943;
NELJÄ PAIVÄNLASKUA (FOUR SUNSETS), 1949; FELIKS
ONNELLINEN (LUCKY FELIKS), 1958; VALTAKUNNAN
SALAISUUS (THE SECRET OF THE KINGDOM), 1959;
IHMISKUNNAN VIHALLISET (THE ROMAN), 1964. His later short
story collections include KUUN MAISEMA (MOONSCAPE), 1953,
and KOIRANHEISIPUU (THE WOODBINE), 1961. In the fall of
1978 to celebrate Waltari's seventieth birthday, the Helsinki
University Library sponsored the publication of a bibliography of all
foreign translations of his works.[1]   The story, *The Apple Trees*,
from the 1943 collection. NOVELLEJA (SHORT STORIES),
represents the quality of his writing and his understanding of a
Helsinki youth.

---

1 BOOKS FROM FINLAND, Vol. XIII, No. 4, p. 174

The Apple Trees (1943)

That spring I received a grade report which entitled me to advance in school from the sixth to the seventh form without any conditions, and I had reason to be happy. For the summer I got a job on the railroad tracks in a small town about sixty kilometers from Helsinki. In those days there was plenty of work for everybody, and the poor pay on the railroad tracks did not attract many workers from the regular work force so they hired students for the light summer jobs. The three marks an hour meant a lot to me, and I was able to save most of it for the winter as I had free board and room with the kind uncle who had arranged the job for me. The dressing room in the sauna was my room, and in the evenings I often sat on the sauna steps, my body weary from being burned by the sun all day, my hands aching, but feeling most content, even important.

There were two of us students working there, but we were not put into the rough and tough railroad track gang, since changing wornout railroad ties for new ones demanded the strength of grown men. Our work was uprooting and raking new growth. We had to pull up by their roots the weeds which grew in the sand on the railroad banks, rake them into piles, and then smooth out the embankments. When this work was finished, with our brush hooks we had to chop the willows growing on the sides of the track embankments. We did a good job.

Showing us how to do our work and generally acting as our boss, as it were, was old Nyberg, who for decades had worked for hourly wages, and for whom the trackmaster tried to arrange regular, year-round easy work as a sort of pension. Nyberg's face was all wrinkled, and he no longer had many teeth. Even in the sun's most scorching heat, he wore a ragged old coat, which puzzled us boys, who had the upper parts of our bodies exposed to the sun. But he told us that in his childhood, during most of his life, he had suffered so much cold he could now never get enough heat. The men made fun of him and told us that during the winters his little cottage at the edge of the town was as hot as a sauna. He bought the wornout railroad ties very cheaply and burned them steadily through the whole winter.

At first both of us were a little afraid of him, for he seemed gruff to us, who were used to considerate and kind treatment at home. But we soon learned that he was extremely good-hearted. He did not scold us for our lack of experience and when we got tired, he let us take short "smoking breaks". Then he would smoke his handrolled cigarets and tell us his little anecdotes, which we soon knew by heart, but which were fun to listen to time after time anyhow. He always told them word for word in exactly the same way, and we always laughed heartily.

But more than anything else, he taught us how to do our work carefully and conscientiously. The raking work offered opportunities to cheat, to just carelessly press down the weeds and cover them with sand so everything looked fine, but after the first rain, the weeds would flourish anew. We had to be sure to get the weeds and their roots out of the ground and to rake them away, even if the work thus progressed more slowly. It was a point of honor with Nyberg that the trackmaster should never have grounds to utter a word of complaint about his work, and the quality of our work was his responsibility.

We had a lot of fun. Our skin turned brown. At first our hands grew blisters, but they soon toughened. The bag lunches tasted just wonderful. Since we had progressed many kilometers away from the station we, of course, could no longer go into the town for lunch. We felt quite important. After all, we were working for the government, and we felt that the track was our responsibility. Outsiders were fined for walking along the tracks, although rarely was this regulation strictly enforced. Once in the early days of our employment, a man came walking along the tracks toward us and my fellow worker shouted angrily at him, "Off the tracks, old Man!" We were a little embarrassed to find he was the track superintendent returning from vacation and had come to inspect our work. Neither one of us had seen him before, and Nyberg tittered quite delightedly over our mistake.

In those days I did not yet understand very much about people, but already in some vague way I was instinctively curious about them. I wanted to learn to know people and to understand their actions. I soon observed that as a person, Nyberg was out of the ordinary. He craved heat even on the hottest days. He kept all his savings with him in a dirty pouch. He had his own unique conceptions of heaven and upper class people. His wife had died some years earlier, and now he lived alone in his cottage, his only companion a big, old cat. The wife had not left him many happy memories; she had been mean to him.

But he loved his cat very much. He would sometimes tell us, who never made fun of him, how pleasant it felt when at night the cat rubbed its cold nose on his cheek when it wanted something to drink. They drank coffee together and they ate together. We were still too young to comprehend the tragic loneliness which all this contained, even though we cared about him. He was afraid of people; some tramp had once assaulted him. He had lived through cold and hunger, and people had treated him badly. His cottage, his savings, and the cat were his only security in life.

But in addition to this, he had a dedication which aroused wonder in us. Once in the middle of our work, he came very quickly toward me, knelt on the ground, dug around in the weeds piled up on the track embankment. "Now you've done something bad." He repeated, "Something really bad!" And from among the weeds I had chopped up he dug up the seedling of an apple tree with its roots cut off. "I don't suppose anything will come of this anymore," he said in a grieved voice but, still, he gathered some dirt around the cut-off root, wrapped it carefully in moss and took it into the shade beside his lunch bag. Following this incident, he always walked some distance in front of us, carefully digging up all the apple tree seedlings that grew on the tracks. And there were quite a number of them among the weeds in the hot dirt of the tracks. People often ate apples on the train and threw the cores out of the windows. Quite often the seeds began to sprout and developed into seedlings. We learned that for years Nyberg had gathered these seedlings and planted them around his cottage. He already had fruit-bearing trees which had developed from this kind of seedling.

I didn't quite understand this interest of his. I was still too young to place my goals in the future. I wanted everything right then and there. It never entered my mind to plant an apple tree in my uncle's garden and remain waiting for years in the hope that it might some day bear fruit. And Nyberg--old, with one foot in the grave--would hardly live to find joy from these seedlings. He didn't even have any relatives to whom he could leave his apple orchard as an inheritance.

Toward fall, I was asked one Sunday afternoon to bring a message from the track superintendent to Nyberg and saw his cottage for the first time.

It was a small, gray cottage at the edge of a heath. It had only one room and a large stove. The room was dirty, it smelled and was hot. The cat was old, shaggy, and deaf. It lay on the table and looked at me with drowsy suspicion. The Nyberg at home was different from the Nyberg at work. He was like a strange, old brownie whose wrinkled face was beaming with friendly smiles. He showed me his apple trees. There was so many of them that the small lot enclosed by a fence seemed overcrowded. There were rows of small seedlings. Here and there was a good-sized tree. They were scattered about in the stony ground, but around each one there was dirt, even though the land was all sand. Nyberg explained how in the evenings he had hauled hundreds of cartloads of black dirt for his apple trees.

He took me back to his cottage, dug two apples from among some rags and offered them to me. I bit into one of them, it was hard as a rock, woody, bitter. Of course I didn't tell him this, for I was polite, but when Nyberg turned his back, I shoved the apples into my pocket with the intention of throwing them away on my trip back. In a worried tone, Nyberg said that the apples were not the best. His teeth were not strong enough to bite into them, and the factory workers' children stole most of them every fall anyway. The overseer at the manor house had told him something about grafting, which could make even poor trees produce excellent, sweet apples. But to him the most important thing was that the trees were safe, and that they grew.

I thought he was something of a fool, this old man. I told him the town would soon grow so he would be forced to give up his cottage.--The trees could, of course, be moved elsewhere to grow, he said, even though it would take quite a bit of work.--But he was already old and sickly, I said, what if he should die.--At least, he said, the trees would still be alive, a little mark of the old man would be left in this world, perhaps as orchards for the children of the factory workers. They could divide the trees and plant them in their yards.

Even if the apples were poor, one can, so he had heard, by planting fifty or a hundred or a thousand trees from their seeds, get one tree which would bear a new, wonderful kind of apple, one which had never existed before. The others might all be failures, but that one single tree would be reward enough. Who knows, one of those seedlings growing over there could be that miraculous apple tree.

I knew nothing about these things at the time nor did I care to discuss them. Later I learned there was some truth to his ideas. But at the time I could not understand how an old man would have the energy or would care to do so much work, to dedicate all his labor and his zeal to growing trees which gave him no apparent benefit and which he would probably never see full-grown.

That summer passed and succeeding summers passed. I graduated, traveled abroad, I received my master's degree. Sometimes during my vacations I would go to visit with my old working buddies in the tool-house next to the station. Occasionally I would also meet Nyberg on the road. He would raise his hat to me and insist on calling me "Sir". This disturbed me but he would not believe me when I said I wanted everything to be as it had been before. He was suspicious of this and perhaps he was right. For the world I now lived in had separated me from the natural feelings of boyhood and the reverses I had already suffered had made me somewhat callous.

Once while out walking, I purposely went across the heath to Nyberg's cottage. The apple trees had grown some, there were fewer seedlings than before, the miserable, deaf, half-blind cat lay on the leaning steps. Nyberg was nowhere in sight and I didn't want to disturb him. He had been ill during the winter and had become irritable.

But walking back as the dusk of evening was falling, for the first time I intuitively realized that Nyberg's life perhaps concealed something rare and noble. Everything in him which appeared distorted and embittered by his life's experiences, everything laughable about him, suddenly dissolved. I saw him as a very lonely person, one whom others did not understand and who, in an effort to make his life worth living, wanted, as a legacy, to leave to strangers something lasting and perhaps rare and beautiful. He nurtured a dream. In all his oddity, he was an artist who had found a means of expression. In the same way as someone who realizes his dream by taming the wilderness with his plow, by draining a huge swamp, by building a house, or by writing a book--in the same way Nyberg in his apple trees would be leaving something behind which distinguished him from everyone else and made his wretched life worthwhile.

Juha Mannerkorpi (b. 1915) [1]

Juha Mannerkorpi was born in Ashtabula Harbor, Ohio, where he lived the first few years of his life until his parents returned to Finland, where his father was a minister in the state church. Mannerkorpi studied theology for a while and in 1945 got his degree in philosophy at the University of Helsinki. He has worked as a translator and free lance writer since. His first publications were three volumes of lyrical verse: LYHTY POLKU (THE PATH OF THE LANTERNS), 1946, EHTOOLLINEN LASIKELLOSSA (THE SUPPER UNDER THE BELL JAR), 1947, and KYLVÄJÄ LÄHTI KYLVÄMÄÄN (THE SOWER WENT FORTH TO SOW), 1954. RUNOT 1945-54 (POEMS 1945-1954) appeared in 1962. Mannerkorpi is often described as a poet on the boundary line between the traditional and the new poetry; he has written rhymed verse and expresses his feelings in older forms. His first prose works were a short story collection, NIIN JA TOISIN (THUS AND OTHERWISE), 1950; AVAIN (THE KEY), 1955, which he called a monologue; another short story collection. SIRKKELI (THE CIRCULAR SAW), 1956, and the novel, JYRSIJÄT (THE RODENTS), 1958, the story of an unhappy marriage from the point of view of the husband. In 1961 he published the novel, VENE LÄHDÖSSÄ (THE BOAT IS LEAVING), in which Mannerkorpi describes differing reactions to the same trivial situation and makes things happen in language as it does in direct experience. A novel, JÄLKIKUVA (THE LINGERING IMAGE), 1965, written after Mannerkorpi had suffered a personal loss, shows a person in the same situation who overcomes his sorrow. His moods and actions are often presented through his surroundings rather than through direct description. The novel, MATKALIPPU KAIKKIIN JUNIIN (A TICKET TO ALL TRAINS), 1967, is a description of a neurotic personality. In concentrated images, Mannerkorpi presents a dark, disconsolate, almost nightmarish vision of the world and seldom indicates the source of his anguished outlook. In his novels the problems of mistrust and loneliness are especially prominent. He chooses the workings of suffering, distorted minds. Seldom in his

1 Juha Mannerkorpi died in September, 1980.

works do people communicate with each other. They wonder about their relations to others, the consequences of their actions, and the meaning, or lack of meaning, in the problems they create for themselves. Mannerkorpi has lived in France and is a well-known translator of French literature into Finnish, having translated Jean Paul Sartre, Albert Camus, Andre Malraux, and Samuel Beckett, who have influenced his writings, particularly in existentialism. He has also written significant modern plays. *The Fur* from THUS AND OTHERWISE, 1950, with its concentrated images has the characters looking for meaning in their lives and wondering about their relations to others as they face an overwhelming truth. *The Monkey* from the 1956 collection, THE CIRCULAR SAW, shows lack of communication between the characters, mistrust and loneliness, and the workings of a suffering mind faced with an overwhelming compulsion--all presented in concentrated images.

The Fur (1950)

It is left there in the evening, on the floor beside the table, an old, worn-out, moth-eaten opossum fur, which had at one time served as a neckpiece. My wife has fitted together old and new, cut into the material with scissors, stitched it here and there. I have been sitting across the table contributing to our feeling of coziness by reading some things out loud. And the opossum fur is left on the floor.

The next morning our son discovers it. We are just drinking our morning tea, my wife and I. The door opens. Wearing only his shirt, the boy runs to our knees, explaining with wide open eyes, "There's a fur. It bites."

"What fur?" I ask.

"It must be that old fur neckpiece," my wife suggests.

Now I also remember. Of course, the old fur neckpiece is lying on the floor with its snout extended and the bone-shiny claws of its hind feet stretched out over the rug.

The boy is impatient. "Come and see! Mother, come and see! It will eat my horses and my cats and everything."

"Wait a minute, please," I request. "Let's have our tea first. Then we'll look."

We drink. The boy waits, but refuses to sit at the table. He just waits.

"There is a fur. It bites. We'll go and look soon."

He is quite obviously shaken up but still wavers between belief and disbelief: a ghost of a smile hovers on his lips but vanishes instantly.

Finally we get to see this strange thing. And there it is, the fur. It must be provoked a little.

"Touch it!" the boy urges. "It bites!"

Stealthily I move my finger near the snout, quickly draw my hand away, shake it and blow upon the bitten finger. The boy laughs.

"Again! Touch it again!"

This time I stealthily move the top of my shoe to the danger zone. The same thing happens. The fur bites. I hop around on one foot, groan and moan with pain. The boy screams with joy.

"Again! Touch it again!"

"I don't dare to touch it anymore. It bites too hard. Now let's get you dressed."

The boy is dressed. Something occupies my mind. I glance through the newspaper absent-mindedly. "Some eight hundred refugees cross the western border." My wife is moving pans in the kitchen.

The boy goes on playing in the next room. From time to time he comes to explain what the fur has tried to eat. Finally he appears in the doorway carrying a horse, a car, a large metal beetle, and a train in his arms. He looks distressed.

"It's going to eat all these!"

"We must take it away," I say reassuringly.

The boy agrees.

My wife takes a knife and a fork, pinches the fur with great care between them and dangles it to the shelf in the closet. A similar procedure has also entered my mind. The matter has been too important to be put on the shelf just like that, matter-of-factly, without illusion.

The boy calms down. But in a short while he finds a fur slipper somewhere. He looks at it for some time and then suddenly throws it to the floor, "A fur! It bites!"

I grab the briefcase on the corner of the bookshelf, open it and trap the slipper into it.

"Now it can't bite."

I place the briefcase on a chair. The boy quickly shoves it to the floor.

"Leather. A fur!"

He is alarmed.

"Now you see furs everywhere," I say helplessly, at a loss to think up a way of getting out of the web, which is beginning to entangle even me.

The boy is on the verge of crying when my wife says, "You haven't even eaten anything yet."

The boy, of course, has no interest in the food, and so the fur is buried under his protests. We do get through the meal somehow. The boy has his coat, and whatever else is needed, put on and he is taken safely by his father into the care of the playground attendant.

On my return, the fur keeps haunting my mind. The fur. "Some eight hundred refugees cross the western border."

I ring the doorbell and my wife comes to open the door. The fur has not left her alone either. We almost forget about breakfast. Both of us are overcome by a clarity of vision. We understand everything. We comprehend man, who creates ever stronger gods as his master. We understand why those eight hundred have fled across the western border. Their reason is fear, which man himself, on that side as well as on this side of the border, has forged into shackles for himself and his fellow man. This is a fur which grows, swells, mocks and bites. The bites are real enough, since reality is part of life only while it directly affects man. We understand why nations rise against nations: there is enough land for all to walk on, but in its midst sprawls a fur, the fur of suspicion, which lies in wait, ready to spring in cruel assault, ready to push everyone aside.

In each other's face and eyes we see the bright and vivid shock of our insight. We understand so much that tiny wrinkles of doubt begin to appear at the corners of our eyes. Even the ultimate becomes clear to us: our very insight has become a fur.

The Monkey (1956)

I hope the boy will not come today either. I vowed the day before yesterday that if he, in his white leather mittens, appears once again on the street corner waving his hands, I will finally get up and say, "You monkey." I have been watching him long enough. He must have been sent there by the devil himself, to make fun of this whole monkey business.

For what else is this anyway? I have been sitting here in this newspaper stall for ages and have as yet seen nothing that would have been anything else. But it's useless to talk out loud about it. They wouldn't listen to me. I don't even imagine they would. I just like to think they would.

Lack of time is not the reason they are not listening to me. Nor is it because I am a shrunken old man nobody would care about. I am a "just". There are such people, many of them, who are inevitably a "just" to everybody. And I am the kind of "just" who just sells newspapers. And I have no other characteristics. At the very most, I might be out of order, like a machine which has developed an irregular noise. This noise they hear and say to themselves, "Silly old man, mutters to himself all the time." I mutter, that is true. What if I were to speak out loud? What if I told each one in his turn, briefly and concisely, "Monkey"? The result would still be the same; no one would accept my proposal. Instead, they would immediately and without further ado, make a counterproposal, "Crazy." They are shaped once and for all. Finished products, finished, altogether lost. That is why they never, under any circumstances, listen to anybody but themselves.

Now, the grocery store across the street opened. The boy will be here soon.

What am I then, that my own muttering doesn't give me satisfaction? They come, buy a paper and go; however, for me that is not enough. I cannot live without them. What I want is precisely this: that they listen. And when they don't, I just keep on muttering and pretend they are listening. And what do I mutter about? That is just it, nothing, absolutely nothing. I mutter because I feel like muttering. Who the devil knows anyhow? I'm certain that I am the only person in the world who has, knowingly and willfully, consented to be a monkey.

That other monkey just doesn't seem to come. He is late. Yesterday he did not come at all, today he is late. What pleasure it would give me to say to him, "Monkey". Since I have not managed to say it to those who are already finished, I want to say it to this five-year old. And yet, he is also finished. He's the one that is really a finished product. But perhaps he wouldn't know right away how to make that counterproposal. Wouldn't he? Again I'm muttering nonsense. Of course he would, with his eyes. And then even with his mouth, after he has first told his mother the old newspaper man had called him a monkey.

Do I no longer have anything else to say, even to him? At first I did, and I did morning after morning. Muttering, of course, to myself, while watching his hands gesturing. Along some invisible wire I needed to send the message to his brain that here, right behind him, sits a person who is cold. For I will not sit here much longer; well, no matter, we come and we go, that's the way it is, no matter. But when one's whole coming and going, and everything in between, occurs without anyone noticing it, it is not good. Thinking about it, one gets so cold no fur coat could help. For I was trapped into sitting in this cold. I was trapped here from the time my legs were shot from under me. It took a cannon, no less. And yet, that is not why I sit here. A monkey is a monkey even if he is elevated on artificial limbs; that is why I am trapped here.

The damned boy, why doesn't he come? I'm beginning to feel that if I have to wait for him until tomorrow, the whole game will start all over again. At first I laughed at his antics; then I suppose I became enchanted by him, and in the end everything spun around. Things spun around because I could not get any kind of message through to his brain. He became the window which, morning after morning, opened up before me and showed me such a view of monkeyshines that I shook with cold for the rest of the day.

He always stands there, on the corner, while his mother is shopping in the dairy store and the grocery store. He wears a blue visored cap and a blouse and long brown trousers, so long and wide only the soles of his shoes show. And he has leather mittens, long white leather mittens. Yes, white ones. He has probably had to whine for them to his mother for days and weeks, for to him these leather mittens meant the ultimate achievement indeed. He has become a god who restrains and releases. He has become a traffic policeman. Right away, he steps to the farthest corner of the sidewalk, lifts the left leather mitten straight up and with the right one begins to signal the cars to move. From time to time, he turns earnestly and ceremoniously, changes hands, signaling now with his left hand. He neither sees nor hears, he sees or hears nothing but the coming and going of the cars and streetcars. Particularly when a blue bus as big as a house comes--oh, oh, we monkeys--he becomes as solemn as God the Father Himself upon seeing the world taking shape beneath His hand. He rises to the very tip of his toes when, with one white leather mitten straight up, he sweeps the bus rolling onward so the exhaust pipe roars. This goes on for ten or fifteen minutes until such a mighty vehicle comes that it doesn't obey even white leather mittens, says only, "Let's go," and grabs the leather mitten held high and leads the little policeman away.

Yesterday the mother came shopping alone. Today even the mother has not come yet. It actually makes me lonely. The boy can't be sick, can he? I certainly wouldn't let boys like him into the cold wearing only a blouse. But he must have had a woolen shirt underneath, of course. I'm babbling nonsense again.

Now, now he is coming. At least the mother is coming. But not the boy.

No, the boy didn't come today either. The mother walks past me to the dairy store. Her face is too rigid; I can't tell anything from it. The boy must be ill. What if I should ask his mother? How foolish. Children do have coughs and colds.

But when the woman comes out of the store, I struggle to my feet. And when she nears my stall, I start, "Madam."

The woman turns. At least she turns.

"Excuse me, Madam, but..."

I begin to hurry, for madam is already apprehensive.

"You have always had a little boy with you, such a little monkey...I mean, his white leather mittens..."

"So?"

"So? So, then, is he, he isn't sick is he, since..."

"My goodness, of course he isn't."

And the woman gives me such an accusing look that I begin to feel as if I were doing something evil, casting a spell on her son to make him sick. I cannot say a word, I cannot explain, and the woman measures me from the top of my head to my feet, has measured me already, has me measured already; I have run out of time. I did not get the time to find the word which would have been the right one. And now the woman is already lost, irrevocably lost.

"What..." once more she measures me... "What do you want with my boy?"

It's too late now for anything. That is why words are easy to find now, but completely different ones, ones you say when nothing matters anymore.

"With your boy? He was my boy."

Never before had I stated my case so adequately. It also had the intended effect: the woman's eyes almost bulge out of her head, then all the blood drains from her face, she gives a little shriek and runs away.

Let her run. She still has her boy. He never was mine. For only a short time I had imagined that I was directing the traffic with such leather mittens as "He was" and "my boy". It almost seemed as if the large busses had for a short while rolled under the direction of my leather mittens. But it wasn't so. The busses were all gone. Gone. God protect us, yes, that's right, God protect us monkeys.

Eila Pennanen (b. 1916)

Novelist, short story writer, critic and translator, Eila Pennanen was born in Tampere, where her father was the superintendent of a factory. After receiving her degree in philosophy in 1940, she worked as a librarian, in advertising, and as assistant to the editor of the Finnish literary magazine, PARNASSO. As a free lance writer she contributed to PARNASSO and other publications. She wrote her first novels during World War II and developed into one of Finland's foremost writers of prose. She is also one of the most accomplished translators in Finland, translating mainly from Swedish and English, and has lectured on translation at the University of Helsinki since 1967. Her first novels, ENNEN SOTAA OLI NUORUUS (BEFORE THE WAR THERE WAS YOUTH), 1942, KAADETUT PIHLAJAT (THE FELLED MOUNTAIN ASH TREES), 1944, PROOMU LÄHTEE YÖLLÄ (THE BARGE LEAVES AT NIGHT), 1945, and LEDA JA JOUTSEN (LEDA AND THE SWAN), 1948, contain realistic elements contrasted with refined artistic symbolism. Her two historical novels, PYHÄ BIRGITTA (ST. BRIDGET), 1954, and VALON LAPSET (CHILDREN OF LIGHT), 1958, the latter about seventeenth century English Quakers, mark a transition between her first novels and her later works. Unlike traditional historical novels, these two center around individuals rather than adventure or setting. In her collections of short stories, TORNITALO (THE HIGH-RISE BUILDING), 1953, PASIANSSI (SOLITAIRE), 1957, and KAKSIN (COUPLES), 1961, and her later novels, MUTTA (BUT), 1963, MONGOLIT (THE MONGOLS), 1966, and TILAPÄÄ (TEMPORARY), 1968, she maintains a mildly critical but understanding attitude toward her characters. These characters, ordinary contemporary people, involved in conflict, tension or maladjustment, are often insecure, bewildered, unaware of their real motives, which are revealed during the narrative. However, Pennanen's stories do not solve the characters' problems. She uses the art of understatement, describing seemingly uneventful circumstances. The story, *Long Ago*, from the 1957 SOLITAIRE collection, addresses itself to a conflict between two women, as in Jotuni's *The Girl in the Rose Arbor*, and demonstrates the antagonist's insecurity, bewilderment, and her lack of understanding of her own motives. Pennanen uses the technique of inner monologue to reveal many of the antagonist's feelings. Both women are contemporary, ordinary people, and the antagonist's problem is not solved when the story ends.

Long Ago (1957)

I went to the woman's house and decided to mince no words. I had found out beforehand where she lived and had no trouble finding my way from the station to the cottage. Or to the house, I should say, for it was rather large and decent looking. The building was quite new, had no siding, and was unpainted. Ahaa, the money must have run out, I thought as I walked along the farm road toward the yard. Crossing the yard, I cast my eyes down so as not to reveal my curiosity. It was fall, the day was beautiful. I glanced at the rosebushes, which were full of plump red rosehips. The path through the yard was but a barely visible track in the yellowed grass.

I lifted the latch and went into the hall. Bright, striped rugs, light in color, lay crosswise on the floor. Somehow, seeing those striped rugs made me angry. My heart began to pound, and I stood there a moment looking at the various doors before I knocked on the one I assumed to be the door to the kitchen.

"Come in!" someone called from within. Could that be she? I wondered. Am I even in the right place? But this is where those two strangers on the bus had directed me.

As soon as I opened the door, I saw that it was she. I began to feel faint, paused on the threshold like a timid stranger. "Come in, come on in," she repeated. "Could I have a glass of water?" I asked as courteously as I knew how. "I'm lost. I've come from Villilä and was to go to the station at Laukeela. I don't know where I got mixed up, but I'm on the wrong road. I'd like to rest a while."

"By all means, rest, rest, sit down--no, sit here, it feels so good to rest in a rocking chair. Oh, so you were on your way to the Laukeela station? Well, you really are lost. Still, you can get to the Kulju station along this road, if only you can manage to walk another five kilometers. Oh, oh, your shoes are all muddy."

"Yes, so they are," I said. She brought me a glass of water, she had even put it on a plate. She stood before me, looked at me inquisitively; I just looked at her. I thought, aren't you the rosy-cheeked and well-fed one. My God, seeing her makes me feel bad. Such smooth skin and bright eyes. So this is what she looks like. I would never have believed it.

She kept chattering the whole time. "We have good water in our well. It's clear, it doesn't leave any stains on the pail. See for yourself." She came and showed me the white pail; it was true, there were no stains in it. This, too, angered me. I could have grabbed the pail and thrown it---. "I missed the bus," I explained hastily. "There's only one bus a day from Villilä." "Well, you can still get to town from Kulju," she said. "You have plenty of time to walk, and at Kulju you might even have to wait. I know, why don't I make some coffee. I guess a cup of coffee would taste good after your walk?" "I guess it would," I said. And I thought, "So, you can spare me a cup of coffee, can you? You just wait."

She began to bustle about making the coffee and I looked around like a thief scheming what to take. Here, too, there were rag rugs side by side, clean, bright. The whole room was cheerful. The window sills were wide, with geraniums still blooming even though it was fall. On the wall an old-fashioned clock ticked away. Where could she have gotten that? Most of the things in the room were new, naturally...and if not exactly new, at least they were not family heirlooms. She hummed while making the coffee. She took the coffee jar from the shelf, gave a quick swipe to the copper pot. She put some wood chips into the stove, where a fire already blazed...She must have had a dish in the oven, since there was no pot or pan on top of the stove. Yes, of course, the family was at work and would come to eat before long...

Then she began chattering again. "When, through the window, I saw you coming, I wondered, 'Who is this stranger?' As a rule no one comes to this place, since it's so out of the way. It gets lonely...I'd love to be able to talk..." She had slipped into the Karelian dialect.

This gave me my glance. "You must be Karelian?" I said in my native Karelian dialect.

She was absolutely delighted. Only a vague suspicion kept her from rushing to put her arms around me, or was it just my imagination?

"Are you, too? Oh, my goodness, how wonderful..." She now slipped even more into the familiar speech from home. But then she switched back into the more standard speech of the people and that was a good thing, for my heart began to act in strange ways again. For already at that time I had a heart condition although the doctors kept saying there was nothing wrong with my heart.

"What part of Karelia are you from?" she asked.

"I'm from Koskisalmi parish."

"From Koskisalmi...? You don't say..." she spluttered. Eyeing me sharply, she asked, "What village?"

"From Valtala. We had to leave there during the war. Where are you from?" I asked, looking her straight in the eye, twirling my glass of water. I could see that hearing the name Valtala had startled her. Was the name familiar? I thought, You just wait, I'll tell you much more.

She said nothing for a long time. She took some cloth for carpet rags into her hands, sat and looked at the cloth as if wondering where to continue her cutting. But she did nothing, she just stared, and I could guess why.

As she remained silent, I decided to go on. "Yes, we fled from Valtala. What about you, did you flee, too?"

Now she had to answer, for my question would not go away. It just hung there, waiting.

"I was never a refugee. I left Karelia long ago. Long ago," she repeated, looking down at her carpet rags.

"Yes, the years slip by," I said in the same kind of voice the director of the Workers' Institute uses when he gives a talk and is quite agitated. "We will have to face old age on alien soil."

Again she gave a start and looked up at me. She looked quite different from a short while ago. As if older. I looked at her, watched her closely, expecting to see the marks of sin on her face. But I could see none. Then she began to speak slowly and gropingly, as one who fumbles in the dark. "Yes, that's so. On alien soil. So you're from Valtala...I, too...visited there sometimes...long ago. It had good land...large, open fields, wide and rolling. Just as if a wave had flowed over them and stopped...What nonsense am I talking...But it was a beautiful village...Mountain ashes in every yard, no less..."

Again she fell into silence and I slipped in, "Yes, yes," as I couldn't think of anything else to say. I couldn't help it that my voice rang sharp and shrill. It was as if a cat had meowed, "Yes, yes." She turned her glance away from the window toward me.

"What did you say? Yes...oh yes...In Valtala you could see very far out of your window; you didn't have to stare at the edge of the forest, as you do here. When we came here the very first thing I told my husband was to chop down those trees and make some space..."

"So, your husband, no less," I thought, "You vulture."

She glanced at me and a question finally came, "Did the Harkonens still live in Valtala when you left?"

"The Harkonens?" I asked, taking my time. "Of course,

they...the Harkonens...where would they have moved to from their home? The war forced us all to leave our homes. Old Mrs. Harkonen died during the evacuation."

"Miili? Miili Harkonen dead?" Her voice trembled. "But then, Miili was up in years, many years older than I. What about her husband, Vihtori Harkonen?"

"Old Mr. Harkonen died long before. Ten years before the war," I said.

"So they're both gone...Miili and Vihtori...And the Nirkkolas? The Nirkkola family? What about them? And the Putkinens?"

"You seem to know all the people in the village," I said. "Your water is boiling." She didn't even notice.

Now she moved clumsily toward the stove. She no longer walked as nimbly as before. Ahaa, old woman, I've taken the props right out from under you, have I?

She measured out the coffee and was very generous. But then she stopped and asked, "Do you know anything about Mikko Tuomaalainen?"

"I suppose I heard them talk about him during my childhood," I answered. I was annoyed that she did not respond to my remark about her knowing all the people in the village.

"Oh that Mikko was quite a musicmaker. He was fairly old when I used to see him and must surely be dead by now. He really knew how to play. And we would dance. You could always dance at Harkonens and play games and have fun. And the crickets would sing when we walked home at night."

"You must have been in Valtala as a young girl?" I asked. I had to get her safely on my hook so she couldn't escape. So, dances, games, and fun. Excellent.

"Yes...as a young girl...I would go to Harkonens...once in a while." Now she was standing with her back to me, watching the pot. Then she shouted, actually shouted, over her shoulder, "Do you know Viljami Tarkiainen?"

Now she bit, I thought. I put my glass on the table and sat down on the bench. I don't care for rocking chairs, you can't think very clearly in them.

I said, "I don't think I remember. Just where in the village did he live?"

"Surely you must remember," she answered. "Right near Harkonens. You just walked down the road and then Tarkiainen's cottage was right on the other side of the road. You must remember the Tarkiainens, since you remember the Harkonens. The house was red, white roses in the yard, a white swing. Two big spruce trees on both sides of the house. Real huge spruce trees...Don't you remember? There was a rusted weathervane on the roof...it always whistled and whined through the nights..."

I was all choked up. So that's how well she remembers everything. Now I would have to watch what I said.

"I do remember the house," I admitted. "It was exactly like that. One of the spruces was chopped down a couple of years before the war. It had started to rot. But the Tarkiainens?" I acted as if I were trying to remember. "Viljami? What was he like?"

"He was tall and strong, a real bear of a man, a little on the heavy side...he was a good provider, he kept the house in good condition...he was well respected...he was even a member of the village council. Surely you must remember..." Now she turned toward me, holding the coffee pot in her hands. She shifted it from one hand to the other for the handle burned her fingers. Her face had a probing look. She had noticed something. She had become a little apprehensive...

"Or perhaps Viljami was no longer at Valtala in your day. Perhaps he had moved away? How old are you?" She measured me with her eyes, but I did not answer. Instead, I asked, "What kind of family did this Viljami have?"

"He had two children...then, long ago...small children, a girl and a boy. The girl was three, the boy was two..."

"And what was the mistress of the house like?" Now my voice grew sharp and shrill again. The woman stared at me. "The mistress?"

"Yes, I might remember the mistress better...I don't look much at men..." I said this in an angry voice, something was choking me. The woman seemed upset as well, she stood there looking bewildered.

"Viljami Tarkiainen's wife? You can't know her. She left home such a long time ago. She left and never returned."

"Why did she leave?"

"She just left...and never returned. Left small children behind."

But now she had regained her composure, although I was almost dying. She began to bustle about again, rushed with the coffee pot to the table, placed the cups, sugar and cream, beside it. She moved back and forth as if in panic. I would not have been able to take a single step. I just thought, Why was I so crazy as to come here like this...I should at least have taken Väino along...he would have cried and prattled and then perhaps she would have given in more easily...

"Please have some coffee," she said in a firm voice. It was

strong for an old person's voice, I thought. I could see my job was not going to be an easy one. This made me even more determined. I have to have some sort of recompense, I thought, and sat down at the table. We sat there across from each other.

"So Viljami Tarkiainen's wife left like that, did she?" I began. My voice was no longer choked up nor did my hands shake. "Did she leave alone?"

"No!" The answer rang like the blow of a fist on a table. The woman stuffed her mouth full of coffee bread and stared at the table. She has decided to answer, I thought, and I continued, "With whom, then?"

"The hired man."

"So, with the hired man." We are really being straightforward here, I thought. I tried to laugh, it sounded vicious. "So, with the hired man. Well, youth and folly. The wife, no doubt, was still a young girl and the husband was, of course, much older? That's how it goes...The hired man was the same age as the wife and so was able to lure her into going with him?"

"No. It was not like that at all." Her face softened again. She began to reminisce, she even had to laugh. "The hired man was a twenty-year old youth, the wife thirty-five. The husband and his wife were of the same age, had even been in confirmation school together."

"So, confirmation school classmates," I said since she didn't continue. "The marriage, of course, was not happy, the man beat his wife or was unfaithful to her. That's why the wife ran away..."

"It wasn't like that either."

"Then how was it?"

Now she looked at me. The woman really had penetrating eyes. They actually made me weak.

"Who are you, anyway?"

"Who am I? Nobody, really."

"You know Viljami."

"Yes, I did know him. Viljami is dead."

"Who are you?"

"I am Viljami's daughter."

She looked at me...I could not look at her. I knew, without looking, that tears welled up into those old eyes. I did not want to feel sorry for her. Why feel sorry for someone like her? She only pretended to be crying. Now she took out her handkerchief and blew her nose. She said nothing. The tears just flowed. Finally, I had to pick up the line of the conversation again. We just couldn't sit there indefinitely, the family might come, the husband or whoever would be coming.

"Yes, Viljami Tarkiainen is dead and the settlement of the estate has been held up for a couple of years since his wife could not be found. She disappeared and despite public notice of her disappearance she was not found, even though she was searched for, actually hunted for by the police. She could not be declared dead since there was no proof of her death. That was the kind of mother the children had, one who was neither alive nor dead. The estate could not be divided, and the boy's wife is demanding that the estate be divided, and right away."

She just kept on crying. She didn't actually cry out loud, but the tears flowed copiously. I began to get angry.

"Don't cry. Crying won't help. It's your daughter who is sitting before you, and things have to be settled. You don't intend to deny who you are? That would be useless. I recognize you from the pictures. Otherwise, I would not recognize you. I would not recognize my mother otherwise. Yes, greetings from Valtala. Greetings from the Tarkiainen home. The second spruce was cut down when I was just a little girl, and Father thought of you then, since you had cared about those trees. Don't cry, just answer. Will you sign the papers or not?"

She just cried. It angered me terribly. I began to dig the papers out of my handbag. I had had them prepared by a lawyer and according to them, the woman had to renounce all claims to the estate in favor of the children. But she didn't seem to hear, nor see, she just cried. I began again to preach; my heart ached. "Twenty-five years we have hunted and searched for you. I found you by accident...complete strangers told me. Two women on the bus began to stare at me and whisper to each other. Finally, one of them asked me outright if I were so and so. And when I answered, they said with one voice, 'Go to this place, if you wish to meet your mother'. I didn't know what to say, they stared at me and their eyes glowed like embers. But I supposed they spoke the truth, and they did speak the truth...you would never have been found if the war hadn't come and moved people around. Well, is the other one still alive, the one you left with? The hired man? Do you live with him now, or have you found another breadwinner? Father would always say in a bitter voice that he could have accepted it but for the fact that his wife left with such a small, bowlegged runt. What for? Father, at least, could not understand it. When he was drinking he always talked about what he would have done to his former hired man if he had ever got his hands on him...He thought you had gone crazy. You had appeared depressed and talked very strangely for a long time before you left, Father said. Well, tell me now, at least tell your daughter, how it came about that you ran away as you did.''

She did not answer. I waited and then in my pent-up anger I poured myself some coffee. I even took some coffee bread, dunked it in my coffee. The old woman just cried.

"Did Father treat you badly, or what? Were there some secrets? Was there something which a man would be ashamed to tell his children? Although he did tell us in detail everything that had happened between you two. When he was drinking he always dwelt upon the bedroom matters between you...How can a woman leave her children? There must have been some reason? Small children, the girl three, the boy two. Have you thought about that? What happened to them? How they must have felt when they grew older and learned their mother had gone whoring with the hired man?"

Now the words came to her. She stammered through her tears. "You are still young." That is what she said. Those were the first words I ever heard from my mother...what she may have said to me when I was a small child, I did not remember. And now she even addressed me using the formal "you".

"Me, young? I am not young, almost thirty. I look older, I am taken for an older woman. People think I'm forty. I am as dry and thin as a broomstick, as sour as a pickled cucumber. The juices drained from me already as a child, when I had to be the mother in a motherless home. Father did not want women in the house. He hated women. He was mad at everybody. He said he would beat the whore out of me. But there was not much to be beaten out of me, nor have I forgotten to be grateful to him. I have never been frivolous. My time was spent working, being a mother to my brother. I am no longer young, I am old, older than you. I don't even talk like a young person, even the director at the Workers' Institute has said that. Yes, I have gone through the Institute and have even studied in the folk high school, although I am just a motherless brat. Yes...and I would also like to know this, do I have brothers and sisters, have you had bastards with this hired man, for I do know the ways of life, even though I am young."

I ranted and raved and although I was not aware of it, the strength behind my determination was dissipating. I would not have permitted it, but that is what happened. The woman realized this too and she stopped crying. She just wiped her face and sighed. And, yet, I tried to continue, but my tirade no longer had any strength. "I have had to suffer so much because of you, I have not become a real person, having grown up without a mother...even psychology says that...I have studied. You should also have suffered...you haven't been poor, one can see that. But now your neighbors will learn that you are not married, that your children are not legitimate...for children you have, I can see that from the clothes hanging on the rack, those girl's slacks are not for you...You have made your bed and now you can lie in it. What was wrong with Father? He was such a good provider and everything. After you left he began to deal in livestock and we had good days..."

She now looked at me quite calmly and remarked, "Viljami was happy and busy slaughtering already in my time." She said nothing else, but the words rang in my ears a long time. Did she mean it bad, that Father slaughtered? Father was a skilled butcher, that was well known, and he even knew how to castrate. Had the woman not liked that? But her face showed nothing, it was just as if she had said whatever came to her mind. I tried to continue as before, but everything was all mixed up.

"You will have to give up the inheritance; you do not deserve it since you left as you did, and even the law..." I did not really dare talk about the law; the lawyer had rattled on and on about all kinds of things which I did not understand. "And so...even the law, and you should ask Väino to forgive you; he is the one who really suffered because of you; he never became a real person, he is a weakling, totally dominated by his wife and he whimpers about every little thing. I know very well that it is your fault, I've studied...You unnatural mother, to leave your children."

It had seemed like such a good speech when I had planned it in my mind walking from the station, but now it didn't sound like anything. The woman looked at me with complete indifference and I knew that I had been defeated. She began to speak.

"If I were to tell you why I left, if I were to explain everything, what good would that do? There are matters which do not show on the outside, there are matters which happen inside a person. When a person's life loses its flavor, when she feels she is moving only toward the grave, when she has no desire to go on living, there comes the thought that she could start again. That is what I thought then. I could not go on with Viljami...that is why I left. I know I was wrong. You cannot start all over again. Don't think that I haven't carried a cross and been punished. For twenty-five years I have yearned for my native land and thought about the children I left. But still, I have done my work and served those who have come afterwards. This time I remembered to be humble, if nothing else."

Humble? I wondered what she meant. Oh yes, she had to be

humble, otherwise the hired man might have left her. Be that as it may, my revenge had been taken away from me. While I was sitting there, my words had dissolved into the air. That baggage, my mother, was not ashamed of anything. I tried once more to speak. "Everything must then have been Father's fault and I have also thought so. But wouldn't it still have been possible for you to stay? Why don't you admit that the lust of the flesh tempted you a little in the figure of that young hired man?" But I could hear it myself...the bitter words, contrived out of nothing, had no strength nor substance. They just sounded foolish.

And she ignored them. She just looked at me, looked with sadness in her eyes. I saw in them a stranger's look, and I shrank farther down at the table. So that was how it was, I thought. I tried to get up but then she reached out her hand toward me, an old, veined hand, but one with plump flesh over the bones.

"Don't go, my Daughter. Please stay, won't you?"

I could guess what she had in mind. I should have risen immediately and rushed away, but I couldn't. I stayed there and my impotence exasperated me. What did I really want from this stranger of a woman?

She went on speaking. "They're coming now, I see them through my window. My husband and my boy. I have two boys with this one and a daughter."

"Oh, do you?"

"Your coming here will turn into something good for all of us. You intended something bad, but it will turn into good."

"Don't you believe it!"

"You'll get to know your brothers and your sister."

"I already have a brother."

"But now you'll get a sister as well. You'll be grateful to me yet..."

"No, I won't."

"Be kind to your stepfather, he always feared that you would come, you or your brother...Or Viljami, Viljami is dead..."

"Now you can even get married."

"That's true, that's true...For a long time we have moved from place to place using different names. Always in out-of-the-way villages...always leaving when someone would start to ask questions...It was good that you came, it was a relief..."

"I don't believe that you have suffered," I hissed. We began to hear the stamping of feet in the hall. I would gladly have jumped out of the window, I was so angry with myself.

"Just wait until you see your sister. She has always asked about her older sister and wondered why you never came to visit."

"They know?"

"How would they not know?" The woman seemed surprised. "But they don't know that we are not married. Young people...they wouldn't understand."

"You better believe I'll tell them."

"You will not tell them and you will now do the only thing you can do."

Somebody had already turned the door handle. There they were, my mother's world of the present. I was only part of the past and that was not worth bringing back to life. I relinquished everything, I stayed, shook hands, probably even smiled.

And that is how I met my mother. And not much time passed before she had talked me and my brother into giving her compensation for her share of the estate, although I had planned things altogether differently. The woman twisted me around her little finger.

But I have not done everything she would have liked me to: visit them all the time and be sweet to her, my supposed sister. I have stayed apart. My brother does visit them, but, then, he is what he is.

My old mother is still trying, but it is useless. I will not give in. The share of the estate I gave, myself I will not. Why did she leave me like that...?

But what I still would like to know is why she left her home although everything there was good. A good husband, a good house, and she leaves. This I do not understand.

Marja-Liisa Vartio (1924-66)

Marja-Liisa Vartio (Marja-Liisa Sairanen) was born in the Lake
Saima Region, in Sääminki, where her father was an elementary
school teacher. She received her master of philosophy degree in
1950 and worked as a free lance writer. She was married to Paavo
Haavikko, one of Finland's most versatile writers. Her first
publications were two volumes of lyrical poetry. HÄÄT (THE
WEDDING), 1952, and SEPPELE (THE WREATH), 1953, but she is
remembered primarily for her prose, which draws on dreams,
fantasy, and myths, avoids personal comments and explanations,
yet contains humor. Her short story collection, MAAN JA VEDEN
VÄLILLÄ (BETWEEN LAND AND WATER), 1955, is poetic but her
novels are more realistic and include SE ON SITTEN KEVÄT (SO
IT'S SPRING), 1957, MIES KUIN MIES, TYTTÖ KUIN TYTTÖ (A
MAN AS A MAN A GIRL AS A GIRL), 1958, KAIKKI NAISET
NÄKEVÄT UNIA (ALL WOMEN HAVE DREAMS), 1960. Her
humor is most apparent in the novel, TUNTEET (FEELINGS), 1962.
Her last novel, published posthumously, is HÄNEN OLIVAT
LINNUT (HIS WERE THE BIRDS), 1967, in which two women carry
on a long dialogue, much in the manner of Maria Jotuni. Most of
Vartio's writing hides a serious purpose beneath its superficial
structure. Her short story, *A Finnish Landscape*, from the collection,
BETWEEN LAND AND WATER, 1955, represents her particular
style of humor, her gift for fantasy, her avoidance of personal
comments and explanations.

A Finnish Landscape (1955)

It is snowing. A man is driving a horse along the ice on the lake,
stunted spruce trees serving as his guideposts. The trees are still
visible above the snow, looking like tired, crouching animals being
slowly covered up. The man drives along the wintry road appearing
to be in no hurry, giving his horses free rein as he sits in deep
thought. Who knows what he is thinking. He finally disappears from
sight.

This view is seen through a sauna window. Two men are stretched out on the sauna benches, one an artist, the other a doctor, both known to be amiable men. The night before, they had met on the street, agreed on this sauna trip, deciding that this time they would ski and enjoy invigorating exercise. But the next morning before going to the bus--the trip to the artist's cabin takes two hours--they had each bought a bottle.

"Well, we're just like most people--we hope to do so much--. But to even think of going on a sauna trip without a bottle!" said the artist.

"And a cold building will take a long time to warm up."

They looked out of the window as long as there was something to see. It was just the natural thing to do.

"It feels like we'll have good fellowship here."

The artist stepped down to produce more steam since he knew exactly where to stand to throw the water over the heated rocks to get the best kind of steam.

"The snow outside is strangely blue, or does it just seem that way. One seldom sees clean snow in the city," the artist reflected as he climbed back up on the bench. The man with the horse was now driving along the shore on the other side of the lake. The artist did not recognize him; he did not know the people living around here nowadays. The shore on the opposite side of the lake was filled with cottages, but no cottages had been built near his even though his cottage had been there almost ten years. He would drop in at his cottage from time to time, even in the winter, to enjoy a sauna, usually bringing a friend. Most often it was the doctor who accompanied him. The two seldom met in the city for both of them had their own work, their own circles, and different interests. Coming here for a sauna had become a habit, a sort of ritual. The older they got the more often they were drawn to the sauna, for it was a place which demanded nothing of them. It was for the sake of the sauna the artist had built his cottage. The cottage was on land that had belonged to his family; in fact, his whole family had its origin in this area. His father, who had been a minister in this very parish, had died young. All the family's lands now belonged to strangers, forfeited and disposed of, the city and progress had swallowed them up. None of the descendants had stayed there to farm the land. Of course, it was not sheer nostalgia that made him buy a piece of the family land, but still, it was satisfying to have his cottage on the same land on which he had roamed as a child.

They needed more steam. The doctor took his turn, with the artist showing him where to stand, how to throw the water, yet the steam seemed to dissipate instantly. Walls deteriorate just as men do. The two men were of the same age, soon fifty years old. They had entered a city school at the same time, a whole lifetime ago. The artist was not successful in school, so after two years he had had enough and quit, and when his relatives got tired of looking at him, the lazy son of the minister's widow, he had left home. Now his travels began, he sailed the seas, he went as a soldier into Karelia, finally ending at the Atheneum Art School in Helsinki with a handful of wood carvings of old men and women. Before he had left for Helsinki, his mother had made him an overcoat from the black coat of a wealthy relative. Wearing his long coat, he marched straight up to the director of the art school and announced that he was there to enter the Atheneum. The director had cleared his throat and trying to make some kind of response to this country boy, asked, "Can you show me some of the art work you have produced up to this time?"

"Oh, yes, I've got it all with me." And he had turned his pockets inside out on the table and there was his complete output, a handful of carvings of old men and women.

"That was in those days," the artist said. "You used to sing then. Yes, and you studied ants."

"I'm still studying them. Every now and then I look at the notes I have written about the life of ants. When I'm not doing anything else, I will take up my study of ants again and I will write stories about them--"

"And yet, you became a women's doctor."

"The family pressured me, although I did want to become a doctor. In those days reason prevailed. But that was back in those days."

"The time I spent as a soldier in Karelia was quite a time as well," said the artist. "I was sixteen years old then, a mercenary soldier." The artist sat up, giving the laugh he was famous for. As he laughed, the soles of his feet touched each other, he rubbed his knees, ran two fingers through his hair, and only then did his full laugh emerge. The doctor had once said the artist wore his clothes out even on the inside, so much did his body move inside his clothing. A mercenary soldier, indeed---.

With the money he had earned as a soldier the artist had bought a pair of trousers; the old ones, the ones issued by the Crown, were so worn out that there was not much left anywhere except around the waist, where the shreds hung as if from a rope. The new trousers were hanging on the wall of the store to which he had gone as soon as he had reached the Finnish side of the border. The pants were of blue serge or some such material. "Those up there," he had told the shopkeeper. "You don't have to wrap them up." The trousers under his arm he looked for the outhouse, which he found behind a rose bush. He stepped inside, closed the door, took off his old trousers, rolled them into a bundle, and dropped them down the hole. Then he proceeded to put on the new trousers but he had trouble getting into them. He pulled and tugged, the seams ripped. Pulling the trousers up as far as he could, he tied them to his shirt with sticks and whatever else he could find and then pulled his coat over them. He rode the train across Finland to Turku, his trousers ready to drop down at any moment during the trip. The jerking of the train constantly threatened the position of his trousers. He had to sit upright throughout the trip. Few return from wars so erect.

The doctor laughed, he had heard the story many times but it was part of their sauna ritual. They remembered the old times and told the same stories over and over. And the laughter was always the same; it was there, ready in their memories, always the same, decade after decade. The first bottle was empty, the artist went to the dressing room to get his bottle; they opened it, they sang, the doctor sang alone, just as he had always sung in the sauna. The artist did not have a singing voice but he sometimes attempted to join in only to stop when the doctor's bass cut off the path of his off-key notes.

It was the moment of the clear winter evening just before darkness suddenly falls over forest, over road. The view from the sauna window was now like an etching: a dark hole in the ice, only traces of the spruce trees, smoke rising in straight columns on the other side of the lake, with the window casings serving as a ready-made frame. There was no one on the ice, the man had gone, the landscape remained.

"Having you been buying any paintings?"

"Every now and then," answered the doctor. "I was offered a work by Simberg--one in which the devil appears with twins."

"I understand his paintings are rather scarce nowadays."

"What kind of man was this Simberg?"

"A pleasant man, I studied under him for a while. He had a black beard, he didn't say very much, he didn't speak Finnish very well." [1]

There was silence.

"His scope was not very broad. But then, who says you need a broad scope?" The artist sat up and rubbed his knees. "The main thing is to paint with all you've got."

1 Hugo Simberg was a member of the Swedo-Finnish minority in Finland.

They were silent, exchanged a few words, were silent again, lifting their feet up to the ceiling. The heated rocks had begun to give off only moist heat, the fire needed replenishing.

Outside it was pitch dark, a wind had risen. The snow dropped with gentle thuds from the branches of the trees around the cottage sounding like the footfalls of soft felt boots in deep snow. The blowing snow struck the warm window and ran down the pane in tiny streams of water. The wind increased, the trees swayed heavily, but occasionally the wind stopped and everything was still.

"I believe we left our skis lying out in the snow beside the wall. We forgot to lean them against the wall."

"Should we heat up the sauna again?"

But neither one seemed to want to get off the boards. They listened to the sounds outside. The long branch of a tree scratched against the wall as if a fingernail had scraped against it. The trees swayed more violently, the wind began to pant like one who is running short of breath, who is struggling fiercely, and then everything was still again. The wind revived, trying to rip something open, then sighing in resignation. Snow struck the warm window and melting, turned into small streams of water running steadily down the glass.

"That man Simberg had strange motifs, devils and death."

"I wonder where he found them--perhaps he saw himself in them."

"But Simberg's devils look so real you actually believe they're walking around, asking for milk for the twins."

"And his devil with a toothache."

"It was probably Simberg's own tooth that ached. It's an old technique, to transfer one's own disease into a painting."

"He painted the devil in every life situation: in confirmation school, stealing roses off a bush, he even escorted the devil on a stretcher to the grave. But he made the devil beg only for milk. The devil should have been given a drink."

"Yes, I guess even the devil has his griefs. The sauna is just like a mother's womb in this evil world."

"You're always in a gynecologist's world."

They fell asleep on the benches. The night was dark, but morning brought the light. The artist was the first one to awaken, he opened his eyes. He felt good, as if he were wrapped in soft cotton, everything seemed to sway before him. He closed his eyes and thought, "I'll sleep some more."

Soon he awakened again. It was full day, the wind had died down. Only the high snowdrifts around the cottage were left as reminders of the night's snowstorm. The sun's rays filtered obliquely through the window. The artist opened his eyes a slit; above his head he saw green blotches, then wooden boards in between.

"It's a ceiling, a sauna ceiling, I am in the sauna," he thought. He closed his eyes, trying to sleep some more. But nothing came of it. He began to shiver, realized he was chilled, and being naked, he decided to get up to get a blanket from the dressing room. He got up and fell off the bench.

About three hours later he regained consciousness, his whole body was shivering. He was lying on the concrete floor, it was cold. Last night the sauna had been a mother's womb but now it was a stepmother. Cautiously, the artist turned his head, the doctor was sleeping on the bench. The artist tried to call his name but could not open his mouth.

"What's the matter with me?" he thought. "I am in the sauna? I wonder whose head this is."

His head felt as heavy as if it was filled with rocks and soon the load of rocks would start to rumble and turn into pain. The artist touched the place where he assumed his forehead to be, felt a lump and looked at his hand. He felt the lump again. It was blood all right.

He tried again to call the doctor's name but was able to manage only a woeful sound. The doctor finally woke up, rose from the bench, and without a word, got a mirror from the dressing room.

"What is this?" asked the artist. "Who am I?"

He had never seen such a face. It was a face, but not a human face. It was as if the Creator had been repulsed by his own work and had rubbed his palm over his finished handiwork when he saw what was being formed. There were horns on both sides of his forehead and a third one growing as reinforcement in the middle of his forehead, his nose was thick and out of place, a long nose, and his mouth, his small mouth--it was at least three times its normal size. It covered his whole face so there was little room left for his eyes. He peered out like a mole out of its hole.

The artist felt the rest of his body as far as he could. It was sore all over just as if his body had been rolled out like a piece of dough; and it was dark, as if singed.

The doctor began to laugh. He had tried to control his laughter, not out of sympathy, but waiting to laugh only at the moment when the other could see himself in the mirror. He laughed, pounded his knees, and repeated, "In all my life I've never seen, in my whole life I have never---"

The artist did not know which part hurt the most, one ache blocked out another. They heated the sauna again and the doctor cleaned and treated the artist's bruises. The sun now shone directly in through the window, revealing a man, black and blue, lying on the lowest bench; the artist no longer cared to lie higher up.

"How are you feeling?" asked the doctor.

"I feel like the Hungarian who was tired of living. An Italian found the Hungarian lying in the forest with a knife in his stomach. When the Italian asked if it hurt, the Hungarian replied, "Only when I laugh!""

The sauna got warm, there was still a little left in the bottle, they drank it up. The doctor drew a bucket of water from the water tub, tossed it over the blackened, heated rocks, stepped away from the hissing steam but then fell arms outstretched against the hot barrel stove. He jumped free, the front of his body covered with rings of red. He turned around and slipped backward against the stove; now his back was as striped as a zebra.

The artist tried to laugh but without success. Neither of them felt like laughing. Each piece of clothing felt as if lined inside with nettles, but they finally got themselves dressed. Silent, they gathered their belongings into their backpacks. In passing through the dressing room, the doctor tossed the two empty bottles under the bench.

The men opened the cottage door, stepped outside. The crusted snow glistened, water dripped from the eaves, a titmouse sang blithely on the branch of a pine tree. The men dug their skis out of the snow and began slowly to ski. They skied across the lake toward the village crossroads. With gloomy faces they stood among other skiers to wait for the bus. They tried to respond to the stares of the people in the same way Napoleon's soldiers did as they retreated from Moscow across Europe back to France.

In two weeks the swelling around the artist's eyes had, like a spring snow, disappeared, his mouth was back in place, his nose had straightened. His beret covered the scar on his forehead, his black and blue marks were now yellow, he was as if of a different race.

One evening the two men went to a casino together. They sought a quiet table at a window overlooking the sea. As he sat down, the doctor patted his buttocks, they were still sore. The waiter came to the table, the men ordered two cognacs.

"It was just ordinary whiskey," said the artist. But the question, "Who knows what special stimulants doctors may add to their bottles?" had already crossed his mind.

"Just ordinary whiskey," said the doctor. "But strong."

"And we really didn't drink very much. There must have been fumes escaping from the stove."

"There were no fumes, I checked the coals."

"What was it then?"

"Who knows what it was."

The men sat quietly for a while. There were only a few people in the restaurant besides them.

"Did you buy that painting by Simberg?"

"I won't take the devil into my house," said the doctor.

They laughed, talked, and laughed again when the waiter brought their order. He wiped the table with a cloth and set the first glass before the doctor, the second before the artist. The third glass he set before the empty seat.

Veijo Meri (b. 1928)

Veijo Meri grew up in a military environment as his father served in the regular army, but Meri himself was too young to fight in any war. He lives today as a free lance writer and has been very prolific. Most of Meri's works describe war situations or have some connection to war or military life. In the 1960's he was considered a classic writer of 1950's modernism: he depicted war with a grim gallows humor and was an anecdotal observer of the urban milieu. The prose in his earlier works built strongly upon the spoken word, on the structure of speech, which naturally led him into the field of drama, particularly radio plays. In his latest novels and short stories he concentrates on dialogue. He has debated about cultural matters and has contributed to the discussion of Finnish and international literature. Meri has written a monograph on the life of Aleksis Kivi based on considerable personal research into the life and works of the enigmatic Kivi. Meri's first work was a collection of short stories, ETTEI MAA VIHERIOISI (SO THE EARTH MIGHT NOT BE GREEN), 1954. Then followed novels on war, his best work being perhaps MANILLAKÖYSI (THE MANILA ROPE), 1957. Other war novels are: IRRALLISET (THE ROOTLESS), 1959; VUODEN 1918 TAPAHTUMAT (THE EVENTS OF THE YEAR 1918), 1960; SUJUT (QUITS), 1961; TUKIKOHTA (THE BASE), 1964; EVERSTIN AUTONKULJETTAJA (THE COLONEL'S CHAUFFEUR), 1966. Among his plays with motifs from war is SO- TAMIES JOKISEN VIHKILOMA (PRIVATE JOKINEN'S MARRI- AGE LEAVE), 1965. Novels with civilian motifs are PEILIIN PIIR- RETTY NAINEN (A WOMAN DRAWN ON A MIRROR), 1963; YH- DEN YÖN TARINAT (STORIES OF ONE NIGHT), 1967; SUKU (THE FAMILY), 1968; NUOREMPI VELI (THE YOUNGER BROTHER), 1970; and KUVITELTU KUOLEMA (THE IMAGINED DEATH), 1974. Meri turns repeatedly to the short story genre as is indicated by the collections: TILANTEITA (SITUATIONS), 1962, LEIRI (THE CAMP), 1972, and MORSIAMEN SISAR JA MUITA NOVELLEJA (THE BRIDE'S SISTER AND OTHER SHORT STORIES), 1972. Meri has shown a great interest in the theory of fiction, often ridiculing classifications and norms. In his own writings, he presents not only relevant details but also many irrelevant ones, which may seem pointless to the reader, but which do present reality as experienced by his characters, who do notice many trivial details. Very often his characters do not communicate with each other, which may cause friction or frustration but never violence or tragedy. Meri's stories are slices of life. *The Proposal*, from a 1965 collection entitled VEIJO MEREN NOVELLIT (VEIJO MERI'S SHORT STORIES), and *Selecting a Play*, from the 1972 collection LEIRI, are both written in dialogue and present a lack of communication among the characters. Also, much of *The Proposal* may seem irrelevant, appearing mainly as one man's monologue. Both stories end in typical Meri fashion: they do not "conclude" in the general sense of the word but seem as if they could continue on and on.

The Proposal (1965)

Lackstrom was eating with a spoon from a bowl into which Regina had cut up the meat and the potatoes. Every now and then he pushed food over the edge of the bowl on to the table. And when he smeared his hand into it, he put out his hand and Regina got a towel or a dishcloth and wiped it clean.

The neglected yard was so full of trees and brush that the sunlight could not shine through. Since the window was open, they could hear the drone and whine of tires as the cars whizzed by on the asphalt road. It sounded as if there was a thin layer of water on the road.

Santavirta was wearing a new black suit and he was sweating profusely. Whenever the sweat dripped from his eyelids into his eyes, he blinked fiercely. With his right hand he held on to Regina's left hand, except when he had to cut his meat. Then he discreetly and quietly withdrew his hand.

Lackstrom was talking continuously now that he had a listener. Santavirta now and then turned his head eagerly and nodded, "Yes, yes, that's right."

But most of the time he looked at Regina, at her red hair piled high on her head. Her hair glistened like new copper wire, and when the sun shone on the back of her hair through the open door of the kitchen, it looked as if her hair were on fire.

The old man was talking about a big storm which had raged in

Helsinki some time during the last century.

"All the big trees in the park around the old church fell to the ground. I went there the next day to see, when the men were sawing them into pieces so they could be hauled away. During the storm I was in Kaivopuisto and there were stones rolling along the ground, stones as large as fists. I have never since seen such a storm. The waves tossed all the sailboats on to the shore and wrecked them, beating them back and forth until they went to pieces. A Mr. Sjöblom asked me to go and sink his boat. I swam out to it and climbed up the mast and tipped the boat over, and it sank so that only the top of the mast showed. This Sjöblom promised to take me to Porvoo sailing on that boat, but someone stole it. When they tried to hoist the boat, they found only a hell of a long pole, which had been stuck to the bottom. But then when another old sea captain, Blomberg, went sailing, he took Mr. Sjoblom along and Sjöblom took me. The captains spent the whole trip below deck drinking. I had to stay at the helm and take care of the sails alone. I was only eleven years old. I had already sailed a lot, but never toward Porvoo. Always when there was a rock in front of us I had to ask down below which side we should go on. They said, to the right or to the left. They knew the whole course by heart. When we reached the shore at Porvoo, Sjöblom said he was not going to come out. "We are drunk. What do you think your mother will say?" "She's been dead for fifteen years," Blomberg said. "For God's sake, did she pass away?" "Let's go to her grave at least, now that we're here," said Blomberg. "We can't go, we're drunk," Sjöblom said. "The boy can go." I had to run up the hill, where they had this graveyard, but how was I to find the grave just like that? I came back and we set out on our way back right away. Those old fellows never once came out of the cabin to the deck during the whole trip."

"Eat now, Papa," Regina said. "Your food is getting cold."

"I won't eat any more."

Regina carried the dishes to the kitchen and brought in the coffee.

"You've got a good memory, Papa," Santavirta said.

"You have to, when you're this old. Otherwise you wouldn't remember old things like this. On the way back from Porvoo these old men told each other the wildest stories throughout the trip, but they were the same stories over and over again. That Blomberg told a story about Bellman that..."

"Is that Bellman, the poet?" Santavirta asked.

"How did you know that, Mauno?"

"I just thought, since it was the same name."

"Papa just called Mauno by his first name," Regina said.

"That's perfectly natural," Santavirta said.

"Papa, your coffee's getting cold," reminded Regina.

"What? Do I have coffee?"

"I poured you some."

"Why didn't you say so?"

"Well, because Papa was talking and not listening."

"Listen, Papa, what Regina and I have been thinking," Santavirta said and glanced quickly at Regina. Regina blushed and looked at him as if frightened, but then she started to look at the sugar bowl so intently that one of the sugar lumps began to roll.

"My brother Alarik went to sea. From the very beginning he earned such a reputation that when he got to the port at Hietalahti the police ran along the shore at Kaivopuisto to greet him. For whenever the boys went ashore, they would start up a real storm. They always wanted to beat up the police when they reached land after a long trip. On the sea, they had thought about how they would beat them up. There was a terrible fight right away at the port, but the police got enough of an upper hand so they managed to take them to the police station at Punavuori. But at the police station the boys started all over again, and there the police were not as brave since there was no one watching, and they lost. The boys shut them up in the police station and locked the door and sent a little boy to take the key to the central police station. The boys themselves went back to the ship and sailed off right away. The chief of police and all the policemen hurried to the Punavuori station. The chief of police sat in a droshky and the policemen ran alongside it. I was there too, watching. Then they unlocked the door of the station. It was the kind of two-story building where the lower story was of brick and the upper story was of wood. The police chief told them off in such a way that everyone heard him. "Six policemen the size of half-grown horses and you let yourselves get locked in. Why didn't you come out?" "Because the door was locked," they said. "Why didn't you come out of the window? The windows are so low the drunks stumble in through them." "We just didn't think of it," the policemen said. "You are so stupid, that you're not smart enough to even be policemen," he blasted at them.

"Papa, Mauno has something he wants to say to you," Regina said.

"I would have gone to sea also, but mother didn't want me to. Father sent me to learn bookbinding as soon as I learned how to read. Do you know who Haapoja was?"

"The name does sound familiar. Just a minute, I'm trying to remember."

"He was a terrible murderer."

"Papa, don't talk about such awful things right after eating."

"This Haapoja died in the central prison. The day after his death the boss sent me to the prison to pick up for binding the book Haapoja had written about all his doings. Among the papers there was a big piece of skin which they had cut off his back. We bound the book in this skin. We tanned the skin and it turned completely black. It was all right, except that it was rather limp, and when we had to put the writing on the skin, the gold letters would not stay on, no way. Human skin absolutely lacks fat, nothing sticks to it."

"He doesn't hear us." Santavirta told Regina. "He's all worked up."

"Talk loud, he won't hear you otherwise."

"Papa! May I interrupt for a little while. I would like to talk a little with Papa about something. I and Regina have been thinking..."

"We even bound books for the colonel who was the commanding officer of the guards. I went there many times to deliver books. If he didn't have anything to do, he would ask me to sit down and would begin to tell me all kinds of stories, and he would give me sugar lumps. I had to eat them. He ate them the whole time also. He once told a story where they were..."

"Papa doesn't give anybody a chance to say anything," Regina said.

"Did you say something?"

"Mauno has something to say."

"The guard was at camp at Tsarskoje Selo, and they were practicing ground firing there. The Russian battalion fired first and the Finnish one was signalling and keeping score. The Russians had pierced the charts beforehand and were shooting in the air. All of a sudden, the Tsar called off the firing because he wanted to know how they were doing. He was kind of a restless and impatient man. 'Well shot. Your accuracy is 140 per cent,' the colonel told the Russian commander. 'For God's sake, don't tell the Tsar that,' he begged. 'You should know, I have a beautiful wife and small children. Report 40 per cent, won't you?' 'Don't instruct me to lie,' the colonel told him. 'I also have a wife and small children. I will report 4 per cent.' 'Is there no way you could report 40 per cent? Isn't it the same to you, whether it's 4 per cent or 40 per cent?' 'I am an honest man, but I am not heartless. You may choose, 4 per cent or 140 per cent.'"

"Papa, don't go yet," said Regina.

"I'm going to rest a little. I ate too much," Lackstrom said and went plodding toward his room.

"Listen, Papa," Mauno said and started to follow him. "He doesn't even pay attention."

"He didn't hear," Regina said.

"He heard all right, but he pretended not to hear. All deaf people are the same. But just say something nasty about them, and they will hear you."

"What are you saying about my father?"

"Did I say something mean? I didn't intend to."

"But you're shouting."

"For heaven's sake, don't start crying. I am thinking about what's best for you. You've got to have your own life too. And what about me? Nobody thinks about me. You're not a prisoner, are you? You're not married to that old buck."

"He's my father."

"Let's go outside. It's so hot in here I can't even think."

They went to sit in the lilac arbor, where it was dark. Their tobacco smoke made long, blue dragons in the air.

"I'll go and talk very nicely to Papa about how things are," Santavirta suggested.

"Papa's asleep already."

But Santavirta got up and went inside. In the hallway he knocked on Papa's door. When there was no answer, he opened the door quietly and peeked inside. Papa was lying on his back in the bed, sleeping with his nostrils pointing straight up. He closed the door as quietly as he had opened it and looked through the hall window at Regina, who was sitting in the lilac arbor smoking a cigarette, her legs crossed. He dropped his cigarette on the floor and ground it out with his foot. Then he put on his hat and went out to the lilac arbor to sit beside Regina.

Selecting A Play (1972)

The play selection committee was meeting Friday night in the auditorium of the workers' hall. It was the end of August, dusk fell, no one remembered to turn on the lights. The stage became dark first, then the floor, then the ceiling. The inside wall held its light the longest. From the side rooms and the attic came the creaking of steps. The watchman had made his rounds there at three in the afternoon and the creaking from his footsteps still lingered.

"Just some short play, but it has to be funny as hell," said Chairman Ranta, a carpenter.

There were old copies of 108 plays in the storage cupboard. Secretary Tammilehto brought about thirty of them to the table. He was the operator of a kiosk.

"Nothing old fashioned," Ranta said.

"I would like it to have love in it," said Mrs. Ranta.

She had a taxi driver's cap on her head and she wore a man's gray summer jacket, a white shirt, and a blue tie. One could see her car through the window. It was in the yard. She always left her car in a place where she could see it from the inside.

"Love is old fashioned," said Mr. Ranta.

"Is that so?" said Mrs. Ranta.

Up until now, Mr. Virta had not said anything. He was new. He worked on a farm as some sort of handyman; he had his pockets full of nuts and bolts, in his hands he carried monkey wrenches; he repaired farm machines. And when they worked, he drove them.

"I know a good one, which has not been put on," he said suddenly.

"Why not?" Mrs. Ranta asked.

"Because it's a little bold. A man used to visit a woman when her husband was away from home. One day the husband came home earlier than usual. The lover hid in the clothes closet. The woman was so frightened that she left. She said she was going to get some starter for clabbered milk from the neighbor. The man was there in the closet, and the husband made himself comfortable. The two men knew each other, and the man in the closet tried to figure out how he could disguise himself so the husband would not recognize him. So he put on the wife's clothes, dropping his own clothes on the floor of the closet. She was a large woman, and she had such large clothes that they fit, I mean they fit the man; of course they fit the woman, since they were her clothes. The woman's wig was also on the shelf. He put it on his head and fluffed it up a little more. The woman's handbag was also there in the closet, and the man painted his face with the makeup he found. He daubed even his eyebrows with lipstick. Just by estimating, he put on enough powder to be sure his beard would not show. The husband was sitting in the easy chair, enjoying the peace and quiet. The lover thought perhaps he had dozed off and came out of the closet cautiously. But then he noticed that he was not much of a woman, since he didn't even have breasts. Through the large armholes he thrust his fists under the dress over his chest, like this.

'Excuse me, I must have come through the wrong door,' he said. 'Does anyone live here by the name of...' In his distress, he couldn't think of any other name, so he said the wife's name. 'I was supposed to come and get some starter for clabbered milk from her.' He was so mixed up that he couldn't come up with anything out of his own head. The husband was so startled that the visitor came in from the closet that he never came to think of it as odd.

'She left only a moment ago to get it; I don't know from where. Won't you sit down?'

The woman was at the edge of the woods, peeking from behind a tree, waiting for either one of the men to come out of the house.

It was so dark the husband could not see very well. He just thought, This is a handsome woman.

'I really have to go now,' she said.

'Please don't go yet,' said the husband and placed his hand soothingly upon her knee.

At that moment the door flew open. The wife entered. 'So, the moment I turn my back!' she yelled.

She drove her lover out and began to scold her husband. Then she opened the window, took her lover's clothes from the closet, and threw them out in a bundle.

'There are your clothes; you go with them!' she shouted to her husband.

The husband tried to calm down his wife and didn't have time to pay attention to anything else. Outside, the lover, in the meantime, pulled on his own clothes and took off.''

"Yes, we'll take that one," Ranta said.

"I second that," Tammilehto said. "It's good, since it has a man in women's clothes, and if we just put in a section where a woman puts on men's clothes, it'll be perfect." They doubled up with laughter.

"What's so funny about a woman dressing in men's clothes?" Mrs. Ranta said.

Tammilehto looked at her jacket and shirt and tie.

"Nothing."

"It's indecent, and there's no love in it," Mrs. Ranta said and she lit a small cigar.

"What if there *was* love between the two?" Ranta attempted.

Tammilehto got the rest of the plays from the cupboard and began to deal them out as if they were cards. Each got 27 plays.

Veikko Huovinen (b. 1927)

Veikko Huovinen received a master of forestry degree at the University of Helsinki in 1952 and worked for some years as a forester in the Kainuu area, following in the footsteps of his father, who served as a forest supervisor. In 1957 Huovinen turned from forestry to a career in free lance writing. He now lives in northeastern Finland, the setting for many of his stories. His first work, a collection of short stories called HIRRI, had appeared in 1950. In 1952, the novel, HAVUKKA-AHON AJATTELIJA (THE THINKER OF HAVUKKA-AHO) introduced a character, a homemade backwoods philosopher, Konsta Pylkkänen, who voices opinions that are a mixture of horse sense and nonsense. The novel was well written, popular, and eventually adapted as a play. The same backwoods philosopher appeared in the 1961 novel, KONSTAN PYLKKERÖ (KONSTA'S PIROUETTES). Huovinen's later books are somewhat humorous but often satire predominates, and some contain sections of pessimism. Biting satire is cultivated in the novels IHMISTEN PUHEET (WHAT PEOPLE SAY), 1955, and in RAUHANPIIPPU (THE PEACE PIPE), 1956, the latter being a satire on war with the main character a typical folk hero who pretends stupidity. HAMSTERIT (THE HAMSTERS), 1957, is a humorous description of winter life in the North, filled with bizarre joking. SIINTÄVÄT VUORET (THE MOUNTAINS IN THE DISTANCE), 1959, is a romantic portrayal of two young people wandering in a wilderness. KYLÄN KOIRAT (THE VILLAGE DOGS), 1962, is an amusing story of dogs in the northern winter. KUIKKA (THE LOON), 1963, is a collection of humorous and satirical stories and yarns. TALVITURISTI (THE WINTER TOURIST), 1965, is pessimistic about man, and in LEMMIKKIELÄIN (THE PET), 1966, a human serves as a pet. Other writings include: LYHYET ERIKOISET (SHORT AND SPECIAL), 1967; MIKÄPÄ TÄSSÄ (WE'RE DOING ALL RIGHT), 1969; TAPION TARHAT (TAPIO'S REALM), 1969; LAMPAAN-SYÖJÄT (THE LAMB EATERS), 1970; RASVAMAKSA (A TASTY LIVER), 1973. The story, *The Frogman's Day*, from the 1973 short story collection, RASVAMAKSA, combines humorous and satirical behavior in a natural setting. *Is My Hair Beautiful?*, from the same collection, satirizes a certain type of modern youth.

The Frogman's Day (1973)

The frogman's cottage stands on an isolated point at the farthest end of a large lake. The frogman lives there with his beautiful, sensuous wife. Their life, particularly during the summers, is peaceful and close to nature. They hardly ever travel to faraway lands because the frogman's work ties them to this dwelling place. During the summer they seldom go anywhere although the frogman himself goes into town every other week to fill his oxygen tanks. Some winters they have flown to Tenerife, but its commercialism did not appeal to them.

The frogman's day is long and filled with work. He has to start early on his morning fishing rounds, before the fishermen arrive to gather their catch. At three in the morning the frogman is awakened by the buzz of his alarm clock. He eats a small roll and drinks a glass of orange juice. Then he puts on his underwear and over this his rubber suit. Before putting on his oxygen mask, he quietly slips in to his sleeping wife and plants a kiss on her cheek. Now it is time to go outside, cautiously, without slamming the doors. His flippers lie in wait on the dock. When he has put on his flippers and opened the valve of the oxygen cylinder, the frogman walks toward the lake on the gently sloping rocky shore. Soon a path of bubbles leads toward the open water.

The frogman swims in the dark green water. He looks around. Ahaa! He sees the net belonging to the summer cottage dweller, Mr. Siven, the engineer. With smooth strokes, the frogman swims along the net. He sees a good-sized whitefish thrashing about in it. The frogman removes the fish from the net and puts it in the fish pouch on his hip. From a smaller pouch he now takes a salted herring and pushes it through the mesh, making sure it is well caught in the net.

And over there! The water bubbles and swishes some thirty meters away, the white belly of a fish flashes. What a fine trout has bitten into fisherman Kaasalainen's long line! The frogman fights a hard battle with the wild fish but manages to subdue it. On the empty hook he again attaches a salted herring. The frogman, you see, never takes anything for nothing from another's catch; he always makes an exchange. Besides, is there anything more delicious than salted herring and new potatoes?

When the frogman's fish pouch is full, he swims to a rocky islet and climbs up to sit on a boulder at the shore. He places his face mask beside him, fills his pipe, and draws in a few gratifying puffs. Then he cleans the fish, thus lightening his wife's work. In this way, his wife's hands remain soft and smooth since she doesn't have to clean fish.

At eight the frogman returns home. He sees his wife sitting on the dock, dangling her legs in the water. The frogman swims under the dock. Suddenly, a cold hand grabs the woman's ankle. "Ouch!" screams the woman, frightened. But no squabble comes from this. The wife understands her husband's mischievous nature.

At ten the frogman has breakfast, which generally consists of rice krispies or cornflakes, a vegetable, fish, much milk, and even meat, when they've been to the grocery van. After breakfast, the frogman goes to the dressing room of the sauna for a nap, and it would be hard indeed to sleep in the cottage, for his wife's loom clatters noisily as she weaves wall hangings and rag rugs. And, of course, the frogman understands that woven things contribute significantly to the level of comfort in their home.

After drinking two cups of drip coffee at noon, the frogman goes on his daytime tour. It is now time for the light-hearted activities in the water. He has a pouch of supplies on his hip.

The lake is calm, the sun is hot, sounds carry far. Holding a fishing rod a man sits in a boat beside a small island. The frogman swims deep, close to the bottom of the lake so he can get under the boat unseen. The fisherman sits dozing in the heat, the fish are not biting. He is roused by a strange noise. It sounds like some insect chewing at the boards of the boat. The sound seems to be coming from the bottom of the boat. And suddenly the fisherman sees the point of a drill coming through the bottom. The drill is pulled away and a stream of water spurts into the boat. There is nothing else the fisherman can do at first but thrust his finger into the hole while he hunts with his other hand for a handkerchief to plug into the hole.

But by then the frogman is far away.

Farther away, at the very tip of the point, two young girls are rowing along, every now and then stopping to chat and laugh. Then their boat jerks in a most peculiar way. The girls see a hand wearing a black rubber glove groping its way over the edge of the boat. The hand disappears as quickly as it had appeared. But on the rower's seat in the middle of the boat is a plastic bag with strips of licorice and letter-shaped lozenges. "How neat!" say the girls after recovering from their fright.

And what about the three schoolboys paddling about in their rubber boat? They have just had a swim and are drying off. Abruptly their attention is drawn to rapidly bubbling water just a stone's throw away. What's this? A bright yellow balloon with the ears and face of a rabbit pops up from the water. The balloon keeps on rising, ascends to almost half a kilometer's height, where the high winds carry it out of sight.

And just how was this feat accomplished? Well, the frogman has helium gas in a small cylinder. He stretches the mouth of the balloon over the cylinder head and the gas escapes into the balloon. With a quick pinch he closes the mouth of the balloon and releases it. So it's quite a simple trick, but it takes many people on the lake by surprise.

The old master of Haukkasaari is rowing to the post office on the mainland to get the mail. Startled, he sees large bubbles rising from the water. In the midst of the bubbles a black, glistening head rises to the surface and a booming voice asks, "Excuse me, but what time is it?"

With trembling hands, the old master digs his America-watch out of his vest pocket and says the time is a quarter after one. But the unknown questioner does not even thank him for the information but vanishes into the depths of the water just as mysteriously as he had risen. "Could that have been one of those UFO's" contemplates the old man for a while and then continues his rowing.

Two men are trolling in the sound. A large wooden lure is attached to the end of their one line. A fish jerks at the line, pulls at it with unusual strength. The fisherman begins a grim struggle with the large fish. The water splashes some distance away. "It came to the surface!" the rower calls in excitement. After a long struggle, the fish begins to tire. The line is drawn in from the deep water. And rising from the water with the lure is--a rusted gasoline can. A plastic case is tied to the handle of the can and inside is a letter:

Dear Sirs:

Greetings from the Water People.

We wish you the best of luck.

For the Water People
Ahti and Vellamo [1]

Just as a bear who walks in the freedom of the forest sometimes gets carried away with romping, knocking down rotten tree trunks, clawing at the ground and roaring, so also the frogman has his moments of unpredictable whimsy. Sometimes in the early evenings, particularly on stormy days, the frogman rises to the land near out-of-the-way fields close to shore. Then he bellows and howls in a hoarse voice, wrecks tens of meters of fences, and tramples the grain or the potato plants. Hearing the frogman's raving, the nearby landowners, trembling, retreat into their houses, lock their doors,

[1] Ahti and Vellamo are known in Finnish mythology as the rulers of the seas.

and do not venture to the lake that evening. In the morning they discover flipper tracks running from the water's edge to the field. Tracks also lead back to the water. The mowing machine has been tipped over near the hay shed, piles of hay have been tossed hither and thither...

At three o'clock the frogman comes home from the lake, sometimes it is as late as six o'clock; he then eats his dinner and listens to the weather report for seafarers...

But the frogman's day is not over quite yet. At eight o'clock he again goes down to the lake, for now it's time for the evening croaking.

The frogman swims close to the row of summer cottages. He climbs to a rock just under the water, lies on his stomach with only his head showing above the water. With suction cups he attaches tentacles the shape of half-moons to his forehead. Seen from afar, he looks like a giant, bulgy-eyed frog staring out the water. The frogman now takes a rectangular box containing a radio set out of his pouch. He has had it made by special order. It has one part similar to one in a Japanese laughing machine but a frog croaks in this one. The best thing about the machine is its powerful amplifier.

The frogman places mufflers over his ears and presses the button. A terrifyingly loud croaking of a frog blares out. The intensity of its sound is equal to that of a chain saw. On a calm night it carries a distance of ten kilometers.

Around the cottages, the people run inside, close their doors and windows, turn their portable radios on loud, and place their hands over their ears.

For his croaking, the frogman has selected a place half a kilometer from the shore, for he has once been shot at with a rifle from the bushes on the shore. Every now and then a speedboat sets out from the shore toward the rock. But the frogman always has time to dive to a spot thirty meters deep right beside his rock.

After about half an hour's croaking, the frogman swims home.

Here the climax of the work-filled day awaits him, a peaceful evening within the confines of his home. On the terrace of their cottage they enjoy their evening coffee; small Japanese lanterns are lit to create a pleasant mood. Now the frogman has a chance to relax and to enjoy his wife's many warm expressions of affection, which he doesn't always notice, but which still delight him. The frogman sits in a canvas chair and reads two-day old newspapers.

The sun sets. The dusk of the summer night spreads to dim the landscape. The many-faceted surface of the lake borrows bright colors from the sky. A light fragrance of perfume hovers about the frogman's wife. The woman casts veiled, mysterious glances at her husband and occasionally there is a glimpse of a well-shaped leg from under her white skirt. The wife goes inside and in the beam of light coming from the door, which is slightly ajar, he sees the brassiere tossed on a chair, the silk panties dropping to the floor. The frogman understands that it is now time for him to go in. On his way he picks up his frogman's outfit, which has been drying outside. The door is closed, the lock clicks shut.

In this way the frogman's summer days pass. With the coming of autumn, the leaves blaze with color and drop to the ground. Dark clouds roll over the restless lake, it rains, the first snowflakes fall. In October, the frogman's level of activity drops markedly. The water is cold and he does not care to venture under the ice. Should the oxygen equipment fail, he risks death by suffocation.

And then the snow falls. It covers the woods along the shore, piles up in deep drifts on the roof of the cottage, lays a cover over everything. The snow also envelops the idyllic existence and smoldering eroticism of those two happy people, the frogman and his wife. Now they have more time to devote to each other, to tell each other of their childhood experiences, to probe into the deeper meanings of life. How they love each other!

Some time in January two pairs of ski tracks lead from the cottage to the forest and then to the edge of the country road. The frogman and his wife have skied there. The frogman has had a suitcase strapped to his back and his wife has carried a shoulder bag and a handbag. They have gone to the capital city for a little entertainment. They will stay there perhaps two weeks, go to the theater once or twice, buy something by Marimekko or have something made at Koponens. The frogman replenishes his supplies; next summer he intends to include a morning croaking in his program. They drink champagne and go to Iberian and Chinese bazaars. On their last day they buy two coffee cakes and some bottles of whiskey. Then they return to their cottage to await the spring. Only during the summer is one really alive there, but blessed also is the winter, white, tranquil, pure...

Is My Hair Beautiful? (1973)

Jarkko is going to the hairdressing salon. He is a strong, handsome brute, six feet tall. By occupation he is a student, planning to take his examinations in the spring.

A long row of customers is sitting in the hairdressing salon. Of the seven customers, two are women. The rest are men who are having their hair done. Jarkko knows two of them.

The hairdresser takes charge of Jarkko. First the hair is washed and then, as the saying goes, it is softened. Jarkko has such beautiful, girlish waves, so beautiful! His hair reaches down to his shoulders.

After the shampoo, Jarkko looks through the hairstyling magazine with the hairdresser. Should the hair be styled this way or that? This is a Swiss artist's creation. That is the present hair style of the slalom gold medal winner. This one a popular TV star uses, that one is a well-known movie actor's favorite style.

After a very thorough and serious study, Jarkko decides on a hairstyle with soft waves on the hair on the forehead and on top of the head, but with more tightly curled hair at the neck and around the ears.

Jarkko seats himself in the hairdresser's chair. He is a strong man with shoulders like a lumberjack's, a neck like a wrestler's, chest muscles like a sheet metal worker's. Here, somehow, a big man has gone to waste, Such a man could do hard work or would have, in former days. He would have carried sacks, dug ditches, felled trees, rowed boats, loaded cannons at a shore fortress, skied with a patrol during years of danger.

But this Jarkko has done no heavy work. Of course, going to school can be work, can really be considered hard work, especially when you carefully observe the teacher's methods, criticize them, and give the teacher a hard time. And yet, today's students cannot get work. Automatic heating takes away even the slightest chance for working with trees; modern water and sewage networks do not bring many problems and jobs. Not very many have vegetable gardens anymore; snow is removed by the apartment house caretaker, and summer work for wages is scarce. For the future, automation threatens to do away with manual labor. And you can get your exercise, too, when you slalom ski and rush down the slopes in Lapland, drive a motorcycle or a car, water ski, and swing in a discotheque.

So why do we criticize the young man, who lives in good faith in a world made by his short-sighted elders...

With the help of the hot air blower, the hairdresser shapes the waves in Jarkko's hair. Jarkko does not read the paper, he just stares intently at how attractive his hair is becoming. He has a strong, intense face, with even a beard, a firm chin, and serious, such serious eyes which, without blinking, watch the birth of the waves...

Jarkko sits at the hairdresser's.

He does not perceive in the least that this in any way should be odd.

Jarkko's hair is arranged in waves. The hairdresser sets the waves. Jarkko observes closely, to see whether she's doing a good job. Jarkko's eyes admire his hair and face. Jarkko will have beautiful hair. Very beautiful.

Curlers are also arranged in his hair. Then Jarkko puts his head under a dryer hood. There they sit in a row, six Finnish heroes, curlers in their hair. The men look a little like auntie or mother as they sit with the curlers on their heads. One almost expects them to have handbags with make-up kits, fingernail files, creams, small neat calendars, and jeweled combs.

That Jarkko will have pretty hair, oh, yes! For sure everyone will notice it and wonder who that tough, handsome brute is.

At last, after a long sitting, it is finished. The hairdresser holds a mirror behind his neck so that Jarkko can see whether his hair is beautiful in the back. And Jarkko does call attention to something. The hair in the back should be a little more fluffy, a little more off the neck. Well, the hairdo is repaired. With a serious look, Jarkko follows, as if bewitched, the final shaping of his curls.

His hair is all right. Jarkko approves of the work. Jarkko feels you have to be firm and demand good work. But now his hair is attractive, it satisfies Jarkko. However, he still looks at the picture in the hairstyling magazine. Did his hairdo turn out the same as the one in the picture? Not exactly. Anyhow, he pays. He puts on his leather jacket and goes out. In his car he looks immediately into the rear-view mirror. He presses the waves with the edge of his hand, turns his head sideways.

He drives home.

In his room he begins to look in the mirror. For he has a large round mirror there and a hairstyling table and bench in front of it. The tall, blond youth looks closely into the mirror. His eyes appraise and approve, question and admire. Golden waves...

Jarkko presses the waves with his palms, fluffs up those on top. He also examines his skin. With his tongue, he pushes out his cheek and checks to see if there are pimples, enlarged pores, or blackheads. He smiles in a friendly way to his image in the mirror. A good looking man. He is now ready to go to a meeting. Jarkko has decided to be a rebel. Power to the workers and the working class! The system must be changed. Even though he is the son of a factory owner, Jarkko has already been a member of the labor organization for three months. Workers and farmers are honest and straightforward. Some time in the future Jarkko plans to go to work on a Soviet Russian collective farm. Even if he doesn't stay there permanently he will, at least, learn what work is...

Whenever he pauses from looking at himself in the mirror, Jarkko plays records. In the resounding workers' songs, Jarkko feels himself one with the workers.

Jarkko takes off his shirt and raises his well-developed arms. He sprays deodorant into his armpits.

After an hour, he meets Miia. Miia is a dark, very beautiful girl. Jarkko has fallen in love with her. Miia is so spirited and dominating. She drives a car better than Jarkko. Most often Jarkko sits in the back when Miia drives. Miia always wins in tennis and darts, she swims faster than he does.

How wonderful it is to stretch out on the sofa with his head in Miia's lap. Miia strokes Jarkko's blond hair, talks about all kinds of things, laughs merrily. Miia never uses a deodorant, she is so natural. That's why Jarkko likes her. Miia is the only natural girl Jarkko knows. Miia smells a little of sweat, excrement, and generally smells like a person, but in no way excessively, just the right amount. Such girls are treasures nowadays, when the manufacture of commercial perfumes and cosmetic compounds tends to drown out all natural smells from the world.

Jarkko. A fortunate man...Goldilocks!

Antti Hyry (b. 1931)

Antti Hyry, born in rural northern Finland, has retained a close relationship to nature and physical activities. Although he received a degree in electronic engineering from the Helsinki Institute of Technology in 1958, he has not worked as an engineer but has devoted himself to free lance writing. He may be one of the most original of Finnish writers, his originality coming from his very commonplace manner of describing ordinary situations. Using an objective, matter-of-fact method of description, Hyry disassociates himself from his writings by withholding his comments and opinions from the reader, offering no social, moral, or political messages, and presenting seemingly meaningless everyday life in his stories. He describes unimportant facts as carefully as he describes the important facts. His practical turn of mind and his technical studies influence his literary style, many of his writings describing work or physical activity. His writing centers around childhood and the countryside of northern Finland. Hyry sees childhood and youth as the period of full, direct experience with the world, the capacity for which he thinks man later loses. He feels that those things which are really important are generally considered too trivial to mention. His characters who have moved to the city from the country often suffer from problems of adjustment because of their estrangement from life close to the soil. They remain rural even in the city and long for the world of their childhood close to nature. Indirectly, Hyry protests against the complex world created by modern technology. His first work was a collection of short stories, MAANTIELTÄ HÄN LÄHTI (HE LEFT THE HIGHWAY), 1958. A novel, KEVÄTTÄ JA SYKSYÄ (SPRING AND FALL), also published in 1958, has as its main character a small boy in northern Finland. KOTONA (AT HOME), 1960, and ALAKOULU (THE LOWER GRADES), 1965, are autobiographical novels. Another short story collection. JUNAMATKAN KUVAUS JA NELJÄ MUUTA NOVELLEJA (AN ACCOUNT OF A RAILWAY JOURNEY AND FOUR OTHER SHORT STORIES), appeared in 1962. MAAILMAN LAITA (THE EDGE OF THE WORLD), 1967, is a novel in which the main character, even in the face of nuclear reactions, reflects that human life actually depends on very small things. Another collection of short stories, LEVEITÄ LAUTOJA (WIDE BOARDS) appeared in 1968 and a novel, ISÄ JA POIKA (FATHER AND SON), in 1971. The stories, *The Pigbitten* and *The Rock in the Sunshine*, both from Hyry's first collection, HE LEFT THE HIGHWAY, 1958, are objective, matter-of-fact, about physical activity, of rural background, present seemingly meaningless everyday life, and offer no special message; the reader is free to draw his own conclusions.

The Pig Bitten (1958)

It was summer.

Valde, a farmer's son, lay alone on his bed in the large living room of the farmhouse thinking about things.

One can't say about Valde, as one can say about many, that if a man cannot get a wife, then he doesn't need one. Valde was in his twenties. He was tall and thin and in his movements and his speech he was hasty and fussy. He had made a cupboard for dishes which he had painted dark green and decorated with red stripes. The cupboard stood against the wall near the stove.

Valde was playful. For instance, in the carpentry courses he might watch while someone made a cabinet: when he saw a poor joint, he would suddenly put his fingers in his mouth, touch the spot with his fingertips and depart quickly.

It was June: it was the kind of afternoon when everything is like a color photograph; the mosquitoes are flying, white clouds float in the sky, the sparrows chase each other in the currant bushes, and quack grass is growing around the currant bushes.

Valde lay there and was restless. He was waiting for a young man, Ville, who was to come over. They were to go fishing at a lake far in the forest with two girls, Anja and Helli. Valde thought about Helli and it was as if he breathed sweet air.

Ville had planned the trip. He wanted to get Valde and Helli together just for the fun of it. Ville and Anja went out together in the evenings. Ville talked to Valde about Helli and the trip, and Valde immediately accepted the plan. Anja spoke to Helli. But when Helli heard she would have to go with Valde, she wasn't going to go. Anja said Ville wanted Helli to go and, besides, they would go as a group, just for the fun of it, and so Helli consented.

Earlier, as a child, Helli had been thin and tall for her age. Her home was far from the road, back of the forest. While the children along the road spoke of their fathers and mothers, Helli and her brothers and sisters spoke to their mother: "Elma, give me some bread," and to their father, "Arthur, the food is ready." Elma was short, fat, and talkative, and she loved to go visiting. Arthur was extremely tall. As a child, Helli had gone to feed the pig. She had leaned over carelessly and the pig had bitten her lower lip. A scar remained on her lower lip, a small lump in the middle of it. After this Helli was called the Pigbitten. Helli was now close to twenty.

Valde heard clatter in the hall and Ville came through the door.

"Get up."

"Which fishing lure? The Professor?" Valde asked and he pulled on his boots and put on his shirt.

"The Professor and the red-tailed one," said Ville.

Ville had his mouth half-closed when he spoke and his voice rumbled from the back of his throat, but one could understand him anyhow. Ville was tall and blond and his eyes were bluish gray.

"I'll take this one," said Valde.

They went out and across the farmyard to the road. At the gate Valde chased away the calves which were coming toward the yard. Waiting at the road was Anja, who said, "Hi!"

"Do you have the coffee pot?" asked Ville.

"Yes, and sandwiches," said Anja and she swung her knapsack.

Valde glanced at Anja and Ville every now and then, but mostly he looked elsewhere. They walked along the main road and soon turned on to the forest road. Anja sang, "I remember a park, the loveliest, the most perfect moonlight night." She wasn't really too fat, her hair was brownish gray, cut short and she had had a permanent. Her face was a little round and her eyes were bluish. She wore slacks and since she was not very thin, she looked a little peculiar. She had on a green blouse and on her back the small knapsack with the coffee pot and the sandwiches.

"...in the beautiful moonlit night
often under the linden tree we..."

"Put some pitch oil on," said Valde. He rubbed pitch oil behind his ears, on his neck, and elsewhere. When they entered the forest the mosquitoes had come at once and they bit Anja's bare arms. Ville and Anja held out their palms and Valde poured oil from his bottle for both of them; soon they all smelled of pitch oil. The forest came to an end, now there were willows and fields, then a tall pine forest; here the road was dry; there were wagon tracks, worn down light-colored rocks, black soil and fine sand. They walked now apart from each other, then close to each other; they broke off birch branches with which they beat away the mosquitoes. Then came fields again, then a forest with spruces and pines and leafy trees, mountain ashes, juniper bushes, and raw blueberries. After the forest came larger fields. Beyond the fields on the left was the house which was Helli's home.

"You go and get Helli," Ville said to Anja.

Anja left, jumping over the ditches and sometimes running along the edges. A drainage ditch ran through the middle of the tilled fields and was easy to cross during this dry season.

The men walked to the edge of the drainage ditch and sat down. Willows grew all along the ditch.

"Helli sleeps in that small log building," said Ville.

"It isn't going to rain," said Valde.

The wind blew over the fields, there were white clouds in the sky, but not near the sun. The singing of birds came from the bushes and through the air.

"It's really good weather; the hay will grow fast now. Does she sleep in that log building?" said Valde.

"She sleeps there alone. If it rains soon it will be a good year for hay," said Ville.

They sat at the edge of the ditch and waited, then they walked about two meters across the bottom of the ditch and sat on the edge at the other side. After a little while the girls came. Helli did not seem very enthusiastic.

"Hi," said Helli and jumped to the road.

"It's nice weather," said Valde.

"How are you?" said Ville.

All four of them started right away to walk along the road. Valde was behind. Helli was wearing a cotton dress with small flowers. She had on a windbreaker jacket. Helli's rubber boots left tracks in the ground where the road was damp. Helli's hair was blond, straight, rather long and fastened somehow behind her ears. She wore a scarf tied in the back. Helli walked with her feet turned a little inward. The small mark from the pig bite showed on her lower lip and enhanced her looks.

As they walked, the field ended and the road led into the forest.

"You put on some pitch oil too," Anja told Helli.

Valde poured a brown glob into Helli's palm and Helli rubbed on the pitch oil. The others also rubbed more on themselves.

"Put some on your legs too," Anja told Helli.

They soon reached a swamp. There the road was of dried mud. The wind blew from the left, and the swamp stretched far in that direction; it also extended to the right. The girls walked side by side in front. Valde looked at Helli, her hair and her dress. Helli's eyes looked at Anja and the swamp, but not for long at anything. Valde tried to think how everything would happen.

"Helli, have you ever gone casting?" asked Valde.

"Helli, are you quick at mi-milking?" asked Ville.

"Mi-milking," mimicked Helli.

The swamp ended and then came birches. But soon they were in a new, large swamp. They walked close together. Valde felt like touching Helli. He bumped into her when they jumped over a wet spot. They were in the middle of the swamp, and sat down to rest because Anja was tired. Valde's thoughts wandered, his chin trembled. The sun shone from the right side of the road.

"I'm going to sleep here," said Anja, and lay down on her back on a hummock.

The sun was pleasantly warm.

"Tickle her," Valde said quietly to Ville.

"Your mare seems very talented, have you trained her lately?" said Ville.

Valde moved away and went to sit near Helli.

"I see a raw raspberry over there," said Helli, and left; she moved farther away. Soon she cried out, "A frog, a little frog!"

Helli picked the frog off the ground, held it between her fingers and dangled it by one leg. She looked at it closely. Anja got up and shuddered.

"That would be a good-sized bait for a pike. Let's take it along," said Valde. But Helli let the frog go.

They walked on. It was still a long way to the lake. They walked to the other side of the swamp, then through a high birch forest, a heath, a slough, another swamp; they finally reached the shore of the lake. The boys each cut down a fishing pole, the girls sat on the shore. The boys came over with their poles. Ville tied fishing line to his pole. Furtively he winked at Anja and said, "Now we've got a good bait."

"A bright lure should do it in this kind of weather," said Valde.

"Anja and I will fish that shore, you fish the other shore. When we meet on the other side of the lake we'll make coffee and eat. There's a good place there. I cooked there last summer. There's a large smooth rock; we can fry pike. I guess Anja has salt. It's also a good place to take a little nap," Ville said and attached his fishing lure.

But Helli was startled. The lake was small, enclosed on the left and the right by swamps, on the other sides by forest. The sun was low. They had come at least eight kilometers. Ville threw his lure into the water. Helli had walked a short distance away. Suddenly she started to run and disappeared without a word.

Helli had been hesitant on the way here. It was as if she had been attached to a red rubber band which stretched the whole time and drew her homeward. She ran back the same way it had taken them hours to come. Valde ran after her.

Helli knew how to move in the forest, she ran and walked quickly through shrubs and brush, through forests and swamps, and got home in the middle of the night. Valde followed behind. At first he tried to catch up with her, and he could have, but he gave up trying. From the edge of the wide field he glanced at the log building where he knew Helli slept, continued on his way, and was soon home.

Ville and Anja stayed at the lake to fish and came back the next morning, when it was Sunday. That same summer they were married.

On Sunday morning Helli walked from the log building to the house.

"Are you planning on becoming the daughter-in-law at a big farm?" Arthur, her father, asked and he sipped coffee at the table.

Helli did not say anything. She took the milk pail, she stood on the steps in the morning air, she walked across the yard to her milking; as she walked, she stepped to the side, on the sauna flowers and on the grass.

On Sunday Valde felt as if he had been sick for a long time and was still a little sick. It was as if he wore poorly fitting, tight clothes among people. During the whole summer he wouldn't let anyone speak to him about the trip; otherwise he was soon the same as he had been before.

When, in July, he was repairing the roof on the barn, and the sun was shining as it does before a thunderstorm, he felt that he was like a human being.

The Rock In The Sunshine (1958)

The boy stepped out of the door of the cottage one summer morning with a knife in his hand. He was wearing knee pants and a shirt with short sleeves. The boy's hair was brushed off to one side, his eyes were dark brown and his eyelashes were long. A boy with lovely eyes, as the gypsy woman said when she talked with his mother. The boy walked to a pile of boards and sat down. He was going to make a new arrow for his crossbow.

The boy sat on the pile of boards and whittled. One end of the long, thin piece of wood was against his chest and the sharp knife moved along the wood. White shavings fell around him, all over his pants and his bare feet. His hair kept falling into his eyes, and the boy constantly had to brush it away.

There was something above his knee. The boy put his knife aside and scratched his skin with his hand, so the hem of his pants leg moved up. He then put his arrow on the boards, and he looked: his leg was bare way above his knee, and the sole of his foot was on the grass next to a rock, bending the blades of grass in many directions against the rock in the warm sunshine. The sun-warmed rock gave off heat.

Something ran through the boy and made him tremble. He looked and wondered: is that mine, the whole leg from the bottom to the top, all of it? And the boy stood up. He walked slowly around the pile of boards to the back of the cottage making each step a separate little event. He walked around the building slowly and went into the cottage. He sat down on a bench and looked at the ceiling and the corners. His thoughts moved and smarted under his knee pants and under his shirt with short sleeves to his hands and to his head.

And this created a restlessness in him, which took him throughout the fields and brought him to the rocky shore of a rapids and to the quiet water. And he saw it all, the smooth reeds, black heads swaying, and the spotted orchids beneath the bank on the shore of the rapids, but they reminded him of something, which seared him. He had his knife with him as he walked and he did everything, which was necessary, but always, when he did something, he looked at himself and his hands as if they were a knife, which makes shavings. And he was like the wings of a hawk returning in the spring, which are light and strong but which have been cut off and don't know where they should go.

But then he got lost somehow, when he had a wife and children, so that he drank coffee peacefully beside the window in the evenings.

And some day his son will discover his leg beside a rock in the sunshine, and other things.

Hannu Salama (b. 1936)

Hannu Salama, after attending secondary school for four years
and then a technical school in Tampere, near his birthplace of
Kouvola, worked as an electrician, as his father did, and also as a
manual laborer. In 1961 he turned to free lance writing. His first
novel, SE TAVALLINEN TARINA (THE USUAL STORY), 1961,
dealing with lovelessness and the contrast of old and new, of
country and city, his first short stories, LOMAPAIVA (THE DAY
OFF), 1962, and his poetry collection, PUU BALLADIN HAUDALLA
(A TREE AT THE BALLAD'S GRAVE), 1963, were promising and
original but attracted little attention. Some of the images in his
poetry collection are very intense and have been compared to Van
Gogh's late paintings. But Salama's novel, JUHANNUSTANSSIT
(THE MIDSUMMER NIGHT DANCE), 1964, in which one of the
characters gives a mock sermon, aroused the opposition of church
circles for allegedly blasphemous passages, and Salama and his
editor were sentenced, fined, and the book censored under a
near-obsolete law, but in 1968 they were pardoned by the president
of Finland. Some critics consider this novel a great one, others
contend it lacks merit and has a number of poorly written sections.
Salama has continued publishing, writing with an almost oppressive
sense of reality. In 1967 he published a volume of short stories,
KENTTÄLÄINEN KÄY TALOSSA) KENTTÄLÄINEN COMES FOR
A VISIT) and an autobiographical novel, MINÄ, OLLI JA ORVOKKI
(I, OLLI AND ORVOKKI), which won the State prize in 1968. Other
publications include the novel, JOULUKUUN KUUDES (THE
SIXTH OF DECEMBER), 1968; short stories, KESÄLESKI
(SUMMER WIDOWER), 1969; two novels, TAPAUSTEN KULKU
(SUCCESSION OF EVENTS), 1969, and LOKAKUUN PÄIVIÄ
(AUGUST DAYS), 1971; a poetry collection, VILLANPEHMEE,
TASKUNLÄMMIN (SOFT AS WOOL, POCKET WARM), 1971; and
a major novel., SIINÄ NÄKIJÄ MISSA TEKIJA (NO CRIME
WITHOUT A WITNESS), 1972, considered an important literary
work of post-war Finland. His short stories are traditional in form
but protest against society quite violently. He describes sexual
activities frankly. Salama's view of the world is almost psychotic,
often leaving unpleasant impressions. His attitude toward others is

one of pity but he cannot seem to bear people who do not accept his pity. The story, *The Drunkards*, from the 1962 collection, THE DAY OFF, delineates the thinking and actions of an alcoholic.

The Drunkards (1962)

I had come to town a little before noon. Marke had been at the station to meet me and we had gone to the room she had rented for me. At two, Marke's shift at work began and I walked with her to the hospital. She went inside quickly so I wouldn't have time to slobber over her with everyone watching. I smiled to myself at this as I started walking slowly downtown.

I would not go to a bar. I owed Marke that much. If now, on the very first day I were to go drinking I would, of course, go every time I had the slightest bit of adversity. I tried to look with contempt at men who were such slaves to alcohol that they had to drink every single day. Even from their outward appearance one could tell they were gradually deteriorating, the most trivial of things irritated them, they went to the bar whenever they got some money. I would stop drinking entirely, it would be easy with Marke near me. Only once in a while would I take a small one, only one or two, if my work did not go well.

I would not go to a bar. I returned to my room, took out a stack of papers and read about one page. After reading it, I knew I would not have the courage to tackle the stack of papers, at least not today. I left it on the table and went out, went back downtown and thought of going to a cafe to wile away my time. Marke would get off at seven. I would buy her flowers or some small thing.

I walked past a large window. On a table in front of the men sitting there were some glasses and two empty beer bottles. They looked at me a little curiously; I guess I had stared a long time. I walked past the window, came back. Perhaps I could have a bottle of beer. Or if I should have one strong drink, then the whole matter would stop bothering me. Even at rehabilitation centers they give you liquor in small doses at first.

I went inside. The bar was almost empty, the room large. I ordered a drink, drank it and asked for my bill when, from the other side of the room, a familiar looking man got up from a table.

It was Mikkonen, the same red-faced Mikkonen, who, upon getting his corporal's stripes, had talked to the girls about his experiences as a pilot. He had such an expansive nature that you could not help liking him. He was one of those men who have enough imagination to live in a grand style and yet not enough intelligence to restrain them. The same red-faced, popeyed Mikkonen. He had once, while serving as an assistant clerk, arranged a furlough for me even though I had been in the garrison only three days. He had signed my request: "Recommended, signed, Sgt. Kontio. Approved, signed Lt. Helminen." Toward the end of the training we had a disagreement over something, what, I don't remember. On the whole, he was a good man, a great pretender, who believed so earnestly in himself that he was able to make his role one of importance. In the past his company had given me pleasure and it seemed to do so even more now as we sat across from each other. Grown men, our lives before us.

"Come over to my table, I'm sitting over there."

"Actually, I was planning to leave."

"You will do nothing of the sort. You will please be good enough to come now and join me at my table."

His very proper use of language amused me. I didn't answer right away. I thought I wouldn't have anything, at the most a bottle of beer. But then it occurred to me that I had an obligation to buy him a drink since he had arranged that furlough for me. I had money, enough to live on for a month. But now we would not think about disagreeable things. If I should go hungry the last half of the month, it would force me to work. And working meant money.

He stood before me, his hand extended. I laughed and gathered up my cigarets and money from my table. We walked to the other end of the room, talking in loud voices. Where have you been? What have you been doing?

"Been in Kajaani."

"In Tampere."

"Same old job."

"Sales representative. Free agent. Good job."

"You're fatter."

"You're thinner."

In no time we tossed down three and ordered more. We discussed politics. I said that Finland's responsibility, her diplomatic duty, would be to call the Scandinavian countries together and conduct preliminary negotiations. I was inspired by my own cleverness. I talked long and eloquently about how this time around common sense demanded our sending diplomatic notes to Sweden and to the other Scandinavian countries. In the end, I realized that I kept repeating the same thing over and over again. I asked whether he had heard anything about Vatanen, our former top sergeant. Mikkonen said he had seen him in Jyväskylä.

"He had gotten thin, he's running the family farm at Saarijärvi."

"He was absolutely crazy."

"After five drinks the top sergeant used to get so drunk I had to help him outside."

"He was really totally insane. He came pretty close to making us crazy too. And he was as homely as a mud fence."

We drained our glasses. I looked at the street through the window. A heavy snow was falling. There was a two-inch layer of soft snow on the sidewalk and a boy, running out of a stairway, left marks like snowshoe tracks on the clean snow.

"Strontium's falling down."

"A slow death in your limbs, in your limbs a slow death. We'd better drink."

On the other side of the window was a park with two bridges over a creek flowing out to the sea. Below the wooden bridge with white rails hung large brownish icicles. The nearest trees were leaning over the creek as if wondering about the black water running between the snowy banks. Beyond the park was a taxi stand. A fat driver got out of the last taxi in the row and ran clumsily to the telephone booth, then he squeezed his body into the first taxi in the row and drove away.

"A nice city," I said. "The people here have a spirit different from the people in the South. Here they aren't as sour looking as back home."

"This is a nice city. How long have you been here?"

"Just a couple of weeks," I lied.

"But say, when are you coming to Kajaani?"

"Well, some time after February. I can't get away before then."

"Listen, you should come to Kajaani. We'll take a trip to Lapland from there. You've got to see Lapland. Have you ever been there?"

"Only to Aavasaksa Hill, and only half way up that. I had to turn back because of the mosquitoes. There were fewer mosquitoes on the ferry, and for the rest of my trip to Lapland I stayed on the ferry. Then a car came and took me to Tornio. From there I went by train to Tampere and stayed there for three years."

"I went on a trip once to see the autumn colors of Lapland. You can't believe what it's like, you can't believe it until you see it."

"A Finn will believe only what he sees."

"What?"

"Nothing. Listen, they're playing Glazunov's "Russian Images." No, it wasn't Glazunov who wrote it. It was someone else. It was Borodin."

I suddenly wanted to go to Lapland. Skiing and sunshine. Health, good humor, and Borodin.

"Let's go in March to shoot a wolf. Do you have a gun?

"Enough to even give you one."

"I'm a poor shot. You probably remember?"

"You didn't even try. No one can shoot that poorly if he tries at least a little bit."

"It would be damned good for me. I have let my body get rusty. In a sedentary job, me! An old fisherman and soccer player. Life should be wonderful. But it isn't if you're not in good health."

"You were the national champion of Finland."

"No, the district champion."

"But you said you were on the national championship team in soccer."

"I lied. Even I had to be somebody."

He did not understand my taunting and seemed a bit stunned, and I knew why. To him it was incomprehensible that I admitted my lie. I took it upon myself to explain, "Now look, it no longer makes any difference whether one says one has been the champion of Finland or the champion of the district. Such details don't matter when one is already a fat pig. Or to put it in another way: when you feel that you are a fat pig and there is no hope that you will ever be anything but a pig. And moreover, when you find that two thirds of the people are fat pigs and that together we constitute a power and propagate our species."

He had to laugh when I said "And propagate our species."

"Ha haa, you always have the same old stories."

"I really shouldn't be talking like this. So cynically, you understand. Nor should I even drink. But I am a drunkard. Listen, now they're playing that tune. What's the name of it again? How do they know I'm here?"

But Mikkonen was still talking nonsense saying. "You'll just have to come to ski in March. We'll take some girls along."

"None of that stuff. I want to be faithful."

I wondered if I was really serious. At least I didn't want office girls with us in the mountains. The whole trip would be wasted. I could not explain this to Mikkonen, he would not have understood. I said, "I'm not a frivolous man, I am a melancholy man. I have become a shit and soon, of course, I will become a moralizing shit."

Mikkonen was silent. Six men sat down at the table next to us, businessmen or salesmen, obviously, judging from their smiles. I looked at them with my most disagreeable look. They were such an affected looking lot. One of them noticed my look and from time to time turned to stare at me. The waitress came to flirt with them and Mikkonen took the opportunity to order another round.

I was getting drunk. I hadn't eaten since I'd had a sandwich and coffee on the train. That was almost ten hours ago. I tried to think of something a sober man might say and said, "In the mountains I could get rid of my shit. It doesn't go away with liquor."

He drained his glass, grunted, and shook his head.

"Huh, four years and drunk almost every day."

"I really have been," he added, evidently thinking I didn't believe him. I felt a little sorry for the exaggerator; he told me he had spent a year in a technical school studying airplane mechanics but had been kicked out.

"I was married by then," he continued. "Even had two children, a girl and a boy."

"You got divorced?"

"It just didn't work out. You remember Birgitta?"

I gave a short laugh.

"So you were Birgitta's husband."

"I was. But not any more."

"And why not?"

"You can guess. While I was at school, Birgitta wouldn't stay at home."

I said nothing. I remembered Birgitta very well. She had been one of the more obvious sweethearts of the soldiers.

"It didn't work out."

"So you went and married Birgitta? But that should be no surprise. Birgitta was a good looking girl."

"She still is. She has remarried. You've been wise not to get married."

"Is that wisdom? With me it has been more a matter of lacking initiative. Or failing to do anything about it. But now I am planning to get married."

He had again ordered another round. We clinked our glasses. He called me his best friend. I thanked him.

"Do you remember that furlough you arranged for me?"

He didn't remember. I told him the story.

"I did it many times, but only for my best friends."

"Well, then, goodbye, sober days."

"Here's to a good friend."

"Why is it that everybody drinks?" I said then. "Or perhaps

they have always drunk. One just exaggerates the drinking of one's own generation. For that matter, I was supposed to stop drinking today."

"You'll never be able to do that."

I glanced at him and was almost incensed.

"And why not?"

"I know your nature. You will never be able to leave liquor alone."

There we were again. One should never start drinking with fools. I did not say anything, however, and emptied my glass. I did it in a little too hasty a manner. I couldn't handle it. I swallowed my spit, poured a glass of vichy water, rinsed out my mouth, and swallowed again. He stared at me calmly, and I got an urgent desire to punch him in the nose.

But I contented myself with restraining my temper, sat up straight, and adjusted my tie. At the same time I remembered why we had had that quarrel in the army. As a trainee leader of the platoon, upon seeing Sgt. Vatanen coming down the hill I called out, "Attention!" Mikkonen had not noticed Vatanen. He had remained standing at ease. I had yelled the command directly to him. Vatanen had given him four days of cleaning the soldiers' canteen and Mikkonen had come whining to me about it.

"So you know my nature," I shouted. "And I can't stop drinking because you have not been able to? And my life would go to hell just because your marriage didn't work out? Is that why I can't get married and stop drinking? For god's sake! Say something, you Fool!"

He looked vacantly at me.

"I'm a salesman. In that kind of work you get used to seeing and handling many different kinds of people."

"Oh, I see. But let's both shut up now and have another round."

I really didn't need any more, but I ordered out of sheer defiance. I decided to still prove something to him. I didn't know what, then pay the bill and leave.

"My good Friend, I..."

"Yes, what is it?"

"I would like to treat you to dinner."

"When? Now?"

"I would like to treat you to dinner tomorrow."

"At what time?"

"At eight."

"And what will you feed me?"

"Listen, now don't get excited."

The same salesman who had been interested in us a short while ago stared at us, his arm on the back of his chair.

"Just keep sucking on your cigaret, your neck won't get tired from that," I shouted to him. The man turned back to his table.

All of a sudden I felt quite sober. I would have left, but I had to wait for the bill. When the waitress came, I left the drink she brought me on the table, put my money into my pocket, and got up. Mikkonen emptied his glass. I told him to drink mine too. He drank it in a couple of swallows and said, "Let's go to my room, we'll have some beer brought over."

"I'm going home now."

"Remember to come tomorrow at half past eight. To this same place. You are my best friend and I want to treat you to a dinner. I don't pay bad with bad."

"Thank you very much."

I told him I would come, even though I knew I wouldn't. I would never come here again nor would I go to very many places in this city.

"And in March we'll go to Lapland," he said as we separated in front of the hotel.

"In March we'll go to hell!"

I took off. I had synthetic rubber heels on my shoes and kept slipping every now and then. A couple of times I fell down and my bare hands groped in the snow. It felt cold. My gloves had dropped out of my overcoat pocket. The squareheads leaning against the bridge railing sneered, "Just so Uncle doesn't fall into the ditch."

When I got to my room I took my suitcase from the cupboard and put the stack of papers I had left on the table into it.

"It's goodbye to another room."

I decided to try to get down the stairs with my suitcase. My suitcase had been the largest one in the department store, I could fit everything I needed into it.

I heard the downstairs door open. I tried to turn around with my suitcase and get back up. But then I remembered that it no longer would matter what impression the owners got of me. I kept on going down.

But it was Marke.

"Where are you going?"

"Away from here. It's impossible to stay here."

She looked at me in surprise. I tried to look sober.

"And why not?"

"I'm leaving here, leaving the whole city."

Marke looked at me for a little while and said, "Let's go and talk about it at least. Then you can leave.''

"No, I'm going now.''

"Why, for goodness' sake?''

"For your sake. It was for your sake also that I came.''

"You've been drinking.''

I sought her eyes. They were slightly accusing.

"I wasn't going to. But I couldn't do anything else.''

"Where are you going to go?''

"Away from here, away from you. I will spoil your life, I'm a drunken pig.''

Marke grabbed the suitcase and brought it into the room, then drew me in through the door.

"Out of the hallway so people won't hear.''

I sat on the bed and tumbled backwards.

"I have been drinking, yes.''

Marke sat beside me without saying a word. Nor could I say anything. She would not understand in the right way anyhow. She would reproach without understanding that it didn't make any difference whether she reproached or not. It was no use to say anything.

"Do you get drunk often?''

"Yes. I'm always drunk. I have always been drunk. I have never been anything but drunk.''

I asked for a cigaret. She dug one out of my pocket and gave me a light. I muttered to myself and said, "It's not that serious. It's not true.''

"What isn't true?''

"Nothing. Tomorrow I will be sober. And even that isn't true.''

"So you will drink tomorrow, too?''

"No I won't. I won't drink for many days, perhaps not for many weeks. That is not the issue. I cannot say what the issue is. Or, yes, I can: I am a drunkard. Nothing else.''

"Say something,'' I said then. Marke leaned over me and said, "Silly boy. Will you promise not to drink any more?''

"I would be lying if I promised. One can't promise something like that.''

"But you must promise me now.''

"All right. I promise.''

I became furious. But she held me in the bed and laughed at my ranting. I got up.

"You have a nurse's view of the world, you expect to cure me, don't you? You believe, you think, think whatever you want to, but I am a drunkard.''

"You promised you wouldn't drink any more."

"Yes, I can be such a great drunkard that I won't drink, if for no other reason than to prove that your nurse's world view is all wrong. Do you understand?"

"Just as long as you don't drink."

"You would be completely unneeded if there were no sick people!" I bellowed. She laughed. I was silent and felt almost sober. I went back into bed, closed my eyes, and talked freely about everything that came to my mind. Then I began to sing.

I woke up some time later. Marke had gone. My mind was clear and bright, as always after drinking if I hadn't made the mistake of mixing different kinds of liquor. I had sweated away the liquor. I didn't have a headache. I knew it would come if I tried to get up. I would try to prolong this false feeling of well-being for many hours by lying absolutely still and not straining my neck muscles with any unnecessary turning of my head. It was difficult. I couldn't stay in bed. I got up and developed a headache, went to my suitcase and found two envelopes of aspirin powder and took them with water. I couldn't keep them down. I took two more and they stayed down. I went back into bed and tried to find a comfortable position. I knew that my hangover would last only till noon. Downstairs the clock struck twelve midnight and it seemed only five minutes later when it struck four. In eight more hours, the length of a full working day, I would again be in good shape, better than during the whole week, even though this week had been one of the best weeks in my life. I had looked forward to seeing Marke and then had seen her. She had left here, had gone away from me, some hours ago.

The next time I woke up it was full day. I dug the stack of papers from my suitcase and began to work. I worked until seven. Then I telephoned Marke and listened as long as she kept on talking.

"Don't talk about that any more," I said, when I realized she had stopped. "Let's go to the theater tomorrow night."

I dialed another number.

"Hello. I'll probably be a little late."

"Well, just so you come. An unexpected reunion like ours needs celebration."

"You can say that again. Especially since we haven't seen each other for years."

"You'll be here as soon as you can then. 'Bye."

" 'Bye. But one more thing. I guess I really blew off at the mouth last night."

"That was nothing. You were just a little drunk."

"That's what I thought, it was nothing else. See you."

"See you."

Marja-Leena Mikkola (1939)

Marja-Leena Mikkola, a writer of short stories and novels with social and political themes, social protest song lyrics, social documentaries, variety shows, and filmscripts, has more recently become one of Finland's leading children's authors. Born in Salo, a city located between Helsinki and Turku, she earned her degree in philosophy in 1963. She worked as a library trainee and served as office manager of the Finnish Writers' Union, 1961-64. Since then she has worked as a free lance writer. In her first writings she describes the youth of the 1960's with calm realism, writing about them in a traditional manner but with her own personal style. Her early collection of short stories, NAISIA (WOMEN), 1962, centers around young women, many of them rootless and dependent. Her early novel of rootless youth, TYTTÖ KUIN KITARA (A GIRL LIKE A GUITAR), 1964, has ballad-like overtones and is the story of the unhappy love between a nightclub singer and her pianist. In her novel, ETSIKKO (VISITATION), 1967, love and politics mingle in a story about two left-wing intellectuals. As she continued writing, Mikkola's social awareness and satire grew stronger; her interests covered social and political themes, especially woman's role in society. In 1971 she wrote RASKA PUUVILLA (HEAVY COTTON), a book of interviews with women workers in a Tampere textile factory. A short story collection, LÄÄKÄRIN ROUVA (THE DOCTOR'S WIFE), appeared in 1972. Her children's books include AMALIA, KARHU (AMALIA BEAR), 1975, ANNI MANNINEN, 1977, and LUMIJOUTSEN (THE SNOW SWAN), 1978. The story *Aila*, from her early 1962 collection, WOMEN, is about the rootlessness and dependence of young women of the 1950's.

Aila (1962)

Riitta sat in the car for a while in front of the country store and waited, but when Erkki didn't show up she got out of the car. Some clothes, two sleeping bags, a red mesh bag filled with provisions, and a separate bag with crayfish traps filled the back seat. Hay was stacked in ricks on both sides of the road. Wild parsley and purple clover grew profusely along the road. Riitta glanced at the top of the hill and saw smoke rising out of chimneys. People were heating their Saturday saunas. In between the hayricks she saw three small girls approaching. They were wearing dandelion wreaths on their heads.

"Come here!" the little girls called, stopping at the edge of the field across the road. "Come here! Come here!"

Riitta started to walk toward them. The girls had white, tangled hair, their lips were red from eating berries. They had some strawberries hidden in the hay. The smallest girl was bow-legged.

"What is it?" Riitta asked.

The girls jumped over the ditch and began to giggle. They put their arms around each other and twirled about on the road, the smallest pluckily hanging on to the other two.

"We weren't calling you!" the girls giggled. Holding back their laughter, they looked at each other, then burst out laughing. Grabbing each other around the neck, they danced about, their heads together, chanting, "We weren't calling you, we weren't calling you!"

The girls became still noisier, dragging each other along the road, their wreaths askew.

"We were calling the cat, we were calling the cat!"

Riitta returned to the car. Bored, she sat in the car, toyed with various knobs and stole one of Erkki's cigarets. The girls were now farther down the road.

Finally Erkki came, a large package under his arm. The little girls came back and stood near the car. Erkki started the engine, the girls watched quietly as Riitta, sitting next to Erkki, sped past them. The smallest one was gravely picking her nose, her flower wreath askew, tipped over one eye.

"What more did you have to buy?" Riitta asked

"I was so busy in the city I didn't get to buy everything there."

They turned on to a side road. Riitta remembered every large rock in it which you had to watch out for when riding a bike over the road; she remembered the oddly shaped birches, the strawberry patches on the southern slope. The river flowed dark green in its bed along an alder grove, past the clothes washing platforms and continued flowing under the bridge of the large farm. Now they turned into a narrow side road and it looked as if they were driving straight into the alder grove. Only when right in front of Aila's cottage did one realize there actually was a cottage there and behind it a garden. Aila was in the garden and hurried into the front yard.

"My goodness, what a surprise!" she called on the way.

Aila is Riitta's aunt, her father's oldest sister and is very much like him. Aila always walks slightly stooped over, clenching her fists even in her old age. She smokes cigarets all day long, sometimes even at night if she happens to wake up. The logs of her cottage are weather-beaten. She lets her garden grow in reckless abandon with thistles, timothy grass, apple trees, a few maples, and it abounds with flowers of all colors and shapes. Most often one will find Aila among the flowers in her garden, wearing the overalls and leather gloves she got used to wearing as a construction worker. Aila enjoys a thunderstorm after a hot day like today.

"Look at those clouds, for goodness sakes," Aila says, sitting in her overalls on the open porch, her legs spread apart, the hoe in her hands. "Riitta, if you're not as afraid of thunderstorms now as you always were as a child, we could eat out here on the porch."

Riitta had not noticed that storm clouds had gathered in the sky. Much of the sky was now dark blue and Aila's large, fiery red flowers on the east side of the garden looked as if they were listening for the rain. Somehow Aila had gotten her flowers to bloom profusely. Many had asked for her secret but Aila always burst into a laugh saying it was all in the hands.

"If you have hands, like mine, like pine roots, then the garden will flourish," Aila would reply.

"Miss Aila, your garden is truly magnificent," Erkki said.

"You don't have to be so formal, young Man, just call me Aila. You'll soon be a member of the family, anyway. When are you two getting married, or shouldn't I even ask such a question? Yes, the garden is pretty nice, but the stems of the flowers could be longer. I'd like to have flowers with stems taller than a person so when you walk among them you only see a small patch of blue sky above."

Riitta went into the kitchen and noticed that the cloth over the dishtowels was still there. "Home Sweet Home" was embroidered in red thread on the towel cover and a girl holding a sprinkling can was watering flowers. The spray of water had been embroidered in short, broken lines. Riitta looked at the hotpads. The red one she had made as a little girl in the sewing class in primary school was still there. And Aila had saved it.

Aila came into the kitchen and put the coffee pot on the stove. Riitta was just opening a drawer in the kitchen chest. She turned around quickly when she heard Aila coming.

"You just look around, my Girl, I've still got some of your old drawings."

Aila went back to the porch. The sky had grown darker. Riitta opened one of the drawers in the chest and saw her drawing on which she had written: *War* to AILA from Riitta. Bombers were flying from all directions at the same time. She had actually been a cubist at that time.

"The boys ripped it," Riitta is crying and brings her drawing, which is torn in two, to Aila. "For god's sake!" Aila says and heads for the yard. Riitta's cousins and their mother live just across from Aila's cottage.

"Keep your brats in line or I'll do it for you!" Aila rages in the yard. She comes inside and says, "They think they can do anything they want to just because their father is dead and their mother works in the city. Damn it! Come with Aila. Aila's making coffee bread. Let's make an S shape with the dough."

Aila came into the kitchen and opened the cupboard. A delicate aroma of spices wafted out. Aila took out a loaf of coffee bread saying, "It's lucky I did some baking today since you brought that boyfriend of yours along. I won't have to serve him stale coffee bread. Come and have coffee now."

They sat on the porch and Aila poured coffee into the cups. On the table she had put thick, yellow cream and coffee bread, which was soft and round, just like Aila. Aila had also placed on the table a low, wide, wooden bowl filled with wild parsley, roses, and daisies.

"My goodness, look at that lightning," Aila says and snuffs out her cigaret.

The garden around them is dark green and a delicate, moist fragrance floats up to the porch. The sky is completely black. Lightning flashes in a long streak, followed instantly by the roar of thunder.

"It's right above us," Aila says and stares up into the sky. "Don't be afraid now, Riitta."

"I'm no longer afraid of thunderstorms."

Riitta gets up and walks to the other side of the porch. Erkki goes to get cigarets from the car. As Riitta turns, lightning flashes again and Riitta sees how Aila is craning her neck toward the sky, her eyes half-closed as if listening for something. During the next roar of thunder the rain begins to pelt down and forms a green haze in the air. Aila's face glistens and it looks as if at any moment she will break either into a smile or into tears, Riitta doesn't know which. The question reaches her lips now no more than before. Unknowingly, Riitta reaches out her hand toward Aila. Aila sees it and turns.

"A fine rain," says Aila, short of breath. "Do you remember when we got all wet on the berrypicking trip?"

Riitta has a fever and is delirious. "There's a goblin in the sewing machine! In the sewing machine!" she cries and Aila runs heavily to her. "Don't be afraid, Aila's little Darling," Aila says and lifts up Riitta's head. "Here, take these drops. Aila will give her little Buttercup some drops."

"Where's Mother?" Riitta cries out.

"Mother's in the city. We'll go there in a couple of weeks."

"Aila has to come too," says Riitta.

"Of course Aila will come too. Take the drops now so the sickness will go away. Aila will come with you. Now Aila will go back to work on the building."

Riitta is well again and Aila carries her to the sauna. Aila undresses Riitta gently and places her in a tub of water on a bench. Then Aila comes and climbs up. Aila looks much larger and heavier naked than with her clothes on. Her stomach is lined with creases. Aila sits on the bench and with a bath whisk starts beating her legs, which are covered with black and blue blotches.

"Black and blue," Riitta says pointing to Aila's legs.

"That's right, black and blue veins, one broken vein right next to another. Now we will wash Riitta so the sickness will go away altogether. We'll tell the evil thing to go back to where it came from."

Riitta splashes the water, her soap drops under the benches.

"Devil, go back where you came from! Go, Devil, go away!" Riitta screams with joy.

"You little Rascal, did you drop your soap again? Now I'll have to go down and crawl under the benches once again. Dear, oh dear, what will I do with you?"

When Riitta has been washed she has to wait in the tub on the lower bench while Aila quickly washes herself. "So Riitta won't get chilled," Aila says. In the dressing room Riitta is wrapped up in a clean towel and Aila, her face red and shining, combs Riitta's hair. "Aila's own little Sweetheart," Aila says and takes her into her arms. "Now we'll warm some milk for you."

"Put some more cream in your coffee," Aila said. "You've gotten so thin, my Girl. Young Man, you better take care of this girl so she doesn't get it into her head to lose weight."

"Girls nowadays talk of nothing but their figures and dieting," Erkki said. "As if there was something wrong with being a little round. At least I find those thin, long-necked fashion models just horrible."

"That's easy for you to say since you stay thin however much you stuff yourself," Riitta said. "Give Aila and me a cigaret. Don't be so inconsiderate."

"My own brand suits me just fine, but thank you just the same," Aila said. "Where do you work, young Man?"

"I have about a year of school still left," Erkki said, a cigaret in his mouth and lighting one for Riitta. "This summer I'm working in an architect's office."

"So you're going to be a builder of houses. You're in the same trade as I am. I've built houses all my life," Aila said and exploded into laughter. "The same trade, the very same trade. Good, excellent."

Even in the city Riitta lives with Aila. "Your mother doesn't earn very much and she has your little brother to support too," Aila says. Not even here are they rid of the cousins. They now live with their mother in the other room of the apartment.

Riitta is sitting on the cellar steps in the stony yard. She is crying quietly. The cousins are scuffling in the yard and every now and then one of them comes to snatch a wisp of hair off Riitta's head. White wisps of hair are floating dolefully here and there in the yard. When Aila, wearing her overalls, comes home from work and appears at the gate, Riitta starts to cry out loud and runs to meet her.

"What have they done to you now?" Aila shouts. Sobbing, Riitta points to the wisps of hair in the yard.

"Damn it!" Aila bursts out, runs to the cousins and beats at them. "You darned brats, one of these days I'm going to knock your skulls together with a bang!" The cousins' mother is watching from the windows and begins to scream.

"You're not putting one foot on our side, not a single one of you!" Aila shouts toward the window. "You're after me like a tail and the old lady can't even keep her brats in line!"

Snorting in anger, Aila picks up the hair from the yard. Riitta follows behind, sobbing. They go inside and still wearing her overalls, Aila sits down on the daybed and takes Riitta onto her lap.

"Oh, what you will still have to suffer in your lifetime, you poor little Devil," Aila says and begins to cry. Riitta looks at the wisps of hair in her hand and sobs along with Aila. Finally, Aila makes potato soup, puts the bowls on the oilcloth and slips a large pat of butter into Riitta's soup.

The rain has stopped and Erkki has gone to check over the gate, which needed fixing.

"Your life is turning out quite nicely, isn't it?" Aila says. "Such a fine boyfriend. Now we'll all have a sauna and enjoy a pleasant Saturday night. Tomorrow you may want to go fishing."

"Well, listen, Aila, we're really on our way to go crayfishing about twenty kilometers from here. We have a tent with us."

"Oh, I see. Well, that's sure a rotten turn of events. Here I was, so happy already. All your visits here nowadays are so very short," said Aila, looking straight at Riitta.

Riitta is with Aila at the Workers' Hall, where a Communist march is being planned. Red banners are standing up at the corner of the building. Some men, who have been drinking, pass by. The wife of one of them stops beside Aila and Riitta.

"Is that your daughter?"

"She's my dead brother's daughter."

"Is she joining the march too? Is she a member of the Young Pioneers? Hello there, Riitta, I remember you, I knew your father. How are you, Riitta?"

"No, I'm not taking her along. She'd just get tired and start whimpering in the middle of everything. And, of course, her father became a Social Democrat. You knew that, didn't you?"

"Yes, so I remember. But he sure was a nice boy, so witty and he always arranged things..."

"And now the girl's mother says she wants his memory honored and so on. Her mother wouldn't like it if I took her on these marches. And, of course, she'd get tired, poor little Thing."

They moved into the hall to practice their songs. The workers' mixed chorus sang and Riitta moved down the aisle in front of the chorus and began to beat time with her foot. On one occasion Riitta recited a poem:

"Meow, meow, little Kitty, where is your home?"

"Of all Kitten Cape's maidens, I am the smallest one."

"Have you any sisters there?" "Yes, no less than seven."

"And brothers are there some as well?" "Yes, one sent to us from heaven."

Aila has tears in her eyes.

When Aila and Riitta went up into the attic, Aila said, "Look at these rugs I've woven." Aila had her loom in the attic. "I'll give them to you when you get married. A kitchen must have proper rag rugs."

"What beautiful colors, so bright and gay," Riitta said, fingering one of the rugs.

The rugs were very bright and of the same style as those covering Aila's kitchen and bedroom floors.

"If you'd rather have other colors, just let me know, and I'll weave them for you."

"But these colors go with everything."

"Since you've been used to this kind of rug from your childhood, I just thought you'd like some for yourself."

"I'd love some," Riitta said.

In the summer Riitta walks around naked in the village, her little belly bulging out like a drum.

"There goes Aila's little sweetheart walking around in her birthday suit again," says Aila. Riitta's belly keeps peeping out through the leaves of the birch trees, which is how she knows it's Riitta.

Many women come to visit them in the summertime. "What is Riitta going to be when she grows up? Are you going to be a construction worker too?"

"For god's sake, don't lay such a curse on the child's future," Aila says.

"I'm going to be the master gardener in God's garden," Riitta says, eating blueberries, her belly covered with blueberry stains.

"What are you saying, Child?" Aila asks, baffled.

"A gardener in God's garden," Riitta says. "Aila is one too."

"What kind of silly nonsense have they been feeding her in Sunday school?" the women ask.

From the attic Aila and Riitta walked to the garden. The rain had stopped. A pleasant fragrance rose from the garden, everything was wet, drops of water glistened on th leaves and branches as the sunlight struck them.

"I have some new flowers. These you've never seen here before," Aila said, stooping over slightly. "They're some new kind of amaryllis."

"Aila, if I ever have a house of my own, will you come and make a garden for me?"

"You bet I will. Can you smell all the different scents? Look, I've put a bench here, let's sit down."

Riitta is walking to school carrying a red shoulder bag. At Eerikki Hill she always stops to look for the Siren boys. There are three of them. They do not go to school yet and that makes them so angry that they throw stones. They are plump, smooth, shiny, very small, tanned by the sun, and always dirty. In her evening prayer Riitta always prays that they not throw stones.

One day there is an accident. One of their stones hits Sirpa in the eye. She is walking home with Riitta. Blood spurts from Sirpa's eye and the Siren boys instantly vanish into their hiding places and the hill is empty. Riitta is alarmed by Sirpa's crying. The blood keeps coming and Riitta feels like throwing up. They walk hurriedly toward home, Riitta holds Sirpa's hand and from time to time she has to swallow so she won't throw up. When they get to Sirpa's house, Sirpa's mother is combing her hair and rushes out to the road, her hair hanging over her eyes, comb in hand. Her face is gray.

Aila marches over to the Sirens the following day and the boys never show themselves on Eerikki Hill again.

"Their mother and father are such wishy-washy people," Aila says, "with three pudgy small trolls always sneaking up on people, like small devils."

"Now when will you come again?" Aila asked when the three of them were once again sitting on the porch.

"When are you coming? You never come to the city anymore."

"I'll be sure to come when you have your own home. I'll come for sure then. And I'll take care of the children whenever necessary. I just don't care to go back and forth to the city nowadays. I have my pension and then I go out to do a little housecleaning around here."

One of the cousins, Mauri, has come to the country with them since he is so wild they cannot keep him at the playground in the city. Mauri is fat, white-haired, younger than Riitta. Mauri says nothing, but does plenty. He rips Riitta's doll apart, throws rocks at the flowers, and snaps the tops off them. But he says nothing, just grunts and runs hard. Riitta is afraid of him. Sometimes Mauri takes the faded, dark red beret he has brought with him from the city and pulls it down over his eyebrows. His eyes glare below the beret. Then Mauri grabs a whip he has made for the cats and brandishes it in front of Riitta. As his beret moves up, he pulls it down in a fury and keeps on brandishing his whip. He circles around Riitta, she doesn't dare to move.

On one occasion when Aila sees this, she rushes at Mauri, snatches the whip out of his hand, gives him a few swats, snaps the whip in two, and scolds him. Aila leads Riitta inside immediately and examines her but finds no marks since Mauri never hits, he just threatens. Mauri isn't bothered at all by the incident and runs away puffing and is back again in the garden trampling the flowers.

"What kind of whipsnapper does that brat think he is? Will his pranks never end? Thinks he's some kind of czar!"

"Now I'm going in to make sandwiches and get you some milk," Aila says. "It's so nice to eat out here now that the sun has come out again."

"Aila, don't make anything, we've got sandwiches and milk in the car."

"Yes, but not country-style bread nor country-fresh milk. You just wait."

"No, but really, Aila."

"You just wait. White flatbread. I made it myself."

When Aila came back her hair was pushed behind her ears and Riitta saw she was wearing her sapphire earrings.

"Now you eat."

Aila has a friend, a widower with five children. He has invited them to his house. It is messy there but cheerful. Aila sits on the sofa, silent, and looks around. The man makes coffee and a girl with thin legs sets the table. Aila is wearing sapphire earrings, the man has given them to her saying they had belonged to his wife. Riitta does not dare to join in the game of train the two smallest boys are playing. They sit at the coffee table and Aila dunks Riitta's coffee bread into Riitta's cup, where it turns into pulp.

"This place is such a mess since there's no grown-up woman here to clean it," the man says as he pours coffee into his saucer and slurps it. Aila says nothing, the sun strikes the earrings which gleam through Aila's shining, rumpled hair.

They sit in the living room, the man says a few words, Aila doesn't speak, just looks and adjusts the ribbon in Riitta's hair. The thin-legged girl sits, restless, in an old red armchair. First she rests her chin in her hands, then raises her arms behind her neck, and finally pulls her legs under her.

"Don't put your feet on the chair while we have company, Girl," the man says.

"Shut your big mouth," the girl says.

Aila looks at the girl, who now leaves. They sit a little while longer and then Aila gets ready to go.

"Thank you and we'll see you sometime. I don't think anything will come of this," Aila says and the man walks irresolutely behind them to the hallway. He doesn't know what to say.

"I cannot bring Riitta into a household where the children speak that way to their parents," Aila mutters. "But thank you and goodbye."

The widower refuses to take back the earrings.

"At least you'll have something for a keepsake," the man says.

"How's your mother?" Aila asks.

"She's just fine."

"And your brother?"

"He's starting sixth grade now."

"Is he still as good in arithmetic?"

"Yes, he gets better all the time."

They still make a few sauna trips together, riding in a blue bus from the outskirts toward downtown. Aila carries her own bath whisks. She is wearing velvet slacks. Riitta has her hair in braids.

"Your mother wants you with her now that her life is in good order again," Aila says. "Your mother has shown a lot of courage. You are going on to secondary school so you won't end up a dumbbell like me."

Riitta is choked up.

"Why don't you go and look at the other rooms," Aila said, "since you won't be coming here for a long time to visit old Aila again anyway."

Riitta got up and went into the living room. She looked at the daybed where she used to sleep during the summers, lifted the bedspread and saw that the old patchwork quilt was still in use. Most of the patches had a place in her memory. She moved to the sleeping alcove and pulled out a drawer in the table. There were photographs and newspaper clippings listing the names of all the students graduating the year she had graduated. Aila had saved her grade school certificate and her drawings. In another drawer she found some of Aila's embroidery patterns and under them a large drawing. Riitta took a closer look. The drawing showed a house, its roof peeping above tall grass and red flowers. The colors were dark green, scarlet, bright yellow. In the midst of the giant-sized flowers something which showed some semblance to a human being seemed to be walking. The sky had been painted pale blue and in the middle of it was an orange sun, a huge, round ball, with broken lines going off in every direction. The sun's rays, painted as if by a five-year old. Aila's painting, her secret primitive dream. The orange sun of a child, hidden away in a drawer.

"Aila dear, now we must go," said Riitta, back on the porch. "Some friends are coming and we're supposed to meet them at one of the side roads. There's a shallow brook where there should be crayfish."

Aila got up heavily and wiped the table. The sapphire earrings glinted through her gray hair.

"I see. Then you have to go. But it would have been so nice if Riitta could have stayed overnight. Someone could have picked her up tomorrow."

Aila remained standing beside the railing of the porch and waved her heavy arm a few times. Riitta turned to wave back and heard Aila's muffled voice, "Damn it, Girl, if you don't come more often to see me..."

They drove quickly to the highway. Erkki whistled and Riitta turned on the portable radio.

"A marvelous individual, your aunt," Erkki said. "You don't often see her kind any more."

"Oh, they're still around."

"She was so uniquely natural."

"So she is."

Beyond the pine forest the road made a turn and then they stopped at a side road. The others were already there, three boys and three girls.

"Hey, we can leave our cars in the large open space at the end of the road and we can put some traps into the brook that runs past there.''

"Hi, Liisa. It's a little cool, isn't it?''

"I really didn't want to come since I'm pregnant but Heikki said I wouldn't have to do anything.''

"When do you expect the baby?''

"I'm three months along now.''

The cars were driven to the end of the road and unloaded.

"The girls can stay here for a while, we'll go look for a suitable camp site.''

The boys disappeared along the path. Some distance away they could see a lake.

"There could be crayfish in this kind of brook,'' Liisa said.

"Look at the bottom, all muddy and slimy.''

"It smells awful. Let's go over to that pine log, we can sit there.''

The girls jumped over the brook and all four settled to sit on the log.

"Let's pick some ferns to chase away the mosquitoes.''

"Well, and how is married life?'' Riitta asked.

"Oh, it's fun,'' said Liisa. "I wouldn't have wanted to have a baby right away though, but now I'm used to the idea that it's coming.''

"The mosquitoes here are just awful. Good god, these everlasting trips to the woods. This hunting and fishing has developed into a regular obsession with the boys.''

"I'm going right to bed as soon as the tents are set up.''

The forest was shady. Spruce trees had been chopped down and the trunks had been left lying on the ground. The road was brand new and was of coarse gravel.

The boys came back.

"We've found a superb spot.''

"Is that right? Right beside an ant hill as last time?''

"No, this place is really splendid.''

"The most beautiful spot in the country, I'm sure.''

"But it is a little windy there.''

"Sure, and then we'll have to freeze all night again.''

"We'll build a campfire of course.''

The boys lifted the packs on their backs and they all started walking along the path. They climbed a small hill and then descended to a heath. In a short while they reached a swamp where a few logs served as a causeway, then a ditch with a narrow plank across it. Suddenly the lake lay before them. To the right was a rowboat, locked to a tree. They walked past it and came to a small point where obviously somebody had been camping some days before. The campfire spot was almost in the middle of the point. There were a few trees here and there. A dead pine tree had fallen across the water, its branches touching bottom. Riitta immediately went to check if it would support her.

"We should take a picture. It's such a grand old ruin."

The lake was gray and in the distance two loons were swimming. The sun set and the wind died down a little.

"Not a single sign that there was a thunderstorm today," said Erkki.

Two tents were up now.

"Are we going to sleep in the tepee too?" Riitta asked.

"Of course."

"Oh, I thought the women would sleep two to a tent and all four men in the tepee."

"You'll see what fun it is to sleep in here with the campfire burning in front," Erkki said.

"Is the tepee going to be left open?"

"Of course. It will be a semicircle, one half will be open. We'll sleep here with Jussi and Irma."

"I see. On the bare ground?"

"No, we'll gather some spruce sprigs to put underneath for warmth."

The boys left to get poles for the tepee and the sprigs. Riitta went to sit on the pine tree over the water and gazed over the lake. The portable radio was playing. After a while she and Irma went to carry the sprigs which the boys had cut on the hill.

"These won't be enough," Jussi said. "These spruce trees are so old it's impossible to cut anything off them."

"Leave the knife with us, we can hunt for the sprigs while you look for poles for the tepee," Riitta said.

"All right, but don't cut your hands, now. And you'd better take the branches from those creeping spruces at the shore, they're fresh."

The girls walked down the hill and found a couple of spruces that didn't look too dried out. They stripped off the lower branches and got armfuls of sprigs. On their way back they circled to the lake and with the knife cut sprugs off the creeping spruces. Then they walked past the rowboat. Beside it stood a strange boy who looked as if he was a farm boy.

"Damn it, somebody's taken my boat from this shore," the boy greeted them.

"Oh, that's too bad."

"I've walked around the whole lake and haven't found a trace of it."

"This is the only boat that was here when we came," Irma said.

"Somebody must have borrowed it," the boy said.

"A friend, perhaps?" Riitta asked.

"No, I don't have any friends here. I have a cabin nearby. Around here they often fill a boat with rocks and sink it."

"Just for meanness?" Irma asked.

"Sure, and then the devils lift the boat from the bottom when the owner has disappeared from the scene."

Fuming, the boy disappeared along the path leading around the shore. The girls went to the tents and threw their sprigs by the campfire. The boys had already found the poles and were pounding them into the ground. The tepee itself lay on the ground, smoke-blackened, full of holes.

"How come it's in such poor condition?" Irma asked.

"It's been used on a number of trips to Lapland, as the young lady very well knows."

"On the shore we met a boy whose boat had been stolen," said Riitta.

"He was here too to ask about it."

"I wonder if he thought we had taken his boat?"

The poles for the tepee were set in and the boys began to hoist the canvas. Slowly they wound it around the poles, leaving the front open. On the canvas someone had painted red and white pictures of salmon and grouse. The top of the tepee was black from soot.

"You didn't use the sprigs we brought," Riitta said. "You've got only one layer of sprigs on the bottom."

"We can still put them in. Give them to me."

"I can do it too," Riitta said.

"Yes, that's exactly how you do it, but let's space them so we get more bounce, then it's better for sleeping."

"All the others are in their tents eating except us, for we always have this tepee, which is so practical," Irma said.

"You'll see how cozy it will be in here when the campfire is burning," Erkki said.

"At least we've got the tent with the most personality."

It was still light. The boys had said it wouldn't be worthwhile putting in the traps until around ten o'clock and they were now fishing in the channel. The campfire was lit and Riitta was making coffee. Deep inside the tepee she had made sandwiches, which were now half-covered with ashes. The coffee water was boiling in a blackened kettle.

"It's smoky in here," Irma complained from the back of the tent.

"What's wrong that half the smoke is blowing in there?"

The boys returned from fishing. Riitta served Erkki coffee.

"Listen, how are we going to sleep in there when it's so full of smoke," Riitta said.

"You lie flat on the ground, then the smoke won't bother you."

"No, we've got to put out the fire before we go to sleep." Irma said.

"And then you'll complain you're cold."

"It's really nice to drink coffee outside," Riitta said. "Look, it's getting dark."

"We're going to set our crayfish traps now. Watch the fire."

The boys had baited the traps beforehand. They picked them up and disappeared in the direction of the brook.

It got dark. The girls gathered around the fire. They could no longer see the lake. From the opposite shore came the voices of other crayfishers. Riitta grilled herself some baloney. After a while the boys came to get their fishing tackle and left again.

"It's just delightful to sit by the fire," Riitta said.

The radio played a Russian folksong.

"What are you doing on your summer vacation? Are you really going to Leningrad?" Leila asked.

"Yes, we've decided to go. Riitta and I have already bought our tickets," Irma said.

"Well, I for one, wouldn't set my foot in that country," Liisa said.

"Why not? I at least am curious to see it. You're not a narrow minded person, are you? Or are you one of those who still have phobias about the Russians?" Irma tossed a branch on the fire.

"Well, just on principle I'm not interested in matters over there," Liisa said.

Riitta threw some berry twigs into the fire.

"Besides, my mother would have a fit if I went there," Liisa continued. "She is a person of principles. She is the authority in our house. Perhaps it's because she's a teacher. For instance, as a child I never used the informal 'you' when addressing her."

"Oh, good god," Irma said. "My mother would consider it a good joke if I used the formal 'you' on her."

"Oh, no, right from the time I was a very small child I was made to understand not to use even the formal 'you'. I had to avoid addressing her directly."

"That is truly odd. I have never before heard anything..."

"You know, my mother is a strong character. But she is better looking, smarter, and has more determination than most people. For instance, the books I could read, the movies I could see, and even my friends were all selected for me. As a child I liked to play with our apartment caretaker's little girl, but when mother found this out, she put a quick stop to it.''

"How terrible. I never had such limits on me when I was a child.'' Irma said. "Riitta, you didn't either, did you?''

Riitta threw more berry twigs into the fire and watched as they slowly began to catch fire.

"No,'' she said.

"I'm certainly going to teach this first child of ours that it cannot use the informal 'you' to me directly but will have to call me 'Mother','' Liisa said.

"I see. And do you think then that this will in some way improve the relationship between you and your child?'' Irma asked.

"I can't say anything about that. It's just that that's the custom in our family.''

It was quiet. The fire crackled.

"Did you have a lot of quarrels, you and your mother?'' Riitta asked after staring into the fire a while.

"Guess how many times,'' Liisa said.

"How did you address her when you were quarreling? You couldn't shout, 'Keep your mouth shut', could you?'' Irma asked.

"No, I said, 'Mother, please, attend to your own affairs.' ''

It was pitch dark. Riitta dug a cigaret out of her pocket.

"In any case, two weeks from now we will be in Leningrad and certainly enjoying it. Russia has always interested me,'' Irma said.

"Yes, and go in peace. I don't want to meddle in other people's affairs,'' Liisa said. "But it's my opinion that a Russian is a Russian and a Communist is a Communist, even if you fry them in butter.''

"If for a short time you had my job and on the home visits saw what I see, you would see a large assortment of very different kinds of Communists,'' Irma said.

Riitta was lying on her back, quietly smoking her cigaret.

On the shore they saw lights from flashlights and they could hear voices and hooting.

"Let's not answer. Who knows what it is.''

"I read in the paper that this year the crayfish are soft-shelled and tiny and will not go into traps.''

The boys had gone to check half the traps but found only seven crayfish. When they came back from the brook they had fifteen crayfish altogether.

"Let's grill some baloney now, we'll eat the crayfish at home,'' the boys said.

Riitta was getting sleepy. The others began to sing around the fire and the boys told their army stories once again. Riitta crawled into her sleeping bag and curled up on the floor of the tepee. Smoke poured in steadily. Her eyes began to smart. She squeezed them shut, but tears began to flow. She crawled to the other side of the tepee but it didn't help. She put her head outside and breathed deeply.

"It's impossible to sleep in here," Riitta said.

Erkki came to her and gave her coffee.

"We didn't come here to sleep."

Irma came into the tent looking sleepy. It was one o'clock. Irma tried to sleep, she even pulled her head down into the sleeping bag but the smoke kept pouring in. The others were singing around the campfire.

"This is awful," Riitta complained. "I should have stayed at Aila's..."

Irma turned and twisted and complained in one corner of the tepee, then tossed her sleeping bag aside and went out for a walk.

"It makes me mad one can't get any sleep here. There's too much noise and too much smoke for the eyes," Irma said as she left.

After a while Riitta came out of the tepee with her eyes all red and walked to the shore. Liisa had already gone into her tent to sleep.

Dawn was breaking, it felt as if the darkness had just brushed past them, withdrawing quickly. The birds had begun to twitter gently. It was as light as on an early winter day. Riitta walked slowly over the bridge, her hands in her pockets. The darkness and the girls' conversation around the campfire seemed distant and unreal.

"Here I am now," she thought. She walked back to the point. The fire had been extinguished and everyone lay quiet. She lay down beside Erkki and burrowed into her sleeping bag. The light filtered through the canvas of the tent and she could not sleep. Finally she turned on her side, her face almost touching the canvas of the tent and she felt sleep coming.

"Tomorrow I will go to Aila," she thought.

Timo Mukka (1944 - 1973)

Timo Mukka, romanticist and pacifist, was born in Sweden, where his parents were war refugees from Finnish Lapland. When he was six months old he returned with his parents to a devastated Lapland. His two older sisters remained in Sweden with their foster parents. He completed elementary school and in 1961-62 studied at the Finnish Academy of Arts in Helsinki. He returned to Lapland, where he wrote slightly stylized novels about life there, attempting new forms of expression and emerging as a social critic. His novels are spontaneous, naive, somewhat melodramatic. Mukka was a romanticist who believed that love was the power that united all humans and influenced their actions, and his writings leaned toward pacifism. His works include a novel subtitled *A Ballad*, MAA ON SYNTINEN LAULU (THE EARTH IS A SINFUL SONG), 1964, a harsh picture of postwar Lapland, which was a great success as a film in Finland after Mukka's death; a book containing two long short stories entitled TABU (THE TABOO), 1965; the novels, TÄÄLTÄ JOSTAKIN (HEREABOUTS), 1965, a strongly pacifist story dealing with military training, and LAULU SIPIRJAN LAPSISTA; (A SONG OF SIBERIAN CHILDREN), 1966; poems, PUNAISTA (RED), 1966; a short story collection, KOIRAN KUOLEMA (THE DEATH OF A DOG), 1967; JA KESÄN HEINÄ KUOLEE (AND THE SUMMER GRASS DIES), 1968, a story of illness. He died in a hospital in Rovaniemi, the capital city of Lapland, at the age of twenty-nine after many years of struggle with poor health. *The Death of a Dog* is from the 1967 collection of the same name. Written in a stylized form, it begins as a poem and develops into a story about illness and death. Mukka does not explain the story, he simply tells it.

The Death Of A Dog (1967)

Summer is coming
god's summer
then father will buy Tuomas a bicycle when Tuomas is big
enough to ride by himself with no one holding on...then Tuomas will
get it
boys
Tuomas will get a bicycle then
he is so happy about it
father went to the church welfare office
father went to work
father is coming in the evening
father is coming in the evening
the clerk at the welfare office tells father: you ought to know that
the township has no funds...what it does not have, it cannot give...
father is coming in the evening
father is coming...Tuomas waits for father so intently, father is
so big other men cannot even compare; father has long arms and a
hairy chest, no one has a father as strong as we have...as strong and
big a father...
the birch is in bud
father will come then in the evening...oh if only evening would
come soon
(the snow has melted from the ground. Everything smelled of
green, blossoming summer: it's *coming* now!) The snow has melted
and most of the moisture from the earth has floated into heaven,
where all the relatives live. These were the first days of summer.
The tarred paper roof of the house was now light in color and hardly
wet at all---just as if the dark and long winter had never existed. The
sun has made everything look so different. And then there were also
the spring winds which devoured the moisture, every last drop of it
and every wet stain. But against the wall of the shed was a bed of
straw on which a mongrel dog lay day after day---the straw was wet
inside. It was decaying and the shavings and straw next to the
ground had molded and rotted and turned to dirt. It's impossible for
such straw to dry out. From it an acrid odor rises along the
sun-warmed wall of the shed. The dog lies motionless. Her fur is
messy and shaggy, like the fur of any sick dog---a perfect nest for
filth and vermin,
Turre is sick,

but when father comes
it will be wonderful!
father will make Turre well

when seven-year old Little-Tuomas, a serious looking boy, brought a
bowl of food to Turre in the morning, the dog got up on her stiffened
hind legs and licked a little at the potatoes and gravy, but she did
this only out of courtesy. As soon as Little-Tuomas had left, the dog
dragged herself back into her hollow in the straw, curled up, lay
there motionless, half asleep, letting the sun warm her coat, matted
and unkempt from the illness. The disease had dimmed Turre's
eyes: disease glowed glimmering red in the whites of her eyes and
matter dripped from them on to her nose. With his stick Tuomas
dug around in the straw uncovering dirty black rot. Then he stirred
up the dog's food with the stick: steam pushed its way through the
congealing grease.

Turre will get well...father is coming tomorrow. Father will make
Turre well, said Little-Tuomas.

He scratched the dog behind her ear.

Turre yelped, thrust out her swollen tongue, licked the boy's
hand, and immediately became ashamed of her behavior.

Don't lick me, don't...you're full of slime like a...stop, stop...

Little-Tuomas picked up his school bag from the steps and went
to school.

The dog was left alone.

Even though they were awake in the cottage and the curtains
swayed from time to time, no one came out yet---it was still early.
The sun slowly climbed up the pale arch of the sky toward its
southern peak. Out of somewhere a bright-eyed magpie flew to the
edge of the barley field to seek and peck at the white, plump grains
of barley left on the ground after the harrowing. As soon as the
magpie spotted the dog's bowl of food in which the ample breakfast
waited in vain for its eater, the magpie's vanity and his impudent
nature emerged. He hopped brazenly toward the dog, moving closer
and closer: teasing and provoking, he hopped right beside the dog's
nose. But when he saw the dog was sick he settled himself beside
the bowl and pecked at the food, still warm. Turre's body trembled
as she breathed---otherwise she was completely still.

A little after noon the woman took the food bowl away. The
magpie had not eaten very much. Turre's eyes followed the
woman's movements as she emptied the bowl into the garbage
dump at the edge of the field. The sun had begun its descent in the
West. It was almost two o'clock. Little-Tuomas meandered
home from school, stayed inside a long time, eating and doing his

homework---finally Tuomas came outside, carrying a piece of sweet roll which his mother had given for Turre. The roll was white and fresh. Tuomas walked slowly: he nibbled at the roll, which became noticeably smaller during the short walk.

Here, Turre. You can have this. Mother gave it...mother said to give it to Turre...mother said that Turre doesn't have to go hungry then...

Little-Tuomas pushed the roll between Turre's lips; the dog took it into her mouth, but did not chew; then she dropped the roll between her front paws. She lowered her nose to the ground and looked at Little-Tuomas, ashamed. The boy took the roll, placed it again into the dog's mouth. After keeping it in her mouth for a few moments Turre let the roll drop again. A fly buzzed against the gray wall of the shed as if in distress.

If you won't eat your roll, I will, Tuomas threatened.

Be a good girl and eat it. Take it...take it, he said exactly as he had heard his father say.

He rubbed the dog's tangled fur and scratched behind Turre's ears but the dog still did not care for the tidbit.

After throwing the roll away, Tuomas went to tend to his own affairs. The dog again was left alone. She whimpered quietly for Tuomas but Tuomas walked straight across the road to the neighbor's without bothering to glance at Turre. She won't eat anything, Tuomas later told his mother.

His mother was ironing her apron on the lid of the box bed, checking with her finger to feel if the iron was hot enough.

Turre will get well...just wait, you'll see.

What if she has to be killed? Tuomas asked.

Turre isn't that sick...who knows what's wrong, what ails her, his mother said in a calm voice, looking for something to keep her hands busy.

Before going to bed that evening Tuomas ran through the yard to the shed. Turre was lying on the straw just as she had lain during the day. Little-Tuomas squatted down for a while looking into the dog's eyes and talking to her; then he got up, ran quickly through the darkening night into the house, slamming the door shut behind him.

Some other dog howled in the village.

Turre twitched her ears, heard the howling and pressed down even deeper into the worn hollow in the straw. Slime drooled from Turre's mouth but she paid no attention to it. The colorless slime flowed along the straw, forming a film over the filth. Voices faded away as the people in the cottages went to bed. The magpie rustled nearby on his own branch as if trying to move quietly without disturbing anyone. By morning death had taken Turre.

On his way to school Tuomas did not go to see the dog. Then the sun rose again in the sky, noontime arrived and the day changed slowly into evening. The woman moved about in the yard, fetched water from the well, washed some clothes. She was preparing for the evening---her husband was coming that evening. Around noon the magpie came to check on the dog's food bowl but it was empty. The black-tailed mischief maker became serious when he saw the dog was dead: its legs stretched out, its hair unkempt. The magpie sat a short distance from the dead dog, his head raised stiffly, his shining bird's eyes staring at Turre. Then the magpie made a few precise hops away from the dog and suddenly took flight.

In the afternoon Little-Tuomas, with a pot in his hand, came to the shed. He set the food on the grass, squatted down by the dog, lifted one of the front paws. It was lifeless. A fly was digging around in Turre's eye.

Now she died! I have to go and tell mother...

The mother came out of the house later leading Tuomas by the hand. The boy was sucking his thumb and buried his face in his mother's apron: his first thought was that it would be best to behave like a baby. His mother stopped a long way from the straw, from which a pungent odor struck their nostrils. The mother saw that Turre's tail lay all stretched out.

Our old faithful watchdog, the mother remarked, wiping her eyes. When father comes...he can bury the dog tomorrow...

Little-Tuomas put his arms around his mother's waist and squeezed her tightly. He stamped his feet on the ground and sang:

Turre died. Turre died.

Now we'll bury her.

Our dog has died...

We didn't have to kill her.

The woman took the boy by the hand and led him away from the shed.

After they had left, the magpie flew down from the roof of the shed and hopped around the pot Tuomas had forgotten, put his beak into the cooled food and swallowed large chunks of the soaked bread. The woman had already reached the steps: then she turned, saw the magpie and hurried back to get the forgotten pot.

When it was almost dark, the husband came.

The clouds floated back and forth in the sky. The wind blew from around the hills cooling the air, portending rain. The loose ends of rope at each end of the clothesline swung to and fro. The birchbark scoop rattled against the wooden frame of the well. The husband came out of the forest stepping along the path from the well. At the window the wife waited for him. The man's shoulders were hunched, his neck thrust downward like the neck of an ox. He bounded effortlessly up the steps in one leap, stopped, took off his backpack. On the steps he looked around, gazed toward the village, sniffed the air, then opened the door. He left his backpack in the hall and in the room he went at once to sit at the table. Little-Tuomas came to sit beside his father: he did not dare to get close until his father with a heavy hand caressed his white hair.

Turre is dead! Little-Tuomas said to his father in a hushed voice.

That night Little-Tuomas woke up many times. Half asleep, he realized the candle was burning. Father had come out of the bedroom and lighted the candle. Father had on a flannel shirt and mother's thick wool cap on his head. His heavy testicles were hanging low between his thighs. He was rubbing his chest with both hands. Sweat poured down father's flushed face. Sleepily Little-Tuomas mumbled something and fell asleep again. The next time he woke up it was dark but he could her mother's voice in the bedroom:

...say something! Say something!...try, try to talk, for god's sake...

Then it was quiet for a long time until he heard father's moaning and a rattling in his throat.

Then Little-Tuomas fell asleep again.

In the morning he woke up to the pattering of rain. The sky was clouded over and the rain was falling in a gentle steady stream. The magpie was sitting on the roof of the shed, despondent, his head drawn into his shoulders. His eyes open just a slit, he waited for the rain to end.

Mother was sitting in the corner beside the stove.

She was crying and every now and then she wiped her eyes with her apron, gasping for breath between sobs. Tuomas looked at his mother, his eyes open wide.

Is father going to bury Turre? he finally dared to ask in a timid voice.

Mother lifted her head, looked at Tuomas as if in anger and burst into sobs so violent that her shoulders and whole body shook.

Father...is sleeping! she screamed.

Tuomas got out of bed, put on his trousers and his warmest shirt. He peeked into the bedroom from the door but father was not up yet. Father lay in bed, a sheet drawn over his head.

On the porch Little-Tuomas hesitated as he listened to the rain greedily striking the tarred paper roof, but then turned up his shirt collar and ran across the yard through the rain to the neighbor's to get Antti and Kalle, both older than he was. Coming back with the boys, Tuomas was carrying the spade he had borrowed from them.

Ignoring the rain they walked to the shed, stood a while staring at the dead dog. The rain had soaked her coat so that only here and there a dirty tuft of shaggy fur stood up.

The boys picked up the dog, carried it a short distance to the edge of the forest and each one in turn helped to dig the grave. Then the woman came out of the house, a scarf over her head and boots on her feet. With great effort, she walked to the neighbor's and soon returned with two other women. They went inside. Little-Tuomas and the other boys looked after their mothers.

What's happened at your house? one of the boys asked.

Nothing.

Your mother was crying, the other boy said.

No she wasn't.

Now let's bury Turre. I'll be the minister.

Can't you let me be...said Little-Tuomas. It was my watchdog!

You don't know how...besides it's our spade, the older boy reminded him.

You can be a relative.

The rain let up a little for the time of the funeral service. The older boy recited the order for the burial of the dead in a loud monotonous voice, his head bowed over the grave. From the house sounded the continuous singing of hymns: the weeping voices rose and fell. Little-Tuomas and the other boy stood at the foot of the grave, their hands folded, their eyes turned on the dog lying in the grave. Tears streamed down Little-Tuomas's face. When the service was over, Little-Tuomas withdrew from the grave letting the neighbor boys fill the grave with the dirt. He sobbed, pressed his head against the trunk of a pine tree.

On the grave mound the boys erected a branch, the shape of a cross. The older boy came over to Tuomas. He nudged Tuomas on the shoulder. Let's go! It wasn't a real funeral...

Tuomas shook his head and released the sob which had been throttling his throat and burst out crying.

One of the neighbor women came out of the house, walked with hurried steps to the grave and stroked Tuomas's wet hair with her palm.

Antti and Kalle...go home and get your schoolbooks...then go on to school at once...and no loitering on the way, she ordered.

Don't cry, Tuomas, don't cry!

At first Tuomas pushes her aside, but when the other boys are gone, Tuomas goes to her and presses his head between her soft breasts and rubs his face against her coarse apron.

Tuomas doesn't have to go to school today, says the woman comfortingly.

Antti wouldn't let me be the minister...

The woman does not respond to this: she shakes her head and smacks her lips together.

The rain drills furrows into the fresh earth piled on Turre's grave and the reddish brown dirt, turned black by the water, runs off the mound little by little, rolls away and sinks into the moss.

Tuomas, go inside...you'll catch your death of cold, says the neighbor woman.

The magpie struggles into flight from the roof of the shed. Restlessly flapping his wings he flies around the small yard and returning to the shed, flies inside. There, quivering with cold, he perches on a pile of hay and through the large open door stares out at the road. School children stop by the cottage, look around and talk among themselves. The bravest of the small boys runs to the bedroom window and peeks inside through the opening in the curtains. Then he returns to the road: the others gather around him, shoving each other to get close to the eyewitness. They walk beyond the bend in the road, beyond the reach of the magpie's eye and sing a simple song.

Sources Consulted For Author Biographies

1. Ahokas, Jaakko A. A HISTORY OF FINNISH LITERATURE. Indiana University, Bloomington, Indiana, 1973.
2. Blankner, Frederika. THE HISTORY OF THE SCANDINAVIAN LITERATURES. Dial Press, Inc., New York, N. Y. 1938, pp. 291-318.
3. BOOKS FROM FINLAND. Helsinki University Library, Helsinki, Finland. Vol. XI, No. 4, 1977, pp. 239-245; Vol. XII, No. 4, 1978, p. 174; Vol. XIII, No. 3, 1979, p. 85.
4. Dauenhauer, Richard and Philip Bingham, Editors. SNOW IN MAY, AN ANTHOLOGY OF FINNISH WRITING 1945-1972. Associated University Presses, Inc., Cranbury, New Jersey, 1978, pp. 5-72; 376-389.
5. FINNISH WRITERS. A brochure. The Otava Publishing Company, Helsinki, Finland. No date given.
6. Haila, V. A., Kauko Heikkilä, and Eino Kauppinen. SUOMALAISEN KIRJALLISUUDEN HISTORIA. Kustannusosakeyhtiö Otava, Helsinki, Finland, 1974.
7. Koskimies, Rafael. SUOMEN KIRJALLISUUS IV, Minna Canthista Eino Leinoon. Suomalaisen kirjallisuuden seura ja Kustannusosakeyhtiö Otava, Helsinki, Finland, 1964, pp. 29-156.
8. Laitinen, Kai. SUOMEN KIRJALLISUUS 1917-1967. Kustannusosakeyhtiö Otava, Helsinki, Finland, 1970.
9. Launonen, Hannu, et al., Editors. SUOMEN KIRJAILIJAT 1945-1970. Suomalaisen kirjallisuuden seura. Sisälähetysseuran Raamattutalon kirjapaino, Pieksämäki, Finland, 1977.
10. Paasilinna, Erno. TIMO K. MUKKA. Werner Söderström osakeyhtiö, Porvoo-Helsinki, Finland, 1974.
11. Pekkanen, Toivo. MY CHILDHOOD. Translated by Alan Blair. University of Wisconsin, Madison, Wisconsin, 1966, pp. vii-xiv.
12. Ravila, Paavo. FINNISH LITERARY READER. Indiana University, Bloomington, Indiana, 1965.
13. Ripatti, Aku-Kimmo, Hilja Mörsäri, and Pekka Tarkka. KIRJAN MAAILMA. Kustannusosakeyhtiö Otava, Helsinki, Finland, 1969.
14. Saarimaa, E. A. ALEKSIS KIVI: KERTOMUKSIA. Suomalaisen kirjallisuuden seura, Helsinki, Finland, 1922, p. 490.
15. Sarajas, Annamari, et al. SUOMEN KIRJALLISUUS V, Joel Lehtosesta Antti Hyryyn. Suomalaisen kirjallisuuden seura ja Kustannusosakeyhtiö Otava, Helsinki, Finland, 1965, pp. 42-92; 140-

166; 385-430; 446-457; 619-626.

16. Tarkka, Pekka. SUOMALAISIA NYKYKIRJAILIJOITA. Kustannusosakeyhtiö Tammi, Helsinki, Finland, 1967.

17. Tarkka, Pekka, et al. SUOMEN KIRJALLISUUS VIII, Kirjallisuuden lajeja. Suomalaisen kirjallisuuden seura ja Kustannusosakeyhtiö Otava, Helsinki, Finland, 1970, pp. 72-131.

18. Viljanen, Lauri, et al. SUOMEN KIRJALLISUUS III, Turun romantikoista Aleksis Kiveen. Suomalaisen kirjallisuuden seura ja Kustannusosakeyhtiö Otava, Helsinki, Finland, 1964, pp. 462-483.

Sources For The Short Stories

1. Aho, Juhani. *Kello* (*The Watch*). KOOTUT TEOKSET I and II, Werner Söderström Osakeyhtiö, Porvoo, 1951, pp. 32-47.

2. ————————. *Kesäinen unelma* (*A Summer Dream*). SUOMALAISIA NOVELLEJA 1, toimittanut Hannu Mäkelä, Kustannusosakeyhtiö Otava, Helsinki, 1973, pp. 14-25.

3. Canth, Minna. *Lapsenpiika* (*The Nursemaid*). SUOMALAISIA NOVELLEJA 1, toimittanut Hannu Mäkelä, Kustannusosakeyhtiö Otava, Helsinki, 1973, pp. 5-13.

4. Häänpää, Pentti. *Joutavan jäljillä* (*The Unneeded Paradise*).. JUTTUJA, toimittanut Helena Anhava, Kustannusosakeyhtiö Otava, Helsinki, 1969, pp. 141-145.

5. ————————. *Sotilaallisen komeasti* (*Military Splendor*). KENTTÄ JA KASARMI, Kustannusosakeyhtiö Otava, Helsinki, 1966, pp. 82-95.

6. ————————. *Viimeinen puu* (*The Last Tree*). HETA RAHKO KORKEASSA IÄSSÄ, Kustannusosakeyhtiö Otava, Helsinki 1947, pp. 108-113.

7. Huovinen, Veikko. *Sammakkomiehen päivä* (*The Frogman's Day*). RASVA MAKSA, Werner Söderström Osakeyhtiö, Porvoo 1974, pp. 123-131.

8. ————————. *Onko tukka kauniisti* (*Is My Hair Beautiful?*) RASVA MAKSA, Werner Söderström Osakeyhtiö, Porvoo, 1974 pp. 52-56.

9. Hyry, Antti. *Kivi auringon paisteessa* (*A Rock in the Sunshine*). SUOMALAISIA NOVELLEJA 2, toimittanut Hannu Mäkelä, Kustannusosakeyhtiö Otava, Helsinki, 1973, pp. 68-69.

10. ————————. *Sianpurema* (*The Pigbitten*). SUOMEN KIR-

JALLISUUDEN ANTOLOGIA VIII, Kustannusosakeyhtiö Otava, Helsinki, 1975, pp. 432-437.

11. Jotuni, Maria. *Kun on tunteet* (*When You Have Feelings*). MARIA JOTUNI, NOVELLEJA, Kustannusosakeyhtiö Otava, Helsinki, 1974, pp. 128-132.

12. ——————. *Kuolema* (*Death*). MARIA JOTUNI, NOVELLEJA, Kustannusosakeyhtiö Otava, Helsinki, 1974, pp. 123-127.

13. ——————. *Rakkautta* (*Love*). MARIA JOTUNI, NOVELLEJA, Kustannusosakeyhtiö Otava, Helsinki, 1974, pp. 59-62.

14. ——————. *Tyttö ruusutarhassa eli kuoleva sisar* (*The Girl in the Rose Arbor, or the Dying Sister*). SUOMALAISIA NOVELLEJA 1, toimittanut Hannu Mäkelä, Kustannusosakeyhtiö Otava, Helsinki, 1973, pp. 155-186.

15. Kivi, Aleksis. *Eriika*. SUOMEN KIRJALLISUUDEN ANTOLOGIA II, Kustannusosakeyhtiö Otava, Helsinki, 1963, pp. 287-290.

16. Lehtonen, Joel. *Ensimmäinen rakkaus* (*First Love*). SUOMALAISIA MESTARI NOVELLEJA, valikoinut Aulis Ojajärvi, Werner Söderström, Porvoo, 1971, pp. 138-143.

17. ——————. *Herra ja Moukka* (*The Master and the Servant*). SUOMEN KIRJALLISUUDEN ANTOLOGIA IV, Kustannusosakeyhtiö Otava, 1968, pp. 407-417.

18. Mannerkorpi, Juha. *Marakatti* (*The Monkey*). FINNISH LITERARY READER by Paavo Ravila, Indiana University, Bloomington, Indiana, 1965, pp. 121-124.

19. ——————. *Nahka* (*The Fur*). NIIN JA TOISIN (Novelleja, lastuja, hämähäkkejä), Kustannusosakeyhtiö Otava, Helsinki, 1950, pp. 5-13.

20. Meri, Veijo. *Kosinta* (*The Proposal*). VEIJO MEREN NOVELLIT Kustannusosakeyhtiö Otava, Helsinki, 1965, pp. 300-305.

21. ——————. *Näytelmän valinta* (*Selecting a Play*). SUOMALAISIA NOVELLEJA 2, toimittanut Hannu Makela, Kustannusosakeyhtiö Otava, Helsinki, 1973, pp. 53-55.

22. Mikkola, Marja-Leena. *Aila*. SUOMALAISIA NOVELLEJA 2, toimittanut Hannu Mäkelä, Kustannusosakeyhtiö Otava, Helsinki, 1973, pp. 135-137.

23. Mukka, Timo. *Koiran kuolema* (*The Death of a Dog*). SUOMEN KIRJALLISUUDEN ANTOLOGIA VIII, Kustannusosakeyhtiö Otava, Helsinki, 1975, pp. 687-694.

24. Pakkala, Teuvo. *Piispantikku* (*The Bishop's Pointer*). SUOMEN KIRJALLISUUDEN ANTOLOGIA III, Kustannusosakeyhtiö Otava, Helsinki, 1964, pp. 190-200.

238

25. ⸻. *Valehtelijoita?* (*Liars?*). LAPSIA-PIKKU IHMISIÄ, Kustannusosakeyhtiö Otava, Helsinki, 1975, pp. 22-26.

26. Pekkanen, Toivo. *Ruokaa talveksi* (*Food for the Winter*). FINN-ISH LITERARY READER by Paavo Ravila, Indiana University, Bloomington, Indiana, 1965, pp. 88-92.

27. ⸻. *Siltaa rakentamassa* (*Building a Bridge*). SUOMALAISIA NOVELLEJA 1, toimittanut Hannu Mäkelä, Kustannusosakeyhtiö Otava, Helsinki, 1973, pp. 225-230.

28. Pennanen, Eila. *Kauan sitten* (*Long Ago*). UUDEN PROOSAN PARHAITA, Kustannusosakeyhtiö Tammi, Helsinki, 1969, pp. 110-121.

29. Salama, Hannu. *Juopot* (*The Drunkards*). TIENVIITTA JA MUI-TA NOVELLEJA, Kustannusosakeyhtiö Otava, Helsinki, 1974, pp. 42-53.

30. Sillanpää, Frans Eemil. *Piika* (*The Hired Girl*). SUOMALAISIA NOVELLEJA 1, toimittanut Hannu Mäkelä, Kustannusosakeyhtiö Otava, Helsinki, 1973, pp. 187-205.

31. Vartio, Marja-Liisa. *Suomalainen maisema* '(*A Finnish Landscape*). SUOMALAISIA MESTARI NOVELLEJA, valikoinut Aulis Ojajärvi, Werner Söderström Osakeyhtiö, Porvoo, 1971, pp. 280-286.

32. Waltari, Mika. *Omenapuut* (*The Apple Trees*). FINNISH FOR FOREIGNERS, READER 3, by Maija-Hellikki Aaltio, Kustannusosakeyhtiö Otava, Helsinki, 1975, pp. 118-122.